Praise for *The Life Experiment*

'Heartwarming and uplifting, *The Life Experiment* will make you think and swoon at the same time!'
Rachael Johns, author of *The Bad Bridesmaid*

'Characters you will embrace from the start. A story you will never forget. A big, bold novel that is not afraid to ask the question: what really matters in this life? And answers: maybe, just maybe, it is love.'
Sophie Green, author of *Art Hour at the Duchess Hotel*

'Heartfelt and thought-provoking, Jess Kitching's characters stayed with me long after I closed the final page.'
Clare Fletcher, author of *Love Match*

'An achingly beautiful, slow-burn romance that will find its way to your heart and stay there. A truly original concept, expertly crafted – one that dares to ask the boldest existential questions about what makes a life worth living, all while grounding you with the sweetest, most unforgettable love story.'
Karina May, author of *That Island Feeling*

'Witty, thought-provoking and brimming with swoon-worthy banter, *The Life Experiment* is a delight!'
Emma Grey, author of *Pictures of You*

'From the very first page, I knew this book was special. *The Life Experiment* is a profound and thought-provoking story about the messiness of life with characters who will instantly capture your heart.'
Christine Newell, author of *Five Seasons in Seoul*

'Aching, tender and hopeful, *The Life Experiment* is a love story that beautifully balances sorrow and light. It will break your heart, then stitch it back together, stronger than before. This book is a reminder that how we spend our time, and who we spend it with, matters more than ever.'
Holly Brunnbauer, author of *What Did I Miss?*

'If you knew how much longer you had on this earth, would you live your life differently? Full of warmth and charm, Jess Kitching is a fresh new voice in Australian fiction.'
Kate Solly, author of *The Paradise Heights Craft Store Stitch-Up*

'A dazzling romance with a fresh and original premise, *The Life Experiment* is equal parts thought-provoking and heartwarming. Brimming with insight, Jess Kitching explores what it means to truly live – asking the big questions and celebrating the small moments that make life worthwhile.'
Anne Freeman, author of *Me That You See*

THE LIFE EXPERIMENT

THE LIFE EXPERIMENT

JESS KITCHING

SIMON & SCHUSTER

New York · Amsterdam/Antwerp · London · Toronto · Sydney · New Delhi

EAST LOTHIAN COUNCIL LIBRARY SERVICE	
5003190	
Askews & Holts	26-Sep-2025
AF	
GU	

THE LIFE EXPERIMENT
First published in Australia in 2025 by
Simon & Schuster (Australia) Pty Limited
Level 4, 32 York St, Sydney NSW 2000

10 9 8 7 6 5

New York Amsterdam/Antwerp London Toronto Sydney New Delhi
Visit our website at www.simonandschuster.com.au

© Jess Kitching 2025

All rights reserved. No part of this publication may be reproduced, stored in a retrieval system, or transmitted in any form or by any means, electronic, mechanical, photocopying, recording or otherwise, without prior permission of the publisher.

A catalogue record for this book is available from the National Library of Australia

ISBN: 9781761630316

Cover design by Emily O'Neill
Typeset by Midland Typesetters, Australia
Printed and bound by CPI Group (UK) Ltd,
Croydon CR0 4YY

MIX
Paper | Supporting responsible forestry
FSC® C013604

The authorised representative in the EEA is Simon & Schuster Netherlands BV, Herculesplein 96, 3584 AA Utrecht, Netherlands. info@simonandschuster.nl

For James Knox and Ross Elliott.
Every day, I'm grateful to have known you.
Every day, I wish you were still here.
Miss you, always.

And for Lily Raiti, who lit up every room she entered.

Do you ever wonder where your life is heading?

Does it feel like everyone around you knows what they're doing but you don't?

Do you ever question if you're on the right path?

We could help!

OPM Discoveries is searching for participants for an exciting research opportunity. Preliminarily named 'The Life Experiment', this scientific study aims to answer all of life's big questions.

Applicants will be required to complete a series of assessments and medical checks to confirm their eligibility. The trial itself will involve a range of tasks over a ten-week period, including submitting diary entries, wearing a monitoring device and 1:1 counselling sessions.

Combining groundbreaking technology with tried and tested research methods, this study aims to revolutionise the way we understand and interpret life, death and everything in between.

To register your interest, click here.

T&Cs: Applicants must be UK residents aged 18 or older. We encourage people from all backgrounds to apply. Participants will receive £3000 compensation for their time once experiment obligations are complete. NOTE: discretion is vital to the success of The Life Experiment. All candidates will be required to follow strict security protocols, including signing an NDA that covers screening and the duration of the experiment.

1
Layla

Legal jargon swam around the stark white background of Layla's laptop screen. She blinked, heavy-lidded, but the words refused to come into focus.

From the desk opposite, Rashida glanced up. 'Go home if you're tired.'

'I could say the same to you,' Layla replied.

Rashida grinned. *Touché*.

Beside her, Sinead laughed, but none of the women moved. As the only people left in the darkened office, an unspoken competition had begun. Who would be the last to leave? There could only be one winner and, as usual, Layla was determined it would be her.

It was a friendly competition, mind you. Layla, Rashida and Sinead were allies, working together to shatter Mayweather & Halliwell's glass ceilings one meeting at a time. It had been that way since Rashida and Layla were allocated desks near each other two years ago, with Sinead joining their cluster earlier in the year. Calling out each other's achievements and being on hand for any workload meltdowns, Rashida and Sinead were the closest thing Layla had to friends in London.

Located in one of the capital's finest heritage buildings, Mayweather & Halliwell was the kind of prestigious boutique law firm where staff generally knew each other through family connections or private education establishments. Layla, Rashida and Sinead were the odd ones out, each from decidedly working-class backgrounds and hustling ten times harder to make it to Senior Partner one day.

And Layla was determined to make it, all right. That very morning her new manager, Michelle Beckett, had taken her aside. 'Nice work on the presentation to Fieldhouse Mews,' she said. 'Keep it up and I can see you making real waves here.'

Layla accepted the compliment, although making waves wasn't usually her style. She much preferred the head down, hard work route. It was difficult for others to belittle her achievements when the results spoke for themselves.

Still, William Addington tried his best to take the shine off the moment. 'It's a good management ploy to side with the weak ones,' he drawled as Layla headed back to her desk.

It was always the same with William. He had a talent for brushing off Layla's success as a fluke or hinting that concessions were made because of her background. Ironic, given that William was only at the firm because his granddad was a Founding Partner. Not that Layla would dare say that out loud. There was almost an unwritten rule in the office – don't acknowledge the fact that Mayweather & Halliwell never was and never would be an equal workplace.

It tried to be, of course. At least performatively. Pink cakes handed out on International Women's Day, posters for mental health helplines in the bathrooms. Name the PR opportunity and Mayweather & Halliwell were on the bandwagon for it.

While the office cynics would do their best not to roll their eyes, others would say that hiring Michelle was an example of genuine progression. As the company's first female Senior Partner, she was a symbol of the future. She had been at the front of every recent promotional photograph as proof of that.

But from what Layla could see, the only thing Michelle had done was stick to the Mayweather & Halliwell status quo. Career progression slowed for women who recently married (God forbid they might have a *baby* soon), late nights were not only encouraged but expected, and relatives of existing employees were inevitably fast-tracked for promotions.

As Layla's jaw clenched, the sensible part of her brain kicked into life. *Office politics don't matter,* it said. *Focus on your career. You know the truth about your place here.*

Sitting taller, Layla straightened her shoulders. The truth was her success was hers, fought for and well deserved. There had been no Daddy to gift it to her, no family connection, no shortcut. Hard work and talent got her to where she was, and she was damned proud of that.

Layla just hoped the early mornings and late nights would pay off soon. Jokes about sacrificing her youth for her career might have made Layla laugh once upon a time, but setting her alarm for 5 am every morning didn't feel funny anymore. Especially when living in London meant using most of her salary on renting a room in an apartment the size of a shoebox.

With Layla momentarily distracted from her screen, her stomach took its chance to grab her attention. Cupping her hand to her rumbling abdomen, Layla fought to suppress the sounds within. Things had been so hectic earlier that she hadn't had time for lunch. Now it was what, six-thirty?

Layla glanced at the corner of her screen.

7:53 pm.

Shit.

Whenever Layla's mum saw her, an admittedly rare occasion – Layla's brain made a note to guilt her about *that* when she was trying to sleep later – she always commented that Layla needed to take better care of herself. Assessing her daughter, Joanna would grimace and say, 'If you don't start putting yourself first, you're going to get sick.'

'Mum's right. I reckon we'll start seeing a few stress-related grey hairs soon,' Layla's sister, Maya, would add. 'Just as well I'm a bloody good hairdresser and can fix them for you.'

Layla knew they had a point. Long days at a desk made her sluggish and bloated. Her skin was dull and prone to breakouts. Even her dark hair seemed tired of being attached to her head. The strands were so lacklustre that no amount of serum or mousse gave them any semblance of vitality.

Another hunger pang tore through Layla, this one too intense to ignore. 'I'm going to the vending machine. Anyone want anything?'

Sinead and Rashida shook their heads, not looking up from their laptops.

Layla stood, wincing as her knees groaned like rusty hinges. What did she expect? She'd barely left her desk all day, despite the wellness prompts HR sent around sporadically. Layla might only be twenty-nine, but some days her body creaked like she was eighty-nine.

Limping to the vending machine in the break room, Layla eyed the artificially lit, sugar-filled contents.

Skimming the names of brands she had come to know better than the names of her school friends' children, Layla selected a can of Coke and a packet of crisps. The dinner of champions. The dinner of success. At least, that's what she told herself as the nutrient-free meal landed with a thud.

Clutching her goodies, Layla headed back to her desk, returning to find Sinead with her head in her hands. 'You okay?' Layla asked as she slid onto her chair.

'Are any of us, when we're still here at this time?' Sinead sighed, the gust of breath so strong it ruffled her strawberry-blonde fringe.

Leaning back in her seat, Rashida linked her fingers behind her hijab to stretch. 'I'm not. I've missed story time again. Aaron sent a photo. I'm not sure he meant it as a guilt trip, but it's working.'

'Show me,' Layla said.

Rashida reached for her phone and turned it to her friends. A photo of her two-year-old son, Syed, wearing adorable aeroplane pyjamas and holding a picture book filled the screen.

'He's so cute!' Sinead cooed.

'He is. It's a shame I'm not around to see his cuteness for myself.'

Layla opened her drink, a satisfying fizz ringing out into the office. 'Go home then. It's almost eight.'

'I can't leave yet. Richard's been at me all week about my billables,' Rashida replied, locking her phone as if the now-black screen could silence her maternal guilt.

'They can't fire you for going home to see your son.'

'No, but they can make my life difficult. You know as well as I do that companies like this look for any excuse to push working mothers out of the office and back into their homes.'

Layla's features twisted, but she didn't argue. Rashida was right. Time and time again, Layla had seen it happen.

Sure, working here is hard, Layla thought, *but what isn't?*

Growing up on an estate in Hull, all Layla ever saw was hard living. The single mother battling to find a job that fit around her childcare needs. The bored teenager who joined a gang because there was nothing else to do. The migrant told their qualifications didn't translate, so all they were offered was a minimum-wage role.

Even in her own family, things had been tough. When Layla was seven, her dad had a near-fatal fall while helping a friend install guttering on his house. The damage to David's body was catastrophic. It took him months and multiple surgeries to recover, not that he ever fully did. Even now, David's movements were creaky and tinged with pain.

The accident put David out of work for years, and government support couldn't make up for the loss of his income. Joanna's part-time supermarket salary just wasn't enough. Money was tight. Grocery shopping was a competition to find the cheapest products. Clothes were bought second-hand and shared between Layla and Maya. Haircuts were done in the kitchen with a pair of blunt scissors and Joanna's best efforts.

Life in the Cannon family might have been filled with love and laughter, but for Layla it was also filled with worry for her stressed parents. David and Joanna were still struggling to pay off the debts they'd amassed during that time. Layla helped where she could, though after rent and living expenses, she never had much money to spare.

But so what if London was a financial drain and her career was an energy vacuum? This was Layla's dream. It always had been.

Ever since Layla could remember, rules, logic and consequences had called to her. Life didn't have to be chaotic, she'd realised. There could, and should, be order in the world.

So, Layla became a lawyer. And not just any lawyer, but a corporate lawyer living in the capital. Sure, Layla once pictured herself defending the rights of refugees or victims of crime, not helping millionaires hoard their wealth, but still, she had made her childhood dream come true.

Layla had been taught from an early age that if you worked hard, you succeeded. If you worked hard, then the place you were born, the school you attended, and the rank of your social class meant nothing.

But if hard work is the answer, why am I getting nowhere? Layla wondered. It was a thought so toxic she wanted to shake her head to dislodge it.

As she popped a salt and vinegar crisp in her mouth, Layla studied Sinead. Dark circles shadowed her colleague's eyes, the bags so embedded that even her expensive concealer struggled to hide them. Layla knew for a fact Sinead hadn't eaten lunch either. It was sad, really. When Sinead joined the firm eight months ago, bright-eyed and fresh from Dublin, she had been the life and soul of the party. 'Always up for the craic,' as she used to put it. Looking at her now, the only thing Sinead looked up for was an early night.

'Wasn't it your anniversary yesterday?' Layla asked, crunching on another crisp.

Sinead groaned. 'Don't remind me.'

'What happened?'

'What always happens – we had plans, but I didn't leave here until after nine.'

'I take it Kirstie wasn't impressed?'

'Would you be if you had to cancel a reservation at La Rosa at the last minute?'

'Ouch,' Rashida winced, but Layla said nothing. For her, romantic dinners were a distant memory.

'If you go now, you could still make a night of it,' Layla suggested. 'Grab some wine and surprise Kirstie. You too, Rashida. Syed might be asleep, but Aaron won't be. When did you two last have a date night?'

'A date night? What's that?' Rashida joked.

'Point proven, so go!'

Temptation danced in Rashida's eyes, but her shoulders slumped. 'I can't. The deadline is Friday and—'

'I'll do it,' Layla interjected. 'I'm staying late anyway, what difference does it make? Seriously, go. We don't all have to be miserable.'

Sinead glanced at the time. 'There is that bottle of wine in the fridge . . .'

'Perfect! Share it with Kirstie. Rashida, go watch a film with Aaron. Enjoy yourselves.'

Sinead wavered. 'Are you sure?'

As Layla nodded, Rashida's left hand hovered above the camel-coloured coat hung on the back of her chair. 'You really don't need any help? Because I can take my laptop and—'

'Don't even think about it. Go, both of you, before I get angry at you for dithering.'

Sinead and Rashida didn't need telling again. Coats and handbags grabbed, they headed for the exit in a flurry of thank yous and promises to repay the favour.

When they were gone, a lonely silence echoed through the wood-panelled office.

Pulling her attention back to her laptop, Layla tried to focus, but the words danced around the screen. Even when she rubbed her bleary eyes, they wouldn't comply. Sighing, she slipped her phone from her pocket and headed to social media for a moment of respite.

As soon as she opened Instagram, Layla wished she hadn't. The first picture on her feed was of Taylina Dare wearing an impossibly small bikini while lounging beside a glorious ocean.

Envy bit Layla's throat. Taylina had been in her year at school. A toxic mix of airhead and bully, Taylina had discovered that when you're beautiful, you can be both and still be adored. Her career since her school days was testimony to that. After amassing a large online following and marrying the footballer she met on series three of *Love Shack*, Taylina was sickeningly rich, even though she'd never known a late night stuck behind a desk

Frustrated, Layla went to close the app, but something caught her eye before she could . . . An advert asking Layla the question she often asked herself.

Do you ever wonder where your life is heading?

'Only all day, every day,' Layla muttered.

Curiosity piqued, Layla read on. Her skin prickled. The advert felt like it was written for her. Like it somehow knew exactly what thoughts she was avoiding.

Was she on the right path or was she as lost as she felt?

Would all this be worth it one day, or was she wasting her time on something that would never provide the happiness and security she was searching for?

Layla sat with her misery for a moment before shaking her head. 'This is ridiculous,' she muttered. So what if the questions felt like they had been plucked from her mind? The pull she felt wasn't fate or divine intervention – it was a skilled copywriter's script.

And an experiment, really? Layla was so busy with work she couldn't find time to cook dinner, never mind commit to a ten-week experiment. Besides, someone else would benefit from the opportunity more. A £3,000 boost to her non-existent savings would be nice, as would using the money to pay off some of her parents' debt, but it wasn't enough to make the commitment worthwhile.

Decision made, Layla went to lock her phone, but at that moment an email pinged into her inbox. The subject line read: *Looks like it will be another late one.*

Layla's heart dropped like a stone down a well. She didn't have to read the email to know what it said. Another insane deadline. Another night of overtime she wasn't paid for.

Another night of asking what the hell she was doing with her life.

Biting back a sigh, Layla skimmed the ad once more. 'Fuck it,' she said, before clicking the link to apply.

2

Angus

The sound of someone using his shower startled Angus awake. He jerked upright, exposing his naked torso from beneath the duvet. A slice of autumnal sunlight peeked through a gap in the curtains, making him wince. Angus had closed them hastily last night, too caught up in passionate activity to care about the morning.

Stifling a yawn, Angus glanced at the time on his phone. 7:47 am.

A groan escaped him. Laying back on his pillow, Angus threw an arm over his eyes to shut out the world, but the woman in the shower chose that moment to start singing. Beyoncé, she was not.

With no chance of sleep now, Angus tossed the duvet aside and found his underwear on the floor. Sidestepping the woman's possessions – Louboutin shoes, Chanel bag – he entered his ensuite.

A miracle of expensive taste and fine craftsmanship, with a large jacuzzi bath that looked out over London, the slick bathroom impressed everyone Angus brought home. So did the rest of his penthouse.

But was living there Angus's dream? Someone once asked him that. The question had stuck with Angus ever since. At the time, he hadn't been able to answer it. Truthfully, he still couldn't.

The woman in the shower smiled when Angus entered the room. Even with traces of mascara darkening the skin under her eyes, she was undeniably beautiful.

The previous night, Jasper had pointed her out as she danced amidst a cluster of similarly long-limbed, bronzed friends. 'I want to marry her,' he swooned, eying the woman up and down.

'I thought you didn't believe in marriage?' Angus replied.

'For her, I'd change my mind.'

But it was Angus who had taken the woman home. It hadn't been his intention, but that tended to be the way things went. People quickly tired of Jasper bragging about his car collection or listing the drugs he could get. Wearied, their eyes wandered until they landed on Angus.

While Angus might present as a humbler alternative to Jasper, his surname told a different story, at least for those in the know.

Despite their gargantuan wealth, a Google search of the Fairview-Whitleys would not bring up a boastful list of business acquisitions and society-page features. In fact, it didn't bring up much at all. The family were not gossip-column fodder. They possessed a level of wealth that rose above all that.

'Did I wake you?' the woman asked, her voice carrying the distinctive croak of a big night.

'Yes,' Angus replied. His body came alive at the thought of joining her, but as he reached for the glass door, the woman turned the shower off.

'I can't stay. I've got to go to work.'

Angus blinked. *Work. Of course.* Not everyone was like him, a 34-year-old with more money than he knew what to do with and no career in sight. Angus knew that statement made him sound like a dick, and at times he *was* a dick, but he wasn't exactly proud of his employment status.

'You're rich. You don't need to work,' Jasper dismissed whenever Angus confessed his insecurities. 'Being loaded is your full-time job. Trust me, you do it well.'

But the truth was that Angus was ashamed. The one time he had gone all-in on a career, Angus lost over two million pounds of his family's money. But back then, when he was twenty-seven and so cocky that 'arrogant' was the first word people used to describe him, it had been fun to wave a cheque in the air and fund the startup of a friend of a friend. Something in tech. Something he didn't understand that sounded cool. Swooping in like a hero made Angus feel powerful, until he realised he hadn't asked the right questions – or any questions at all.

Before Angus could spiral further, the woman spoke once more. 'Can you get me a towel?'

Nodding, Angus grabbed a fresh towel from a concealed cupboard and handed it over.

'Thanks,' she said, wrapping it around herself. Shuffling out of the shower, the woman caught sight of her reflection in the semi-steamed mirror and laughed. 'Good job I saw this. I can't go to work looking like a panda, can I?'

As she wiped the smudged makeup from her eyes, Angus realised he had no idea what work she was referencing. 'What is it you do again?'

The woman stopped. 'I told you last night. I plan bespoke, high-end birthday parties for dogs.'

Yes, that was it – a career so ridiculous Angus had laughed into his drink when the woman said it. She went on to explain how her father had given her a small loan to start the business. *Only eighty-thousand pounds*, she had said, as if it was spare change.

The woman then described the services her company provided: catering from London's finest restaurants, entertainment from award-winning dog trainers and handcrafted puppy-party costumes, to name a few. She informed Angus that she'd arranged six parties so far, each for pets belonging to her mother's friends. No cats – she didn't do cats, or any other animals for that matter. When she had finished her monologue, the woman took a smug sip of vodka soda.

Angus remembered sitting in the club, wide-eyed. The absurdity of the conversation seemed to be lost on everyone but him. Not for the first time, Angus wondered what he was doing, existing in a world that made no sense to him.

What was he *doing*?

Focusing on the woman once more, Angus studied her sharp shoulder blades as they jutted from the top of her towel. Shame twinged his stomach. He shouldn't judge her. At least she'd done something with her life.

'So, what's on the agenda for you today?' the woman asked him.

Angus smiled, painfully aware that he couldn't answer the question. The day stretched ahead of him like a blank canvas. The problem was, he had no paint to fill it with.

Ever since the startup debacle, Angus had lost all trust in himself. Bad habits crept in. Within months, Angus was living a life no different to the one he had at eighteen.

'A cowardly way to live,' he once heard his mother mutter, but Angus didn't care if doing nothing made him a coward. Cowardice was better than failure. Sure, the empty days drove Angus insane, but what could he do? Figuring out what to do with your life at the age of thirty-four was embarrassing.

'Your day?' the woman prodded, when no answer was provided.

'Oh, you know, this and that,' Angus replied. 'Head to the gym, catch up with friends. Chill.'

'But it's Wednesday,' the woman pushed. 'Don't you have a job to go to?'

'Not exactly. I mean, not in the traditional sense.'

The woman cocked her head. 'What does that mean?'

Heat singed Angus's cheeks. What was he supposed to say – *It means fucking around aimlessly every day, killing time until I can fall asleep*?

When the silence dragged on, the woman raised her eyebrows. Angus found himself wishing he had done more with his life. Anything. Even starting a business planning birthday parties for dogs.

Bored, the woman walked through to the bedroom. Angus followed. He found her scooping her belongings from the floor. Plucking her skimpy dress from the pile, she shimmied it over her head. Without the club atmosphere and alcohol, the dress looked more tacky than enticing.

Suddenly, the woman met Angus's gaze. 'A few friends are heading to the Cotswolds this weekend, if you fancy it,' she said. Even if Angus's lack of drive was unattractive, he was still rich. 'Think skinny dipping in an indoor pool, cocktails by a fire, that kind of thing.'

'Sounds good, but I can't this weekend,' Angus replied.

'Oh?' The woman looked at Angus expectantly, waiting for a reason, but he said no more. He'd never been one to come up with excuses or spare people's feelings. He simply said yes, or he said no. Either way, people listened.

When the silence verged on awkward, the woman hooked the straps of her high heels through her fingers. Approaching Angus, she angled her face towards him. 'This was fun. We should do it again sometime.'

'Sure,' Angus replied. As the woman's face erupted into a smile, he panicked. He meant another casual hook-up. She knew that, right?

Angus didn't have long to worry about that, though, because the woman grabbed the back of his head and pulled him in for a kiss. The pressure was wrong, more desperate than passionate, and both could have used a toothbrush. Still, Angus reciprocated the gesture.

Eventually, the woman pulled away, breathless and grinning. Angus took it as his cue to walk her to the door. 'See you soon, Angus Fairview-Whitley,' she chimed.

Realising he couldn't remember her name, Angus waved goodbye and watched the woman slink into the lift. She blew him a kiss, the doors closed, then she was gone.

Briskly, he shut the door of his twenty-seventh-floor haven, trying not to think about how little connection he had to the outside world.

For a moment, he debated making a coffee, but caffeine meant waking up properly, and that would mean more of the day to fill.

Sloping back to his bedroom, Angus flopped onto the unmade super king. The faint odours of sex and perfume lingered on the sheets, but Jinny would be here at twelve to clean it away. By tonight, Angus would slip into bed and find no trace of the woman he had spent the night with. He would fall asleep how he spent his days – alone.

When a yawn bubbled up Angus's throat, he glanced at the time. It was barely 8 am. What to do?

What to *do*?

He could go to the gym early, he supposed, but at this time it would be busy. What if he couldn't use the machines he liked?

He could cook. Sort dinners for the week or try out recipes he'd learned when he last visited Japan. Cooking was Angus's favourite way to de-stress, something he craved now the startup failure was on his mind again. But cooking in the morning meant he would have nothing to do in the evening. It only delayed his boredom.

Maybe he could go out for breakfast instead, but who with? Angus's closest friends were probably still asleep, and he couldn't go *alone*. Imagine if someone saw him.

Angus sighed. Once, living like this had been fun. Growing up in a house with no rules or limits was freeing. Impromptu shopping trip? Take Father's card. A last-minute holiday? Where to, and how long for? Studying was for those who needed a job. Consequences were for those who didn't have connections in high places to smooth things over. Angus knew his privilege, and he enjoyed the fruits of it – until he realised how hollow the fruits were.

Memories of parties and puppy love swept through Angus. The stately homes with endless bedrooms. The taste of fruit-scented lip gloss mingled with spirits stolen from parents' alcohol collections. The names and faces seemed so transient now. Drunken moments that had promised happiness but delivered none.

Angus knew this wasn't something he could ever say out loud. After all, how could anyone feel sorry for him? But Angus didn't want pity. He wanted . . . What *did* he want?

Anything. Anything but this.

Propping himself up on a pillow, Angus grabbed his phone. Plenty of notifications were waiting. Money might not buy happiness but it certainly bought friends, although Angus suspected his definition of 'friend' was more transactional than most.

Hitting Instagram, he learned he had gained a new follower request. Strange, given that his account was private. Someone clearly wanted to find him.

Opening the notification, Angus saw it was the woman from last night.

Her bio informed him that her name was Fiona 'Fifi' Fortston. His finger hovered over the 'follow back' button, but he didn't commit to the gesture. Instead, he went back to his homepage. There, something caught his eye.

Do you ever wonder where your life is heading? an advert asked.

Swallowing hard, Angus read on. The more he read, the more the blank stretch of days ahead filled with colour. This experiment would last ten weeks, and that wasn't including the application process. That meant that for at least ten weeks, he would be busy. He would wake up with a purpose.

Before he could talk himself out of it, Angus clicked the link and submitted his details. *There*, he thought, settling into his pillow. *You've done something with your day, after all.*

3

Layla

Layla flicked through the thirty-three-page document loaded on the iPad before her. As question forty-nine caught her eye, she raised an eyebrow: *How would you describe your appetite for sex?*

Gulping, Layla glanced at the woman sitting at the other end of the long assessment room table: Dr Saira Khatri, head of The Life Experiment. She would soon know more about Layla than Layla's own mother did.

Layla knew she shouldn't be surprised by the intensity of the questions. She had researched OPM Discoveries thoroughly after they got in touch about her application. A globally renowned research hub, they trained leading scientists, produced Nobel Prize winners and created lifesaving vaccines. Naturally, their process would be rigorous.

Layla was flattered to have made it this far. After the initial expression of interest, she had been sent a lifestyle questionnaire to complete. Next came an hour-long video interview with Dr Khatri and two senior members of the research team. After that there were a series of online tests, food and exercise diaries and a family history report to complete, as well as a week of sleep monitoring.

Today was Layla's first in-person session at OPM Discoveries headquarters on the outskirts of Birmingham. Taking personal leave to attend made Layla break out in a cold sweat, but the examinations and interview with Dr Khatri could only be completed in person.

If she passed this, Layla would receive one more set of online tests and complete another in-person interview. After that, she would be invited to be part of the study. She would find out the aim of the research and have a week to decide if she'd like to proceed.

Then, on the 2nd of October, the experiment would begin.

A nerve-racking thought, but any apprehension Layla felt dissolved as soon as Dr Khatri greeted her, fresh off the train from London, with the warmth of an old friend.

Layla's nerves about the medical side of the process soon disappeared too. Shortly after arriving, she was taken to a lab where she underwent a series of physical examinations, including blood tests, an eye test, an ECG, and finally a full body scan. The scan had required Layla to step into a machine that looked like it came from the set of a sci-fi film. While she stood still, whirring sensors swept over her body. Whatever they were scanning for, they were doing a good job of hunting for it.

Layla turned her attention back to the questionnaire. She marked herself highly throughout, because admitting the truth would have been mortifying. Confessing her lack of travel would make her seem less cultured; owning up to her lack of fitness would seem unhealthy. OPM Discoveries clearly wanted solid candidates, and Layla was determined to appear more solid than anyone else.

'Here you go, Dr Khatri,' she said, handing the iPad back after submitting her answers.

'Thank you,' Dr Khatri replied. 'And please, call me Saira.'

'Saira,' Layla repeated, testing the name.

Saira was older than Layla – early-fifties, if she had to guess – but she had the style of someone younger. Dressed in an orange blazer, a white t-shirt and a pair of patterned trousers, she looked significantly trendier than Layla.

Her sense of style wasn't the only thing Layla admired about her. When Saira had taken Layla on a tour of the OPM Discoveries complex, everyone they met seemed to adore and respect her. Layla knew that balance was hard to strike, but Saira made it look easy. The fact that she was witty and charming didn't hurt, either.

On the table, Saira's phone buzzed. She checked the notification. 'I hope you don't mind, but I might push our one-to-one back. The gym instructor is available earlier than expected. It would be best for you to complete your fitness test now.'

Layla faltered. 'A fitness test?'

'Is that okay? Don't worry, it's one of the last things you need to complete today.'

Layla instantly regretted scoring her fitness eight out of ten on the questionnaire she had just submitted. 'That's great,' she replied, wondering if Saira could detect the lack of enthusiasm in her voice. 'The thing is, I haven't brought any workout clothes with me.'

'That's okay,' Saira said, rising to her feet. 'You don't need them.'

'Oh, perfect,' Layla replied, sinking into dismay at whatever *that* might mean.

'I promise it's nothing to worry about. A few weights, some reflex work, a little running, that's all. If at any point you need to stop, let the instructor know.'

Layla nodded, silently trying to figure out when she had last been to a gym. Was it two years ago? Three? Longer than that?

Sports had never come naturally to Layla. Compressing her body into a pair of lycra shorts and heading out for a run never sounded fun. Working out was for people with an athletic body type and time on their hands. Layla had neither.

And now Saira wanted Layla to showcase exactly how poor her fitness was. *Get ready to say goodbye to your spot in the experiment,* her brain grumbled.

Silencing her thoughts, Layla forced a smile. 'Fitness test time it is,' she replied.

Saira led her out of the assessment room and to the gym. As soon as Layla entered, a woman with the energy of a labrador puppy bounded over. 'You must be Layla. Hi, I'm Phoebe.'

'Nice to meet you,' Layla said, shaking the woman's hand and trying not to marvel at how perfect she looked. Phoebe had the proportions of a supermodel and the physique of an athlete. Next to her, Layla felt positively grotesque.

'So, has Dr Khatri told you what we'll be doing in here?' Phoebe asked.

Layla nodded. 'A fitness test, weights, that kind of stuff.'

'Exactly! The only thing I'll add is that you need to wear a monitor the whole time so we can track things like your heart rate. Do you consent to wearing it?'

'I do,' Layla confirmed.

'Great! Now, I'm going to need you to strip to your underwear, then I'll place the electrodes on your body.'

Layla's blood froze. 'Excuse me?'

Phoebe pointed to a machine in the corner. 'To do the tracing, we need the electrodes to access different parts of your skin. You'll need to be in your underwear so we can reach them. Don't worry, it's nothing I've not seen before!' Phoebe explained, but Layla couldn't muster a reaction that was anything but horrified.

'You want me to be in my *underwear*?' she said, looking around the room. When she saw the mirror directly opposite the treadmill, she winced.

'Is there a problem?' Phoebe asked.

Layla didn't know how to answer that. Of course there was a problem – did this woman know how unsupportive Layla's bra was?!

But it was more than a poor choice of lingerie that caused Layla such horror. That honour went to coming face to face with the body Layla did her best to avoid.

Throughout her childhood, Layla had watched her mother obsess over diets and listened to her grandma warn her she was getting 'chunky'. It got worse as a teenager. Friends, complaining about bloating, wobbly thighs and cellulite, pushed Layla further along the journey of being painfully, achingly aware of her body and all that she needed to change about it.

Layla might have buried her head in books and pretended to be immune to the critique, but she was only human. The ever-changing, impossible beauty standards and edited photos on social media still got to her. Even with a list of achievements longer than her arm, in her most vulnerable moments Layla still wished for a magic wand to shrink here and grow there, tweak this and change that.

'Layla?' Phoebe asked, butting into her thoughts. 'Is everything okay?'

'Of course,' Layla replied, straining a smile. 'I'm just trying to remember the last time anyone saw me in my underwear, that's all,' she joked, but the words made her cringe.

Great, now you've admitted that not only are you mortifyingly insecure, but you're a romantic failure too.

Ordering herself to stand to her full height, Layla looked Phoebe in the eye. 'Ignore me. I'll do it.'

Pushing herself to be brave, Layla stripped to her underwear. Under the unforgiving lights, the dimples of her cellulite seemed to glow.

'Perfect,' Phoebe said, now Layla was undressed. 'Let's get you hooked up to the monitor.'

As Layla approached the machine, with her arms crossed over her chest, Phoebe presented her with a series of wires. Round stickers were attached to the end of them. 'These pads will be stuck to you throughout your time in here. Try not to interfere with them. I warn you, they're a little cold.'

Phoebe was right about that. Layla gasped as the first electrode was stuck to her temple. Methodically, Phoebe moved around the rest of Layla's body, attaching electrodes until she had none left.

When Layla got on the treadmill, Phoebe took her position beside the monitoring machine. 'There's a program loaded onto the treadmill called "Fitness Test". Click that and press "Go". Whenever you're ready, you can start.'

Layla followed Phoebe's instructions. Beneath her feet, the track began to move. She set off, matching her pace to the machine. As she stared her reflection down, Layla chose not to look at her thighs or wobbling stomach. Instead, she focused on the fire in her eyes telling her that right here, right now, was exactly where she was supposed to be.

4

Angus

'What are you doing?'

Jasper's plummy voice tore through Angus's concentration like a bullet. *Great. You've fucked up your answers now*, his brain scoffed. Stifling a sigh, Angus looked up from the memory test he was working through to find his best friend leaning against the doorframe of his bedroom, chewing a packet of crisps so loudly it sounded like he had his mouth beside Angus's ear.

'Didn't I tell you I needed ten minutes?' Angus huffed, focusing back on the task at hand.

'You did, and I said we needed to get going. Dinner's at eight,' Jasper replied.

'If dinner's so soon, why are you eating?'

'I'm a growing boy,' Jasper replied, patting his rounding stomach. Tipping his head back, he polished off the remainder of his crisps and entered the room. When he could find no bin, Jasper scrunched up the crisp packet and left it on Angus's bedside table.

'Don't leave it there,' Angus said, re-reading the question on the screen. It asked how many yellow balls were in the picture on the previous page. Angus's forehead scrunched as he tried to remember, but it was no use. Jasper's interruption had wiped the image from his mind.

'It's fine,' Jasper said, steamrolling Angus's concentration once more. 'Jinny will clean it when she's next here.'

Sighing, Angus typed the number '2' and submitted the answer. A random guess, but it was better than nothing. 'Jinny's job isn't to pick up your rubbish,' he said irritably.

'She's a cleaner,' Jasper replied, flopping onto Angus's bed with his shoes on. 'Picking up rubbish is literally her job.'

A rebuttal was on Angus's lips, but he swallowed it. Getting into it with Jasper was annoying at the best of times. Besides, the progress bar on the latest OPM Discoveries test informed Angus he was 76 per cent of the way through the task. So close to finishing, yet with Jasper around, the end seemed further away than ever. Even more annoyingly, Angus couldn't save what he'd done so far and return to it later.

'Give me a minute, would you? I'm in the middle of something,' Angus said.

'Yeah, yeah,' Jasper drawled, engrossing himself in his phone. As his oldest friend fell silent, Angus read the next question. This one asked how many posters had been in the scene. The question felt like a trick. The image he was supposed to have memorised was of groups of people in a park. Angus couldn't remember any posters in the scene, but then again, he couldn't remember much about the picture anymore.

Hedging his bets on it being a trick question, Angus responded '0' in time for Jasper to speak again. 'What are you doing, anyway?'

Ignoring him, Angus tried to recall how many children were playing hopscotch. Was it four? Five? There was someone with pigtails stood nearby, but were they playing or were they doing something else? Angus concentrated harder, waiting for the image to appear through the mist, but the sound of Jasper shuffling along the bed pulled his focus.

'How many children were playing hopscotch?' Jasper read, laughing. 'What the fuck, Angus? Why are you answering questions about children? What is this?'

'It's nothing,' Angus grunted. His cheeks fired red as he rushed to minimise the tab, but Jasper pulled the laptop from his desk.

'A memory test . . . Why are you completing a memory test? Worried you're going senile?' he teased.

The speed and ferocity with which Angus snatched the laptop back surprised both men.

Jasper handled it with a tense laugh. 'Steady on, Angus. I'm only asking.'

'Well, don't. I told you I needed ten minutes,' Angus snapped, but when he retook his seat at his desk, he sighed. 'Look, I just need to get this done.'

'What's it for?' Jasper asked, flopping back onto the bed.

The Life Experiment's strict confidentiality warnings flashed in Angus's mind, as did the wording of the airtight NDA he had signed. While it promised a range of benefits for accepted candidates, it also warned of fines and lawsuits should the subject of OPM Discoveries' research be leaked prematurely.

'It's for a course,' he lied. 'Business skills. It's teaching me how to read a room.'

'You don't need to read a room. You're Angus Fairview-Whitley, you probably own the room. Don't bother with the course.'

'I want to do it,' Angus replied, surprised to find he was speaking through gritted teeth.

'Fuck, you're weird. I'm getting a vodka. Hurry up and tell me when you're done.' Bored, Jasper exited the room, leaving behind only the pungent smell of his aftershave and the burn of his derision.

Tension remained in Angus's jaw as he focused back on his laptop. Even with Jasper gone, it was no use.

Maybe he had a point. Maybe Angus shouldn't bother. This wasn't a business skills course, but it was an experiment that required time, commitment and effort. While time was something Angus had plenty of, commitment and effort were not. His startup investment failure was just one example proving that.

With slumped shoulders, Angus went to close his laptop, but at the last moment, he stopped. *You're over 76 per cent of the way through,* his brain reminded him.

Angus bit his lip. He couldn't remember the last time he'd been 76 per cent of the way through anything. Anything good, at least. Usually, he either didn't try, or he gave up.

And look where that's got you, a crueller part of his brain snarled.

Angus hated it when his brain turned on him like this. It happened often, and always led to the same thoughts of failure, disappointment, and reasons why he disgraced the Fairview-Whitley name. Scarier still, that negative voice in Angus's head was getting louder each day.

Lifting his gaze, Angus looked at the test's progress bar once more. It was the eighth online test he'd completed. He had an in-person session at OPM Discoveries booked in for two days' time. Were he to miss completing this, that session would be cancelled. His application would be withdrawn, and Angus would be back to square one.

As Jasper blasted music from a speaker in the living room, Angus flinched.

It would be easy to slam the laptop shut and join his friend. Good times and high-quality liquor were calling, after all. But Angus had spent the last few years answering their calls and it turned out they had little to say. More than that, Angus wanted to know what it felt like to reach 100 per cent.

Standing to close his bedroom door, Angus breathed in the quiet. A faint beat thudded in the background, but it was soft enough that he could hear himself think.

He sat back down and continued with the memory test. The park image was well and truly out of his mind now, but that was okay. There were only a few more questions to go before a new image would load. A second chance for Angus to get things right would appear.

When it came, he steadied his breath. He focused on the image. And, most importantly, he assured himself that he would do better this time.

5
Layla

Layla's foot tapped against the leg of the chair she was sitting on. It was her second visit to the OPM Discoveries headquarters in two weeks, but this time, there were no fitness or medical tests to complete. This time, it all came down to one conversation with Saira.

The problem was, Saira was nowhere to be found. Layla had been alone in her office for fifteen minutes now and was starting to wonder if she'd been forgotten.

As far as places to be left waiting went, Saira's office was a great one. A serious, grown-up workspace, just being in it made Layla feel important. Her desk was a chunky wooden thing of beauty, the walls behind it lined with framed qualifications and books on psychology, the human body and scientific theory. At the back of the room, two cream sofas faced each other, inviting deep, meaningful conversation. An added bonus was that the office smelled amazing. A mix of spices and vanilla, the combination was surprisingly soothing.

Right now, Layla needed to be soothed. Her nerves were at an all-time high. This session was the last part of the application process. The occasion she needed to impress Saira the most.

It shocked Layla how much she wanted to be accepted onto the study. Applying had been a spur of the moment decision, but the more rounds she made it through, the more invested she became. The layers of secrecy surrounding the experiment were simply too alluring.

Besides, to get this far and not make it? The rejection would be crushing.

That's why you can't mess up now, Layla's brain hissed. Then another thought sprang to her mind – what if leaving her alone was a test? What if Saira was watching to see how Layla reacted to things not running perfectly to schedule?

A quick scan of the room assured her there was no CCTV camera, but the idea that Saira could be watching made Layla sit straighter. She painted her face with a pleasant expression. When Saira eventually came back, that's how she would find her – calm, composed, patient. The perfect candidate.

As if conjured by Layla's thoughts, Saira breezed into the room. 'I am *so* sorry for the delay! Another interview ran over. I got here as fast as I could, but clearly not fast enough.'

'I completely understand,' Layla replied, doing her best to showcase the smile her mother described as 'winning'. Layla hoped Joanna wasn't a victim of maternal blindness. 'These things happen.'

'Still,' Saira said as she took a seat at her desk. 'I'd like to apologise for keeping you waiting. Tardiness isn't a true reflection of my character.'

'Don't worry, I can see how seriously you take your work.'

Appeased, Saira took a moment to log in to her computer, then settled her gaze on Layla. 'Let's get straight to it. How do you think everything is going so far?'

Layla was caught off guard. How was she meant to tailor her response when she didn't know the aim of the study?

Thankfully, Layla's job had given her plenty of practice at being put on the spot. 'Obviously I'm not fully aware of what you're looking for in a candidate, but from my perspective I would say it's going well. I've completed all tasks in a timely manner and in detail. On top of that, I'm really enjoying the process.'

'I'm glad you've enjoyed the experience, tests and all,' Saira joked.

'What I propose we do next is run through your results so far. Does that sound good to you?'

Layla nodded, trying to display an appropriate level of eagerness. While she knew it wasn't her most attractive trait, finding out test scores was one of Layla's favourite things.

'I'm pleased to report that you scored highly on the tasks you completed at home,' Saira said. 'Some of your results were the best we've seen, particularly with comprehension and memory. Signs of suitability so far are positive.'

Layla's smile faded when she realised Saira wasn't done.

'There is one thing I'm concerned about, though,' she said, turning her monitor to face Layla. A copy of the questionnaire Layla completed during her last in-person day filled the screen.

'Is there something wrong with my answers?' she asked.

'There is no right or wrong answer to these questions, Layla, but your results are a little anomalous.' Saira scrolled through the document and stopped at a self-rating section. Layla remembered it well. She'd wanted to appear confident and well-rounded, aware and thoughtful. She marked herself highly because high scores were highly regarded, right?

The expression on Saira's face told Layla that, in this instance, she might have been wrong about that.

'In the friendship section, you marked yourself as a nine out of ten in most aspects, yet in your preliminary application you mentioned you didn't have time for friendship.'

The memory of Layla's early interactions with OPM Discoveries burned her cheeks. She had been angry when the first questionnaire came through. Working late, yet again, had made her bitter. Resentful, even. Outing herself as a loser hadn't seemed like a big deal, but Layla didn't know how much she would want to be part of the study back then.

Saira scrolled to another question. 'Here, when asked to score your sense of humour, you put eight out of ten, yet you left the name of your favourite comedy show blank. Now, I don't believe television habits indicate personality, but most people can think of one show they laugh at.'

Layla flushed. 'I mustn't have seen the question.'

'But someone who scores ten out of ten for detail orientation would.'

Layla hung her head. She had never been caught out like this, mostly because giving people answers she thought they wanted to hear had never been a bad thing before.

Reading her distress, Saira continued. 'Layla, these answers are yours and yours alone. Only you can rate yourself, but when analysed they could be interpreted as disingenuous. As the person in charge of this study, that worries me. For our work to have the impact it needs to, we can't have inaccuracies in our recording. With that in mind, I need to ask if you would describe your responses as honest?'

Layla bit her lip. 'I suppose I could've been more open about my flaws. I was trying to impress you.'

Leaning forward, Saira pierced Layla with the intensity of her stare. 'Layla, you are impressive exactly as you are. I hope you know that.'

Out of nowhere, a lump appeared in Layla's throat. She tried to swallow it, but it wouldn't budge.

While her parents simmered with pride over all she had achieved, no one else had ever called Layla impressive before, and definitely not impressive as she was. She was, at her core, the definition of a work in progress. Someone who had great potential if she dared to use it. Someone who could break free of the poverty she had grown up in and soar, but only if she worked hard enough.

From school to university to Mayweather & Halliwell, Layla had pushed and pushed. There was always another assessment to complete, another task to tick off, another goal to chase. Never the opportunity to appreciate who she was at that moment.

Saira's features softened. 'You don't see yourself for all the wonderful things you are, do you?'

'Not really,' Layla admitted, surprised at how emotional the confession made her. 'At work, I'm the kid from Hull they let into the building. When I go home, I'm the girl who abandoned everyone to make something of herself. I guess I don't fit anywhere.'

'I see. What does fitting look like to you?'

Layla pondered the question for a moment before replying. 'I suppose fitting means being at peace. Belonging in the place you are, and within yourself too.'

'Have you reached a place of peace within yourself?'

Saira's question earned a laugh from Layla. 'Has anyone?'

'Believe it or not, they have. There is always more for a person to do, more to learn, but that doesn't mean you can't be at peace with who you are along the way.'

'I don't know what peace looks like for me,' Layla admitted, chewing her lip. 'I know I don't want to struggle like I did growing up, but I'm not sure what I'm doing now is what I want either. I guess . . . I guess I don't know what I want.'

Saira leaned closer. 'Shall I let you in on a secret, Layla? Not many people do.'

The first genuine smile of the day graced Layla's lips.

'I mean it when I say you are incredible. You wouldn't be here if you weren't,' Saira continued, 'but this study requires complete trust in participants. To have that, we need honesty. We need to know how participants are feeling and what they are thinking. There is no room for error. It could be the difference between life and death.'

Beneath her shirt, Layla's heart began to thud. 'What is the purpose of this study, exactly? And before you say it will be revealed to accepted candidates, I think after weeks of tests and time I deserve to know. Being honest works both ways.'

Saira paused, then nodded. 'You're right, it does. I haven't practised my delivery of this yet, so forgive me if I'm a little blunt, but the truth is we believe we have found a way to determine when someone is going to die.'

Layla, usually never short for words, couldn't find any.

The corners of Saira's mouth flicked upwards. 'It's a lot to wrap your head around, I know, but it's true. We believe we have found a way to determine when someone is going to die, and in some cases, how.'

Layla's forehead creased. 'I . . . How . . . Is this for real?'

'It might sound like a fantasy, but I promise it's not. You've completed the tasks so far, Layla. You're a smart woman. Would we collate so much information if we didn't need to?'

'But . . . But how can you tell when I'll die from that?'

'Science,' Saira replied with a knowing smile. 'We've made the most incredible advances in recent years. More advances than the average person would dare to believe.'

'But finding out when someone will die? Surely not.'

Saira gestured to her surroundings. 'Would we be here right now if it weren't true? Would The Life Experiment be wrapped in so many layers of confidentiality if it wasn't researching something so huge?' Seeing Layla's shock, Saira smiled with understanding. 'I realise it's a lot to take in. Trust me, we've been working on it for a long time and still can't believe what we've discovered. You're more than welcome to research OPM Discoveries' credentials for yourself, although I imagine someone as studious as yourself has already done that.' When a blushing Layla gave a sheepish nod, Saira laughed. 'Don't worry, I'd have done the same. But after researching us, you'll know we're legitimate.'

'I do. I just . . . I . . . I can't believe this is possible.'

'I have an information pack that might help your understanding, if you'd like to read it?' When Layla nodded, Saira reached into a drawer of her desk and removed a brochure. 'If you have any questions, let me know.'

Turning her attention to the information in front of her, Layla began to read. Cutting-edge procedures and cellular testing, state-of-the-art technology, a high success rate when trialled on multiple species of animals . . . Maybe OPM Discoveries really could calculate when a person would die.

When she reached the end of the document, Layla's lips parted. 'This is crazy.'

'It's a lot to process, but as you read, our clinical trials showed a 98 per cent success rate in estimating a biological date of death in animals. Now it's time to test humans. People of all ages, races and backgrounds. People like . . . well, people like you, Layla. Our work here has incredible implications. Think how this knowledge could help people living with health anxiety or the terminally ill. Even people simply wanting to plan their lives better. Layla, this research could change everything.'

As the weight of those words hit Layla in the chest, she nodded. There was no denying the possible ramifications of this experiment, both good and bad. Something like this could quite literally change the world.

'Is it . . . Is it ethical?' she asked. 'To tell people when they'll die, I mean.'

'Only those who want to know will find out their result. If this trial is successful, people would have the choice to access the service. They would also be able to leave the process at any point before results are handed over. Counselling is mandatory too. We take our duty of care seriously. Nobody wants to tell someone this news unless it is absolutely what they want to hear. That's why we give participants a week between participation offers and their decision. We're not immune to the gravity of this knowledge, Layla. Whatever result we pass on, we cannot take back.'

The more Saira spoke, the deeper Layla was pulled into intrigue. Sure, there was a dangerous element to the study, a 'playing god' complex she was sure her mum would hate, but to know the map of your future . . . Who wouldn't be curious about that?

'With the highly sensitive nature of this study, I'm sure you can understand why we need complete transparency from our participants,'

Saira continued. 'With that in mind, can you understand why your responses concerned me?'

Sheepishly, Layla nodded. 'I'm sorry I messed up.'

'You haven't messed up. If anything, you've made me more determined to have you in this study.'

Layla smiled at the compliment, but a wobble of insecurity wiped her smile away. 'Can you . . . Can you really tell me when I'm going to die?'

'We can't factor in accidents or natural disasters, but we can pinpoint your biological death date from your current health, lifestyle and DNA makeup. If you want us to, that is.'

As Layla closed her eyes, her life passed before her. The run of late nights and ready meals, her aching joints and ever-growing mental load. Before this conversation, she would have said it was worth it, but now someone was saying they could *actually* tell Layla if it was.

Desire flickered in the pit of Layla's stomach. She wanted – no, she *needed* – to know. Every early alarm, every skipped meal, every cancelled plan . . . Would the sacrifice one day outweigh the cost?

Leaning forward, Layla levelled her gaze at Saira. 'If I redo my questionnaire, will you reconsider me?'

Grinning, Saira pulled an iPad from her desk. 'I was hoping you'd say that.'

6

Angus

'So I told her to get out or I'd call the police!' Jasper roared, banging the table with his fist, making the patterned china and silver cutlery jump in the air.

While the rest of the diners guffawed, Angus stifled an eye-roll. How anyone could believe Jasper's story, that he once dated a woman who tried to rob him, was beyond Angus, but when someone shouted loud enough, people tended to believe what they said.

Sipping his whisky, Angus glanced across the garden to the main house. His parents and their friends sat on the veranda, no doubt having similarly insincere conversations. The only difference was they were at the grown-up table, and he was at the children's one.

No one called it the children's table anymore – not now that most of those seated at it were keeping wrinkles at bay via botox or staring down the barrel of a divorce – but that's what it was. Pushed off to the side, under the embrace of an oak tree and surrounded by portable heaters due to the autumnal weather, everyone at the table was the offspring of one of his parents' friends. Partygoers, socialites and travellers burning through their inheritance like the money was theirs to spend in the first place.

Suddenly, a hand trailed up Angus's thigh. Glancing to his left, he locked eyes with Clarissa Dowess. Set to inherit an expansive property empire when her father died (probably of a heart attack, judging by

Archibald's rich diet), everyone expected Angus to marry Clarissa. She was, after all, an 'eligible' match. The daughter of Peter's best friend, four years younger than Angus and classically beautiful, his mother called her 'a darn catch'.

She was also a tedious bore with a crippling cocaine habit. As Angus placed his hand on top of hers and gently pushed it away, she pouted. 'Aren't you in the mood for a little fun?'

'You mean this isn't fun enough?' he replied, gesturing to their surroundings.

Smirking, Clarissa picked up her champagne flute. 'It's a riot. Who doesn't love Jasper's stories? Although this one gets more outrageous every time I hear it,' she said, leaning so close to Angus that her lips brushed his ear. 'One wonders if perhaps our dear Jasper isn't exactly forthcoming with the truth.'

As if sensing he was the topic of conversation, Jasper looked across the table. When his gaze met Clarissa's, he winked.

Triumphant, she turned to Angus. 'At least someone's keen for a good time.'

Angus shrugged. 'Maybe you should sit with Jasper instead.'

With a haughty glare, Clarissa snatched her embellished bag from the table. 'You know, you can be a real dick sometimes,' she snapped. Rising to her feet, Clarissa's theatrical exit was hindered by the legs of her chair, which had sunk into the grass. Furious, she battled with them until finally, with a squelch, she was free.

Angus watched Clarissa sweep to the other side of the table. There, she slid onto Jasper's lap, twisting her body until her silky dress pulled tight across her chest. As his cheeks flushed red, Jasper couldn't hide his delight at the surprising turn of events.

Angus knew he should feel something. A kick in his gut or some ounce of anger. After all, he and Clarissa had been hooking up for years, but seeing her entangled with his best friend, Angus felt nothing.

'Someone's playing her usual games,' Fergus quipped beside him. 'When will you two make it official and save us from this never-ending drama?'

Angus downed the rest of his drink. 'Never going to happen.'

'My friend, marriage comes for us all eventually. Especially those with parents concerned about continuing the family name.'

'And you think Clarissa is the right woman for me?'

'Angus, you and Clarissa have more money behind you than most of this table combined. If that doesn't make her the right woman, what does?'

Angus's mouth twitched, the only response he could muster to such a depressing statement. 'Excuse me,' he said, standing abruptly. Without another word, he strode across the grass towards his parents' impressive Buckinghamshire estate, aware of Clarissa's eyes boring into his back as he went.

It would have been quicker for Angus to head to the kitchen via the veranda, but he entered the house through a side door instead. Anything to stop his mother stretching out a slender hand and drawing him into stilted conversation with whichever friend she wanted to belittle.

Inside, Angus drifted through grand room after grand room. With tasteful, opulent interiors, the stately home was luxury in its purest form. Everyone agreed that Gilly Fairview-Whitley had done an exquisite job with the latest renovations. Angus wondered if his mother would ever admit to using a top interior designer for the task.

The kitchen was a hub of frantic activity as a team of caterers rushed to ensure everything sent out met Gilly's exacting standards. The chaos was overseen by the Fairview-Whitley's housekeeper, Ms Tillman. Employed by the family for the last eleven years, Angus's interactions with Ms Tillman usually centred around her rustling up a hangover cure for him.

When she saw Angus enter the kitchen, Ms Tillman frowned and moved towards him, but a chef arranging a selection of delicate desserts got to him first.

'Is everything okay with the food, sir?' she asked.

'Everything is wonderful. I only came inside for a beer.'

'Haven't they been served?' she replied, shooting a withering glare at a passing waitress.

'There are plenty of drinks outside, thank you. I just fancied getting away from it all, you know?'

The woman nodded, but her expression indicated she had no idea what Angus was talking about. Get away from what – a lavish party? Being waited on hand and foot?

Shying away from the judgement, Angus headed to the fridge. As his hand wrapped around the neck of an ice-cold beer, he heard his father calling him from somewhere inside the house. Angus paused, debating whether to shout back or hide in the kitchen, but as he turned, Angus discovered Peter had already found him.

Even with his casual suit rumpled, Peter Fairview-Whitley was a man with presence. His broad frame and thick head of hair marked him as good looking despite his sixty-plus years, but even without such strong physical attributes, he would still command attention. There was something in the way he strode into every room, like it should be grateful for his presence, that made people stand straighter and try harder. Not for the first time in his life, Angus wondered how someone like Peter could have a son as pathetic as himself.

The hubbub in the kitchen doubled now Peter was there, but Angus wanted to tell the staff not to worry. Peter Fairview-Whitley was a teddy bear. Gilly, on the other hand . . . Well, the less said about her ability to reduce people to tears, the better.

'Did you come inside for a drink too?' Angus asked.

'Actually, I followed you. I thought we could talk.'

Angus tried not to react, but in his surprise, the beer nearly slipped from his hands.

'Don't look so worried, son. Come on, let's get out of the kitchen.' Peter clapped his hand on Angus's shoulder and steered him away.

Angus expected Peter to take him outside to join an exchange with one of his boorish friends, but instead Peter led Angus to his office. Traditionally styled with wood panels, it was filled with antiques and rare first editions. Fiction had provided escapism for Angus as a child, so his father's book-lined office became one of his favourite places. Not that Angus had often been allowed in.

The contents of that room are far too precious to be handled willy-nilly by someone so reckless, Gilly would scold whenever she caught Angus inside, usually when Peter was away on business. *Go play elsewhere.*

For the most part, Angus obeyed the 'stay out' rule. But on his more rebellious days, sneaking into the room that smelled like Peter and curling up in an armchair with a book was the closest Angus felt to being at peace.

When the office door was closed behind them, Peter led Angus to the window. Side by side, the pair observed life on the other side of the glass. The garden seemed alive. Four of Angus's schoolfriends lay on the grass, watching a drunk member of the party try to do a handstand. At the main table, Gilly was entertaining her audience with another carefully constructed story. Over by the oak tree, Jasper was doing the same. Two expert hosts, two larger-than-life personalities.

Two people who fit in exactly where Angus didn't.

'Clarissa's looking well,' Peter commented, taking a bottle of whisky from his desk. He poured two generous glasses. 'Your mother would be happy if you pursued her.'

Accepting the drink, Angus stayed silent. In the distance, Clarissa chugged her champagne, held the empty flute in the air, then whispered suggestively in Jasper's ear.

'I, on the other hand . . .'

From the corner of his eye, Angus caught his father's dubious expression. The pair exchanged a smile.

Peter took a long drink before facing his son. There was a mistiness to his eyes that Angus had never seen before, and for one terrifying moment he thought his father was going to cry.

'This isn't real, you know,' Peter said. 'This party, this life . . . it isn't real.'

It took Angus a moment to process the words. Another passed before he could speak. 'What do you mean?'

Turning back to the window, Peter absorbed the scene before him. 'When I met your mother, she was unlike anyone I knew. Opinionated and passionate, at times she verged on arrogant in her disdain for everything you see outside right now.'

'Sorry, are we talking about Gilly Fairview-Whitley here? The woman who insists on throwing these god-awful parties?'

Peter let out a sad chuckle. 'Believe it or not, yes. We both grew up in this world, but we didn't relish it. Not like the others. Once, your mother would have laughed at today and called it a charade. She would probably have stolen a bottle of brandy and hidden in the woods until her parents called a search party to find her.'

Angus raised his eyebrows. '*My* mother did that?'

'Yes. You're not the only one with a talent for going rogue after a few drinks, let me assure you.'

Angus studied Gilly, taking in her perfectly styled hair and the neat scarf tied around her neck. He searched for a sign of the person his father was describing, but all he could see was the same buttoned-up soul he'd always known.

When Angus looked back, Peter's face was clouded with sadness. 'This life can consume you, if you let it. Who has the latest car, who went where on holiday, who makes the most money. It's a competition you're signed up for at birth, and it's exhausting.'

Suddenly, Angus's own exhaustion seeped into his bones, making everything seem so heavy, so pointless.

'After what happened to Hugo . . .'

As his father trailed off, Angus's throat tightened. Hugo wasn't mentioned within these walls. Ever. Sometimes, Angus liked it that way. It was easier to push away the hurt of losing someone you loved when you weren't allowed to talk about it.

But even if his name wasn't mentioned, Hugo was always there. He was the big-brother-shaped stick Angus measured himself against. His shadow covered everything Angus did, reminding Angus of everything he could never be.

'I shoulder the blame for how things turned out,' Peter said. 'Things happened in our family that changed us forever, but it's more than that. When your mother and I married, I insisted we host the parties and dinners and grow our connections like my parents had. I never realised the expectation I placed on Gilly, but this world is hard. You either fit in or you're cast out. How else was she meant to survive?' Suddenly, Peter turned to Angus. 'Angus, you remind me so much of your mother, it's scary. I see the way you sit at these tables, wishing you were anywhere else. I see the way you don't belong.'

Angus flinched, the casual delivery of his failure a knife to the chest, but Peter shook his head.

'I mean that as a compliment, believe me. I've watched you today. You're here, but you're not *here*. I know this life might not be what you want, but I also suspect you don't know what you do want. That's just as dangerous. Things might not have worked out as you'd hoped in the past, but don't let one bad investment keep you down. Put it behind you and look to your future.'

'What future?' Angus heard himself mutter.

'That's for you to decide, son, but you can't tread water forever or one day you'll wake up a lonely old man full of regrets. You have all options open to you. All the support a person could ask for, but what you're doing now? Angus, it's no life. You're miserable, I can see it.'

Softening, Angus absorbed his father's words. Peter Fairview-Whitley was always an engaging conversationalist, but he had never spoken to Angus like this before – so plainly, so openly, so full of love. For Angus, life simply wasn't the same as it had been five minutes ago.

Angus opened his mouth to respond, but at that moment his phone rang.

'Sorry,' he said, fumbling in his pocket for the device. When he saw Saira's name on the screen, Angus's stomach flipped. 'I need to take this.'

With a nod, Peter's controlled persona slotted back into place. 'Sure, son. I'll see you outside.'

Angus watched his father walk away. The departure created an ache in his soul that he couldn't put words to, but Angus's phone ordered him to push those feelings aside and answer the call.

'Angus,' Saira said when he picked up. 'I'm glad I caught you. I'm calling with what I hope is exciting news.'

'Oh?'

Through the window, Angus saw his father return to Gilly's side. He kissed her cheek. She leaned her head on his chest. Together, they stood tall, like two people who belonged in their world completely.

'I'm pleased to say we'd like to invite you to participate in The Life Experiment. Congratulations!' Saira cheered. 'If you're still on board, we'll set up a meeting to run through the aim and expectations of the study, then send the contract for you to read over. As previously mentioned, you have seven days to think—'

'I'll do it,' Angus interjected. 'I want to do it. I want to be part of the experiment.'

'Angus,' Saira replied sternly, although he could hear the ghost of a smile in her voice. 'While I appreciate your enthusiasm, you need to be sure that this is something you want to do. The work we're doing could change your life.'

Dry-mouthed, Angus studied the scene outside once more. The glasses full to the brim, the tables stuffed with uneaten food. The abundance, the insincerity, the privilege – it was all he could see. It was everything he needed to change.

As Angus's gaze settled on his father, something in his chest tugged. Whatever Peter was hoping for him to find, Angus was going to do it. The Life Experiment would be the catalyst. From there, Angus would bloom. Anything to make his father, and himself, proud.

7

Layla

'Layla, have you got one? Layla? Layla!'

It was only when Rashida clapped in her face that Layla realised she had drifted into a daydream. Startling, she looked to her friend. 'Sorry, what?'

'Michelle wants an updated witness list for the Iso-Marks hearing. Do you have one?'

Straightening, Layla searched her computer. The names of clients and codes for current matters flitted across her screen. When she found what Rashida was looking for, she mailed it across.

'Thanks,' said Rashida, before flicking her gaze to Layla once more. 'Are you okay? You seem distracted.'

'I'm fine,' Layla replied, but the words weren't entirely true. In three days' time, she was heading to OPM Discoveries headquarters again, but she wouldn't be completing a test.

This time, she would find out when she would die.

Goosebumps lined Layla's arms. Initially, they had been the markers of excitement, but now only nerves hummed through Layla. And who could blame her for being scared? All her life, she had followed a plan and ticked off her goals one by one. Sure, a lot of hard work went into making them happen, but Layla wasn't afraid of hard work. No, she was afraid that her hard work might be for nothing.

Knowledge that The Life Experiment could provide.

Discovering when you were going to die was not a decision to make lightly – Saira had stressed that multiple times. For every positive it could bring, Layla worried that there were three negatives. When Layla felt as tired and beaten down as she did, was there room in her brain for more pessimism?

As if to illustrate that point, Sinead chose that moment to return to her desk. Layla could tell she'd been crying.

'You okay?' she asked as Sinead took a seat.

'I'm fine,' Sinead replied, in a voice that sounded anything but.

Rashida and Layla caught each other's eye. It wouldn't take much time out of their day if they took Sinead for a coffee. They could use the machine in the breakroom if they didn't want to leave the office and be back at their desks in twenty minutes.

But as Layla's attention drifted to the forty-three unread emails in her inbox that had arrived in the last hour, she stamped down those thoughts and got back to work. Across the pod of desks, Rashida did the same.

Opening a draft of a briefing, Layla skimmed what was written so far. William Addington was taking the lead on this one, and his work was sloppy as usual. Part of Layla wanted to leave it and let William stumble over his own incompetency, but she couldn't do that. Not when Mayweather & Halliwell demanded perfection.

So, silently and resentfully, Layla got to work improving what was written. With each letter she fired through the keyboard, the anger Layla spent her days suffocating smouldered. Soon, her lungs were aflame. What was she doing?

Seriously, what was she *doing*?

Covering for colleagues who wouldn't think twice about throwing her under the bus and ignoring the pain of someone sat two desks away . . . Was this the life Layla wanted? Was this the person she wanted to be?

Earlier that morning, she had watched a woman with a baby try to get onto the tube, only to be pushed aside by people rushing to work.

Layla didn't want to be one of those people, but as she watched Sinead discreetly dab her tears, she wondered if she already was.

Narrowing her eyes, Layla turned back to her laptop. She polished the briefing until it was good. Better than good. William would likely take the credit for the work, but Layla told herself it didn't matter. What mattered was that she had done the job well.

But it does matter, her heart screamed.

If Layla's work was never attributed to her, was it really hers?

If William was passing off her voice as his own, did Layla even have a voice within these prestigious walls?

As she wrestled with these questions, Layla's phone buzzed. A photograph of her mum taken two Christmases ago filled the screen, and she fought the urge to sigh.

No matter how many times they had the conversation, Joanna never understood that a social call in the middle of the day wasn't acceptable. Her shifts at the supermarket seemed to make her think that everybody's working hours were malleable and subject to a rota. It often meant Layla missed her calls, then it was too late when she returned them.

'Nine o'clock is midnight at my age, Layla,' Joanna would say. 'I'm in bed by then.'

But when else was Layla meant to call?

Eventually, Joanna's call rang out. Moments later, a text came through. *I forget how busy you are*, it read. *My little lawyer! Hopefully speak soon. Miss you xx*

Cursing herself for reading the message, Layla let the last two words eat away at her until she could take it no more. *Miss you too,* she replied.

Turning her phone facedown, Layla tried to escape into her work, but now that the tentacles of her mother's love were reaching for her, the comfort of personal statements and decisive language had lost its appeal.

Clicking her mouse a few times to appear as though she was busy, Layla allowed her thoughts to drift to her family. As always, whenever she thought of them, her chest hurt.

Casting her mind back, Layla tried to remember when she had last seen them. It was Joanna's birthday, she realised. Back in May, when everyone was waiting for summer with bated breath. Now, with the imminent arrival of October, sunny weather was a distant memory.

How had Layla let so much time pass without seeing the people she loved?

As that reality sank in, Layla's brain tortured her with the worst thought: Was she a stranger to her family now?

Sometimes it felt like it.

Layla had learned to accept it for what it was – her choice to leave had put her on the edge of Cannon family life. Now, she watched from afar. The photos of days out posted in the group chat, the events she heard about long after they happened, the in-jokes she wasn't part of. Even when she was in the same room as them, she felt separate.

It's your choice to be here, her brain reminded her. The statement wasn't a lie, but that didn't stop her mind wandering to what could have been had she stayed in Hull.

Every success, every moment Layla navigated on her own, was tainted with melancholy because her family weren't there to share it with her. As she deepened her roots in London, she felt the roots of her hometown crack, sometimes snap. Guilt seeped into her exchanges. Loneliness became second nature.

'I don't want to be lonely anymore,' Layla whispered before she could stop herself. Cheeks burning, she glanced around the office to see if anyone had heard her, but her colleagues' eyes remained fixed on their screens.

Relief was quicky replaced by the familiar burn of shame.

However uncomfortable the experiment made her, Layla knew she had to do it. She couldn't not. This was a turning point. The experiment would give her an answer, and around that answer, she would craft a life.

Squaring her shoulders, Layla decided she was going to say yes to Saira. Then, in three days' time, Layla Cannon would find out when she was going to die.

8

Angus

Angus drummed his fingers on the arm of the chair, then on his knee, then the chair again. Nerves buzzed around his body. How else was he supposed to feel? In a few minutes, he might find out he was going to die next week, or that he was going to live forever. Angus couldn't decide which thought tightened his chest more.

Last week, when Saira first told him the purpose of the experiment, Angus had laughed. His laughter died in his mouth when he realised she was serious.

'Well . . . wow,' was all Angus could reply in the end. Or, the only polite thing he could think to reply, anyway.

After mulling things over, Angus decided to accept his invitation to participate in the study and approach his result with an open mind. It wasn't like there was anything else filling up his calendar. Nothing as intriguing as the experiment, at least.

While he waited for Saira to return to her office, Angus checked his phone. A text from his mother caught his eye.

Angus, your father and I are hosting a dinner on Saturday. A small get-together with the Haywell-Newtons, the Smythes and the Markingtons. Be there at seven. I mean it, Angus. Seven.

Angus sighed. There was no question or acknowledgement that he might already have plans on Saturday. Fuck, there wasn't even a kiss at the end to suggest Gilly felt any affection for her son. Instead, the message read as a summons.

Confirming his attendance, Angus squirmed as he imagined how the night would go. He could already hear Richard Smythe's booming voice and feel Corinne Smythe's roving eyes on him. She might be a close friend of his mother's, but that hadn't stopped Corinne from slipping a hotel room key into Angus's jacket pocket when he was eighteen.

And Bruno Markington and Henry Haywell-Newton . . . Angus shuddered. Bruno's eldest son was an MP and Henry's was a CEO. Next to them, Angus looked more pathetic than ever.

Sighing, Angus opened another message, this one from Jasper.

You, me, vino, tonight . . . ?

Angus grinned as he imagined the dim lights and warming reds of his favourite wine bar. The perfect antidote to the stress of his mother's message, and the best way to end the day. After all, Angus might be celebrating once he learned his death date. That or drowning his sorrows. Either way, wine would be a welcome addition to the evening.

As Angus hit send on his reply, Saira entered the office. Two research assistants, Greg and Isa, were with her. Angus stood to greet them. Isa was carrying a large box so couldn't accept the handshake, but they each said hello like Angus was an old friend. He took that as a good sign. They wouldn't be so cheerful if they were about to reveal he had two weeks to live, after all.

'Angus, how are you?' Saira asked as she took her seat.

'Good. A little nervous.'

'I'd be worried if you weren't. This is a big day. Now before we proceed, I want to confirm your decision to participate in the experiment one final time. I know contracts have been signed, but I wouldn't be doing my job if I didn't check again.'

Angus knew all too well that if he changed his mind, Saira would understand, but he didn't want to back out. Not now he'd made it this far.

Admittedly, Angus had debated withdrawing from the study once or twice over the last few days. After all, no one wanted to think about death at the best of times, but to carry on living, knowing exactly when your time would be up . . . How could anyone do that?

But the longer Angus sat with the knowledge of what he could learn, the more curious he became. The idea of knowing exactly where he was headed had wormed its way into his brain, leaving him unable to sleep. He'd tossed and turned, wondering if he had enough time to make the changes he wanted. If he could become the person he dreamed of being.

'I'm all in,' Angus confirmed for the final time.

Saira beamed. 'Excellent! Now, before we share your results, I'd like to remind you that for the next ten weeks, you cannot tell a soul outside of OPM Discoveries what you learn today. Breaking your contract would leave you ineligible for the benefits of this study, as well as land you with a hefty fine and potentially a lawsuit. Is that clear?'

Angus nodded. Who would he tell? Jasper wouldn't want to ruin a good time, and emotions were practically banned in the Fairview-Whitley household.

In the end, it seemed to Angus that keeping the news to himself was going to be the easiest part of the whole process.

'I understand,' he confirmed.

'Perfect!' Saira enthused. 'Before we hand over the results, there are some things we need to pass on for you to complete your side of the experiment.'

Taking the box from Isa, Saira pulled out a watch that looked identical to a Fitbit.

'You must wear this watch at all times for the next ten weeks. It will track your bodily responses to everyday life. Things like your heart rate, sleep pattern, exercise habits and so on.'

Nodding, Angus slipped the watch onto his wrist. Jasper would probably ask why he wasn't wearing a more expensive one, but Angus could tell him he was on a fitness kick. Maybe he'd even joke about the quality of Jasper's watch. That would stop him talking.

Next, Saira handed Angus an iPad. 'Questionnaires will be sent to you on this device. The app you will use to log responses is already downloaded, ready to go. One questionnaire will be sent in the morning, the other in the evening. Think of them as journal entries, shared directly with me. Your answers can be as short and as informal as you like, but you must complete them every day. On top of that, your answers must be honest, and they must address each question. If you're struggling, we need to know. If you make any lifestyle changes, tell us. Do you understand?'

Angus nodded. This part of the experiment would be harder to complete, given Angus's penchant for late nights and lie-ins, but he'd figure something out. Maybe the experiment could finally get him into a routine.

As Angus concocted a plan to complete his questionnaires, Saira continued. 'This tablet will also give you a direct link to video call me. If I'm unavailable, it will connect you to Isa, Greg or another senior researcher. If you ever need to speak outside of our sessions, call. I cannot stress that enough. What you learn may lead to negative thoughts. You may consider self-harm or even suicide. If anything like that crosses your mind, even for a moment, you must contact me. Is that clear?'

Angus tried to swallow, but his mouth was too dry. Life and death, that's what this was all about. The two biggest questions humanity has: Why am I here and when will this end?

What Angus was about to discover was huge, but the aftermath of that discovery was still very much unknown. Pressing his palms against his chair, Angus prayed he was strong enough to face whatever came next.

'I understand,' he confirmed.

Saira continued to provide Angus with items to use throughout the experiment. A stress ball, a pillow spray, playlists of relaxing music. Everything he was given seemed designed to calm Angus down, which made him worry more. Surely you would only give someone who was going to live to one hundred a round-the-world ticket and a thumbs up?

As Angus's underarms dampened, Saira handed him an envelope with 'Candidate 11 – Angus Fairview-Whitley' written on it.

He gulped. 'Is this . . . Is this it?'

When Saira nodded, the air thickened. No one spoke. No one breathed. They just sat, staring at the envelope.

Angus flipped it over in his hands, marvelling at how light it was. This thing with the power to smash his world in two. How easy it would be to scrunch it up and throw it in the bin, or tear it into tiny, indistinguishable pieces.

Biting his lip, Angus read his name and candidate number once more. Ten people had been before him. Ten people had sat in this chair and found out when they would die.

It was only when Angus noticed the envelope looked like it was vibrating that he realised he was shaking.

'Take your time,' Saira said. 'There's no rush. Remember, you can walk out of here, leave the envelope behind and never look back. You never need to see what's inside.'

Angus nearly laughed. Saira made it sound so simple, but it wasn't simple at all. Leaving the envelope wouldn't really *leave the envelope*, would it? There would always be some part of Angus that yearned to know.

Temptation snapped at his heels, with fear close behind it. But fear had always been there, hadn't it? It had stopped Angus telling Jasper no to a fourth night out in a row. It had stopped him admitting how much he was struggling. It had stopped him from trying again when he lost all that money.

But Angus didn't want to be scared anymore. Ripping open the envelope, he pulled out the papers, ready to learn his fate.

9

Layla

Layla didn't know how long she'd been slouched on the squat, wooden seat, but it was starting to get uncomfortable. The slats pressed into her spine, prodding her bones with every wobbly inhale she took, but Layla was glad of the pain. It told her she was alive, something she hadn't been sure of since opening that envelope.

The envelope...

Layla blinked her surroundings into focus in a last-ditch attempt to stop herself from crying. A hipster cafe was hardly the place she wanted to break down in. With tiny pots of brown sugar on each table and single flowers reaching out of small glass vases, it was like a 'cool aesthetic' Pinterest board come to life. But when Layla stumbled out of OPM Discoveries, she didn't care where she ended up. She just needed somewhere to sit in solitude and process the news.

The news.

Her face crumpled at the memory. *Hold it together,* she scolded herself.

Desperately, Layla forced herself to count the cutlery in the mason jar on the table. Three knives, four forks, four spoons. Once she'd counted them, she counted the cutlery on the next table, then the one after that.

When she could no longer make out the silverware in the distance, Layla reached for the latte she had ordered. She flinched when her hand brushed the mug, now cold. How long had it been sitting there? How long had *she* been sitting there?

Wasting time, yet again, her brain muttered, and that was it. That was the moment Layla realised there was no avoiding the truth. When she was thirty-one years, eight months and six days old, Layla Cannon would die.

Thirty-one years, eight months and six days.

That was Layla's death date. Her horribly short, impossibly devastating death date. The words 'BELOW AVERAGE' were printed beside it, to really kick Layla in the gut, but that wasn't the worst part. As Saira promised, in certain cases the data was strong enough to predict a cause of death. Layla was one of those lucky, or unlucky, cases.

Candidate 8's organs and cells show significant signs of damage thanks to prolonged, heightened stress. Combined with her lifestyle responses, it is highly probable that a stroke will be her cause of death.

Groaning, Layla ran her hands through her tangled hair. A big, screaming part of her wanted to dismiss the study as bullshit. After all, OPM Discoveries weren't God or fate, they didn't *know*. But, like a true top-of-the-class student, Layla had researched the organisation thoroughly. It was impressive, ground-breaking and in a league of its own. In short, the team knew what they were doing, meaning they knew when Layla was going to die.

And now so did she.

In two years' time.

Everything paled into insignificance when Layla read her horrific timeline. Everything.

Before meeting with Saira, Layla had fretted about taking the afternoon off work. Taking leave meant missing important meetings. It meant falling behind. Even sat outside Saira's office, Layla had been mentally calculating how many emails she would miss because of their meeting.

As if reminding her that she had dared to take time away from the office, Layla's phone rang. She closed her eyes. How could she talk to clients now, without telling them that their legal disputes weren't worth it? How could she care enough to go in early and stay back late when all her hard work was going to be for nothing?

Sighing, Layla picked up her phone to throw it across the cafe, but she stopped when she saw Michelle's name on the screen. Despite every instinct telling her not to, Layla accepted the call.

'Layla, hi. Just wondering if you're coming back to the office today? There's a bit of a crisis. You see, the . . .'

With zero fucks to give, Layla zoned out until she became aware of silence on the other end of the line. 'I won't be back today, no,' she heard herself say.

'Oh, okay. Well, that's fine. We'll manage without you somehow.'

Layla's nostrils flared at Michelle's not-so-subtle guilt trip. Once upon a time – a few hours ago, even – it would have worked, but as Layla squared her jaw, she told herself, *not anymore*. 'I need to go,' she said, ending the call before Michelle could speak again.

Setting her phone on the table, Layla folded her arms. She had been rude, but she didn't care. In two years' time, nothing would matter anyway.

Numb, Layla focused on life outside the cafe. The world looked different now. Scarier, less certain. Everything felt different too. Layla's smart clothes itched her skin. Her high heels pinched her toes. Layla was even talking differently. Years ago, when she'd grown tired of her colleagues teasing her for her northern accent, Layla trained herself out of using it. She'd copied phrases her privately educated colleagues used and rolled her vowels like she'd grown up with the richest of them.

But now? Now, fuck it. She would use contractions and slang and every profanity she could think of. Let her sentences be short and clipped and as blunt as she could make them. Who cared what anyone thought anymore?

Who cared about anything anymore?

Suddenly, all Layla wanted was a hug. A pair of strong arms wrapped around her to prove that she wasn't as alone as she felt.

I want my mum.

The words rattled through Layla. She hadn't had that thought in years, but at that moment, it was true – Layla wanted her mum. She wanted her mum more than she wanted anything. Even to live past the age of thirty-one.

Joanna was a good mum, a great mum . . . Had Layla ever told her that? Had she ever thanked her, or her dad? Her dad with his round tummy and bald spot at the back of his head, who battled for years to overcome the physical and mental trauma of his accident, to get back to work. He drove a taxi part-time, even though sitting for so long made his joints stiff. He worked nights, even though it meant he was always tired. But pain and exhaustion meant food on the table. It meant a better life for his family.

Layla's heart broke as she thought of the people who not only gave her life, but a great life at that. And Maya, the sister who'd been an ally through it all . . . Had Layla ever thanked her? Had she ever sat her family down and told them how grateful she was?

Grief pushed up Layla's throat as she thought about how desperate she'd been to leave Hull. Determined to prove the world wrong when it tried to limit all she could be, she ran, but she hadn't meant to leave her family behind in the process. Over the years it just . . . happened. Work got busier, her ambition grew hungrier. Recently, all Layla's energy was spent by the time Friday rolled around. Who wanted to take the train to Hull and back again at the weekend when they could barely keep their eyes open?

Who had time to cook, work out, read a book, go on a date? All those things had been on Layla's 'one day' list, but now she couldn't deny it would be nice to have someone there when she came home after a long day.

The shock of her sudden desire for romance tore through Layla. Love hadn't been on her radar for a long time. Not since her most serious relationship ended six years ago.

Once upon a time, Layla believed she would marry Trent Otello. After meeting in the university library, Trent would joke that he knew Layla was the one because she was more interested in books than booze. It had been a cute line. One that, like their relationship, hadn't stood the test of time.

Their natural end came around the time Trent realised that to be in a relationship, you actually had to see the other person. He tried to sit Layla down three evenings in a row so they could break up. Each time, she was home so late that it was dark outside. For a week, they slept side-by-side with Trent's packed suitcase in the wardrobe and Layla too tired to notice.

Now, she could barely remember his face.

You cried when he left, Layla's brain reminded her. *You must have cared.*

But Layla knew the real reason for her tears. The moment the door closed behind Trent had marked Layla's choice to commit her life to her work. A choice that now seemed even more final, thanks to her death date. There would be no wedding bells for Layla. No children, no joint bank account. She didn't have time for any of that.

She didn't have time.

10

Angus

Angus didn't know the area around OPM Discoveries well, but Google Maps promised him a cafe was nearby. With the equipment for the study deposited in his car, he set off walking. Life erupted around him with every step he took.

Life he was going to experience for a very long time.

For ninety-three years, two months and fifteen days, to be exact. An impressive lifespan by anyone's standards. No one would turn their nose up at that.

Only Angus *had* turned his nose up. His initial reaction wasn't joy or elation or even mild enthusiasm, but a dull, aching, cavernous nothingness.

'How are you feeling?' Saira asked, unable to hide her excitement. After all, a longer-than-average lifespan, and the money to enjoy it? It was the thing of dreams!

Angus did his best to sound equally enthused. 'Good. Great,' he replied, but then he remembered Saira saying that for the experiment to work, participants had to be honest. Shifting in his seat, Angus leaned forward. 'I'm a little shocked, actually,' he admitted. 'Ninety-three is pretty much sixty years away. What am I supposed to do with all that time?'

Saira smiled at him like it was simple. 'Whatever you like.'

Angus didn't have the heart to say that for his entire life, he'd been able to do whatever he liked, and it transpired that what he liked wasn't very much. Sleeping, drinking, fucking, floating but feeling like he was sinking. Day in and day out, that was what he did. To do that for another sixty years . . . Angus's blood ran cold.

You selfish prick, he berated himself. *What's wrong with you?*

So many people would kill to be in his position, yet the thought of such a long lifespan struck Angus like a snowball to the face.

Suppressing a shiver, Angus spotted the cafe ahead. He sped up, practically running by the time he reached it. With navy and gold decor and bronze fittings, the cafe gave the illusion of sophistication. Angus wasn't sure the suburban spot quite managed it, but sitting in there was better than sitting alone with his thoughts.

Shimmying his coat from his shoulders, Angus moved towards the counter.

That was when he saw her.

Two tables over from the window, wearing a smart red coat and looking like she wished it would swallow her whole – a striking woman. Turbulent thoughts were painted so clearly across her face, mirroring Angus's own. Try as he might, he couldn't look away.

His heart rate quickened, beating so fast he wondered if OPM Discoveries was wrong and he was going to die of a coronary right here, right now. While Angus stood there floundering, the woman stared into the distance as if the meaning of life could be found somewhere on the street outside.

Angus had never seen an expression like it before. Everyone he knew smiled constantly, all dazzling teeth and unshakable perkiness. He never knew what was real with them and what wasn't, but this woman, this stranger? She was real, all right. Real, raging, lost . . . exactly like Angus.

'Excuse me, I need to get past,' said a voice.

Angus turned to the hunched, craggy-faced old man beside him and stepped aside. 'Sorry.'

'Thank you, son. Have a good day.' The man's chirpiness contrasted with the slow, laboured way in which he moved. Angus watched him go, wondering how old he was. Eighty? Ninety? Older?

The old man's jerky steps made Angus shudder. A long, empty life was one thing, but a long, empty life with your body falling apart was something else entirely. Swallowing his unease, Angus made his way towards the counter, doing all he could not to look at the woman in the red coat.

'A large soy cappuccino, please,' he said to a flame-haired barista.

'To have in or take away?'

'To have in, thanks.'

Angus blinked as the response left his lips. His plan had been to grab a drink then wander the streets to process the news of his extended life. Now, apparently, he was staying.

There was no reason he shouldn't enjoy his drink indoors, Angus thought while paying. No reason he shouldn't be in the vicinity of the woman who had given him butterflies for quite possibly the first time in his life. No reason at all.

When the card machine chimed to confirm the transaction, Angus turned from the counter, doing all he could to drag his eyes away from where they begged to look.

Roughly half of the cafe was free. Angus could sit at the empty table in front of him. Or, if he fancied eavesdropping, the couple nearby appeared to be having an intense conversation. A break-up, perhaps? Sitting beside them, he could immerse himself in someone else's life for a while. Or . . .

Or he could sit with her.

Angus's legs didn't wait for his brain to say no. As the woman's gravitational pull drew him to her, Angus's heart beat in his throat. His brain begged him to turn back, to remember that Angus Fairview-Whitley didn't do shit like this, but he continued.

The woman was inches away now, so close Angus could see the freckles dotted across the bridge of her nose. So close he could tell she had a habit of biting her nails.

So close that he might have to speak to her.

·

The realisation swiped Angus's confidence, but it was too late. His large frame was in front of the woman, looming over her table.

Clearing his throat, Angus found his voice. 'Excuse me, is this seat taken?'

It took a moment for the woman to register that he was speaking to her. It took another for her to look at him. When she did, her eyes – dark like the night sky, but more beautiful – met his blue ones. Angus's stomach flipped, and for one awful, panicky moment, he thought he was going to be sick.

The woman blinked. 'You want to sit here? With me?'

Angus's toes curled at her sharp tone. Warning lights flashed in his mind. *Abort, abort!* they screamed, but it was too late. He had approached a lone woman minding her own business. He'd committed to the role of creep in the coffee shop.

The woman scanned the cafe, eying the multitude of empty tables. Suddenly, coming over seemed like the worst idea Angus had ever had.

'I'm sorry, I shouldn't have interrupted you,' he rushed. 'Sorry, forget I said anything.'

Angus backed away, so focused on his humiliation that he didn't take in his surroundings. Knocking into the table behind him, he sent a jar of cutlery tumbling to the floor where it inevitably smashed.

The sound alerted people to Angus's epic failure. He felt their eyes on him, cold and calculating as they assessed the situation. *Who is that man? Is he harassing that woman?*

'I'm so sorry,' Angus said, flustered, as the barista approached with a brush. She batted his apology away, but her kindness only made the moment cut deeper. As hot, sticky shame prickled Angus's skin, his body twisted to flee, but then he heard a voice.

'Wait!'

Turning, Angus's gaze met hers. The woman's brows were still furrowed, but she nodded to the chair opposite. 'You can sit.'

Angus moved quickly, sinking into the seat in one fluid movement. Finally, he allowed himself to breathe. 'Thank you.'

'Well, I couldn't have you knocking into more tables, could I?'

Angus couldn't tell if the woman was joking or not. Her face remained serious. He was about to ask if she was okay when a waitress set down his cappuccino. 'Thank you,' he said. By the time he managed to get the words out, she was gone.

Picking up his drink, Angus forced himself to take a sip. The cappuccino scorched his tongue. Fighting a grimace, he placed it back down. That's when he noticed the mug encased in the woman's delicate hands. Its contents were barely touched.

'Did you not like it?' he asked.

She blinked. 'What?'

'Your drink,' he said, nodding at the mug. 'Did you not like it?'

'Oh. Something like that.'

Angus studied the woman. Up close, he could see the finer details of her face. Her lips were full, but the bottom one was bigger than the top, making the balance of her mouth ever so slightly off. There was a small scar beside her right eyebrow. Angus wondered how she came to have it. He hoped one day he might find out.

Suddenly, the woman pinned Angus to his chair with her gaze until his stammering broke the silence.

'I'm Angus, by the way.'

Her lips flicked into a wry smile. 'That's a posh name. Are you posh?'

'No,' Angus replied. One simple word, one enormous lie.

The woman's eyes narrowed. 'Are you sure? You seem like the men I work with.'

'Are they posh?'

'Oh, the poshest. But none of them have hair as posh as yours.'

It took everything in Angus not to touch his hair. 'What kind of hair is that?'

'Hair like a blond Hugh Grant. The poshest hair of all.'

As the woman giggled, Angus lit up. 'As flattered as I am by that comparison, I'm afraid there's nothing Hugh Grant about me. I'm just . . . well, I'm just me.'

'You're just you. Well, I guess that makes me just me. Whoever that is, anyway.' At that, the woman laughed again, but this time it wasn't a happy sound. 'So, Mr Not-Posh-But-Looks-It. Humour me. Do you think people are happier if they're rich?'

The question floored Angus, partly because it was unexpected, but mostly because it was one he searched for an answer to most days. 'You ask deep questions, don't you?'

The woman shrugged. 'Maybe I'm tired of wasting time with nonsense.'

'I know what that's like.'

The corner of the woman's mouth dragged into a smile. 'In that case, I can't wait to hear your answer.'

With those words ringing in his ears, Angus did something he hadn't done in a long time – he looked inward for an honest answer. He thought of his grand, empty penthouse. His privileged, directionless friends. His endless days and piles of belongings and full phonebook that contrasted sharply with his disconnection to everything and everyone.

'No, I don't think you're happier if you're rich,' he replied. 'In short-term ways, maybe, like enjoying buying something you want, but those highs don't last forever.'

'But if you're rich, you never have to worry about losing your home or not being able to afford to eat,' the woman pointed out.

Angus blinked. Never in all his thirty-four years had he had those worries. He couldn't imagine what they felt like. With shame burning his cheeks, Angus forced a smile. 'Very true. Maybe the secret is having enough money to live a good life, but not so much that it's all you desire. That's when I imagine it doesn't make you happy. Not properly, anyway. People always say that money can't buy happiness.'

'That could be something people with no money tell themselves to feel better about being poor.'

'Maybe, but I don't think it would be a saying if it weren't true.'

The woman tilted her head. 'Is that how you decide if something is true or not – if there's a phrase paired with it?'

Angus laughed. 'It's not my go-to tactic, but in this case, I stand by it. Money might buy things we're told will make us happy, but when everything ends, it's not objects we want around us. It's people. So if that's the case, how can chasing money lead to happiness?'

'You're right. Who wants to get to the end of their life and see they wasted it chasing the wrong things?' the woman replied, so quiet her voice was almost a whisper.

'Exactly. That's got to be the worst end-of-life realisation there is.'

Angus meant the comment to be flippant, but when the woman's eyes flicked to him, he was alarmed to see sorrow in them. He yearned to take her sadness away, but she spoke before he could try.

'I used to think having money meant I'd be happy. That working hard and chasing security really mattered, you know?'

Angus nodded, but he didn't know. All his life, Angus had been secure.

'Now I wonder if it's worth it,' the woman continued. 'I mean, what's the point? Why are we here, buying overpriced coffee and acting like it's a good way to spend our time?'

Angus looked around, the frivolity of his surroundings taking on a new significance in the shadow of her words.

'Do you ever wonder why you get out of bed in the morning?' she asked. 'What it is that drives you to keep going?'

Angus tightened his grip around his drink as the directness of the questions set his soul on fire.

Suddenly, the woman's face transformed. Shutters went down, covering her rawness with a bright, happy mask that looked painful to wear. 'I'm sorry. I'm being maudlin.'

'Not at all. Granted, the topic is a little dark.'

The woman laughed at this.

'But it's more interesting than the *what's your name, where are you from* chats you usually have when you meet someone like this.'

The woman bit back a smirk. 'Do you meet a lot of people like this?'

'No, actually. I've never approached someone in a cafe before.'

'Does that mean they usually approach you?' she quipped.

Angus coloured. 'That's not what I meant.'

'I wouldn't care if it's what you meant.'

Angus fell silent, flummoxed by the knowledge that he wanted her to care because, weirdly, he cared. He cared more than he should for a man who had been speaking to a woman for less than ten minutes.

Angus's spiralling was interrupted by the woman leaning forward, so close he could smell her perfume. Sweet, but not overpowering. A scent he wanted to bury his face in.

'Have you ever had a bad day, Angus?' she asked.

The sharp change in conversation threw Angus off for a second, but then he nodded. 'Sometimes it feels like I'm having a run of bad days. A bad day marathon, even.'

Angus hoped the woman would laugh at his joke, but she didn't.

'I mean a really, really bad day. The worst day. The kind you fall apart over. Ever had one of those?'

Angus's thoughts went to Saira's office. The news she delivered had blasted him apart, and he didn't know why. 'Honestly? I think I'm having one of those days today.'

The woman smiled a beaming smile, blinding Angus with her beauty. 'Well, that's the first thing anyone's said today that's made me happy.'

A burst of laughter escaped Angus. 'My misery makes you happy?'

'Is it wicked if I say yes?'

'Definitely, but what's the saying? Misery loves company?'

She giggled. 'Another saying! Although I'm guessing not many people would want an invite to our pity party.'

Angus's heart lurched at her use of 'our'. He opened his mouth to fire off a witty retort, but the woman's phone began to ring. At the interruption, reality flooded back into focus. The sound of cups hitting saucers and people speaking over each other seeped into Angus's consciousness, and he hated it.

When she saw who was calling, the woman grimaced. 'I should take this. In fact, I should go.'

'You're leaving already?' Angus said, fighting the urge to ask her to stay.

The woman gathered her things as if she hadn't heard him, then paused. 'Isn't timing funny? On the worst day of my life, you appeared and made it seem not so bad.' The woman paused again, digesting her words. Then, shaking her head, she stood to leave.

'Wait,' Angus cried. 'May I have your number?'

The woman froze. 'You want to speak to me again after all I've rambled on about?'

'I do.'

Cautiously, she studied him. Angus could see her calculating the pros and cons of saying yes. Then a miracle happened – she reached out her hand. 'If you give me your phone, I'll put my number in it.'

As Angus handed his phone over, their fingers brushed. A jolt of electricity passed through him. His eyes flicked to the woman, wondering if she'd felt it too, but she was busy typing out her number.

'You have to agree to one thing, though,' she said. 'You can only contact me when you have a bad day. Not a "my boss shouted at me" or "I spilled coffee on my shirt" bad day. I mean a really, really bad day. You said it yourself – misery loves company. The way I'm feeling, I only want to be surrounded by people who are as miserable as I am.'

Angus faltered. 'Are you okay? Is there anything I can help with?'

At this, the woman gave a watery smile. 'I don't need you to fix anything for me, Angus. I don't have time for a hero, and I don't want one.'

Angus's heart twisted at the blunt certainty of her words, but he felt himself nod. 'Okay, deal,' he said. 'When I'm the most miserable I've ever been, I'll call you.'

'I look forward to it,' the woman replied before walking away. Angus watched her go, wishing she would turn around so he could get another glimpse of her face, but she never did.

When she disappeared from view, Angus looked at his phone and read the digits he was certain would change his life forever. Above the number was her name.

'Layla,' he said. Angus loved the way her name sounded and how each letter rolled across his tongue. Most of all, he loved the way he felt himself come to life when he said it.

11

Layla

The curtains were closed. Layla didn't know what time it was, nor did she care. She was in bed, as she had been for the last two days.

She'd missed work. She'd missed calls from her family. And that morning, she'd decided she wasn't going to fill out any more of OPM Discoveries' stupid surveys. What was the point? In two years' time, none of it would matter anyway. Besides, what did Saira expect her to say – 'I feel happy knowing that I'm barrelling towards my untimely death'?

Groaning, Layla rolled onto her side. Her hand reached for her laptop, but at the last moment, she stopped herself. Why research OPM Discoveries again? It wasn't like it helped.

Ever since finding out her result, researching was all Layla had done. Scrolling through endless results, she had been consumed with trying to find a flaw in the company's work history. Something, anything, to delegitimise their claim that they could predict her death. In all those endless searches, Layla found nothing. Worse still, those fruitless hours added to the 'Days Layla Has Wasted' tally she was collating. The only thing more terrifying than seeing the number of wasted days was realising how quickly a new one was added.

Burrowing her face into her pillow, Layla let out a frustrated groan. She was grateful that her flatmate Rhi wasn't there to hear her. A junior doctor who worked even harder than Layla, Rhi used the apartment as a place to sleep and little else. Usually, the two women's schedules meant they were like ships that pass in the night, but even their fleeting interactions over the last few days had concerned the elusive Rhi, who normally didn't bother herself with Layla's life. *Hope you're feeling better. Text if you need me to pick up more paracetamol*, Rhi had written on a Post-it note stuck to the bathroom mirror. Layla had politely ignored it.

On the bedside table, Layla's phone buzzed. It had been sporadically ringing for the last few hours, but the effort required to pick it up was too much. All Layla wanted was to let her duvet swallow her whole. But when the intercom to her apartment buzzed moments later, all hope of fading into oblivion was shattered.

Shuffling to the door with her duvet wrapped around her shoulders like an empty hug, Layla spoke into the intercom's microphone. 'Hello?'

'Layla, it's Saira. Can you let me in?'

Layla blinked, waiting for the appearance of the head of The Life Experiment to make sense, but it didn't. Saira lived in Birmingham, not London. Layla wasn't supposed to see her until their counselling session in two days' time. And, as someone who had read the terms and conditions of the experiment in detail, Layla didn't remember anything about house calls.

'Layla?'

Nudged into action, Layla buzzed Saira into the building. Moments later, dressed in the same pizza-stained pyjamas she had been wearing for days, Layla opened the door. 'What are you doing here?' she asked, blinking to check Saira wasn't a mirage.

'You didn't turn in your questionnaire this morning. Given the news you received the other day, I was worried.' Saira paused before speaking again. 'Can I come in?'

Dumbstruck, Layla let Saira into her apartment.

Compact and functionally furnished, the space looked as though she had only recently moved in, not lived there for three years. But welcoming decor was for someone who had time to shop. With Layla's work hours, she was barely ever at the apartment, despite paying eye-watering rent for the privilege of living there.

After circling the room and studying the closed curtains and empty pizza box on the coffee table, Saira faced Layla. 'I would ask how you are, but I think I can answer that.'

'I have two years left to live. How do you want me to be?'

Saira's lips pressed together like there was more she wanted to say, but instead she went to the window and threw back the curtains. Light burned Layla's bloodshot eyes, even though the grey October day couldn't exactly be described as bright.

With the open curtains inviting the day into the apartment, Saira moved about the room, picking up an abandoned wineglass and empty bottle of shiraz.

'What are you doing?' Layla asked.

'I figure the sooner I help, the sooner you get back on your feet and keep going.'

It took everything in Layla not to choke on the statement. 'Keep going? How am I meant to do that?'

Saira stopped. 'What else are you supposed to do?'

When Layla couldn't answer, Saira headed for the kitchen.

Layla followed. 'You can't seriously expect me to carry on like I haven't been given a death sentence?'

'What else are you going to do – try every takeaway pizza London has to offer?' Saira challenged as she dropped the rubbish in the bin. 'Believe it or not, Layla, the aim of this experiment isn't to tell people how to die. It's to show them how to live.'

'But I only have two years left.'

'So? Some people only have two minutes. Do you think they're spending it in the dark, drowning their sorrows?'

'Maybe,' Layla replied, but she cringed at the petulance in her voice. With a sigh, she rubbed her eyes. 'I don't know what to do, Saira. How am I meant to get out of bed? How am I meant to go to work? I feel like I should be on a beach somewhere downing cocktails, not stuck in an office.'

'Okay, let's start with that. Do you want to quit your job?'

'Yes. No. I don't know,' Layla admitted. 'Being a lawyer is all I know. It's all I've ever wanted to do. I don't know who I am without my career, but the idea of sitting at that desk and carrying on like there isn't a countdown ticking in the back of my mind . . .'

As Layla trailed off, Saira softened. 'Now isn't the time for hasty decisions, Layla. There's a lot to think of, especially in terms of practicality. Do you have the finances to support yourself if you did leave your job?'

Layla couldn't help laughing. 'Not even a little bit.'

'Well then, it looks like you need to stay in work. For now, at least, but that's okay. We can figure things out around it.'

Layla searched Saira's face for a trace of uncertainty, but everything about her was composed. 'Saira, I can't,' she whispered, feeling the all-too-familiar burn of tears once more.

'Why not?'

'Because everything is so pointless now. Every meeting, every phone call . . . They mean nothing.'

'Things might seem that way, but they're the opposite,' Saira replied. 'Time counts now more than ever. Each decision you make can craft your life into exactly what you want it to be.'

'But I don't know what I want it to be, and two years is nowhere near long enough to figure that out.'

Leaving Layla's wineglass to soak in the sink, Saira approached her. 'I know your death date was a shock, but you don't need to destroy the life you have to make your future a good one. Look at the foundations you've already built! A job you've strived for and a home in one of the greatest cities in the world. You've crafted something amazing, Layla. Now you need to figure out how to utilise it. We can work that out together.'

Saira's passionate speech shone with possibility, but after so many days of darkness it was hard for Layla to see it. 'How?' she asked, her chin wobbling.

'By taking it one day at a time. Small step after small step until this feels achievable.'

Again, Layla waited for doubt to creep into Saira's tone, but it never did. Lifting her chin, Layla met Saira's gaze. 'Do you really think I can do it?'

'Layla,' Saira replied, taking her hand. 'When I read your application, I knew you needed to be part of this study. I knew we would learn so much from you. With your drive and your mind, you are unstoppable. You've proven that a hundred times over. Why not prove it once more?'

'I don't know if I can.'

'Well, I do. Throughout your life, there hasn't been a single obstacle placed in front of you that you haven't successfully climbed. Granted, this is your biggest challenge yet, but the woman I met four weeks ago was not one to back down just because something was tough. Why not let her take the lead for a little bit?'

When she couldn't come up with a single reason, Layla swallowed her tears. 'And you'll really help me?'

'Absolutely. I'm going to check on you every day. Expect a text. Multiple texts, even. All you need to do is respond with a number, marking your mood out of ten. Any less than seven, I'll call you there and then. Any less than five, I'll be on the next train to see you. How does that sound?'

'That sounds like a lot for you to take on,' Layla joked weakly.

'Well, this is my experiment. I have a duty of care. But more than that, I want you to be okay.' Moving closer, Saira let her features melt with sympathy. 'Layla, however alone you feel right now, you're not. You will get through this. I will be with you every step of the way.'

To prove her point, Saira squeezed Layla's hand reassuringly. It was almost enough to make Layla believe that things might be okay after all.

12

Angus

The Life Experiment: Daily Questionnaire
Property of OPM Discoveries

How would you rate your level of contentment today? (1 represents low contentment, 10 represents high)

1   2   3   4   5   (6)   7   8   9   10

How would you rate your energy level? (1 being very low energy and 10 being very high energy)

1   2   3   4   5   (6)   7   8   9   10

What are two things you are grateful for today?
1. Cafes in Birmingham
2. This questionnaire giving me something to do. I would have been watching Netflix until I hit the gym with Jasper later otherwise

What are you struggling with today?
The fact that I met someone incredible the other day, but can't contact her yet

Do you have any additional notes on what you would like to discuss in your upcoming counselling session?
No

The Pinot Noir slid smoothly down Angus's throat. His fourth glass of the night was no doubt staining his teeth, but boy was it needed. His parents' dinner party was as tedious as Angus had predicted. More so, in fact. Richard Smythe seemed intent on making sure his voice was heard in all four corners of the room. Imagining another sixty years of events like this made Angus want to reach for the the bottle of wine and down the rest of it.

As her husband recounted a tale of his accountant's canny ability to cut his tax bill to criminal levels, Corinne caught Angus's eye. Her pencilled eyebrow kinked suggestively. Angus found himself turning to Bruno beside him before he could see the wink that would follow.

'So,' he said. 'How is the family?'

If Bruno was surprised at his friend's usually reserved son making conversation, he didn't show it. Dabbing his mouth with the corner of a napkin, Bruno nodded. 'They're good, Angus. Tabitha's wedding plans are coming along nicely, and Phineas is making a name for himself in parliament. Have I told you he looks set to run for a second term?'

'You must be proud,' Angus replied, cursing himself for inviting the conversation. With talk of Phineas's success, it would only be a matter of time before Bruno swung the focus onto Angus.

Although Bruno was one of Peter's friends that Angus liked, he still didn't trust his questions. Not when Angus knew he was considered the measuring stick of failure among his parents' friends.

At least our little darling hasn't been as big a disappointment as the Fairview-Whitley boy, Angus imagined people saying. *All that money and opportunity, yet he's done nothing. Gilly and Peter must be awfully ashamed.*

If only Hugo were still around, their counterpart would add. *He knew where he was headed. Angus is as lost as they come.*

Excusing himself from the table, Angus headed to the nearest bathroom. There, he splashed his face with cold water to drown out the worst of his derision.

But as he closed his eyes, Angus was greeted with a vision of Layla's wry smile. Instantly, his heart pounded. Opening his eyes, Angus levelled his gaze at his reflection. When he was with Layla, it hadn't mattered that he wasn't Hugo. All that mattered was that Angus was himself.

In that moment, all Angus wanted to do was leave and find her. Talk to her. Check she was doing better than when they met. Anything, as long as it meant being around her.

Reaching into his pocket, Angus pulled out his phone and found Layla in his contacts. As it had done many times over the last few days, Angus's thumb travelled to the call button. He itched to pull the trigger. Something inside him said Layla would be happy to hear his voice. Maybe even laugh and say, 'What took you so long?'

But another part of Angus warned that calling now was not what had been asked of him. For the first time in his life, Angus wanted to follow the rules. No shortcuts or steamrolling ahead because his surname allowed it, even if the wait killed him.

Sliding the phone back into his pocket, Angus looked at his reflection again just as someone knocked on the bathroom door. Panic struck, imagining Corinne leaving the table to proposition him, but when a familiar voice called his name, Angus relaxed. Slightly, at least.

'Angus, what are you doing in there?' Gilly asked from the other side of the door.

Jolting, Angus emerged from the bathroom in such a rush he almost collided with his mother. Gilly stepped back, resting her hand on her bony chest.

'Why the haste?' she asked.

'You sounded like you needed to get inside,' he replied, but the comment made Gilly's nostrils flare.

'I don't need the bathroom, Angus, and for goodness' sake don't be so loud when you say things like that. I came to see where you were. You practically ran from the table as if you were being chased.'

'I needed the toilet,' Angus replied.

Gilly saw straight through the lie.

'Did Bruno say something to upset you?'

'No, nothing.'

'Are you sure?' Gilly pushed. 'He's not known for his tact. And he's forever showing off about his idiot son, like we've all forgotten how Phineas streaked across the lawn at the Barrington summer social.'

As Gilly sniffed in disapproval, Angus wilted. If the tame partying days of Phineas Markington made his mother shudder, then Angus dreaded to think what she said about him.

'We should get back to your guests,' he said stiffly. 'I know you hate to keep people waiting.'

The pair ventured through the house in silence, their bodies inches apart until the dining room was in sight. Only then did Gilly slip her slender arm through Angus's. 'Smile, dear,' she said, before stepping them both back into the spotlight.

'There you are! We were about to call a search party,' Peter joked, standing to pull back Gilly's chair.

Letting go of Angus, Gilly slid silkily to her husband's side. Her hand graced Peter's arm in thanks, a tender smile shared between them.

Again, Angus thought of Layla, and he lost the ability to think straight.

'Angus chatting to you about another business venture, eh?' Richard boomed before polishing off the rest of his drink. 'You want to be careful after last time.'

The joke landed with a thud, but Angus was too numb to register its impact. All he wanted was to head back to the bathroom and barricade himself from the world.

'Richard, behave,' Corinne said, giggling nervously.

It was only upon seeing his wife's panic that Richard realised his faux pas. His already red cheeks flushed. 'What a silly comment,' he blustered. 'Ignore me. Too much wine!'

'Actually, we weren't discussing business,' Gilly retorted, piercing Richard with an icy glare that sobered him up in an instant. 'But Angus did mention that he hadn't seen Penelope for a while. Tell me, is she still in Italy?'

The sip of water Gilly took after her question was delicate, but her eyes sparkled with the knowledge that she was touching a nerve. As Richard became flustered and Corinne burned with silent indignation, Angus felt the atmosphere swell.

'She's having a lovely time,' Richard muttered, reaching for his empty wineglass.

'How wonderful. Perhaps you could ask her to send me a postcard? I'd love to hear about her travels,' Gilly pushed, but it was a prod too far for Peter.

Rising to his feet, he clapped his hands to signal the end of the conversation. 'I'm sure Penelope is having a lovely time. Now, shall I see about asking Ms Tillman to fetch dessert?'

The table murmured in agreement, but Angus stayed silent. He caught his mother's gaze, flinching at her smug delight. Sure, Gilly had rescued him from public ridicule, but only by highlighting another family's shame. Everyone knew that Penelope Smythe wasn't touring Italy; she was in rehab in Kensington. The partying that had been funny when she was eighteen wasn't met with the same affectionate eye-roll now that she was twenty-eight. After stealing and crashing Richard's Bentley while high on a cocktail of drugs that would have killed most people, Penelope's family's patience had finally snapped.

And there Gilly was, using that pain as a weapon. Slicing someone else down to make Angus seem tall. Pushing his plate away, Angus's shame deepened. He should be used to how it felt by now, but it crushed his chest until every day felt impossible.

At least, it had until the moment he sat opposite Layla.

For the umpteenth time that night, Angus's mind wandered to Layla and the sparks that flew during their brief conversation. Stripped of all pretension, it was the most honest interaction he had experienced in recent memory. He craved another hit. Another moment where Layla's smile made time stand still.

13

Layla

The tannoy crackled, announcing the next stop, but Layla barely registered the information. She didn't need to. She knew there were another ten minutes left of her train journey. The route from London to Hull was drilled into her, even if she hadn't taken it recently.

With her forehead resting on the window, the world whizzed past Layla in short flashes. A skeletal tree, a crumbling house, a barren field. Flash, flash, flash, the train's speed blurred the surroundings. Layla preferred it that way. The distorted world mimicked her erratic mind – she didn't need to see where she was going, she just needed to keep moving.

In the seat beside her, a balding man shifted his weight with a sigh. Layla tried not to be irritated by his presence, but it was hard when his spread legs meant he was taking up most of her room. He had got on the train six stations ago, smelling mildly of a meat pasty.

As if the space invasion and odour weren't bad enough, the man had made a call as soon as the train set off. 'Gazzaaaaa,' he bellowed down the line, seemingly oblivious to the carriage full of people surrounding him. From there, it got worse. Loudly and disdainfully discussing asylum seekers ('Don't they realise we don't want them?'), then his mother's ill health ('Looks like I'll be coming into my inheritance soon, mate'), every second spent beside him had been torture. The worst moment was when the man left his seat to collect one of the train's free newspapers then practically sat on Layla's knee upon return.

'Sorry, love,' he said, winking as if his butt cheek against her thigh was harmless fun. When Layla's nose wrinkled in disgust, all joviality left his face. 'Miserable bitch,' he muttered, not at all quietly.

Since then, the man had ensured he took up as much space as possible. Flipping the pages of his newspaper with unnecessary force, his elbow dug into Layla's forearm with each turn.

The sound of rustling paper reminded Layla of Sunday mornings. Her dad stifling a yawn as he read the newspaper cover to cover. Maya extracting the gossip section so she could look at outfits worn by her favourite celebrities. Her mother serving breakfast, something sweet for a weekend treat.

Layla's mouth watered at the memory. Then, like it always did when she thought of those days, her heart hurt.

Inside her pocket, Layla's phone buzzed. She pulled it out with difficulty, narrowly avoiding brushing her arm against the man, and checked the notifications. There was a message from Sinead asking if she could call Layla for advice, and Saira's daily check-in text. It had been five days since her unexpected visit. Five days of *Are you okay?* messages and muddling through work until something inside Layla snapped and told her to book some personal leave.

I'm fine, Layla replied. *I'm on my way to Hull. I think seeing my family might help.*

Saira's reply was fast and in agreement with Layla's plan. Clicking out of their exchange, Layla allowed herself a second to hope that another message was waiting. A message from someone else entirely.

Someone who, quite inexplicably, possessed the power to make Layla's mind wander away from her impending death.

But she had no other messages. In fact, in the time that had passed since Layla had met Angus, no contact had been made at all.

Layla knew she shouldn't be surprised. She'd hardly been good company that day, what with finding out she only had two years left to live, but Angus didn't know that. All he knew was that he'd taken a seat opposite an odd, grumpy stranger.

Layla's toes curled at the directive she'd given him . . . *You can only call or message when you have a really, really bad day.* Layla wasn't even sure why she said it. That day, she had wanted the world to be as miserable as her, but now Layla wanted to be consumed by anything other than the ticking clock in her mind reminding her how little time she had left. And Angus, with his thick hair and kissable lips, was someone Layla would have no issue being consumed by. No issue at all.

In her most desperate moments, Layla had tried googling him, but it was useless. All she knew was that he was called Angus and that his smile shone with the radiance of the sun. As good as Google was, it couldn't pull off a search that obscure.

Pressing her body back into her seat, Layla scolded herself. Why was she so bothered that Angus hadn't been in touch? She'd never sat waiting for a man to call before. Truthfully, she wasn't even sure she wanted him to. Aside from the obvious fact that nothing could happen between them, given her death date, there was something about Angus that made Layla hesitate.

Perhaps it was because he reminded her of the men at work. He had the same self-assured, privileged air about him. He spoke like the boys on *Made in Chelsea*. But even with those off-putting attributes, there was something about Angus. Something . . . intriguing. Layla didn't know what it was. Maybe it was his outlook or his humour. Or maybe it was that for a brief moment, on the darkest day of her life, Layla had felt a glimmer of joy, all because of him.

When the tannoy announced her stop, Layla turned to the man beside her. 'Excuse me.'

Closing his newspaper in a motion that could only be described as pissy, the man shifted his legs, providing enough room for Layla to pass, but not without touching him.

Layla's nostrils flared. How often had she been in this situation over the course of her adult life? She'd lost count. The tube was the worst.

Men shuffling unnecessarily close, brushing their bodies against hers and blaming overcrowding. It made her shrivel.

As Layla squeezed out of her seat, the man's stomach grazed the back of her legs. She withered with that all too familiar burn of shame.

But why are you ashamed? her indignation spat. *He's in the wrong, not you.*

For once, Layla listened to her fury. After pulling her overnight bag from the overhead storage, she faced the man. 'Next time someone asks you to let them past, do it in a way that doesn't result in your crotch touching them. It's really not pleasant,' she stated, before marching to the carriage doors.

God, it feels good to stick two fingers up to the world, Layla's brain sang as the platform came into view. No more silent compliance. No being nice and polite because it's expected. If Layla only had two years left to live, why spend it being quiet, small and ashamed?

Hopping from the carriage, Layla made her way to the taxi rank outside the station. After giving the driver her parents' address, she sat back and looked out at her hometown.

Even though she hadn't been back for months, Layla could navigate the streets of Hull with her eyes closed. Around here, things didn't change much. Despite pre-election promises, there had been no government investment or boost to the city centre. The place almost felt forgotten, stuck in a time warp of its poorest days.

That's not to say that everything was the same as when Layla was a child, though. There were more empty stores than she remembered, and more discount and charity shops on the high street than big brand names. Things looked dirtier, which was alarming considering they'd never been that clean in the first place.

But underneath the faded facade, it wasn't all bad. In fact, there was a charm to life here. Children played outside, using their imagination to transform their surroundings into something fantastical. Elderly couples went about their business holding hands. Groups of mums pushed prams together, talking and laughing in a way Layla never had with anyone in London. The council had planted flowers along the roadside. Despite the cold, they bloomed. Their beauty welcomed her back. Welcomed her home.

As the familiar houses of Thorpe Estate came into view, Layla's palms began to sweat. Whether it was nerves or excitement, she couldn't tell, but it didn't matter. This was where she needed to be.

When the taxi slowed to a stop, Layla looked at the redbrick semi-detached house of her childhood. It was exactly as she remembered it, with patchy grass in the garden and the vase gifted by Layla's grandma visible from the living room window. Beautiful in its consistency and comforting in its familiarity. Home.

After paying the taxi fare, Layla slipped out of the car. Pausing to take in the sounds and smells of home, she willed herself to approach the door. Her feet moved slowly at first, but soon picked up their pace like they couldn't reach their destination fast enough.

When Layla's knuckles rapped on the door, a shout of 'Coming!' rang out from inside. A few seconds later, the door opened and there she was.

'Mum,' Layla exhaled.

Joanna's temples were greyer than ever. The pink and white apron she'd had since Layla was in secondary school was wrapped around her generous waist, a sauce stain splashed across it. She never was the tidiest cook, but that didn't matter when she was a great one.

Joanna gasped at the unexpected sight of her daughter. 'Layla! What are you doing here?'

Layla's answer stuck in her throat, but Joanna didn't need it. She simply pulled Layla into a fierce hug.

The hug, which Layla had been craving ever since opening that envelope, exceeded every expectation. Layla breathed her mum in, the scent of coconut and that damned floral air freshener she insisted on using tickling her nostrils.

'Hi, Mum,' she whispered thickly.

Taking Layla's head in her hands, Joanna ran her eyes over her eldest daughter. Layla could almost hear her assessment: *Beautiful, but sad. So sad.*

'What is it, baby? What's wrong?' Joanna asked.

Layla's mouth opened, but she didn't know where to begin. So, instead, Layla settled on the simple truth she knew deep in her bones. 'I missed you,' she said.

Joanna's face twisted once more as she pulled her daughter into the house.

Stepping through the front door, Layla's past and present collided, making her dizzy. She'd experienced so many memories within these walls, both good and bad. She had cried on the bottom step of the staircase after schoolyard fallouts with friends. She had strung a banner across the wall to welcome her dad home after his fourth spinal surgery.

'Go upstairs, pop your bag in your bedroom and take a bath. I'll have dinner ready for when you're done,' Joanna said, squeezing the top of Layla's arm.

'My old bedroom is Jayden's room,' Layla croaked, but Joanna shook her head.

'The room is yours for as long as you need it. Don't worry about a thing, Jayden will be happy to bunk with his mum for a bit. Just go and get yourself settled.'

With someone else taking control, Layla found it easier to move, even if she did walk upstairs with jerking, zombie-like steps. She paused at the second door on the landing. A faded 'keep out' sticker was embedded into the wood. Layla remembered sticking it there when she was thirteen.

Her throat tightened as she pushed open the door, revealing a space that was at once hers and not hers. The walls were now painted dark green instead of the bright lilac she'd chosen when she was nine, and there were miniature dinosaurs everywhere. Tiny pyjamas were flung on the floor, clearly discarded earlier that morning.

Swallowing hard, Layla stepped into the space. How wrong it felt to be in this room that was no longer hers.

How right it felt to be back with the people who loved her the most.

Dropping her bag to the floor, Layla let peace wash over her.

14

Angus

'Tilda said we can use her parents' villa next month. The place is incredible. Shame we need to invite her too, though.'

Angus stirred the pho in front of him, watching chunks of chicken bob up and down in the broth.

'She sent me photos earlier,' Jasper continued. 'Six beds, eight baths, a pool and a jacuzzi. Golf course nearby, naturally.'

The couple at the next table giggled, their heads so close their foreheads almost kissed. Angus was too far away to hear the joke they shared but close enough to know he wanted what they had.

'So, what do you say? Are you in?'

Taking another mouthful of pho, Angus observed the couple's intimacy. The last time he had clung onto someone's words like that was twelve days ago. He'd been in a cafe after learning he would live to ninety-three. The memory plucked at his chest. Again, he debated calling Layla, but today wasn't a really bad day, was it? Today was a day like any other.

'Angus? Angus, are you even listening to me?' Jasper clicked his fingers in Angus's face.

Dropping his spoon, Angus locked eyes with his oldest friend. 'Sorry, what?'

Jasper sighed, irritated. 'Jesus, Angus. I shouldn't have to fight to get your attention. Next month. Tilda's parents' villa.'

'Oh. Cool.'

'Cool? That's all you have to say about leaving this miserable weather behind for a trip to Saint Lucia?'

Angus rubbed his temples. 'Sorry, my mind's all over the place today.'

'Your mind's always all over the place,' Jasper grumbled, taking an angry bite of food.

As the atmosphere simmered, Angus forced himself to smile. 'Sorry. Saint Lucia sounds great. Thank you for organising it.'

'A bit of gratitude, that's more like it. You'll be even more grateful when I tell you the guest list. You, me, Locke and Anderson are going, of course, then there are the girls to think of. Don't worry, Clarissa will be there.'

Angus found he couldn't muster any enthusiasm. Not even the fake kind. Pushing his dinner away, he nodded. 'Let me sort the bill. My shout for not listening,' he said, striding away before he had to engage in more empty conversation.

Bill paid, Jasper and Angus headed to Jasper's favourite night-time haunt. Set in a converted warehouse, Luca and Carlo's was exclusive enough to meet Jasper's exacting standards, but it wasn't discreet. Music pounded down the street, audible before the men even reached the club.

Bypassing the queue of well-dressed, shivering people, the men were waved inside by the bouncers.

Jasper rubbed his hands together. 'It's going to be a good night,' he enthused.

Angus wished he could share his friend's excitement, but the pounding in his head said otherwise.

Luca and Carlo's was dimly lit and decorated like secrets were buried in the walls. The place screamed 'Let's sin and spend lots while doing it.' From the back of the venue, the VIP area beckoned to Jasper's ego.

The men approached and were once again granted access as if they owned the place.

'Look at the talent on the dance floor,' Jasper said over his shoulder with a wolfish grin.

'It's so dark I can barely see the dance floor,' Angus grumbled, but Jasper was busy greeting the tall, distinguished man waiting for them in the cordoned-off area.

Archie Locke, another school friend, rugby squad alumnus and now property developer. So cocky he was excruciating company, Locke had a different date on his arm each week, despite also having a wedding planned for two months' time. But when someone was as rich and influential as Locke, people tended to look the other way at such indiscretions.

Grinning, Locke held up a bag of white powder. 'Fancy some?'

Jasper didn't need to be asked twice. He took the bag to the table and poured out the contents, cutting lines of cocaine with more care than Angus had seen his friend give to anything else.

As the VIP attendant pretended not to notice what was going on, Jasper laughed. 'Imagine anyone else doing this. They'd be arrested before they even cut a line.'

Locke howled, then dipped towards the table. Angus watched him hoover drugs into his right nostril, then throw his head back and roar to the ceiling, 'We're untouchable! We're un-fucking-touchable!'

Suddenly, Angus felt sick. Never had he been more aware of how stomach-churning his friends were. Hidden in the corner of some sleazy bar, downing drugs, safe in the knowledge that while other people would lose their livelihoods for this behaviour, they would be fine.

It was wrong.

It was all wrong.

And Angus was part of it.

As Jasper inhaled a line then looked at Angus expectantly, Angus noticed for the first time how his friend's mousy hair was thinning. His skin wore the signs of too many nights like this, but still, Jasper held out a rolled note for Angus to join him.

Angus stepped backwards, but an arm slipped around his waist and stopped him. 'You made it,' someone purred into his ear. He turned to find a glassy-eyed Clarissa behind him, vodka and a sweet mixer clinging to her breath.

'Jasper wouldn't let me miss this,' he replied, catching the eye of his irritated friend, who pointed to the drugs waiting on the table.

'I can always count on Jasper to get you where I want you to be.' Clarissa spoke of seduction, but her tipsy slurring ruined the effect. Grinning, she ran her hand down the centre of Angus's chest. 'You better come to Saint Lucia. I have my eye on a room beside yours.'

Her words plunged Angus underwater. He could picture the trip already. Too much sun, too much alcohol, too much everything. Jasper, louder than ever now he had an audience for two weeks. Clarissa creeping into Angus's room in the early hours of the morning, pretending to be lost, though that had been her destination all along.

As if reading Angus's mind, Clarissa pushed her body against his. 'I'll bring my smallest bikini,' she whispered, biting his earlobe to demonstrate her intentions.

Angus's reaction was instinctive. He stumbled away, hands in the air to protest his innocence, with only one thing on his mind . . . Layla.

Layla whose searing honesty would cut through this bullshit.

Layla who could save him from these people, this place.

Layla who might even save him from himself.

Laughing to downplay the sting of rejection, Clarissa grabbed Angus and tugged him towards the sofas, but it was too late. Angus was gone, consumed by thoughts of Layla.

As Clarissa pulled harder, Angus made his choice. 'Excuse me,' he said, breaking free of her grip and heading for the rope marking off the VIP section.

'Angus? Where the fuck are you going?' Clarissa shouted, but after a few strides her voice melted into the music.

Pushing through the bodies on the dance floor, Angus made a beeline for the exit. The closer he got to it, the quicker his movements became, until suddenly the dance floor and all its intoxicated revelry was far behind him.

Cool air kissed Angus's flushed cheeks as he stepped outside, but he didn't allow himself time to enjoy it. Instead, he paced down an alleyway beside the club and pulled out his phone.

She picked up after six rings. 'Hello?'

Layla's voice vibrated through Angus, making him nervous. 'Layla, it's—'

'Angus. You called.'

Melting against the wall, Angus closed his eyes. The smile in Layla's voice told him all he needed to know.

'I take it this means you've had a really bad day?' she said.

'Yes. It's been marginally worse than the others, at least,' Angus replied, then he shook his head. 'Look, Layla, I need to be honest. I was waiting for a really bad day like you said, but the problem is, they're all bad days. I know I've bent your rule of contact, but I was hoping you'd take a mathematical overview of the situation.'

'And what does a mathematical overview look like?'

'Well, the way I see it, a series of lifeless days surely equates to one really bad one.'

'I don't know,' Layla said, her tone teasing. 'Rules are rules . . .'

'What if I argue my case?'

Layla laughed. 'All right then. Convince me your sadness qualifies.'

Filling his lungs, Angus began. 'I wake up every day not knowing who I am. I've spent my whole life avoiding working it out because

I'm scared I won't like who that person is, but I'm tired of being scared.'

Angus trailed off and looked up at the sky. A sea of stars dotted in inky blackness stared back, witnessing him bearing his deepest, darkest thoughts. Angus wondered how many people throughout history had been in the same position as him. Lost, lonely and looking to the sky for answers.

'I can't do it anymore,' Angus admitted. 'I can't follow this path, waiting for things to get worse while knowing you're only a phone call away. I'm ready for change, you see, and I think you might be part of that. I know it sounds crazy to think that about a person I barely know, but I've spent so many years not listening to my gut. It's time I listened to it. Right now, it's saying I want to talk to you. A lot.' The words left Angus's mouth before he had time to think about how intense they might sound to someone he had only met once. Cringing, he scuffed the toe of his shoe across the cobbled ground. 'And I want to change too, of course. Be a better man,' he added for good measure.

'Me and change,' Layla replied slowly. 'Well, they're two great things.'

Angus couldn't help but laugh. 'I'm glad you agree. I'm also glad my ramblings haven't terrified you.'

'How could they? Do you not remember how odd I was when we met?' Layla joked, then she let out a sigh that fluttered through Angus's chest. 'Angus, this call? Every thought that's come tumbling out of your head? They're the first things I've heard in a long time that make any sense to me.'

'Really?'

'Really.' When Layla next spoke, her voice was soft like she was about to share a secret. 'Do you want to know what my gut is saying to me?'

'What?'

'It's saying that talking to you is exactly what I need to do too.'

Closing his eyes, Angus soaked in those words until the promise of what tomorrow might bring lit him up from the inside.

15

Layla

**The Life Experiment: Daily Questionnaire
Property of OPM Discoveries**

How would you rate your level of contentment today? (1 represents low contentment, 10 represents high)

1   2   3   4   (5)   6   7   8   9   10

How would you rate your energy level? (1 being very low energy and 10 being very high energy)

1   2   3   (4)   5   6   7   8   9   10

What are two things you are grateful for today?
1. My family not asking a million questions about why I'm home
2. Impromptu phone calls

What are you struggling with today?
The fact that I am going to die just as my life starts to get interesting

Do you have any additional notes on what you would like to discuss in your upcoming counselling session?
Why I feel so different in Hull compared to London

Layla knew that someone was watching her before she even opened her eyes. She could feel the intensity of their stare and hear their gentle breathing. Silencing her weary body's pleas for more sleep, she peeled her swollen eyes apart.

'Aunt Layla,' Jayden said, beaming his gap-toothed smile as soon as their eyes met. 'You're awake!'

'I didn't have much choice with you in the room,' Layla grumbled, trying to roll onto her side, but Jayden grabbed her arm and pulled her back.

'No! Grandma said no more sleep. She sent me to wake you up.'

'I don't have a choice in this, do I?'

Jayden's giggle told Layla all she needed to know.

With a sigh, she rubbed her bleary eyes and hauled herself to a sitting position. 'Thanks for waking me, I guess. I'd have slept all day otherwise.'

'That's what Grandma said, but you need to come downstairs.'

Layla's forehead creased. 'Why?'

'Because breakfast's ready. Grandma made pancakes for a Sunday treat!'

With that joyous shout, Jayden scampered out of the room. Layla watched him go, wondering when she last had that amount of enthusiasm for anything in life, never mind breakfast. When no such memory came to mind, she sighed and reached for her phone.

No matter how often wellness influencers despaired over the habit, Layla couldn't help herself. Every morning, the first thing she did was check her phone. Usually for work emails, but today it was for a different reason.

Today it was to see if Angus had replied to her message.

When the screen lit up, Layla grinned. Waiting was a wellness check from Saira. Beneath that were two messages from Angus. Wishing Layla sweet dreams, they were sent after another night of deep, and perhaps flirty, conversation. In their chat, Layla had touched upon how lost she felt. She hadn't intended to, but there was something about Angus that made doing so seem easy.

'Things are just hard at the moment,' she had confessed in a wave of vulnerability. 'Ever since that day in Birmingham . . .'

The news The Life Experiment had delivered bubbled on the tip of Layla's tongue. Sense forced her to swallow it away, but not without her heart putting up a fight first. The experiment had exploded any certainty Layla had in life, and at every opportunity, her body willed her to share her burden.

But instead, Layla stayed quiet long enough for Angus to ask, 'Why were you there that day?'

'Um. I had a work meeting,' she replied, heat burning her cheeks. 'You?'

'Same,' Angus replied. 'Is it work that's getting you so down?'

'Partly,' Layla admitted, calmer now she was less periously close to revealing the real reason she had been in Birmingham. 'I feel like I've been so focused on following one path that I've blinked and life has passed me by. I don't know if my job is the right fit. I miss my family. I wish I had more friends. I'm just . . . I'm lost, Angus. Lonely, too, I suppose.'

Angus hadn't shied away from Layla's vulnerability, or mocked or belittled her feelings. Instead, he had listened. He had understood. 'Loneliness is the worst,' he replied. 'It's all-consuming, but there's a stigma around it, like it's embarrassing to talk about.'

'That's why I never do, but I don't feel exposed when I talk to you. I like being so . . . naked.'

'Careful, Cannon,' Angus teased. 'That sounded a lot like flirting.'

The laugh that burst from Layla felt freeing. It was the strangest thing. Despite everything, Angus always found a way to make her laugh.

He was just so . . . kind. Considerate. Attentive. His gentle nature made it easy for Layla to open up. Aside from hiding her death date, she didn't edit herself when they spoke. She was silly and honest and brave. The mix made Layla feel more alive than she'd felt in a long time, an irony that wasn't lost on her, given her circumstances.

And when Angus called Layla 'Cannon', her stomach flipped. It felt like an in-joke. A nickname that indicated a kind of intimacy.

Giddily, Layla's thumb moved to reply to Angus, but at the last second, she stopped herself. *What's the point?* she wondered. *Seriously, what's the point?*

If Layla only had two years left to live, she didn't want to waste time on meaningless flirting. She didn't want a fling, not even with someone as great as Angus. Besides, something about their interactions told Layla that if anything happened between them, it would not be a fling.

It was selfish to reply quickly and let Angus believe that they could have a future, Layla decided. Cruel, even. Almost as cruel as fate showing Layla a life she could have had if it weren't for her impending death. The injustice of that thought bit hard.

Resting her phone on the bedside table, Layla dragged her body from the safety of bed and plunged her feet into Maya's spare pair of fluffy slippers. Reaching for a bra, Layla began to dress, cursing herself as her mind wandered to thoughts of Angus once more.

Maybe we can be friends, she reasoned. Friends was better than nothing. It meant she could have Angus in her life in a way that didn't end in heartbreak. Maybe theirs didn't need to be an epic love story. Maybe friendship was enough.

As she fastened her bra, Layla settled on a plan. After breakfast, she would reply to Angus. They would talk, they would meet, but they would not fall in love. She would be clear with him about that, and even clearer with herself.

Decision made, Layla headed downstairs to the hustle and bustle of the kitchen.

'Jayden, you don't need that much syrup,' Maya called over the chaos.

Layla entered the room in time to hear Jayden's protests.

'But syrup makes you strong, Mum!'

Briefly, Layla glanced at Joanna; the act was muscle memory, thinking the only mum around here was hers. But then it hit Layla, as it did whenever she was around her family – Maya was a mum too. The little sister, who had snuck into Layla's bed when she had a nightmare and sung pop songs in front of the mirror, was grown up. So grown up she was someone's mum.

It was a strange thing to see a sibling become a parent. Part of Layla mourned the definitive loss of childhood, but mostly she was proud. Witnessing Maya blossom into this new role was incredible. Different sides of her sister's personality had come to light. Maya was softer now. Kinder. She laughed harder, loved more fiercely. She noticed things Layla didn't. Twice over the last few days, Layla had watched Maya point out an interesting cloud to Jayden, anchoring him in the small marvels that were all around him. It made Layla stop and notice them too. It made her proud of her sister and the way she chose to view the world.

Have you ever told Maya that? her brain asked, but her father kicked out a chair for her to join them.

'Come on, kiddo,' he said. 'Hurry, before all the pancakes are gone.'

'Or drowned in an ungodly amount of syrup,' Maya muttered, dropping two pancakes onto a plate and handing them to Layla.

'Thanks,' Layla said. She took a moment to marvel at how pretty Maya looked. It was barely 9 am, but Maya's hair was perfectly styled and her beloved red lipstick was firmly in place. Layla often felt plain and dumpy next to her sister, and the contrast felt sharper than ever that morning. 'This looks amazing, Mum,' Layla said as she took her seat.

'Thank you, sweetheart. I thought a nice breakfast would set us all up for the day. I was thinking we could go for a walk later, if you'd like?'

'Not me, love,' David replied, patting his hips.

'Are you okay, Dad?' Layla asked, adding syrup to her pancakes. 'Do you need to see a doctor?'

'I'm fine, it's just the cold,' David explained. 'My bones and joints always play up around this time of year.'

'That's what happens after you fall and break them all,' Maya joked.

Everyone laughed, but Layla couldn't join in. Coming home was always a confronting reminder of what the Cannons had been through. Even all these years later, Layla couldn't dismiss her dad's injuries. As soon as she stepped through the front door, she transformed into the scared little girl visiting him in the ICU, worrying that he could be here one day but gone the next.

'Do go for the walk, though,' David said. 'See if you can beat Jayden in a race.'

As Jayden launched into a passionate speech about how fast he could run, Layla glanced at Joanna. She'd only meant to check if her mum was worried about her dad, but now she was concerned for her mother.

Despite the generous spread on the table, there was only a small fat-free yoghurt in Joanna's hands. To most people, it would simply look like Joanna wasn't hungry, but Layla knew her mum. She knew that there were only two reasons Joanna would semi-starve herself – either money was tight, or her body image was at its worst. With fresh fruit on the table and two choices of fruit juice laid out, Layla guessed it was the latter.

'Aren't you having pancakes, Mum?' Layla asked.

'No. One bite would be on my hips for the next five years,' Joanna replied, laughing as if to brush off the self-deprecating comment.

'Oh hush, love. You're perfect,' David said, reaching across the table for a bowl of bacon. Even through the cloud of worry, Layla couldn't help smiling. After all these years and all they'd been through, love still bloomed between her parents. It might not be loud, showy, Instagram-worthy love, but it was real.

It made Layla think of Angus. Ducking her head before her family could see her blush, Layla added a few strawberries to her plate then handed the bowl to Maya.

'Layls needs to come home more often,' Maya quipped as she heaped the fruit onto her plate. 'We never get fancy treatment when it's just us.'

'Excuse me, I treat you all like kings and queens,' Joanna admonished, rising to her feet. 'David, have you had your tablets?'

Mid-wolfing down a mouthful of bacon, Layla's dad shook his head.

'For goodness' sake,' Joanna muttered, reaching for a pillbox from the cupboard. Setting it on the table, Joanna watched David remove the tablets he needed from the AM section. Layla did the same. Her eyes widened as she counted the five tablets in his hand.

'Jesus, Dad. How much medication are you on?' she asked.

'Too much,' David replied, tipping the tablets into his mouth and swallowing them with a mouthful of tea.

'That's just his morning meds,' Maya added. 'Wait until you see how many he takes before bed. With all the pills Dad has in him, he rattles when he walks.'

Maya grinned as David pretended to clutch his sides to stop them splitting with laughter, but Layla couldn't smile. While Layla knew David's health wasn't in top condition, she hadn't expected this. Biting her lip, she looked to the pillbox and tried to count how many tablets were in the PM section.

'Don't fret, love,' David said when he caught her. 'These pills keep me fighting fit, don't they, Jayden?'

As David mimed boxing with his grandson, Jayden laughed. 'Grandad's silly,' he said, his mouth half-full with pancake.

'Jayden, manners,' Maya said, reaching to add more syrup to her own pancakes.

'Well, now I see where Jayden gets his sweet tooth from,' Layla joked, trying to be present.

'Stop getting me in trouble,' Maya said, pulling a face at her sister.

As Layla returned the gesture, warmth filled her. *This is what you've needed,* it said. *This is what you've missed.*

The temptation to berate herself for leaving so long between visits beckoned, but for the first time in days, Layla chose not to sink into her most miserable thoughts. Instead, she chose to focus on the fact that she was here, in the moment, with her family. Better late than never.

16

Angus

His father was calling to him from another room, but all Angus could focus on was the exchange on the screen before him.

I've had dinner and can confirm – fish and chips in the north is superior to fish and chips in the south x

By superior, do you mean greasier? x

The grease is what makes them taste so good, Angus, don't you know anything?! x

I did not know that. Clearly my palate isn't as sophisticated as yours . . . x

I'm glad you can admit it. Don't worry, I'll educate you x

I look forward to your tuition, Cannon. How about when you're back from Hull, we meet for dinner and begin my education? It would be great to see you again x

When he sent that message to Layla, Angus felt brave. Alcohol always had that effect on him and he had consumed a bottle of wine over dinner with his father. Plus, while his mother was away in the Cotswolds, Angus was free to be unfiltered.

But rereading his text as he sobered up on his parents' sofa, Angus couldn't believe he'd ever thought that asking Layla out via text was a good idea. The wording was juvenile, the tone blasé, and he couldn't help worrying he looked cowardly by not asking to her face.

Angus's concern didn't appear to be unfounded. As soon as the message was delivered, the playful conversation Layla and Angus had enjoyed all day ended. Two hours later, Angus was still waiting for a response. Cursing himself, he reread the messages for clues about where he went wrong.

Were his jokes about the north of England offensive?

Was dinner too formal? Too casual? Too boring?

Was Layla unnerved by him reminding her that they had only actually met once?

Tipping his head back, Angus let out a pained groan.

'Someone's in a terrible mood,' Peter said, stepping into the living room. No longer dressed in a sharp suit, his monogrammed robe and pyjamas made him look older, less powerful. The fact that he was clearly tipsy only made it worse.

Angus never knew how to read this version of his father. In some ways, Peter felt more approachable without his formal armour. In others, it was like interacting with someone who wasn't his father at all.

'I'm just tired. A little frustrated too,' Angus admitted.

'About what?' Peter asked, heading to the drinks cabinet. There, he poured two whiskies before joining his son on the sofa. 'I take it from your silence that this is a romantic frustration?'

'I guess so,' Angus replied, accepting the glass of amber liquid.

'Well, well, well,' Peter said, unable to hide his smile. 'I don't think I've ever seen you in one of those. You've always seemed capable on that front. With the short-term kind of love, at least. So, who is she? She must be special to have you in such a tangle.'

'Her name is Layla.'

A wave of vulnerability swept over Angus. Up until now, Layla almost felt like a figment of his imagination. The fact that they'd only met in person once added to the sense of intrigue. What they shared was too incredible to spoil with reality. When he talked to her, Angus wasn't Angus Fairview-Whitley, but the person he wanted to be.

Maybe it was because Angus had tweaked details about himself here and there. Nothing big, but big enough. Angus had said he lived in London but hadn't gone so far as to say that he lived in a multi-million-pound penthouse. Angus had said he liked to travel, but he hadn't quite admitted to having unlimited funds to do so.

The core of what you've said is the truth, his brain pointed out. It was the only way Angus could calm his nerves.

Things with Layla were so magical, he didn't want reality to taint them with his failures. He didn't want to admit to bad investments and the ever-present ache of loneliness. Their relationship was a fantasy land Angus could escape to, fuelled by instant attraction and a good phone network.

But now that Angus had told Peter about Layla, his two worlds were colliding.

'And what does Layla do?' Peter asked, after taking a long gulp of his drink.

'She's a lawyer.'

The answer earned an impressed nod from Peter. 'Smart, then.'

'Very. Too smart for me,' Angus joked, but he wondered if it could be called a joke if it was the truth.

'Don't put yourself down, son. You have more to offer than you think. You've just got to find the thing that makes you tick.'

'Any idea what that might be?' Angus asked, grimacing into his glass.

'That's for you to figure out. Besides, I'm not someone you should take advice from, especially on the dating front. I wouldn't exactly call myself husband of the year.' With those words, Peter closed his eyes.

Angus frowned, studying his father. 'Are you okay?'

Opening one eye, Peter settled his gaze on his son. 'Why wouldn't I be?'

Peter's tone was sharper than Angus expected, cutting him down to size. 'You don't talk about your marriage usually, that's all,' he mumbled while staring into his drink.

'Yes, well, there's a lot we don't speak about in this house,' Peter said, draining his glass.

Angus's frown deepened, but he didn't have time to ask his father what he meant. Peter leaned forward to set his glass down on the coffee table, but missed his target. The glass fell to the floor, splashing whisky onto Gilly's prized cream rug.

'Uh-oh,' Peter sang, his voice wobbly and strange.

There was something about seeing his father so out of sorts that unsettled Angus. He had only seen Peter this way once before, and that was after Hugo's death.

'Maybe you should go to bed,' Angus suggested.

'Maybe I should.' Peter paused for a moment before standing. His body swayed slightly, then he flashed Angus a sad smile. 'Is Layla someone special?' he asked.

Though he was taken aback by the question, Angus nodded. 'She is.'

'In that case – hold onto her tight and never let her forget how much she means to you. Ever.'

With those parting words, Peter began to walk away in small, unsteady steps. Angus watched him go, too surprised to speak.

'Goodnight, Angus,' Peter called over his shoulder.

Before Peter reached the living room door, Angus called out to him. Stopping, Peter turned around. 'Yes, son?'

'Do me a favour and don't tell Mother about Layla, will you? I don't think she'd understand.'

Sadness covered Peter's face. 'I won't say a word, but you should think twice about that. Your mother is a better person than you give her credit for.'

Silenced, Angus watched his father amble away, a strange sense of guilt overcoming him. He didn't like the way it sat on his chest. Reaching for his phone to distract himself, Angus's eyes widened when he saw that Layla had replied.

Angus, I would love to go to dinner with you, but I need to be honest – it would be a 'friends' thing. There's a lot going on in my life right now. I don't have the capacity for anything more.

I love talking to you and don't want to stop, but I also don't know if you are hoping for more . . .

All I can offer at this time is to be friends. If that works for you, then YES to dinner. If not, I understand x

It took Angus three reads of the message to fully digest what it said. It took five seconds for him to find air after that.

The pain that hummed through Angus felt like it was alive, tearing chunks from him with its sharp, pointed teeth.

But there was something accompanying the pain that Angus didn't expect – understanding.

The day he met Layla, it was clear she was going through something. In all their interactions since, Angus had felt the undertones of sadness. Just two days ago, Layla described her day as 'heavy'. Angus wanted nothing more than to lighten that load, but Layla was guarded about the cause.

Angus knew that Layla didn't need any added pressure. She needed a friend. And, if that was the only way he could be in her life, then Angus would be the greatest friend Layla ever had.

Besides, she said 'at this time', his brain pointed out. *That doesn't mean never.*

A small smile lifted his mouth. Angus could wait. He had all the time in the world. Almost another sixty years, in fact. If that was how long it took Layla to deal with whatever she was going through, he would wait. Then maybe, if he was lucky, some of those years could be spent with her.

I understand, say no more. When you're back in London, we'll make plans x

As a yawn escaped Angus, he dropped his phone on the sofa. It was time for bed.

Dragging his lethargic body out of the living room, Angus began the ascent to his childhood bedroom where Ms Tillman had laid fresh bedding for his arrival. His shoulders relaxed as his mind wandered to thoughts of the bed that awaited him, and the dreams that would accompany it.

17

Layla

Icy wind slapped Layla's cheeks as she walked with Joanna towards the bypass that led to the estate they called home. She had been in Hull for a little over a week, but it felt like the temperature had dropped by at least ten degrees in that time. Winter was well and truly coming.

Usually, winter meant going to work in the dark and coming home in the dark. It meant months of daydreaming about sunshine and brighter days. But with Angus in her life, winter didn't seem as dull as it once had. Especially considering what could happen if – *when*, Layla's brain snapped – she returned to London. The run-up to Christmas was the most magical time in the capital. That's what tourists were told, anyway. Layla was usually too busy to participate in the frosty revelry, but this year, she hoped for something different. And, judging by their recent exchanges, it sounded like Angus was determined to make those wishes a reality.

Just wait, Cannon – dinner is only the start of our festive plans. I'm picturing roaring fires, toasted marshmallows and of course, mulled wine x

Layla had almost squealed reading that. Her mind filled with visions of cosy, intimate dates. Only as friends, of course.

'Come on,' Joanna said suddenly, picking up her pace. 'We can get home and out of this cold faster if we hurry.'

Layla copied her mum, moving so fast her arms swung with determination. The walk back from the neonatal unit of the local hospital wasn't far. Thirty-five minutes, if that. However, the pink tip of Layla's nose indicated that thirty-five minutes of walking on a freezing day was not exactly comfortable.

Joanna had refused to get the bus, though. 'The exercise will be good,' she insisted.

Although Layla suspected her mum's personal motivation for the walk was to punish herself for eating pasta last night, she hadn't argued. The only reason Layla was out of bed was because of Joanna.

Since Layla had arrived in Hull ten days ago, Joanna had filled her time with odd jobs. A skirting board that needed painting, a grocery shop she could not complete alone. And earlier, when Joanna announced that she was dropping off another batch of knitting to the neonatal unit, she'd asked Layla to tag along.

Layla knew it was all a ploy to get her outside and moving, but she didn't mind. Fresh air sounded appealing, as did seeing the place Joanna visited every month to drop off the fruits of her labour.

Joanna had been knitting items for premature babies for the last nine years. The project started when Layla was at university, Maya was in her partying phase, and David was working through a new physio regime. Layla had never questioned her mother's sudden love of knitting. In fact, she'd almost forgotten it was something Joanna did until she saw her making a tiny yellow hat while watching TV.

But as Layla watched Joanna being greeted like a hero by the staff at the hospital, she'd felt a surge of pride for her mother. She had seen an opportunity to make a difference and learned a new skill to do it. In a world where it often felt like people were more self-serving than ever, Joanna was bucking the trend. Her way of helping might not be huge, but it definitely wasn't small.

'Why do you do it?' Layla asked when they approached a set of traffic lights near a busy intersection.

'Do what?' Joanna replied.

'Knit the hats and blankets.'

'It's simple: someone needs them.' Joanna pushed the button at the pedestrian crossing like what she had said was the easiest thing in the world to understand.

'But so many people need things. You don't see everyone else going out of their way to help.'

'Maybe I'm not like everyone else,' Joanna said, flashing Layla a cheeky grin, but then she shrugged. 'I guess I know what it's like to go through life thinking everything is fine, then one day it's not. You lose all confidence in your footing. People you thought were friends are suddenly nowhere to be found. When your dad had his accident, it was the kindness of strangers that got me through. Sometimes, I just needed that person at the bus stop to talk about the weather and make me feel normal. Then there were times when people went out of their way to help. Like once, at the supermarket, I was a pound short for the weekly shop. The cashier wanted me to put something back, but an old lady in the queue gave me the money. She saved me from breaking down at the end of aisle five.'

'Oh, Mum,' Layla breathed, slotting her arm through Joanna's. 'I had no idea.'

Joanna squeezed Layla's hand. 'Your dad and I tried to shield you from it as best we could, but I'll never forget the kindness of that woman. She was a pensioner, she probably needed the money as much as I did, but she still gave it to me. She helped when she could have chosen not to. Since then, I've tried to be that person for someone else whenever I can.'

As the traffic lights changed colour, Layla leaned her head on Joanna's shoulder. 'You really are the greatest.'

'And so are you,' Joanna said, pressing a kiss to Layla's hairline.

Layla replayed her mum's words as they continued their journey home. The more she thought of them, the more Layla wondered if they were the truth.

Layla didn't feel great, and not just because of her death date. In fact, she hadn't felt great in a long time. As they reached the familiar street of her childhood home, Layla wondered why that was.

Work was the first thought that came to mind. Life at Mayweather & Halliwell was tiring and stressful, of course it made her feel not-great, but Layla knew it was more than that. Within the walls of that office, she wasn't the person she wanted to be.

You only have to look at how you are with Sinead to know that, her brain pointed out. Day after day, Layla sat beside a woman who was struggling. Sinead had migrated from Ireland to be with her girlfriend. She didn't have the support network of her family and hadn't been in London long enough to make solid friendships. With her work-life taking over and her relationship crumbling, Sinead needed a friend. Layla hadn't been one for her, or for Rashida.

Guilt tugged at Layla as she thought of how, by running off to Hull, she had abandoned her colleagues at one of the busiest times of year.

The day she decided to hop on a train home, Layla had booked personal leave and told Mayweather & Halliwell that there was a family emergency. At first, everyone was understanding – Michelle even sent an email saying she was thinking of Layla – but by now the caring bubble had burst and the hounds were calling. People needed information about clients and cases, and answers about when she'd reclaim her workload. They needed her back, but Layla couldn't help thinking, *So what?*

For years she'd used all the energy she should have spent on herself on her job. It took everything in Layla to not burst into tears at that realisation.

'Maya, are you home?' Joanna called as they entered the house.

'In the kitchen,' Maya responded. 'I've got work in an hour, though.'

'Want me to make you some lunch, Mum?' Layla asked, slipping her feet free from a pair of boots she'd borrowed from Maya.

'No thanks, sweetheart. I'm not hungry.'

Layla frowned. 'You must be. You only had an apple for breakfast.'

'You wouldn't think that to look at me,' Joanna joked, patting her stomach. There was something about the gesture that made Layla want to shout at her mother. Her hands itched to grab Joanna's wrists and beg her to stop being so cruel to herself, but as Joanna headed upstairs, the moment slid through Layla's fingers.

In the kitchen, Layla found Maya leaning against the fridge, flicking through her phone.

'All right, Layls?' Maya asked before taking a bite of a cheese sandwich.

'Yes. No. Is Mum okay?'

Maya looked up from her phone at the unexpected question. 'What do you mean?'

'She's not eating.'

'Oh, that,' Maya replied. 'She's in another of her I-want-to-be-thin stages. She thinks some article she read in 2012 about fasting is the answer.'

Reaching into the cupboard for a biscuit, Layla tried not to shake her head. 'Should we be worried?'

'Layla, this is Mum. She always thinks there's something wrong with the way she looks, and she's always hunting for a diet to fix it.'

'I know, but it's so sad to see.'

'I agree,' Maya replied, taking another bite of her sandwich. 'But that's what years of societal brainwashing does to a person. It makes you hate yourself, then look back at photos and think, *Wait, why did I? I looked great!* Besides, Mum's spent years on the bottom of her own priority list. She's never had time to care for herself in the way she wants to.'

'Because of Dad's accident?'

'Because of life, Layls. Being a mum isn't easy, never mind being a mum and the partner of someone who became disabled overnight. Mum's doing the best she can. If this makes her feel like she has some control, then who are we to judge?'

The chocolate biscuit Layla was eating soured in her mouth. 'I wish we could make her feel better about herself, that's all.'

'Make who feel better?' Joanna said, bustling into the room with the laundry basket.

Like two guilty children, Layla and Maya stood taller. 'A client from the salon I was telling Layla about,' Maya lied. 'No matter what I say, she doesn't think she looks good.'

'Poor woman,' Joanna replied, opening the drum of the washing machine. 'This world doesn't tell you how to be confident. It only wipes away whatever confidence you have.'

Layla's eyes met Maya's. In them, she saw all the times they had heard Joanna speak negatively about herself. All the times they'd seen her get flustered and upset in a fitting room if an item of clothing didn't fit. All the times she'd moved to the background of photos rather than be at the front, or not be in them at all.

As Layla's mouth opened to say something, an alarm went off on her phone, reminding her that it was almost time for her weekly counselling session with Saira.

Experiment rules stipulated that sessions were held virtually one week, and in person the other. Saira had bent this rule for Layla while she was in Hull – but at a compromise, her counselling sessions were upped to twice a week. Layla hadn't battled against the new structure. If anything, the extra time to talk was needed. Sometimes, the sessions with Saira felt like the only time anything in Layla's life made sense.

'I've got to make a call,' Layla said, putting her phone away. 'Sorry, it's important.'

'Another call with the mystery man?' Maya teased.

Tempted to stick out her tongue in juvenile retaliation, Layla instead let the comment slide. 'Not quite. A work call.'

'I was wondering when you were going to get in touch with them. I can't imagine they've loved you disappearing.'

'Maya,' Joanna admonished, whipping her with a pair of Jayden's pyjama trousers. 'Ignore her, sweetheart. Go talk to whoever you need to.'

Excusing herself from the kitchen before more Angus-inspired comments could be fired her way, Layla headed to her room. Pulling her laptop from under the bed, Layla powered it up. Her eyes found her inbox, the red notification bubble indicating a nauseating number of unread emails, but Layla forced herself to look away. Opening Zoom, she joined the meeting.

Seconds later, Saira's smiling face filled the screen. 'Layla,' she said in a tone so upbeat it was practically a cheer. 'You're looking well.'

The compliment mirrored a similar one Saira had made at the start of their last session. Back then, Layla had been so dismissive she almost didn't hear it, but this time she did. And, after thinking for a moment, she nodded. 'I feel well. Not perfect, not there yet, but better.'

'I'm glad to hear it. Remember, take things one day at a time.'

'That's my mantra,' Layla joked, but it wasn't really funny. 'One day at a time' was what Layla told herself when she woke up. She repeated it in her wobbliest moments. One day at a time, bringing her closer to the end of her life, and hopefully closer to the person she was destined to be.

18

Angus

Relief came the instant Angus closed the door of his apartment. Finally, he could breathe.

For the entire ten-minute walk to his flat, Jasper had tried to convince Angus that fun could be found within the strobe-lit walls of a nightclub. Each time, Angus had been adamant it could not.

'You've turned boring, my friend,' Jasper hollered as Angus headed for the lift. Angus didn't fight him on it. Instead, he let his friend go.

Moving through his apartment, Angus pulled out his phone. He needed to complete an OPM Discoveries questionnaire, but it could wait. There was only one thing he wanted to do with the evening, and it didn't involve rating his energy level.

Scrolling for Layla's contact details, Angus paused. He took a breath, and prepared himself to lie.

Angus knew he only had himself to blame for the predicament he was in – he was the one who told the lies – but in the cafe, when Layla asked if he was posh and he denied it, the lie didn't seem like such a big deal. The more they spoke, though, the more Angus stretched the truth.

He said that Peter owned a business, but he didn't specify that it was worth tens of millions.

He told Layla anecdotes about his friends, but he didn't admit to meeting most of them at an elite private school.

And, perhaps most damningly of all, Angus's cushy unemployed life became enduring a vague IT role, because even Angus knew that saying 'I work in IT' was a sure way to fend off any further questions.

In no time, Angus had become someone who was so distanced from the life he lead, he was unrecognisable to himself.

'I can't believe I ever thought you were posh,' Layla giggled when Angus remarked that a Senior Partner at her work sounded like 'a typical entitled prick'.

While Layla hadn't explicitly stated that she hated wealthy people, she'd dropped enough hints about the vapid, unfair nature of the world for the subtext to be clear. Angus couldn't exactly argue with her. How could he protest workplace privilege when so many of his friends were only in their senior positions due to family connections? How could he do anything but agree with the injustice of the 2 per cent holding most of the country's wealth? It was a serious problem, as Layla rightly pointed out. The issue was it was a problem Angus himself was part of.

Silencing that nagging thought, Angus flopped onto his sofa and pressed dial.

'Well, isn't this a surprise!' Layla chimed when she answered his call.

Angus smiled. 'I'd have thought by now you'd be used to me calling at this time.'

'I suppose there are worse things to get used to,' Layla teased.

The muffled sound of footsteps told Angus she was moving. 'Is everything okay? You sound like you're running.'

'I'm heading to my room. Mum and Dad are watching a film. It's the first time I've seen them relax since I got here. I don't want to spoil it by giggling over the top of it.'

'I make you giggle, do I?' Angus grinned, his words laced with unashamed delight. 'What are they watching?'

'*Pretty Woman*. Dad suggested it.'

'The Julia Roberts film?'

'Don't sound so surprised. It's a classic, and Dad loves a happy ending. He's a softie like that.' In the background, a door clicked. Layla was safe to talk freely.

'Tell me about your dad,' Angus said, settling deeper into the sofa.

'What do you want to know about him?' Layla replied.

'I don't know. Everything, I guess.'

The sound of Layla's laughter lifted the corners of Angus's mouth again. 'I'm hurt, Angus. I thought I was the one you wanted to know.'

'You are, but your dad is a huge part of you. I can tell by the way you speak about him. There's a smile in your voice.'

'Really? You can hear that?'

Angus grinned at Layla's disbelief. The fact that he could read her tone shouldn't come as a shock when he spent his days living for their conversations. 'What can I say, I'm good at reading people. Besides, everything about you screams adoration for your father.'

'I guess you could say I'm proud of him. More than proud, even. After everything that happened, how could I not be?'

'Everything that happened?' Angus questioned. 'Tell me more.'

The inhale Layla took before speaking told Angus that her story was a heavy one. As he prepared himself to listen, Angus realised how privileged he was to have it shared with him.

'My dad has always been, and will always be, my hero,' she began. 'When I was little, he carried me on his shoulders and took me on days out. He taught me to climb trees. He showed me I could go higher even when I was sure I couldn't. I was his little adventurer.'

The smile in Layla's voice was back and wider than ever, but when she next spoke, the happiness had gone.

'Dad worked in construction from the age of seventeen,' Layla continued. 'He was a big, strong man. The life and soul of the building site. He was forever helping his friends and doing extra jobs to bring in more money. He wanted to take us to Disneyland, he said. But one day, when I was seven, everything went wrong.'

The moment suspended, elevated by a thread of vulnerability that ran between Layla and Angus. Delicate and fragile, it was so newly formed that to be suspended by it felt scary, but Angus knew he wouldn't allow it to break.

'Dad was helping a friend install guttering on a house,' she said. 'A few hours of work over the weekend, off the books, cash in hand. He'd done it a million times before. He should have been able to do it a million times more, but that day he lost his footing. He . . . he fell.' She paused. 'Dad shattered his pelvis, slipped a disk in his spine and broke more bones than I knew the human body had in it. In a second, my family's life changed forever.'

'Jesus, Layla,' Angus breathed. 'I'm so sorry.'

'It's fine,' Layla replied, but the catch in her voice told Angus it wasn't fine. His chest ached, wishing more than anything that he could hold her.

'Did he recover okay?' Angus asked gently.

'Dad was in hospital for months. He had surgery after surgery. For so long, we didn't know if he was going to walk again, never mind do anything else. We thought that was the hardest time, but things only got worse from there. Dad couldn't go back to work. He couldn't get compensation either because the accident happened in his own time, not on the job. My parents had to sell our home. We moved to a tiny house on a council estate, but we even struggled to afford that. Overnight, Mum became Dad's carer. She worked at a supermarket too, which meant my sister and I had to take on jobs around the house. Dad hated it. He was so angry that our childhood was cut short.'

Closing his eyes, Angus tried to picture his father dealing with the same horrific fate Layla's dad had endured. It was hard to imagine how someone as proud as Peter would react to his freedom and autonomy being taken. Most of Peter's confidence came from the life he provided his family. If that role were gone, what would he have done?

'Things were tough,' Layla admitted. 'It was hard watching Dad struggle to adjust to his new life. It was hard losing our money and our home and knowing we were getting into more and more debt. It was hard turning on the news and seeing people talk about families on benefits as if they were scum. I wanted to scream that it wasn't Dad's fault. If it weren't for the government support Dad got, I've no idea where we'd have been. Hungrier than we already were, probably.'

Shame burned in Angus's chest as he thought of all the times he had been around people who looked down on families like Layla's. And if he was honest with himself, he had too. It was easy to see a clickbait headline about a person taking advantage of government aid and forget about the thousands who weren't.

Angus's voice was like sandpaper when he next spoke. 'Is your dad okay now?'

'Honestly? I don't know,' Layla replied. 'He's still larger than life, but now I'm here, I'm seeing firsthand how he struggles. After the accident, Dad's health spiralled. He gained a lot of weight. He fell into depression. He has type 2 diabetes now and is on medication for his heart. He's in so much pain, Angus. When it's cold, his hips are stiffer than ever, but he still insists on going to work.'

Angus's eyebrows arched. 'He's back in work?'

'He drives a taxi a few shifts a week. He says it makes him feel useful. Mum says he's a workaholic.'

Angus smiled at this. 'Is that who you learned your hard-working ways from?'

'Do you know something? I think it is.' There was a pause while Layla digested this. 'It's funny, isn't it, to reflect on the things we learn from our parents? So many people want to be the opposite of them, but in the end we all take on some of their traits. Good and bad, I suppose. But I know my best bits are things I got from my parents.'

'They sound like wonderful people,' Angus said.

The smile was back in Layla's voice when she replied. 'They really are. What about you? What traits did you get from your parents?'

With the conversation flipped to him, the cushions surrounding Angus became suffocating. Emerging from their padded embrace, he sat tall. 'I don't know. I've never really thought about it.'

'Well, now's your chance.'

Gripping the sofa, Angus thought of his parents. Had he inherited Gilly's cold, distant demeanour? Or Peter's ability to glide through a conversation without ever getting to the deep stuff, the real stuff?

How had being a Fairview-Whitley shaped him?

'Cooking,' Angus heard himself reply. 'I love cooking, same as my mum. Well, she prefers baking, but she was the one who first showed me around a kitchen.'

The answer surprised Angus, mostly because memories of baking with Gilly were not ones he thought of often. They only made Angus remember how special those vanilla-scented afternoons in the kitchen with his mother and Hugo were. The baking stopped when Hugo was gone. His mother's smile vanished too, as did any closeness Angus felt towards her.

'I love that you can cook!' Layla enthused, her chirpiness jarring with his sudden swirl of nostalgia. 'What's your favourite cuisine?'

'That's impossible to answer. They all have their own unique flavour profiles.'

'Check you out, using words like "flavour profile",' Layla teased. 'Well, speaking as someone who can barely boil an egg, colour me impressed. If you ever feel like teaching someone how to cook, I'll be your student. We'll have to cook at your place, though. I think I only own one pan.'

Angus should have pounced on Layla's offer, but he couldn't. Blood was rushing to his head, drowning out her voice.

Angus could never teach Layla to cook because she could never come to his apartment. One look at the penthouse and Layla would know he had lied about a lowly IT job.

Placing his feet on the carpet to steady himself, Angus rested his forehead on his palm and listened to Layla ask about his favourite dishes. His answers were short and noncommittal, but it was impossible to reply in any other way. The severity of what he had started with that first lie was too great to see past.

For the rest of the call, Angus listened to Layla's beautiful voice while feeling sick. He ended the conversation early, claiming tiredness and promising to rest. Angus wasn't lying this time – he was tired. Shattered, even. The problem was, he was tired of himself.

19

Layla

The Life Experiment: Daily Questionnaire
Property of OPM Discoveries

How would you rate your level of contentment today? (1 represents low contentment, 10 represents high)

1   2   3   4   5   6   (7)   8   9   10

How would you rate your energy level? (1 being very low energy and 10 being very high energy)

1   2   3   4   5   (6)   7   8   9   10

What are two things you are grateful for today?
1. Mum trying to teach me how to cook. I made a terrible omelette this morning (apparently, they're meant to be easy . . .) but spending time in the kitchen with her is so nice
2. A strong phone signal and Angus's jokes. Today he told a great one about The Flintstones. I can't remember the punchline, but it made me laugh so hard I nearly cried

What are you struggling with today?
That I can't hide out at my parents' house forever

Do you have any additional notes on what you would like to discuss in your upcoming counselling session?
Angus. Specifically the timing of his appearance in my life and what it could mean

With a biscuit perched on the sofa arm and crumbs from the two she had already eaten scattered across her jumper, Layla read over her latest conversation with Angus.

*Remember when we met and you told me to only
call when I'd had a really bad day?
Well, today's been one of those x*

> *I thought I was the one who had the bad days!
> In all seriousness, what's up? Is it anything
> I can help with? x*

Are you sure you can handle it, Cannon? It's a lot x

> *I'm sure x*

*Prepare yourself.
My favourite Indian restaurant has removed
my favourite curry from the menu . . . x*

> *Angus!
> My heart was in my throat reading your message!
> You made me panic over nothing haha x*

*You don't think this is a serious issue?!
What will I order when I feel like vegging
out in front of the TV? x*

> *I take it back – this is a travesty x*

Layla suppressed a smile as best she could, but it kept creeping in at the corners of her mouth. It was always the way with Angus. Their conversations, even the serious ones, coaxed out a level of happiness Layla hadn't known she could possess.

Exiting the conversation, Layla headed to Instagram. Ever since finding out her death date, doomscrolling had become her nightly routine, bringing a strange mix of nostalgia, envy and mild irritation.

She flicked past weight loss ads and videos of strangers dancing and photos of people's dinners, but what Layla was looking for, she didn't know. Fulfilment? Beauty? Anything that wasn't trying to get her to buy something or click something or be angry about something?

'That was a big sigh,' Maya said from the opposite end of the sofa.

Layla looked up, staring blankly at her sister. 'Did I sigh?'

'Shit.' Maya giggled. 'That's when you know you're depressed.'

'I'm fine,' Layla replied, but Maya looked at her like she knew better. She didn't say anything, though. Instead, she turned back to the TV and continued to watch *Friends*.

Although the sisters had seen the entire series several times already, they would never stop rewatching it. There was comfort in the familiar dynamics and jokes. When life was chaos, Layla needed that.

When the episode ended, Maya yawned exaggeratedly. 'Time for bed, I think.'

'It's not even ten o'clock! You've changed, Maya Cannon,' Layla teased.

'I know, but I have a four-year-old to entertain. We can't all be like you, taking endless time away from our responsibilities,' Maya said, leaning over and ruffling Layla's hair.

'Shut up,' Layla said as Maya stood and walked to the stairs. 'Night,' Layla called.

'Love you,' Maya replied.

The words knotted in Layla's chest. She opened her mouth to say them back, but it was too late. Maya was already upstairs.

Not for the first time in her life, Layla wished she was more like her sister. Someone who could say 'I love you' freely and wear her heart on her sleeve. Maya might have been the younger sibling, but she was the one who lit up a room. Her wit was quick and her personality sunshine yellow. She had a vast friendship group to prove it.

As Layla thought of her own empty social calendar, the difference between herself and her sister had never seemed starker.

Like many things in Layla's life, her friends seemed to have slipped away over time. Life pulled the people she'd had water fights and sleepovers with in different directions. In her early university days, Layla tried to keep in touch with people back home, but her assignments stacked up. With the part-time waitressing job she worked around her studies, she had little time to reach out. There was no definitive line in the sand to explain the end of Layla's childhood friendships. No falling out, no argument, just the gradual, growing distance between people who no longer had anything in common.

Truthfully, part of the reason Layla hated coming home was because it forced her to see people who had once been integral to her life look at her as though she were a stranger. It felt like there was an invisible barrier around her that said, 'You're not one of us anymore.' She wondered if she ever had been.

Another sigh bubbled in Layla's throat, but she swallowed it.

Snuggling deeper into the sofa, she returned to texting Angus.

I'm glad you understand the severity of the situation.
I think I've finally learned what heartbreak is x

My red flag detector is waving at that statement . . .
But let's ignore it so we can talk food!
If we were going for Indian, what would you order? x

What wouldn't I order!
First of all, we'd have to get poppadums and
a chutney tray x

Agreed.
It should be illegal to go for a curry and not order all the sides x

You're a lawyer, do you think you can make that law enforceable? x

Between each giggly exchange, Layla devoured the mind-numbing peace of social media. She watched videos of women styling outfits, wishing she had their confidence. She watched a baby with a cochlear implant hear their mother's voice for the first time. Crying, she wondered how she could ever feel down when life had moments that were so beautiful.

As she sniffed away her tears, the front door opened. 'Hello?' Layla called out.

'Only me,' David replied.

His tone was peppy, but Layla heard what lay beneath it. Stuffing her feet into a pair of slippers, she shuffled into the hallway in time to catch her dad wincing as he removed his coat. 'You sound tired,' she commented.

'Because I am. You would be too if you'd spent six hours driving.'

'You work too hard, Dad.' The comment earned a laugh from David, one Layla responded to with an eye-roll. 'Is the "Layla works too much" joke ever going to get old?'

'Don't get it twisted, love. A hard worker is a good thing to be. You learned it from me.' David offered Layla a wink before moving to the kitchen doorway. 'Biscuit?'

Layla hesitated. She knew a treat at this time of night would only spike her dad's blood sugars, but as his eyes sparkled cheekily, Layla gave in.

'Go on then,' she replied.

Together, the pair entered the kitchen. As Layla turned on the light, David picked two biscuits from the tin. A bourbon for him, a chocolate digestive for her. As he handed it over, Layla's eyes prickled. Even after all this time, her dad still remembered her favourite snack.

'Why do you work if it makes your pain worse?' she asked after taking the first bite.

David blinked at the question. 'What else am I going to do?'

'I don't know, Dad. Rest? Relax? Hang out with Mum? You don't need to push yourself so hard. Sitting for so long is bad for you.'

'Sitting for a long time is bad for anyone. How often do you leave your desk?'

Layla grinned at her dad's playful barb. 'Not often enough, but I'm here now. Here to ask why you aren't retiring and putting your health first, anyway.'

As he polished off his biscuit, David looked past Layla as if searching for an answer on the wall behind her. 'I don't know, Layla. It doesn't feel like it's on the cards for me right now. All my life, I've worked. Or when I couldn't work, I've wanted to. I'm a grafter. I always have been. Apart from after the accident, of course.'

'We don't really talk about it, do we?' Layla nibbled her biscuit, watching her dad's reaction.

'What's there to talk about? It wasn't a good time in our lives.'

'Still,' Layla pressed, 'it hit you more than anyone else.'

'I don't know about that, but it was tough,' David admitted. 'Suddenly, all the things I prided myself on were taken from me. I lost the best parts of myself, as well as parts I'd taken for granted. I couldn't stand, couldn't wash myself, couldn't provide for my family. I couldn't be the husband or dad I wanted to be. I couldn't even like myself.'

'Dad,' Layla's voice cracked.

David smiled gently. 'Don't be upset, Layla. I'm here now, aren't I? I got better. I pushed through.'

'But you shouldn't have to work so hard, Dad. Every day doesn't have to be a battle. You've fought for years, when most would have given up.'

David laughed. 'You say that like it's a bad thing.'

'It's not, but . . . don't you ever get tired? Don't you ever wonder if it's worth it?'

David took a moment to respond, eying his daughter. 'No one can tell you what is or isn't worth it, kiddo. You're the only one who can do that. And what I'm doing right now? Putting food on the table and making it so your mum isn't carrying this household on her own? My body tells me that's worth it.'

'Well, I think getting an early night every now and then is worth it too.'

'Maybe,' David replied with a chuckle. 'But I like my job, Layla. I really do. I watch life happen every day. I see first dates and break-ups and people on their way to weddings and funerals. I've talked to doctors, professors, comedians, scientists, tourists from places I've only ever seen on TV. Do you know, I've even driven two people to hospital to give birth.'

'I didn't know that,' Layla marvelled.

'Well, now you do. Imagine that, eh? Somewhere out there, someone's telling the story of how their child came into the world, and I'm the taxi driver who told them it would all be okay. That right there is a little moment of magic,' David said, but when he saw Layla's still-dubious expression, he softened. 'I know you worry, love, but don't. Driving gets me out there. It gives me stories. It makes me . . . well, it makes me feel like me again.'

There was something to her dad's tone that twisted Layla's steely resolve. Stepping towards him, she wrapped her arms around David's neck, hugging him close. 'I love you,' she whispered.

'Love you too, kiddo,' David replied, squeezing Layla tight until she felt like she was five again and all was right with the world.

Layla could have stayed nestled in her dad's arms forever. She was tempted to. The hug felt safe. Soul-reviving. But when David yawned, it was time for them to break apart.

Stretching, David stifled another yawn. 'And with that, I think it's time for bed.'

'You go ahead,' Layla replied. 'I'll lock up.'

Planting a kiss on his daughter's cheek, David moved to leave, but at the kitchen door he stopped. 'Layla?'

'Yeah?' she replied, turning back to him.

'I don't know what it is exactly that you're going through, but I know if you're here it's because you're struggling. I just want to say I'm sorry for that.'

'That's okay, Dad,' Layla said, but it was clear there was more David wanted to say.

'When things were tough after the accident, I . . . well, I never thought I'd get through it.' Resting his finger on the doorhandle, David stared at the dull metal as he spoke. 'A nurse at the hospital taught me something that helped. Maybe it can help you. In the worst times, when sadness was all I could see, it felt like happiness would never find me again. But it tried to, in small bursts. Usually with you and your sister. When you weren't arguing, at least. You'd tell me about your day or come into the hospital all excited because you'd drawn me a picture.'

Layla smiled. She remembered those times well. Running from school, desperate to see her dad. Looking past the wires and the hospital gown to find the man who once carried her on his shoulders.

'The nurse told me about the power of those small moments,' David continued. 'She told me they were healing. So, when they happened, I used to stop and focus on them. Really focus. I'd pay attention to what I could hear, what I could smell, how the clothes I wore felt against my skin. I'd take a mental picture that was so vivid, the memory lived in me. That way, when the sadness came, I could look back on the moment. Feel it. Know that while things were dark, I carried happiness in me wherever I went.'

Emotion danced across Layla's chest, peaking when her dad looked back at her shyly.

'I thought that might help, that's all,' he said softly before offering her a nod. 'Goodnight, sweetheart.'

As David walked away, Layla listened to the sound of his footsteps. She noticed the fridge gurgling and the scent of floral kitchen spray lingering in the air. In that moment, Layla took her own mental picture, saving the knowledge her dad had imparted. She knew that when her time on earth was up, his shy smile would be one of the last things she saw.

20

Angus

*I always used to dismiss the saying 'it's grim up north',
but I can confirm . . . the weather today is grim x*

*I don't want to brag, but it's a glorious day here.
Blue skies and everything . . . x*

*You're lying.
This is some cruel, weather-based trickery to
make me come back to London . . . x*

Ignoring the way his stomach knotted over the word 'lying', Angus's fingers fired another message Layla's way.

*Hand on heart, it is a day that would make
anyone want to run back to the capital x*

Jasper took his attention off the road to glance at Angus. Spotting the phone in his friend's hand, Jasper's thin mouth settled into an even thinner line. 'Will you stop?'

'Stop what?'

'Not listening to me so you can talk to whoever it is you're always texting.'

'Sorry,' Angus replied, slipping his phone away.

'Who is she, anyway?' Jasper asked.

'Who's who?'

'The woman you keep messaging.' When Angus said nothing, Jasper shot him another sideways glance. 'I'm not stupid, you know. Being glued to your phone can only mean one thing – you've met someone. So, who is she?'

Again, Angus said nothing.

'Is it Clarissa?'

Angus didn't mean to laugh, but the idea was so absurd he couldn't not.

Jasper sniffed. 'Well, whoever she is, you can't keep her hidden forever. I'm running out of patience. You need to either stop cancelling on me to speak to her or you need to introduce us.'

'You can't meet her,' Angus replied, panicked.

'Why not? Scared she'll prefer me to you?' As Jasper's mouth curled into a leer, Angus shuddered at the thought of him ever smiling at Layla like that.

He was about to reply when his friend's attention was caught by a sign up ahead. 'Prepare to have your soul sucked dry,' Jasper muttered as he turned onto the long driveway that led to Haven Hospice.

Situated on the outskirts of South London, Haven Hospice was a detour on the way to Jasper and Angus's lunch plans, but Angus didn't mind. He had another six hours to fill before calling Layla. If it took driving to Scotland and back to make those hours pass quicker, Angus would do it.

A crisp blue sky shone down on Jasper's Tesla as it crept through the grounds of the hospice. Gardens ran along both sides of the long driveway, with a bandstand in the centre of the clipped grass on the left. Beside it, a grey-haired man in a wheelchair watched two children playing. A woman sat on the bench next to him, clutching his hand. The similarity of their features suggested they were father and daughter.

'Why are we here?' Angus asked. 'Can't your dad transfer his donation?'

'My family are sponsoring a wing, Angus,' Jasper replied, breaking sharply when they reached the car park. 'It's the kind of generosity you want known. Dad needs photos for the company website. It's PR 101, my friend. Don't worry, it'll only take a moment.'

As Jasper readied himself to leave the car, Angus looked at the building ahead. The imposing structure was made of thick sandstone, but it was welcoming, not intimidating.

'Stay in the car. This place is depressing as fuck. Besides, if you go inside, they'll only hound you for money. Bloody charities,' Jasper muttered as he exited the vehicle.

Angus watched his friend disappear into the building, then opened his conversation with Layla to read her response.

Photo or I'll never believe you x

After snapping and sending a photo of the sky, Angus locked his phone. In Jasper's absence, he debated completing this morning's questionnaire, but instead he found himself looking back at the family in the garden. The youngest child was showing the man something she'd found in the grass. Angus squinted, watching as she lifted the object higher.

A flower.

The man marvelled at it like it was the best thing he'd ever seen. Tucking the flower into the pocket of his shirt, the man patted the fabric, showing he was keeping it safe.

Inexplicably, Angus's throat closed. The intimate moment was full of vulnerability. And fear. And hope.

Angus remembered the last time he'd allowed himself to feel emotions that raw. It was years ago, stood on damp grass, watching Hugo's coffin lower into the ground. Willing someone to say it was all a mistake, that someone else was inside that box. Terrified his mother's tears would never step falling. Hollow at the thought of a life without his brother.

Staring at the family, all Angus could think was that he wanted to enable them to share more moments of joy. Suddenly, staying in the car felt like the worst way a man with Angus's resources could spend his morning.

Gravel crunched beneath his feet as he strode towards the entrance of the hospice. Nerves simmered under his skin, but as soon as Angus stepped inside, they faded. Whatever he expected to find, it wasn't this. Haven didn't seem like a hospital. There was no chemical smell, no greying paint, just a smiling receptionist, a few early Christmas cards tacked to the walls, and a strange sense of calm.

'Hi there,' the woman at reception said. 'Are you here to visit someone?'

Glancing at the ID badge clipped to her shirt, Angus read that her name was Britta. He opened his mouth to respond to her question, but words failed him. What *was* he doing in this place where people came to die? Why hadn't he stayed in the car?

Britta's face softened. 'First times aren't easy, I know. I can take you somewhere quiet if you need to gather your thoughts?'

Angus shook his head, suddenly aware of how wrong it felt to be here when he had no reason to be. He wasn't sponsoring a wing. He wasn't visiting someone. He was . . . what?

'Come on,' Britta said. 'I'll take you to our Memory Tree Room.'

'Memory Tree Room?' Angus echoed.

Smiling, Britta nodded to a corridor on the left. 'Follow me.'

Angus followed Britta down a long hallway. Floor-to-ceiling windows ran along the left-hand side of the corridor, looking out onto the garden. The old man was still there with his family. The flower was still in his pocket.

Upon reaching a set of double doors, Britta stopped. 'Here we go. The Memory Tree Room. Our families have contributed to it for years. Stay inside for as long as you like.'

Angus nodded. 'Thank you.'

'Anytime. We all need to sit with our thoughts every now and then, don't we?' Britta replied before leaving Angus to explore on his own.

When her footsteps no longer echoed down the corridor, Angus looked to the double doors. A vivid forest scene was painted onto the wood, giving an otherworldly impression. There was something inviting about the design. Something that told Angus to enter.

So, he did.

As Angus pushed open the doors, an intricate mural of a tree came into view. The trunk started at the doorway and extended all the way to the top of the wall opposite. Portraits of animals were painted into the trunk. Branches extended across the ceiling, reaching out to all four corners of the room. The detail and size of the illustration was incredible, but the most breathtaking part was the leaves. Hung from the ceiling by thin pieces of thread, each leaf varied in colour, shape and size. Twirling gently, they gave the impression that the tree was a real, living thing.

Moving deeper into the room, Angus's eyes widened.

The leaves weren't just pretty decorations – they were dedications. Some contained inscriptions, some displayed photographs, some simply named a date, but all were unique, and all were dedicated to someone.

Someone who was loved.

Someone who was gone.

Someone who was remembered.

A lump formed in Angus's throat. When his neck swivelled to take in the room once more, a leaf glinting in the sunlight caught his attention. Made from silver card, it was almost holographic. Tilting it to get a better view, Angus saw that a photograph of an old woman holding a baby was glued in the centre. Beneath the image, written in childish script, was the word *'Gran'*.

As the burn in Angus's throat intensified, he moved about the room, reading as many inscriptions as he could.

'You said our love was written in the stars. Now every night, I know where to find you'.

'You'll always be mummy's special boy.'

'A love that is lost is never gone. It lives on forever, in every beat of my heart.'

Each declaration landed heavy in Angus's chest. *Who would write a leaf for me?* he wondered. His parents, he supposed, although it was hard to imagine Gilly displaying such uninhibited affection. She'd used up all her emotion when Hugo died.

Jasper and his friends, perhaps, although sentimentality wasn't their strong point.

Layla, he hoped, although once she learned of his lies, would she even want to remember him? As the thought made Angus's shoulders slump, the doors to the Memory Tree Room opened behind him.

'Sorry,' came a Scottish accent. 'I can come back later—'

Grateful for the interruption, Angus turned to the short, stocky man in the doorway. 'Please, come in,' he said.

Nodding, the man entered the room and closed the doors. Moving through the space like he knew exactly where he was going, he stopped beneath a purple leaf near the far wall. Angus tried not to watch, but he couldn't help it. There was something in the man's shimmering eyes that he couldn't look away from.

'I'm Chris, by the way,' the man said after a moment.

'Angus.'

'Really? I wanted to call my son Angus, but the wife said over her dead body. There was an actor she fancied with that name. Said she couldn't name her son after someone she'd had a sex dream about.' Chris laughed, then nodded to the leaf. 'We lost her a year ago today.'

Angus blinked, taking in the youth of the man before him. A man who had known love and loss, yet did not look a day over forty. 'I'm sorry,' was all Angus could think to say.

'Aye, me too. I don't think I'll ever stop being sorry about it, but I come in here and talk to Fearne whenever I visit. She never replies. Rude, don't you think?'

'Maybe she's too busy telling Angus the actor about you to talk.'

Chris laughed again, but this time his laugh mingled with something that sounded a lot like tears. Angus searched his brain for something to say to make things better, but what words had the power to do that?

'I woke up today and didn't know what to do,' Chris admitted. 'A year without her . . . It's flown, in some ways. In others it feels like a lifetime. Most days, I still can't believe she's gone. I thought seeing this today might help.'

Angus glanced up at the leaf. 'Has it?'

'Does anything help when you wake up to an empty bed in a house you bought with someone you thought you'd grow old with?' As if remembering where he was, Chris glanced back at Angus. 'Sorry, you don't need me depressing you.'

'It's fine. I'm fine.'

'Well, that makes one of us,' Chris joked. 'You know, before she passed, Fearne said to me, "If you don't live every day like you're lucky to be here, I'll come back and haunt you so bad you'll wish you were dead." Sometimes I feel like wasting the day in front of the TV in my underwear just so she'll come back and tell me off.'

The men settled into a companionable silence before Angus broke it. 'Do you, then?'

'Do what, watch TV in my underwear?'

'No, live every day like you're lucky to be here?'

As Chris mulled over the question, he reached out and touched Fearne's leaf. 'Is there any other way to live?'

With that, he spun the leaf, sending it swirling as if it had a life of its own. Watching it, something inside Angus split open, but instead of the pain he expected, something else appeared.

Peace.

Purpose.

Clarity.

Life didn't have to be a series of mind-numbing events if Angus didn't want it to be. He had the means to create something amazing. Not only for himself, but for others too. After all, what was the point of having so much money if not to do good with it?

For years, Angus had spent his life in hiding, but maybe it was time to stop being scared. Maybe it was time to stop watching life slip by and actually *do* something with it.

Turning to the double doors, Angus set off, ready to follow the instinct he'd spent years ignoring.

'I didn't mean to upset you,' Chris called, stopping Angus before he could leave.

'You didn't. If anything, you woke me up.'

'Did I? Well, I'll make sure I tell Fearne that. Maybe she'll reply this time.'

A look passed between the men. Angus willed himself to say something meaningful, something that would help, then he realised what he should do. Stepping out of the room, Angus closed the doors and left Chris to sit with thoughts of his wife in peace.

Back at reception, Britta looked up when she heard Angus approaching. 'Back so soon,' she said. 'How can I help?'

'Actually, Britta,' he replied. 'I think I might be able to help you.'

21

Layla

'I smell a little boy . . . Where is he . . . Where could my yummy snack be?'

Jayden's muffled giggles rang out as Layla crawled across the floor of her parents' living room, sniffing the air as if she were a dinosaur on the prowl. Grunting, she banged into her dad's empty armchair.

'I'll find him soon and when I do, I'll gobble him up,' she added for good measure.

Layla could spy the top of Jayden's back poking out from behind a sofa cushion but pretended otherwise. Even if she was new to the whole 'being a present aunt' thing, Layla knew that games had to last longer than thirty seconds.

As she sniffed under the sofa, Jayden's giggles became hysterical.

'My lovely lunch, come out, come out, wherever you are,' she growled.

'I don't know where your lovely lunch is, but I know where my son's is,' Maya said, sweeping into the room with a swish of her colourful skirt. She set a plate containing a ham sandwich on the coffee table, then pried the sofa cushion from Jayden.

'Mum, you're ruining the game,' Jayden protested. 'Auntie Layla will eat me now she's seen me!'

'No, she won't. Not now a bigger, tastier snack has entered the forest,' Layla replied, pretending to bite Maya's leg to prove her point.

Roaring with laughter, Jayden slid from the sofa. 'Gobble her up so you've no room left for me,' he instructed before tucking into his sandwich.

Pulling herself up from the floor, Layla flopped onto the sofa beside her sister. 'I don't know how you do it, Maya. Keeping up with a four-year-old is intense. I'm sweating harder than after any workout.'

Maya plucked at Layla's arm. 'Since when do you work out?'

'You know what I mean. Raising Jayden and working at the salon? You're a hero.'

'I don't know about that.'

Layla nudged her sister. 'Take the compliment.'

'Fine, but I'll let you in on my secret. Don't let anyone who says they never let their child have screen time fool you. This is my motherhood hack.' With that, Maya flicked on the TV. A riot of colour and puppets filled the screen, entrancing Jayden straightaway.

Layla laughed. 'It's that easy?'

'Well, it works for a while. Long enough to give you a moment of peace, at least.'

'Maybe I need to distract you with the TV. You talk more than anyone I know,' Layla teased.

'Someone's got to be the social sibling.'

Just then, Layla's phone buzzed on the coffee table. She reached for it, but Maya got there first.

'Although I hear you're being uncharacteristically sociable these days.' Maya smirked when she saw who was contacting her sister. 'Angus, huh? That's, what, the millionth text today?'

'Very funny.' Layla reached for her phone, but Maya continued to hold it hostage.

'Is he funny? A funny man, is that the kind of guy you're after?'

'Behave, Maya. We're just talking.'

'Just talking? Is that what they call it down in London? Around here we call it falling in love.'

'Shut up,' Layla said, shoving her sister, but she couldn't fight her smile. While Maya's description of their exchange wasn't quite accurate – this wasn't Angus's millionth text, not yet – the latest message wasn't their first of the day, and Layla knew it wouldn't be their last. Talking to Angus had become as much a part of her life as breathing. In fact, talking to Angus felt like the only time Layla could breathe.

Trust you to find someone who makes you feel alive, just as you're about to die.

As soon as the thought appeared, Layla reminded herself of her vow. Angus would be her friend, no more, no less. It was all they ever could be.

But as Maya handed over Layla's phone and she opened their exchange, Layla suddenly hated the 'friend' label she had insisted on.

How is today going? Are you still a dinosaur? x

I am. *roars*
I think I have bitten everything in sight . . . x

Hey, no judgement here. I don't kink shame x

As Layla giggled, Maya rolled her eyes. 'My God, this is sickening. It's like living with a lovestruck teenager,' she teased. 'Who is he, anyway?'

Ducking behind a curtain of her hair, Layla shrugged. 'Just a guy.'

'That's it? "A guy", that's all you're going to tell me?'

'There's not much more to say. He's someone I met a few weeks ago, that's all.'

'But you're Layla. You don't meet guys.'

Layla tried not to be hurt, but Maya's honesty highlighted how much of life she had missed out on over the years, and it stung.

'Where did you meet him, anyway?' Maya asked, trying to peek at Layla's messages.

'At a coffee shop.'

'Nice. A real meet-cute.'

'If you want it to be, yeah.'

Maya shot her sister a sideways glance. 'That's really all I get? Angus is a guy from a coffee shop. A guy you talk to all the time, giggling and keeping Mum and Dad up all night.'

Layla's cheeks flamed. 'I do not!'

'Say that to Dad's eyebags. The poor man looks more exhausted than ever.'

'Maybe Dad should think about working less if he's tired.'

A bellow of a laugh burst from Maya. 'That's rich, coming from you,' she replied, throwing her arm over Layla's shoulders before she could be offended. 'I'm happy for you, Layls. We all need a bit of romance every now and then.'

'Maya, stop! We're just friends.' Layla squirmed in her sister's embrace, but Maya held tighter.

'I'm telling you I'm happy for you! Take the well wishes like a normal person!'

'You're so happy you're putting me in a headlock?' Layla said, wriggling free then biting her lip. 'Thanks, though. I guess I am happy. The happiest I've been in a while, at least.'

That truth struck Layla somewhere deep inside. Despite everything, even the aching sadness that clawed at her whenever she thought of her short life, in the bubble of her parents' house, Layla was happy. She was happier still, now that Angus was on the other end of the phone. Waking up to him asking how she slept and ending her day with him wishing her sweet dreams were the greatest bookends to a day.

'I'm glad,' Maya said. 'You had us worried, you know. When you rocked up out of the blue, Mum thought you'd had a breakdown.'

Both sisters paused as the words hung in the air.

'Have you?' Maya asked.

'Have I what?'

'Had a breakdown?'

Layla laughed, even though there was nothing funny about the question. Had she had a breakdown? On the one hand, it certainly felt like it. She'd cried for days after learning of her death date, and now she was sleeping in a room barely big enough for a four-year-old. The career she prided herself on was hanging in the balance and she'd left a full fridge in London, the contents of which would surely be rotten by now if Rhi hadn't sorted it. That list screamed 'breakdown'.

But on the other hand . . .

On the other hand, Layla now knew how magical it felt to hold Jayden's hand while they snuggled on the sofa. She was eating home-cooked meals for the first time in forever. Her dad doted on her with tea and hugs and, thanks to Angus, Layla was daydreaming for the first time since being a teenager.

'I don't think so,' Layla replied eventually. 'A breakdown sounds like a bad thing. This feels positive.'

'Staying in your nephew's bedroom and borrowing my clothes is positive, is it?'

'No, but gaining a fresh perspective on life is.'

'Does this mean you're going back to work soon?'

Layla met Maya's gaze. 'Is that what you want? Am I in the way here?'

'Relax, no one's saying that. Mum would have you home forever if she could, you know that. I'm just asking. No one goes from Miss Corporate to Miss Sweatpants overnight.'

'What if that's what I want to do?'

'Well, you can't.'

Layla blinked at Maya's bluntness until her sister nudged her.

'Come on, Layls. You know as well as I do that you have to go back at some point. If not for yourself, for the colleagues you've left high and dry.'

Anxiety churned in Layla's stomach at the thought of the work she had abandoned. Mayweather & Halliwell, the big, suited elephant in the room.

'Layls, whatever you're running from, you have to face it at some point,' Maya said.

The statement made Layla pull away. 'Who says I'm running from anything?'

'Why else are you here, crawling on the floor like a dinosaur?'

'So much for enjoying spending time with Jayden,' Layla huffed.

Sensing she'd touched a nerve, Maya reached for her sister. 'You know we love having you here, but this sleepover at Mum and Dad's can't last forever. Sooner or later, you're going to have to get moving again.'

Layla's chin dimpled. 'What if I don't want to?'

'I'm afraid you don't have a choice. Jayden and I can't share a room forever. Besides, you're Layla! Where most people see the impossible, you see a challenge. No one ever expects a kid from an estate to amount to much but look at you! Look at all you've achieved. That only happened because of your stubbornness and this mega-brain.' Tapping gently on Layla's forehead, Maya grinned. 'Whatever is causing you this much pain, you can fix it.'

Layla burned at Maya's naivety. *You can fix it* . . . like it was that simple. Like having two years left to live was something a person could accept.

But there was something about Maya's words that shone like a beacon of hope. Layla couldn't help wondering what would happen if she changed her attitude towards work. Her results said her cause of death was likely to be a stroke induced by stress. What if she removed that? What if she learned how to balance her life? Without that stress, without that tunnel-vision, would those two years become ten, twenty or more?

If Layla put herself first, instead of her clients, could she be saved?

Jayden chose that moment to tire of the television. Turning, he caught Layla's eye and smiled at her like she was the best thing he'd ever seen. Layla smiled back at him, but her happiness froze when the worst thought came to her mind.

You'll only live to see Jayden turn six.

The realisation pummelled Layla's stomach, but the questions that followed hurt even more. Would Jayden remember Layla when he grew up? Had she wasted precious years of bonding time?

But as Jaydan reached for Layla to play dinosaurs once more, she pushed her pain aside. *Two years*, she thought, as Jayden pulled her to her feet. *You've got two years to make every second count.*

Layla knew she wouldn't waste a single one.

22

Angus

The Life Experiment: Daily Questionnaire
Property of OPM Discoveries

How would you rate your level of contentment today? (1 represents low contentment, 10 represents high)

1   2   3   4   5   6   7   (8)   9   10

How would you rate your energy level? (1 being very low energy and 10 being very high energy)

1   2   3   4   5   6   7   8   9   (10)

What are two things you are grateful for today?
1. Recently, it's hit me how lucky I am. I should probably acknowledge it more
2. Taking a chance when I first went to Haven. Maybe there's something to the whole 'lean into life' thing, after all

What are you struggling with today?
Jasper constantly trying to get me to go out. He can't sit still and it's driving me crazy

Do you have any additional notes on what you would like to discuss in your upcoming counselling session?
Maybe we could talk about what attributes make a person become successful

For the second time in a week, Angus found himself pulling up outside Haven Hospice. This time, though, he wasn't there to wait while Jasper dropped off a donation.

This time, he was there to volunteer.

Britta had told him that patient-facing roles wouldn't be possible without clearing a few safeguarding checks first, but that there was room in the organisational sphere for a volunteer. If Angus had time, they needed assistance prepping for Christmas events. Angus offered his services before Britta even finished her sentence.

Excitement propelled Angus towards the doors. For a moment, he thought of the watch that was tracking his pulse. He wondered what Saira would think when she saw how it was racing.

For the first time since joining the experiment, Angus was excited for their upcoming counselling session. Usually, he dreaded them. Conversations with Saira often centred on Angus's family, the lies he'd told Layla and his feelings towards himself.

'Sometimes, the hardest things to discuss are the ones we most need to,' Saira said towards the end of their last session, six days ago. Angus had remained silent at that comment, but he felt different now. Now, he had lots to say. He wanted to talk to Saira about Haven Hospice. In fact, he wanted to talk to everyone about it. Layla especially.

The problem was, Angus had told Layla he worked in IT. Where having the time to volunteer midweek would fit into that narrative, Angus didn't know. And so, another lie was added to the list. A list that was so long, Angus could barely keep track of it anymore.

Swallowing his unease, Angus entered the building.

'You made it,' Britta enthused when she spotted him, then she turned to the man beside her. Older than Angus, he was wearing a polo shirt that read 'LTC Plumbing'. 'Angus, meet Aleksander. He's volunteered here for eight years.'

'Nice to meet you,' Angus said, shaking the man's coarse hand.

'I thought it might be nice if you and Aleksander worked together today,' Britta said. 'He can show you the ropes.'

'Haven's hosting a Christmas crafts day in a few weeks for residents and their loved ones,' Aleksander explained. 'Our job is to package the craft kits. Think lots of glitter.' Aleksander's grin was wide and his voice had the distinctive lilt of a Polish accent.

Angus liked him immediately. 'I think I can handle that,' he replied.

After signing him in on the hospice's registration system, Aleksander led Angus down a corridor to a room near the end. Inside, they were greeted by a large table and crates stuffed with crafting materials.

'There's a list of what each bag needs to contain,' Aleksander said, plucking a set of instructions from the top of a crate. 'How about we group the items first. Then, if we divide them, I can put the first half into a bag, pass it to you and you can add the rest?'

'Like a manufacturing line,' Angus replied, examining a stencil for a set of antlers.

Aleksander grinned. 'Exactly.'

For the next few minutes, the men set about grouping glitter pens, pompoms and glue sticks. Then they began to construct the packs. Soon, they found their rhythm, assembling bags at speed. Angus was so in the flow of the routine that he didn't stop to think what the kits were going to be used for until he heard a child laughing in the corridor outside.

This is going to be someone's last Christmas, he thought. As his stomach plummeted, Angus's death date flashed before his eyes. He had so much time left, while the people he was making kits for had so little. Leaning in, he handled each item with care, hoping that the recipient would feel some joy from them.

'So,' Aleksander said, once the men had packaged fifteen bags. 'What brings you to Haven?'

'Curiosity, I guess,' Angus replied. When he caught Aleksander's raised eyebrow, he smiled. 'It's not as strange as it sounds. For a while, I've been wondering what to do with my life. I stumbled across this place, and something clicked.'

Aleksander nodded then handed Angus another bag. 'So you want to volunteer?'

'Not exactly,' Angus admitted. 'I'm here to learn what the hospice does. How they help and what more can be done. If there's a gap, I'd like to use my resources to plug it.'

'You have money.' Angus expected a question, but it was a statement. Aleksander grinned. 'I can tell, and not just because of the car you drive. You seem well-off.'

Angus laughed. 'I don't know if that's a good or bad thing,' he said, adding a glue stick to a bag. 'What's your story? How come you're here?'

As soon as Angus asked the question, he regretted it. Lulled into a false sense of security by the friendly conversation, Angus had forgotten where they were. But, as Aleksander's smile faded at the edges, Angus realised his error.

'My daughter, Mia,' Aleksander said after a moment. 'She was diagnosed with cancer when she was seven.'

'I'm so sorry,' Angus exhaled.

Aleksander flashed him a smile. 'It's okay. We were lucky. We never had to use a hospice.' Relief surged through Angus. 'Mia's eighteen now. A grown-up, or so she tells me. She goes to university soon. Once, her being well enough to leave home was all I dreamed of. Now the time is here, it might just break my heart.' A half-smile softened Aleksander's features. 'I come here to honour the people who aren't as lucky as my family. I have to do something. Pay it back. Help the ones who need it.'

'That's brave. It can't be easy, being around a place that reminds you of the hardest time of your life.'

'It's not,' Aleksander admitted. 'But part of me thinks that if I do this, I can keep Mia's cancer away. Silly, yes?'

'That's not silly at all,' Angus replied. 'I'm really sorry your family went through that.'

Aleksander shrugged in an 'it is what it is' way. 'I'm not the only one. I see it in you too, you know. The sadness that only comes from knowing pain like this.'

For a moment, the men only looked at each other, but then Angus gave a small confirmational nod.

'I am sorry for your loss,' Aleksander replied. 'That's life, or so they tell me. Knowing that never makes it easier, does it?'

'No, it doesn't.'

'Sometimes that time feels like it was all a dream,' Aleksander said as he reached for a new bag to fill. 'I came to England alone at sixteen to build a better life. I never thought one day I would have a sick child, or that I would raise her on my own. I had no family support, no one to help with money, no one to tell me things would get better.'

Angus's eyebrows raised. 'How did you do it?'

'Do what?'

'Well,' Angus began, his mind whirring. 'If you were a single parent with no family, how could you be with Mia? Who looked after her when she was sick and you had to work?'

Aleksander smiled ruefully. 'It was tough, my friend. Back then, I lived in Scarborough, not London. The hospital near us didn't have a children's cancer ward. We had to commute to the one in Leeds, an hour and a half there and back. Money was tight. Some weeks I worried I couldn't pay for the petrol to get there, but my boss was a good man. He gave me time off and extra work when he could.

It was hard, though. All I ever worried about was money. It's not what a father should think about when his little girl is sick.'

Aleksander lost himself in packing another bag, holding a stick of pink glitter for a moment longer than necessary.

'Mia always says that her cancer went into remission, but my worry never did. It's true, I think. When something like that happens to someone you love, you don't forget. You can't, can you?' The bright blue of Aleksander's eyes glinted when he looked at Angus. The spark dared him to be brave.

'My brother Hugo,' Angus began, clearing his throat. 'We lost him when I was eleven. In a way, it feels like I'm here for him. It's silly, really. He didn't die of cancer. He drowned. But there's something about the families here. The feel of the place. I don't know why, but it helps.'

'Grief needs no labels. It follows no rules. If Haven is where you heal, then it's where you need to be. We all know sadness here. We know loss. That's why we come – so that the living know to remember, and the dying know we won't forget.'

Struck by the importance of those words, a sudden, unexpected sense of urgency overcame Angus. *This is it*, he thought. *This is the crossroads.*

What came next, Angus didn't know. The path was still hazy, but one thing was clear – fate was calling. This time, Angus knew he would answer.

23

Layla

Jayden's bed looked less welcoming now it was stripped of the sheets Layla had been using. The room looked less inviting too. Gone were Layla's trinkets – her necklace on the bedside table, her moisturiser beside it. In their absence, the room transformed back into a space that belonged to a four-year-old boy.

'You can do this,' Saira said during their last counselling session. 'You are ready to return to London.'

Exhaling a wobbly breath, Layla plucked her bag from the bed and left the room. Closing the door gently behind her, Layla drew a line under her time in Hull.

'Are you ready, kiddo?' her dad asked when she made it downstairs.

'Pretty much,' Layla replied, but her mum shook her head.

'You're not going anywhere without a packed lunch,' she said, jumping up from the sofa.

'Mum, you don't have to,' Layla protested.

'She already has,' David replied, switching off the TV. Gripping the edge of his armchair, David hauled himself to his feet. A grimace betrayed his pain, but Joanna was back before Layla could comment on it.

'It's only a cheese sandwich, but it should last you until you get to London. Do you want me to make extra? You could take them to work tomorrow, if you'd like.'

Layla wanted to smile at Joanna's fussing, but her lips wouldn't comply. The idea of being back in London in a few hours was overwhelming enough; the thought of returning to work the following day was something else entirely.

But the decision to go back had been made. Maya gave Layla the first nudge, Saira the second. 'Life must continue, Layla,' she said. 'What that looks like is for you to decide, but it all starts with facing what you had before. Your family have provided the healing space you needed. Now it's time to stand on your own again.'

Layla didn't know how stable her footing was anymore, but with her bag packed and a train ticket booked, she knew she had to try.

Besides, her brain pointed out, *once you're back, you'll see Angus.*

Layla's stomach jittered as she thought of their earlier messages.

I can't believe we're going to be in the same city again soon.
London's missed you x

> *I've missed London too, I think.*
> *I'm happy to be heading back.*
> *Well, 95% happy x*

Because you get to see me again? x

> *Awkward. Seeing you is the 5% that means*
> *I'm not happy . . . x*

Ouch. I walked into that one didn't I haha?
There I was, thinking you thought I was a
blond Hugh Grant! x

> *That was before I knew you better ;) x*

Grinning, Layla let her mind wander to what it would be like to see Angus again. How would they greet each other? Would it be awkward? Would they hug? Kiss?

Layla admonished herself for the thought. She hated how easily it had crept up on her. Even more than that, she hated how it dared her to imagine a future that didn't involve an end.

Before a mix of pain and butterflies could take hold, Joanna raised her hand to Layla's cheek. Brushing Layla's skin with her thumb, she said, 'You are strong even when you feel weak. You are loved even when you feel unlovable, and you can get through tough times even when you think you can't.'

No other words were said after that. A hug said what both women were feeling better than words could, anyway.

When David cleared his throat, Layla and Joanna drew apart. 'Sorry, but we'd best head off if you want to get to the station on time,' he said.

The temptation to say 'forget it' and miss the train altogether was strong, but Layla knew Maya was right – it was time to face the life she had fled.

The main reason Layla was going back to work was that if she didn't, she would lose her job. Her extended hideout in Hull had pushed her luck with management. Layla didn't think she could push it any further, even if the thought of stepping into the office made bile rise in her throat.

But as much as Layla resented Mayweather & Halliwell, she couldn't let her biggest, and only, achievement fall apart. Not when she'd worked so hard to get here.

As Layla watched David reach for his coat, another reason to re-enter the workforce came to mind. If she carried on working and saved hard, she could leave her family a lump of cash in two years' time. Combine that with the life insurance payout OPM Discoveries would provide as a result of Layla participating in the experiment and their lives would change forever. Maybe they could leave the estate. Maybe Maya could open her own salon like she'd always dreamed of.

The thought pushed Layla out of the house and into her dad's car.

David let the radio do the talking as he drove to the station. Layla didn't mind the silence, though. There was a comfort to her dad's presence that didn't require words. Right now, Layla needed all the comfort she could get.

It felt to Layla that they reached the station car park in no time. Seeing the imposing Victorian structure ahead, her stomach cramped.

'Here we are, then,' David said after a moment.

Layla knew that she should move. Or, at the very least, she should respond, but all her energy was going towards keeping it together.

'Do you want me to walk you in?' David offered.

Layla shook her head and glanced at the clock on the dashboard. She had fifteen minutes until her train was to depart. Fifteen minutes to calm down and go or panic and stay. The seconds were trickling away.

They're always trickling away, Layla's brain grumbled, but then it hit her – that was the point. That was the fact of life that no one could fight.

Time was passing. It was always, always passing. Staying still wouldn't change that.

Reaching for her handbag, Layla made her choice. However scary it was, she must go back to London. She must face her life there because she *did* have a life there. Whether it was one Layla wanted was for her to decide. Improvements and changes couldn't be made from the passenger seat of her dad's car.

'Thanks for the lift, Dad,' she said, kissing David's cheek. 'I'll be fine.'

'Oh, I know you will,' David replied.

As they shared a smile, Layla realised that she knew the words to be true. Whatever came next, wherever she decided to go from here, she would be fine. Nervous? Of course. Scared? Absolutely, but fine nonetheless. She was her father's daughter, after all.

24

Angus

For the second time in five minutes, Angus checked his appearance. Opting for a lightweight blue shirt, black jeans and distressed leather boots, the outfit was casual but smart enough that Layla would know he'd made an effort. Sure, his clothes had been tailored to fit him perfectly, but they were high street brands. Angus hoped that would be enough to make him seem less heir-to-the-estate and more normal-guy-out-with-a-woman-he-couldn't-stop-thinking-about.

Because Angus had to seem normal. Anything else would be catastrophic.

Smoothing down the front of his shirt, Angus tried to self-soothe. *It's not all been lies*, he reminded himself. *Layla likes you when you're being yourself.*

Layla liked the way Angus laughed without hesitation. She liked that he asked questions and liked even more that he listened to her answers. She liked the music he liked, the films he watched. She liked all the bits of Angus that were completely and utterly himself.

Himself minus the privilege she knew nothing about, of course.

The thought threatened to drag Angus under, but he knew he couldn't give in to his worries if he wanted to be on time.

Angus took a taxi to his destination, a boutique but inexpensive restaurant named Bella Vino in Camden that Aleksander had recommended. 'I go there with Mia for a treat,' he said. 'It's a hidden gem.'

As the taxi stuttered through the bustling streets of London, Angus hoped Aleksander was telling the truth. He jiggled his leg. Angus didn't think he was someone who felt nervous around women, but seeing Layla again? Talking to her in person? Well, Angus finally learned what pre-date jitters felt like.

Not that this was a date, Angus reminded himself. It was a meeting between two friends. Angus just happened to think about this friend twenty-four seven. That was all.

As the well-lit front of Bella Vino appeared ahead, Angus exhaled. The restaurant looked inviting, but not ostentatious. Casual enough that their non-date wasn't intimidating, but intimate enough that if it veered into date territory, the setting was still perfect.

Hopping out of the car, Angus headed towards the restaurant just as Layla stepped out of a taxi further down the road.

He froze.

Layla looked even more beautiful than Angus remembered. How that was possible, he didn't know, but she did. A leather jacket hugged her figure and a pair of heeled boots elongated her legs. Her hair was pulled back, exposing her features in all their radiance.

Captivated, Angus could have observed Layla readjust her handbag all night, but then she spotted him. As her face lit up, he felt his world tilt.

Somehow, Angus found the courage to approach her. 'Would you call it fate, arriving at the same time?'

'That depends. Were you waiting for me so you could say that and seem smooth?'

'Not quite,' Angus replied. 'Although I do like the idea of you thinking I'm smooth.'

Then, all of a sudden, there were no more steps to take to bridge the distance between them.

'Hi,' Angus said, unable to fight a smile.

'Hi, yourself,' Layla replied.

That was all it took for Angus to envelop Layla in his arms like he was welcoming her home. She leaned into him, nestling against his chest. Angus's heart pounded. No doubt Layla would feel it beating against her cheek, but Angus didn't care. Let her see how much this night meant to him.

When someone walking past whistled, Layla pulled out of the hug, blushing. 'Let's go inside. I'm starving.'

The pair headed towards the restaurant, their coat sleeves grazing in the most tantalising way. When they reached the door, Angus opened it. A gust of oregano wafted from inside.

Bella Vino was a hive of activity, all cramped tables, groups of friends and raucous laughter. The place was more of an assault on the senses than the exclusive, dimly lit establishments Angus was used to. It took a moment for him to adjust, but as a waitress carried two delicious-smelling pasta dishes past him, Angus found he preferred this vivid environment.

After greeting them, a baby-faced waiter grabbed two menus and steered Angus and Layla to their table. Close to the window, away from the bathrooms, with an elderly couple to one side and a group of three friends to the other, it was a good spot.

Before Angus could get there, the waiter pulled out Layla's chair. 'Can I get you some water? Still, sparkling or tap?' he asked.

Angus opened his mouth to reply 'sparkling', but Layla got there first.

'Tap's fine, thanks.' When the waiter slipped away, she turned to Angus. 'I always say tap, I hope you don't mind. It's a waste of money otherwise, isn't it? Although admittedly London water is vile.'

Angus nodded even though he had never taken the 'tap' option. In fact, most places Angus went to didn't even offer tap water. Suddenly, the evening stretched out like a long, pothole-filled road, with the opportunity to fuck up and reveal his true nature in every bump. As a bead of sweat rolled down the back of his neck, Angus wished more than anything that he'd never told that first lie.

'I'll be quiet for a few minutes, I'm afraid. I take ordering far too seriously,' Layla said, without taking her eyes off the menu. 'I promise I'll be sociable soon.'

'Take your time. Choosing what to eat is the most important decision of the night.'

'I'm glad to be out with someone who understands that.'

As a grinning Layla debated her options, Angus scanned the restaurant. His gaze lingered on the glowing candles and generous glasses of wine. *Maybe coming here was a mistake*, he thought as he cracked his knuckles. This wasn't a date, after all – Layla had been adamant about that – yet dinner came with a host of romantic connotations. Plus, restaurants carried with them an array of potential disasters. Bad food, bad service, awkward silences . . .

And Bella Vino . . . Angus cursed himself. What was he thinking, bringing Layla somewhere he'd never been before? Suddenly, the restaurant transformed before Angus's eyes. The decor turned from traditional to naff, the waitstaff from busy to disorganised. Even the layout seemed wrong, the tables so close together that Angus felt like he was on a date with the elderly couple beside them. It was as if the man's comments about the garlic mushrooms – 'Lovely sauce, isn't it?' – were directed at him.

As Angus dug his nails into his palms, Layla set down her menu. 'Right, I've decided. I'm ordering the ravioli, unless that's what you're having? Because we can't order the same thing.'

Angus grimaced. 'I was going to pick the ravioli too.'

'No!' Layla wailed. 'That's my cue to check the menu again.'

As she peeled it from the table, Angus laughed. 'I'm ordering lamb ragu really. And, even if I wanted ravioli, I'd pick something else so you could have it.'

The corner of Layla's mouth hooked into a smile. 'How kind. That almost makes up for your treachery, but not quite.'

As Angus laughed again, his hands unfurled. There was something about Layla that made him feel like he was sinking into a warm bath. He'd bathe in it forever if he could.

'When did you decide on the lamb, anyway?' Layla asked. 'You haven't checked your menu once.'

'I looked at it online beforehand.'

'Angus, no! If I'd known you were a menu-hunter, I wouldn't have said yes to dinner.'

Grinning, Angus settled into the rhythm of the conversation. 'I thought lawyers loved planning and preparation?'

'We do, but as someone whose meals are usually from a vending machine, restaurants are a treat. That's why I go all-out, surprise menu and all. The spontaneity adds to the fun.'

'I prefer to think the fun comes from the company, not the food.'

Layla toyed with the stem of her yet-to-be-filled wineglass. 'But this is our first meeting since the cafe, and I was miserable that day. How do you know the company is up to scratch?'

'Judging by how much we speak already, I predict we'll be fine.'

Layla made no attempt to hide her smile. 'We have spoken a lot, haven't we?'

'We have. Surely we're at the "tell me your darkest secret" or "meet the parents" point by now?'

'It's funny you mention parents,' Layla said, cocking her head. 'I was thinking on the way over that I don't know much about yours, even though you know all about mine.'

Angus's leg twitched to kick himself. How could he be foolish enough to steer the conversation onto this territory?! 'Oh, they're like anyone else's parents,' he shrugged, trying to catch the eye of a passing waiter so he could distract Layla with ordering.

'If I know anything in life, it's that every family is weird and wonderful in their own way. So come on, tell me about your parents.'

With his heart in a vice, Angus racked his brain for something to tell Layla that matched the openness of her anecdotes, but it was hard to know what to say when there were so many parts of himself that Angus was ashamed of.

Could he tell Layla about his mum's constant redecorating of the house? How he never knew what he was stepping into, meaning that the concept of somewhere feeling like 'home' was lost on him? How when he was a child, Gilly went through his toys and threw away his favourites because they didn't go with her new colour scheme?

Or perhaps Angus could admit that knowing he would never match up to his father meant he never tried to? That doing fuck-all was easier than being in Peter's shadow?

But as Angus heard himself speak, he realised he wasn't saying any of that. 'My parents have been together since they were teenagers. They're childhood sweethearts.'

'That's nice. Are they happy? Did they grow together, not apart?'

Angus whistled. 'What a question.'

'Thank you, now answer it.'

Angus smiled, then thought of Gilly and Peter. Two people who would never deconstruct the life they shared, even if they were miserable. After all, what would people say if they did? Was there love there, underneath it all? In their private moments, did they still laugh, still cuddle, still conjure dreams together?

Or, like most things in Angus's life, were they one big glossy charade?

'They're as happy as two people who have been together forever can be,' Angus replied, thumbing the corner of his menu. 'I don't know if that means they're happy, but it's what they have, and I don't think they'll ever change it. They're a tight unit. They've been that way since my brother died.'

It was hard to say who was more surprised at Angus's revelation. Layla, at hearing it for the first time, or Angus, at saying it so freely.

The words didn't come easy. In fact, in the Fairview-Whitley household, the words weren't allowed at all. But ever since that day at Haven Hospice with Aleksander, Angus hadn't been able to stop thinking about Hugo.

As Angus's childhood came flooding back to him, his surroundings faded until all he saw was the brother who was there until suddenly, he wasn't. The empty seat at the dinner table. The bedroom at the end of the hallway, locked as if to capture Hugo's ghost inside. The person who taught Angus rugby passes, who roamed the gardens with him, who showed him the best hiding places in the house, gone.

As Angus's vision blurred, Layla reached across the table for his hand. 'I'm so sorry, Angus. When did he die?'

'When we were kids. He was thirteen, I was eleven.'

Sadness burned in Layla's eyes. 'That's so young.'

'I know. He had his whole life ahead of him.'

'Of course. But I meant you. You were so young to know such pain.'

Pressing his tongue into the back of his lower lip, Angus nodded. There was so much he wanted to say about that time. So much he knew Layla would understand if he shared, but the words would not come out. They were too painful.

Layla's calm gaze travelled over Angus. 'Thank you for telling me about your brother. I'd love to hear more about him, if you'd like to share. But I also understand if you need more time.'

'Maybe not tonight,' Angus replied, swallowing the knot of grief in his throat as best he could. 'But I'd like to tell you more sometime.'

Layla squeezed his hand. 'Whenever you're ready, I'll be here.'

I'll be here . . . Angus wasn't alone anymore. It was a feeling he hadn't been able to shake since meeting Layla, sour-faced and furious in a random cafe, the same day Angus found out he was going to live to be an old man. Thanks to her, life didn't seem quite so dark. It had transformed into something to grab, something to chase . . .

And being with Layla, spending time with her? Well, Angus would grab and chase every opportunity he got, even if that meant lying along the way.

25

Layla

With her stomach stuffed with ravioli and aching from laughing so much, Layla grabbed her coat from the back of her chair. 'I'm so full, I can barely stand,' she said.

'Me too, but we need to leave. They're going to kick us out,' Angus replied.

Glancing around, Layla realised he had a point. She and Angus were the last people in Bella Vino and had been for a while. The waitstaff had politely started tidying around them half an hour ago, but in the last ten minutes their movements had become more aggressive. Layla could hardly blame them. It was after eleven, they wanted to go home. But that meant Layla and Angus had to leave too. It meant ending a night that, if she was honest with herself, Layla wished would never end.

'Thank you again,' Angus said to a passing waiter, who smiled widely in return. Layla suspected it was because of the tip Angus left. Layla hadn't seen how much it was – Angus had been adamant about paying for dinner – but from the way the waiter's eyes widened with delight, she guessed it was sizeable.

Layla loved that Angus tipped generously, mentally adding another tick to the chart she pretended she wasn't keeping in her head.

With his hand resting gently on her lower back, Angus guided Layla through Bella Vino. Layla had no idea how her legs were moving.

Her brain certainly wasn't telling them to – it was too busy focusing on the fireworks exploding where Angus's hand touched her skin.

It had been like that throughout dinner. Every innocent brush of hands as they reached for a drink, every moment their eyes met for a second too long, made Layla lose the ability to think.

This is bad. Bad, bad, bad, her brain flustered as Angus opened the door for her. Layla wished she could shut the voice out. How could something that felt so good be bad?

But Layla knew the answer to that. She was dying. In two years' time, to be precise.

No, she could not let herself go there with Angus. Dating was messy. Complicated. More drama than Layla could handle right now.

Plus, Angus was not a fling. He was not a one-night stand. He was . . . well, he was more than Layla had words for. Dinner had only cemented what Layla had come to suspect – one kiss from Angus and she would never be the same again. When her death date had thrown so much of her life into chaos, it wasn't a risk Layla could take.

Standing on the street outside the restaurant, Layla braved a look at Angus, then wished she hadn't. It was easy to pretend that she could stick to her 'friends only' rule with her back to him. But one glimpse of that crooked smile and those twinkly eyes? Well, she was done for.

'I should go,' Layla said at the same time Angus said, 'Would you like to go for a drink?'

Biting her lip to try to control the ferocity of her blush, Layla lowered her gaze. 'I'd better not. I have work tomorrow.'

'Work. Of course. Me too.'

A moment of silence rang out, disturbed only by the sound of traffic passing beside them.

'I wish we could stay out, though,' Angus admitted. 'I feel like I've only scratched the surface of knowing you.'

Although she willed herself not to, Layla flicked her gaze to Angus once more. Her knees almost buckled as their eyes connected. Fuck, he was handsome.

The perfect distraction from death, her brain chimed, but Layla stamped out that thought. She would not – could not – invite romance into her life.

Pulling her phone from her pocket, Layla ordered an Uber. 'Two minutes away,' she said, keeping her gaze on the phone because it was easier than keeping it on Angus.

'That's quick,' Angus replied.

As the time turned to one minute, Layla gulped. She looked up, staring deep into the eyes of the man who made her laugh so hard at dinner she'd snorted.

'I had a wonderful time tonight, Angus,' Layla heard herself say.

The smile that took over Angus's face was dazzling. 'Me too. Tonight might go up there as one of the best nights of my life.'

'One of the best? Not *the* best?' Layla teased.

'Top five, at least,' Angus replied.

As their smiles widened, Layla felt her resolve waver. It would be easy to cancel the Uber and head for a drink. Or, if she were feeling extra bold, cancel drinks and head back to her place. Rhi had a night shift, so they would have the apartment to themselves. All Layla had to do was be brave and suggest it . . .

But ever since opening Saira's envelope, all Layla's energy had been zapped. Feeling so drained took more out of her than she could admit.

As her phone pinged to announce her Uber's arrival, Layla shrank into herself. Standing on tiptoes, she kissed Angus's cheek, her face warming when her lips met Angus's skin. 'Thank you for tonight.'

As she pulled back, meeting his eyes, Layla cursed herself for closing the gap between them. Up close, the scent of Angus's aftershave was intoxicating. His mouth was so close that if she tilted her head slightly, she could meet it with her own. All it would take was one small movement . . .

'Good night,' Layla said, rushing away before Angus could say it back.

Blindly, Layla entered her Uber. As it peeled away from the pavement, she braved a look back at Angus. He stood on the pavement, staring at the car as if dazed. Slowly, his hand raised to wave goodbye.

Only when her Uber rounded a corner did Layla force herself to turn around in her seat.

Breathing air into her lungs, Layla looked to her phone. With shaking hands, she sent a message:

I'm feeling a 1 out of 10 right now

Within minutes, Saira was calling.

'I'm sorry to contact you so late,' Layla said as soon as she heard Saira's voice.

'Please don't apologise. My job is to be here whenever you need me. It's a good job I don't sleep much,' Saira joked, then she paused. 'Is everything okay?'

'I . . .' Layla began, but she had no idea how to answer that question. 'Yes. No. I don't know,' she admitted. 'I've just had the greatest date of my life.'

'I see. And why is that a 1 moment?'

'Because I'm dying, Saira. I was shown a glimpse of happiness straight after finding out when my life will end. How is that fair?'

The Uber driver glanced at Layla in the rear-view mirror, alarm flashing in his eyes. Layla tried to offer him a reassuring smile, but her features wouldn't obey.

'Layla, the purpose of life isn't to focus on death,' Saira said. 'It's to focus on the journey in between the beginning and the end.'

'I guess,' Layla admitted, her shoulders falling. 'Is it selfish to want Angus to be part of that journey?'

'I'm not sure selfish is the right word. Many people believe that the key to happiness is surrounding yourself with as much love and connection as possible, no matter how long it lasts for. If that's the case, then having Angus in your life could be the greatest gift of all.'

Settling into her seat, Layla looked out the window. Everything about Angus's presence in her life felt karmic – like he was sent at a time when she most needed to recognise how great life could be. Layla just wished she had more time to enjoy it.

26

Angus

It wasn't like Angus to cut out early on plans with Jasper, but he had no choice. The four Savile Row tailors Jasper had dragged him to meant their outing was now dangerously close to interrupting Angus's time with Layla.

'You should stick with Mulhoneys,' Angus said as he reached for his coat. 'Your family's been going there for years.'

'Which is exactly why I fancied a change,' Jasper replied, eying the cut of a pair of trousers in the mirror. 'If I was a stately home, I would be in dire need of a renovation.'

'Don't be ridiculous. You dress well.'

'Angus Fairview-Whitley, are you complimenting me?' Jasper teased. He flicked his gaze to Angus in the mirror. 'Do you have to rush off? There's still another tailor to visit.'

'Jasper, we were meant to finish shopping an hour ago.'

Checking the time, Jasper could only laugh. 'Still, I thought we could grab a bite to eat when we finish.'

'I can't. I have plans.'

'With who?'

At that moment, a text arrived on Angus's phone.

Be there in 15. Dinner is on whoever
arrives last . . . x

Grinning, Angus's body moved on autopilot, heading for the door and the promise of the evening ahead. It was only when Jasper shouted his name that Angus realised he was leaving without saying goodbye.

Jasper shook his head. 'She's got you in a chokehold, my friend. Be careful. It's not like you to lose your head over anyone.'

'Maybe she's not just anyone,' Angus replied. Jasper's eyebrows rose, but before he could say anything, Angus pointed to a smart jacket on a nearby mannequin. 'Try that on. I reckon you'll like it.'

Shaking his head, Jasper tutted. 'Trying to distract me with fine tailoring? That's low, Angus. I'm afraid it won't work. I'm too invested in your mysterious love life.'

'It's not mysterious.'

'Angus, I am your best friend and all I know about this woman is that you're obsessed with her. If you don't let me meet her soon, I'm going to have to ask your mother to get involved. If there's anyone who can bully you into doing what they want, it's Gilly.'

Angus's smile tightened, but he couldn't tell which part of Jasper's response made him cringe the most. The idea of Jasper and Layla being in the same room, or the idea of Gilly meeting Layla and firing one of her dismissive putdowns her way.

'That sounds a lot like blackmail,' he replied curtly. Angus didn't mean to sound quite so terse, but the strain of keeping Layla on the edge of his life was fraying him in ways he couldn't control.

'If there's one thing I've learned from my father,' Jasper said, straightening his tie in the mirror. 'It's that there's no such thing as blackmail between friends. It's simply a nudge in the right direction.'

'Spoken like a true Machiavelli,' Angus retorted, before pointing to the mannequin once more. 'I've got to go, but I mean it – you should try this one on.'

'Will do. Enjoy another night with the mystery woman,' Jasper called, waving goodbye as Angus left the store.

According to Google Maps, Hyde Park was a twenty-minute walk away, but Angus knew he would get there faster than that. At the prospect of seeing Layla, his body went into superspeed. While listening to the latest Gillian McAllister thriller, he weaved through crowds enjoying the chilly evening. Soon the traditionally styled storefronts of Savile Row made way for chic restaurants and bars.

As Angus walked, he made note of places that Layla might like. An Italian restaurant that smelled divine as he passed it. A curry house that promised modern takes on classic dishes. Street after street, Angus mapped out potential dates with Layla until he reached Hyde Park Corner. There, Angus pulled out his phone. Jasper had texted to say he'd bought the jacket. *You know me well! Anyone would think we'd been friends for years*, the message said. Grinning as the words proved that all was well between them, Angus had just set about replying when a call from Clarissa came through.

Seeing her name on the screen was like being struck over the back of the head with a hammer. Angus hadn't talked to Clarissa in weeks. He hadn't thought of her in that time, either.

'Clarissa, eh? Should I be jealous?'

Jumping so hard he almost dropped his phone, Angus turned towards the teasing voice and came face-to-face with Layla. 'No, no, not at all,' he blustered.

'You sure she isn't a secret girlfriend you've hidden away?' Layla prodded, lifting her eyebrow.

Angus knew Layla was only joking, but the thought of admitting to the toxic dynamic he and Clarissa had engaged in for years made him shrivel. Angus didn't want Layla to think he was cavalier about sex and relationships. Nor did he want her to know that for years he had been such a shell of a person, offering anything more than a casual hook-up felt like adding another name to the long list of people he'd disappointed.

'It's a work thing,' Angus heard himself blurt out. 'Clarissa's my colleague.'

For the life of him, Angus didn't know why he'd said that, but the words had burst free before he could stop them.

Oblivious to his pain, Layla smiled like she knew all about after-hours work calls. 'Take it if you need to. I don't mind.'

'No, it's okay,' Angus replied, declining the call and slipping his phone away. 'Work shouldn't be contacting me at this time.'

'Oh, how I would love to be able to say that about my job!' Layla cried before nudging Angus. 'Hello, by the way.'

Loosening his shoulders, Angus strained a smile. 'Hello to you too.'

Angus's body moved with a mind of its own, drawing Layla into a hug and pressing a kiss to her cheek. His lips tingled from the contact, as they did every time he greeted Layla that way. With Layla's arms around him, Angus felt his body soften. At peace, all thoughts of Clarissa melted away.

'Shall we set off?' Angus asked, reluctantly pulling away when he became aware of how long they'd stood wrapped around each other.

'Why not? A twilight stroll is tonight's plan, after all.'

Angus didn't know whose idea it was to link arms as they walked, but he was delighted by it.

Hyde Park was, like always, a hive of activity. People meeting after work, rushing home or squeezing in a workout. It was an eruption of life, but the only thing that Angus cared about was beside him, tucked into his arm.

'How was your day?' Layla asked.

'Boring,' Angus replied. 'Yours?'

'You don't want to tell me more about your boring day before I fill you in on details of my busy one?'

Angus let out a strangled laugh. 'Not at all. I already spend too many hours at work. The less I think about it later, the better.'

The lie slid out smoothly, quadrupling Angus's self-loathing. He tightened his grip on Layla's arm. Clinging to her, the world beneath his feet felt solid. In fact, these days, being around Layla was the only time anything felt solid.

As Layla burst into an anecdote about a new client, Angus took a moment to study her. She was so incredibly beautiful. Every time Angus saw her, he had to bite his tongue to stop himself from saying it. But in this moment, pink cheeked and chatting animatedly? She was something else entirely.

'Are you listening to me?' Layla said, pinching Angus's arm.

'Of course I'm listening to you. You're the most interesting person I know.'

Layla's right eyebrow kinked. 'Really? I take it that means you usually only befriend boring people?'

'Not at all. All my friends are fascinating. You're just the best one.'

Tipping her head back, Layla let out a throaty laugh. Instinctively, Angus tightened his grip on her, his heart bursting at the sound.

As Layla continued recounting her day, Angus walked beside her, stroking his fingers back and forth on her arm as he listened. All the while, he lied to himself that he was worthy of Layla's time, even though he knew, deep down, he wasn't.

27

Layla

The Life Experiment: Daily Questionnaire
Property of OPM Discoveries

How would you rate your level of contentment today? (1 represents low contentment, 10 represents high)

1 2 3 4 5 6 7 8 (9) 10

How would you rate your energy level? (1 being very low energy and 10 being very high energy)

1 2 3 4 5 6 (7) 8 9 10

What are two things you are grateful for today?
1. Living in London. I've never given myself time to appreciate all there is to do here, but now I'm hanging out with Angus, I see how amazing it is. We could do three activities every day and never run out of things to do. How incredible is that?
2. Dad's texts. His photos are always blurry and he's so slow at replying I almost forget we're chatting, but I love the insights into his day

What are you struggling with today?
Going to work and acting like everything hasn't changed. I need to figure out what to do about that, but how? All ideas welcome, Saira

Do you have any additional notes on what you would like to discuss in your upcoming counselling session?
Lifestyle changes that could help with my stress level. I'm debating a gym membership (I know, it's a shock to me too!)

Glaring sunlight sliced through the office, not that anyone but Layla seemed to notice. They were too busy focusing on the screens in front of them as if they were the most important things in the world.

You'd have been like that a few weeks ago, Layla thought.

How Layla had changed.

On cue, a message from one of the reasons for that change pinged onto Layla's phone. Opening it, a picture of a takeaway coffee with 'Anus' written on the cup filled her screen. The caption made her giggle.

I don't know if the barista can't spell or if they're trying to insult me x

'Stop,' Rashida said as Layla typed a response. 'You laughing in the office is making me uncomfortable.' Rashida grinned to show she was joking, but Layla couldn't laugh along.

Don't let this place steal your happiness! she wanted to shout. *Mayweather & Halliwell might charge clients exorbitant fees for your time, but they have no respect for it!*

After sending her reply, Layla looked to Rashida. 'Surely we shouldn't be miserable at work? I know it can't always be perfect, but we shouldn't be so downtrodden we can't find the energy to smile.'

'Did you forget what this place was like while you were away? A defeated workforce is how leadership likes it. You're less likely to rebel when you're too tired to protest.' Rashida chuckled, but Layla wondered if she heard the sadness in her words.

'Surely we shouldn't only feel good on payday?'

'Layla, I have a son in day care and a mortgage. There's no payday happiness for me.'

Another grim truth that tore through Layla. 'Well, I still think management should work harder to support their staff.'

Dubiously, Rashida studied her colleague. 'Maybe I need to take a trip up north. You've returned a new woman.'

Layla might have rolled her eyes, but even she could admit that there was an undeniable truth to Rashida's observation. It was the strangest thing. Since finding out her death date – and with the help of a few nudges from Saira – Layla had stepped out from the shadow of her desk. The result had been transformative. Life in all its complex, amazing glory invited her to feel, enjoy and take part.

Sometimes the mix of conflicting emotions gave Layla a headache. The joy of Jayden's laughter coupled with the sadness of knowing she didn't have long to hear it. The rush of love she felt when sitting with her parents, knowing that their newfound closeness would bring them more pain when she was gone. The perfection of her friendship with Angus, knowing she could never allow it to become more.

The constant dance of the brilliant and the brutal was so overwhelming it often made tears spill down Layla's cheeks, but the intensity proved one thing – she was alive. For now, at least.

'Seriously, what's gotten into you?' Rashida pushed. 'First you disappear, then you come back like . . . well, I don't even know. Did you have a lobotomy or something?'

'Smiling means I've been lobotomised?'

'It does in this office.'

Layla looked around and realised how deep a line had been drawn between her and everyone else. The experiment started it, but it couldn't take credit for everything that came after. It hadn't instructed her to read Jayden bedtime stories in silly voices or spend time with Angus – she had done that.

But is this fair on Angus? her brain nagged. It was a voice Layla had been doing her best to shut out. The problem was, the more she came to accept her limited lifespan, the louder the question shouted.

As her heart cracked, Layla busied herself with her laptop. Skimming over her inbox, she calculated which emails were most important and ranked them in a to-do list. Some she would respond to today. Others, she would push to tomorrow. Some things could wait, Layla had come to realise. Some things weren't that important, and spending all your time obsessing over them meant there was a danger of overlooking the things that were.

Watching Layla calmly work through her to-do list, Rashida shook her head. 'That's it,' she said. 'You've been lobotomised. It's the only explanation.'

'It wasn't a lobotomy. It was a much-needed reset.'

Rashida raised her eyebrow and readied herself to say more, but something over Layla's shoulder caught her eye. Immediately, Rashida was silenced.

'Layla?'

Spinning in her chair, Layla turned to find Michelle Beckett standing behind her. Dressed in a suit that likely cost more than Layla earned in a month, Michelle looked every bit as impressive as her credentials suggested she was.

'Can I have a word in my office?'

Rashida's head snapped to Layla, wide-eyed. A word with the boss was either good news or bad. There was no in-between. Given Layla's recent attendance, there could only be one outcome.

With a nervous nod, Layla rose and followed Michelle. Walking behind her, Layla couldn't take her eyes off Michelle's shoes. They couldn't be comfortable when the heel was both impossibly high and alarmingly thin, but Michelle walked in them as if they were a pair of slippers. Confident, strong, with no hint of a wobble. A woman who knew what she was about to do.

Yeah, fire you, Layla's brain snapped.

As Michelle opened the door to her office, Layla bit the inside of her cheek. It was all going to come down to this. Layla and Michelle in a sleek, wooden office, with Mayweather & Halliwell taking the best years of her life and dropping her when she dared to take her foot off the gas.

Everything Layla had worked for, gone.

It was as she walked towards Michelle's desk that Layla realised that although her relationship with her job had shifted, it still mattered to her. Being successful was always going to be an important part of who she was. It was just the way she was built. Besides, Layla's achievements weren't void because she only had two years left to live. If anything, they were more important than ever.

But, as Layla took a seat opposite Michelle, it looked like her achievements were about to come to an end.

'Layla,' Michelle began, smoothing the sleeves of her suit. 'How are you?'

'I'm good, thank you,' Layla croaked. 'Yourself?'

Michelle waved her hand. 'Oh, constantly on the go and permanently tired, you know how it is.' Michelle laughed, giving Layla permission to smile weakly. Then, as quickly as Michelle's laughter had started, it stopped. 'I'm guessing you know all about those feelings though. That's why you've been away so much recently.'

Fear flooded Layla. This was it – the moment she was going to lose it all. A moment she had spent her entire life trying to avoid.

Something in Layla's gut kicked. Something that felt similar to the time Joey Marron accused her of cheating in a maths test because she'd beaten his score. The feeling reminded Layla of all the times others had used their status or power to minimise hers. Making her feel small, like she should be grateful to have a seat at the table, even though she had worked damned hard to get there.

Squaring her shoulders, Layla sat taller. 'I know I haven't been as committed recently as I have in the past, but I don't think current personal circumstances should override years of hard work. I am an asset to Mayweather & Halliwell. If you look at my stats—'

'Layla, please,' Michelle cut in. 'I know how hard you work. Trust me when I say I'm more than impressed with your output. In fact, I see a lot of myself in you. That being said, I have noticed a change in your performance. Specifically in regards to your attitude. You're no longer the first one in and the last one out.'

Layla opened her mouth to explain, but she stopped when she saw that Michelle was smiling. 'I don't understand. Are you . . . are you firing me?'

Michelle's finely plucked eyebrows lifted. 'Firing you? No! I really need to work on my tone if you think that.'

Layla's lips parted to let out a sigh of relief. She didn't know whether to laugh, cry or run down the corridor cheering.

Michelle watched her reaction with an unreadable expression before leaning back in her chair. 'You know, it's not easy to get to a position like this,' she said, gesturing to her surroundings. 'A lot of people want it, but not many make it. I was determined to be one of the ones who did. I nearly destroyed myself trying to show people I was worth it. My relationship with my job was the biggest factor in my first divorce. Some nights I even slept under my desk – can you believe it? That's how much I wanted to prove myself, but that was over twenty years ago. Things should change in that time. People shouldn't be losing friends or ending relationships because of their workload, but it's happening. Day in, day out, it's happening.'

Instinctively, Layla nodded. Sinead's 'sick day' to try to save her relationship after Kirstie threatened to walk out last night was proof of that.

'Layla, when I look at your record and read your sign-in times, do you know what I see?' Michelle asked. 'I see that instead of changing for the better, things have got worse. The world has endured a global pandemic yet we're still expecting the impossible.'

As Michelle's phone beeped with a notification and interrupted the conversation, Michelle rolled her eyes.

'And don't get me started on those things.' She sighed. 'People know you have a phone, therefore think you can be contacted at all hours. The nine-to-five no longer exists, yet we pay people as if it does, all the while expecting a twenty-four-seven workload.'

Too shocked to speak, Layla could only let out a small laugh in response.

'I believe that in order to make change, you have to be the change,' Michelle continued. 'So now I'm here in the office I once dreamed of, I'm going to be the person I wish I'd worked for. Someone who says "go home" instead of offering a pillow for another night on the floor. That's where you come in.'

Layla blinked. 'Me?'

'Yes, you. I don't want to sit back and watch young, talented people like yourself jump through the same hoops I did. I didn't rise to this rank to watch women have to give up jobs they love because they have children or be overlooked for promotions because they might go on maternity leave. I don't want to turn a blind eye to the racism, sexism and classism that has grown wild in our sector. Do you know, when I examine the biggest contributions to cases in the last year, it's the same few names mentioned each time. But then when I look at promotions and pay rises, those names are nowhere to be found.'

Layla held Michelle's gaze. 'Do you want me to say I'm surprised by that?'

'No,' Michelle replied, then she leaned closer. 'But I want you to say you'll help me lead a team to change it.'

Layla felt her jaw slacken. 'You want my help?'

'Why shouldn't it be you? You're talented, intelligent and well-respected. You've also been pushed to a point where you're ready to walk away. I know that can't have been an overnight decision, but it's a useful one. Mayweather & Halliwell can't lose you, and it can't lose all the people like you who are going to be the future of this industry.'

For the second time since Michelle asked to speak with her, Layla found herself in a daze, this time for entirely different reasons.

'You've worked hard for this place, Layla. It's about time you got recognition for that. I want us to revolutionise the way we work. I want days off to be taken, not lost. I want people to log off before midnight. I want recruits to be supported, not lost to burnout. I want to make this company better, and I want you to help me do it.'

'But Michelle, I'm exactly what you want to change,' Layla replied. 'Check my timesheet – I never left on time. I lost more annual leave than anyone.'

'Which is why you're the perfect person to lead the charge in showing us how we can be better. Something's changed in you over the last few weeks.'

'I guess you could say I've seen the importance of having a life outside the office.'

'Good. Great!' Michelle said, throwing her arms in the air in celebration. 'Now let's make it so everyone else sees that too.'

As Layla's short timeline flashed before her, panic flickered across her face. Seeing it, Michelle leaned forward.

'Layla, every night I go home to an incredible house, but I'm greeted by a husband who is surprised if I'm back before he's in bed. My children can access every activity they want thanks to what I earn, but they have little to no access to me. I can schedule a meeting with the biggest businesses in the country at the click of my fingers, but find time for a doctor's appointment? A haircut? Never. Life shouldn't be like this, and I shouldn't be making it this way for those working under me. Things need to change, and I'm going to drive that. Hopefully with your help. Be the person I wish I'd had the courage to be when I was your age. Someone with their whole life ahead of them, bending it to their will, not the other way around.'

The sad irony of Michelle's speech wasn't lost on Layla. Her whole life ahead of her was a dream Layla had been forced to let go of. But still, Michelle's words set off a firework inside Layla that said even if it wasn't a lifetime, the next two years could be better than any that had come before.

'What would you change if you could?' Michelle asked, her eyes sparkling. 'Who would you ask to work on the project? What ideas would you pitch? Tell me.'

Being brave didn't come easily to Layla these days – all her bravery was spent on putting one foot in front of the other. But in that moment, she dared herself to find her voice.

'It starts with listening to staff. All staff, not a select few. There's no point in a detached leadership making changes they think people want. We need to hear what people *actually* want. Build a team that is reflective of the entire staff, not just the children of those in charge.'

'Who would you include in that team?'

'People like Rashida Allamad,' Layla replied. 'Not only is she a hard worker, but she's also a parent. Every decision made directly impacts her family. We can't do a project like this without the input of people like her.'

'Hmm,' Michelle said, tilting her head. 'Is Rashida a little quiet for a changemaker?'

'Is she quiet, or has she been silenced? Don't mistake keeping your head down for not having ideas.' Part of Layla baulked at the audacity of challenging Michelle in this way, but when she remembered her talks with Rashida about all the things they wished they could change, she silenced her inner critic.

The colleagues she spent her days with weren't her competition, Layla realised. Not if she didn't want them to be. And if doors were being opened for Layla, she was damned sure she wasn't going to close them on someone else.

Michelle studied Layla before her mouth curled into a smile. 'Well done. You passed my little test. So, what do you say? Fancy helping me take on workplace culture and winning?'

Layla didn't have to think twice. 'I'm in.'

28

Angus

No matter how comfortable Saira's office was, Angus couldn't relax. Something about this session felt different to the others. Angus sensed it as soon as Saira invited him to take a seat. The feeling only grew when Saira skimmed over his data from the last week, which she usually lingered on.

She wants to get to the good stuff, he thought, knowing all too well what that meant.

Tilting his head to his chest, Angus inhaled the scent of Layla's perfume, which had lingered on his jumper after their hug goodbye the evening prior.

Saira glanced up from the iPad that was balanced on her knees.

'I must say, Angus, you're a different man to the one I first met,' she said. 'Lighter in many ways. Heavier in some.'

'Is that a comment about my weight?' Angus joked, but he knew what she meant. Saira read the questionnaries he filled out as part of the experiment. She knew all about Layla.

More importantly, she knew all about Angus's lies.

'This is our sixth counselling session,' Saira said. 'By now I think we know each other well enough to delve a little deeper, don't you?'

Even though this was expected, Angus still shifted in his seat.

'Deeper how?' Angus lowered his gaze. 'You mean about the things I've told Layla?'

'I'm more curious about why you've said those things when doing so jeopardises the relationship you want to establish.'

'Do you think she'll hate me if she finds out?'

'Angus,' Saira replied with a sympathetic tilt of her head. 'I can't predict how Layla will react, but I can say that no one likes being lied to. And with lies, it's rarely a case of "if" someone finds out and more a case of "when".'

Angus studied his hands. Saira's honesty confirmed everything that, deep down, Angus already knew – the best thing that had ever happened to him was going to come to an end, and there would be no one to blame but himself.

Angus thought back to last night. Another evening spent in Layla's company, this time attending a West End show followed by Thai food. Another night trying not to stare at the lips he wanted to kiss.

But Angus knew Saira was right. His lies would come out sooner or later. And Angus could only imagine the consequences.

'I don't want to lie to Layla,' he admitted, 'but I'm in too deep now.'

'It's never too late to tell the truth, Angus. Being honest doesn't always have the catastrophic repercussions we tell ourselves it will.'

Angus met Saira's gaze. She was so sincere that for a moment he almost believed her, but then he imagined Layla crying at the falsehoods he'd fed her. He thought of her walking away. As soon as Angus pictured that, it was like all oxygen left the room.

'Why do you think you've lied, Angus?' Saira asked.

'I don't know,' he replied, but the way Saira stared told Angus she didn't believe him. Swallowing his shame, he cleared his throat. 'I didn't lie about things like what school I went to because I want to delude Layla. I lied because I don't want to be me.'

There, he'd said it. His most painful truth, released. It didn't feel good to hear it out loud, but it didn't exactly feel bad, either.

'That's a bold statement, Angus.'

He shrugged. 'It's an accurate one.'

'Why don't you want to be yourself? On paper, you have a lot going for you.'

'Well, on paper no one can tell how much I've messed up. It's not like anyone wants me to be myself, anyway. They never have. They want me to be—' Angus stopped, alarmed by how easily he had broached the subject. But ever since he'd touched on it with Layla and Aleksander, Hugo's name had been on the tip of his tongue.

As he shifted uncomfortably, Saira tilted her head. 'They want you to be who, Angus?'

'Hugo,' he whispered.

Angus might have said his brother's name quietly but it triggered a stream of memories he hadn't allowed himself to think of in years.

Gilly refusing to leave her bedroom, her agonised cries echoing down the hallway.

Peter telling Angus he had to be the 'man of the house' before he went away on business.

Coming home from boarding school to find every trace of Hugo removed from the house, as if he'd never existed at all.

Angus's lonely childhood, even lonelier now there was no one to share the burden of expectation with.

'Who's Hugo?' Saira asked gently, breaking into the chaos of Angus's mind.

'You know who he is. I listed my immediate family members in my application.'

'Yes, but I'd like to hear about him from you. I get the feeling it might do you good to tell me, too.'

Angus held Saira's gaze, waiting for her to back down, but she didn't. 'Hugo is . . . Hugo was my brother,' he said, swallowing the betrayal he felt at referring to his brother in the past tense. 'He drowned when he was thirteen and I was eleven.'

'How terrible, Angus. I'm so sorry.'

'Terrible is one word for it. Everything about that day feels like a scene in a film gone wrong. The fancy charter boat, the staff serving my parents champagne ... My mother screaming when she saw Hugo facedown in the water.' Angus shuddered as he remembered a skipper on the boat pulling Hugo's limp body from the water. 'My parents sued the boat company and did everything they could think of to make it better, but nothing brought Hugo back. They've never recovered from it.'

'And you? Did you ever recover from it?'

Angus blinked. He'd never really thought of Hugo's death solely in terms of himself, but of course, what happened to Hugo impacted Angus. He was his wickedly funny big brother. There one minute, gone the next.

'I was never allowed to talk about Hugo,' Angus admitted. 'My family is the definition of stiff upper lip, so all thoughts of Hugo had to be pushed away. In that sense, no, I never recovered from it. How could I? You can't recover from something if you're made to pretend it never happened. Or, in Hugo's case, never existed.'

'Keeping those feelings to yourself must have put a terrible strain on you.'

Angus shrugged. 'It's not like I had much choice. The fallout from Hugo's death was inevitable. Overnight, I went from being the youngest sibling to the only child. Everything my parents ever wanted fell to me.'

'That's a heavy load for a person to carry.'

'Maybe, but it's not like I carried it well.'

Saira's eyes bored into Angus, willing him to continue pulling at this thread. He could feel the calm she exuded spreading across the room, inviting him to talk.

It's okay, he thought. *Just say it.*

For once, Angus listened to himself. 'My parents have a vision of who Hugo would have become, and it's everything I'm not. I mean, look at me, Saira. I've done nothing with my life. The one time I bothered to try something, I failed in the most spectacular way. I lost so much money. Hugo would never have done that. He was strong and confident. He would never have fallen for such a stupid scheme, but I did.' Shaking his head, Angus sank into his self-loathing. 'With Hugo gone, I was expected to become everything he was. I tried, I really did. I became Head Boy. I joined the rugby team and made the right friends, but none of it came naturally to me. I couldn't fit in those spaces. I couldn't become the son my parents wanted.' Angus winced at the shame of saying that out loud. 'When I met Layla, I didn't want to be a failure anymore. I wanted to be someone different. Someone who worked a nine-to-five and went for runs and had beers with his friends at the weekend. I wanted to be normal.'

'Some people think we should remove the word "normal" from our discourse,' Saira said. 'They argue that "normal" can't exist because normality is dependent on unique personal experience. One person's normal is another's abnormal. So, when we compare ourselves based on "normal", we're creating limits that don't exist.'

'The only limit I've ever tested is how badly I can mess up,' Angus replied, picking at the skin on his thumb.

'Listening to you is interesting, Angus. You see yourself as a directionless, unambitious failure, but I don't see that when I look at you. I see someone who is scared to try in case they let people down, not someone who *is* a letdown. They are two very different things. It seems to me you need someone to tell you that it's okay to fail, so long as you try.'

'That is what I need,' Angus admitted. 'Before I took part in this experiment, my father told me he could see I wasn't happy. He told me to make a change. He's never said anything like that before. I can't stop thinking, what if he'd told me that sooner? What if he'd given me permission to find my own path instead of worrying I could never follow his or Hugo's? Maybe I wouldn't have wasted so much time.'

'What ifs are wonderful tools of thought, but they're damaging ones. No one can go back, no matter how much we wish we could. All we can do is look to the future.'

'But I don't know what my future looks like.'

'Well, why don't we imagine it? What does the perfect future look like to you?'

Angus closed his eyes and turned his thoughts inward. As soon as he did, the guilt over his lies stole his breath.

'Your perfect future,' Saira said, her measured tone offering his mind a life raft. 'Who's in it?'

'Layla,' Angus replied immediately.

'Who else is there?'

'My father. He's smiling at me. He's not worried anymore.'

'Why isn't he worried?'

'Because I've figured it out. Who I am. What to do. How to use my time.'

'And what is it you're doing in this future?'

'I ... I don't know, but it makes me feel good. I'm making a difference.'

'Well, someone with your connections has a lot of power to make a difference,' Saira commented. 'And you've started volunteering. You could do a lot of good there.'

Angus opened his eyes. 'I've had an idea, actually. Well, half an idea,' he admitted, then he shook his head. 'It's silly. It probably won't work.'

'Tell me,' Saira said.

Sitting forward, Angus clasped his hands together. 'I met a man at the hospice. His daughter had cancer when she was little. He told me how hard it was to take her for treatment around his job. Their house was miles away from the nearest children's cancer ward. I was thinking I could help with that.'

'How?' Saira pressed.

'Well, while people are receiving hospital care, the demands of life don't stop,' Angus replied. 'But the disruption of needing treatment is huge. People have to attend appointments, sometimes far away, while still going to work and earning enough to pay their bills. It seems to me that something could be put in place to bridge the gap between people's everyday lives and their medical needs.'

'And what would that be exactly?'

'I'm not entirely sure. I'm still thinking through the details, but I think there's an opportunity to ease the burden.'

'There definitely could be,' Saira agreed. 'It sounds like if you can figure that out, it might help you find the purpose you mentioned earlier. Become the person you envision.'

'I don't know what to do to get there, though.'

'Shall I let you in on a secret, Angus? One no one admits? There are very few people out there who know what they're doing. Most of us are simply making it up as we go along.'

'You don't seem like you're doing that.'

Saira laughed. 'Trust me, I am. But something I've learned while working on The Life Experiment is that the people who do know what they're doing have one thing in common. They listen to themselves. They're honest about their desires and they share that honesty with those around them.'

Angus lowered his gaze. 'You want me to tell Layla the truth.'

'What I want doesn't matter, Angus. What *you* want does. I know Layla is top of that list, but a relationship shouldn't be used as a distraction from the things you don't want to face. You've told me how much you value what you have with Layla. I read it in your questionnaires and see it in your face when you speak about her. The best way you can honour that is by working to become the man you describe. Shut out the weight of expectation, listen to your heart and figure out who Angus Fairview-Whitley is. Do you think you can do that?'

Angus thought about his heart and how it had kept him alive for thirty-four years. How it had powered him through rugby finals and all-night parties. How he increasingly suspected it belonged to Layla, even if he couldn't brave showing her his true self.

But most of all, when Angus thought of his heart, he thought of how he'd been so scared to break it, he'd never given himself permission to try.

'I guess there's no better time to start than now,' he said, offering Saira a small smile.

29

Layla

Sinead's harried voice rang out across their pod of desks. While she had every right to be stressed about a deadline being brought forward, Layla found it hard to care about the new timeline. She cared even less about the potential strain to business relationships if someone were to inform the client it wasn't doable. Mayweather & Halliwell weren't miracle workers. They couldn't invent extra time, even if they wanted to. Layla's about death date was proof of that.

But when Sinead pressed her palms to her eyes to stop herself from crying, Layla realised that she did care about something.

Leaning to one side to peer past her screen, Layla tried to grab her friend's attention. 'Sinead, nothing at work is worth getting this upset over,' she said. 'Just tell them the timeline isn't reasonable.'

Sinead's head lifted from her hands. 'Tell Clayton-Parkes their demands are unreasonable? Do you want me to lose my job?'

'No, but if we don't start saying no, the expectations clients have are only going to increase. Then where will we end up?'

'Working until midnight three weeks in a row?'

'Or dead from a stroke at thirty-one.'

Sinead shuddered at the suggestion. 'Imagine.'

Layla watched her friend brush off the awful prediction like it was a cobweb on her sleeve. Envy panged in her stomach. Gone were the days of Layla dismissing thoughts of death. Ever since learning her death date, nothing could distract her from her depressing fate.

At least you're out of bed today, Layla reminded herself, sitting taller.

Saira had taught Layla to count the wins in the day, no matter how small they seemed. Now that Layla was back in London, so much about life felt intimidating. So much was overwhelming. But still, Layla woke up.

Still, she got out of bed and went to work.

Still, she saw Angus.

Before a smile could betray her happiness at that, Layla's phone buzzed against the desk. Snatching it up, Layla grinned when she saw the name on the screen.

I was thinking – last night's dinner was such a success, how about we go again tomorrow?
Maybe for Vietnamese? And the cinema afterwards? x

Layla knew without looking at her calendar that tomorrow was a big day. Three client-facing meetings were booked in, not to mention a stack of work for the project with Michelle. But as thoughts of seeing Angus infiltrated her mind, Layla found she wasn't bothered by her insane to-do list. When an evening that promised to be soul-filling could be had afterwards, anything seemed doable.

Layla began typing an excited response, but when Sinead let out a distressed whimper, she paused. 'What's up?' she asked, leaning over again for a better view of her friend. When their eyes connected, Layla was alarmed to see Sinead was in tears.

'I can't do it, Layla,' she whispered. 'I can't keep up.'

'It's okay. We can send an email saying—'

'It's not just Clayton-Parkes,' Sinead cut in. 'It's everything. I'm failing at every aspect of my life. I'm being pulled in a million different directions and even though I try and try, I keep letting people down.

Kirstie is going to leave me, but can I blame her? I'm so busy with work, I'm never present. I'm going to break, Layla. I can feel it. I'm going to break.'

As Sinead bit her trembling lower lip, Layla swore she would react differently this time. She would actually *do* something. Start making the changes she was discussing with Michelle and stop perpetuating the same cycle that was ultimately going to lead to her death.

When the pool of tears in Sinead's eyes deepened, Layla reached for her coat. 'Come on. You're coming with me.'

Sinead blinked. 'Where?'

'Away from here.'

As Layla shrugged her coat over her shoulders, Sinead looked around. 'But no one else is leaving yet.'

'So? It's after five and you need to talk to a friend. We're going to go somewhere and do that. Preferably a pub.'

'But what about Clayton-Parkes?'

Layla shrugged. 'What about them? You know as well as I do that you won't do your best work if you're upset, and you won't feel any better if you don't let this out. So, let's go.'

Layla's directness was a shock to both women, but there was something about the commanding words that Layla liked. It made her feel like she was in control, for once.

When Layla's eyebrow cocked in a friendly challenge, Sinead's lips stretched into a smile. 'I like this new Layla,' she said, grabbing her coat too. 'She's fun.'

Together, the women left work at a reasonable hour for the first time since they could remember. As Layla stepped out into a mild London night, she didn't know if this version of herself was one she liked. It was too new, too fragile. But what Layla did know was that if she didn't try to be her, she would die in two years' time with more regrets than a person should amount in a lifetime. That was enough to push her to try.

30

Angus

The Life Experiment: Daily Questionnaire
Property of OPM Discoveries

How would you rate your level of contentment today? (1 represents low contentment, 10 represents high)

1   2   3   4   5   6   7   (8)   9   10

How would you rate your energy level? (1 being very low energy and 10 being very high energy)

1   2   3   4   5   6   7   8   9   (10)

What are two things you are grateful for today?
1. Finally having a clue about what I want to do with my life
2. Nabbing Coldplay tickets. They're going to be a great surprise present for Layla!

What are you struggling with today?
I could do with Layla's advice on so much right now, but I can't open up to her. My own stupid fault, I know

Do you have any additional notes on what you would like to discuss in your upcoming counselling session?
Not really. If you could make me feel better about the above, that would be great

It had been a long time since Angus felt nervous approaching his parents' house. The last time was in his early twenties, sheepishly returning home from a trip to Portugal that went awry. Jasper and Angus had hosted a party that resulted in their accommodation being trashed. When the bill for repairs hit tens of thousands, Peter demanded to know what Angus had been thinking by inviting strangers inside.

Back then Angus wasn't thinking, but now he was.

Hopping out of the car, Angus headed inside. It was after dinner, so his parents would be relaxing in the snug. A title not entirely fitting for a room bigger than the floorplan of most homes. His knuckles rapped on the door twice before he pushed it open. A crackling log fire greeted him, as did his surprised parents. Sitting on opposite couches, Gilly curled under a blanket, Peter with a book, the pair straightened at the arrival of their son.

'Angus, what a lovely surprise,' Gilly said, rising to her feet. 'Is everything okay?'

'Everything's great.'

She brushed a lock of hair back from Angus's face. 'You certainly look well. A little flushed, but well.'

'That's the flush of excitement,' Peter said, slotting a bookmark into his book. 'Is there something in particular you're here for?'

'Actually, there is.'

Peter nodded like he expected as much, then indicated for Angus to join him on the sofa. When Gilly retook her seat, Angus obliged, although the energy rattling through his frame made him want to pace the room instead.

'Well,' Peter said after a moment. 'Spit it out, son.'

'We own two townhouses near Great Ormond Street Hospital, don't we?' Angus asked.

Peter nodded. 'We do, yes.'

'Good. Well, I'd like them.'

The glass of water Gilly was about to drink from hovered inches from her lips. The sight would have been comical were it not for the seriousness of the moment. 'You'd like them?' she repeated.

'That's right, yes.'

As Gilly choked on a startled laugh, Peter fixed his gaze on Angus. 'May I ask what for?'

'I'd like to set up a charity specialising in short-term housing for people receiving ongoing hospital care and those supporting them. A bit like a hotel, but one people can stay at with no cost.'

Angus waited for his parents to react, but it was like someone had pressed pause on the scene.

'I've drafted a proposal of how it would work,' he continued. 'I'd like your input, but I have a clear idea. We would still own and maintain the properties, but their use would not be for domestic rentals anymore. We'd convert each room into a self-catering unit as well as provide free access to counselling and other resources for residents, should they wish to use them. The building's function would simply be to support families in these situations.'

'Situations . . .? What situations?' Gilly asked, confused.

'People visiting loved ones in intensive care. People who've suffered strokes or are undergoing chemotherapy. Anyone who needs it, really. You've no idea how expensive the disruption is for people enduring treatment, never mind those trying to support them through it. Frequent hospital parking alone is more than most can afford, and that's without factoring in things like petrol, childcare and time off work.'

Gilly blinked. 'So you want to host these people in our properties for free?'

'As a charitable enterprise, yes,' Angus confirmed.

'For goodness' sake, Angus. Can't you write a cheque like everyone else?!' Gilly cried, laughing to process her shock. She looked to Peter, waiting for him to fall in line, but he was too busy studying his son. Gilly scoffed. 'This is ridiculous! Where on earth has this idea come from?'

'From listening to people living through what I've described and realising how many resources we have to help them.'

'And where have you met these people?' Gilly said, picking an imaginary speck of dust from her skirt. 'What sob story have you naively fallen for?'

'I've started volunteering at a hospice,' Angus stated, another sentence that made Gilly baulk. 'Don't look at me like that, Mother. Please. This matters to me.'

'But a hospice is where people go to die!'

'I know, but it's not like you imagine. Haven is incredible. They're there for families from diagnosis to death and beyond. Accessing support from somewhere like that would have been so useful when Hugo died.' The atmosphere shifted at the mention of his brother, but Angus didn't stop. 'I know it sounds strange, but after four shifts there, I've learned more about living than I have in the thirty-four years I've been alive.'

Angus's words were met with a strained silence. Gilly broke it with a haughty sniff. 'Angus, if you're bored, we know plenty of people who will give you a job.'

'I'm not bored, Mother. I'm tired of living a life with no meaning. I only have the things I do because of the family I was born into. Worse than that, I've had everything given to me and done nothing with it. I don't want to live like that anymore.'

Angus hoped his impassioned speech would silence his critics, but scepticism reigned strong. Angus supposed he should have expected it. After years of aimless wandering, how could anyone take him seriously when he came to them with a plan this ambitious?

'This is incredibly insulting,' Gilly snapped, two pink circles burning her cheeks. 'You want me to feel guilty for having a beautiful home and owning nice things? For giving you everything a person could possibly wish for? Well, I refuse.' Gilly's pale eyes scoured her son. 'You are selfish, Angus. You insult the life I gave you, then have the cheek to ask for two properties. And the best part is, you want them for free! Do you have any idea how much they are worth? Any idea how much they earn? If you despise the position you were born into so much, then don't ask to use its benefits.'

'I don't despise the position I was born into – I despise what I've done with it.' Angus's voice strained. 'I despise that I've spent years only thinking about holidays or partying. I despise that I've never done anything because I never had to. I could never be Hugo, so why try?'

Gilly's head snapped back. 'Don't you dare bring your brother into this!'

'But Hugo is part of this. He's part of everything I am and everything I have failed to become.'

As Gilly flew to her feet, Peter leaned forward. 'Let's take a minute to calm down,' he began, but Gilly cut him off.

'My son died, Angus. He *died*,' she hissed. 'For you to blame him for your shortcomings is, quite frankly, disgusting!'

'I know Hugo was your son, but he was also my brother,' Angus replied. 'He's the person I measure myself against, but we never got to see who Hugo would become. It's like measuring myself against a ghost.'

'Stop talking about him in this way!'

Gilly's hurt filled the air, but instead of hiding from it, Angus leaned into the emotion his family had long suppressed. 'Don't you see? Hugo wouldn't want me wasting away, scared. He'd want me to do something with my life. Something good.'

Turning pale, Gilly stepped backwards, eying her son as if he were a stranger.

'Mother, please,' Angus implored. 'I know what I want to do now. I know who I need to become. I'm asking for your help.'

From the sofa, Peter spoke up. 'Free short-term housing, you say?'

Angus turned to his father. 'That's right.'

'And what would we earn from that?'

'Nothing.'

'Nothing?'

'Nothing,' Angus confirmed.

'Angus, this is absurd,' Gilly cried. 'Those houses are premium properties! There is no way your father and I will let you have one room in them, never mind both buildings.'

'But you don't need them,' Angus protested. 'So why have them?'

Gilly turned to Peter, slack-jawed. 'I cannot believe what I am hearing. Can you believe this, Peter? Peter!'

But Peter wasn't listening to his wife. He was looking at his son as if seeing him for the first time.

Angus inched closer to his father. 'You have more wealth in this room than most have in their lifetime. Whatever monetary value those properties bring you, the value they would bring to others is exponentially greater. There are people out there you could help—'

'Since when do you care about helping people?' Gilly snapped.

'Since I realised that all this means nothing if you aren't happy with who you are,' Angus cried. 'I've spent years not knowing what to do and hating everything I've been given. I was wrong to hate it, but I'd be even more wrong to keep it all to myself. We have the ability to do so much for so many. Why aren't we?'

'This hospice sounds like it's made quite the impression on you,' Peter commented.

'It really has. When I'm there, I think of Hugo. I know it's silly when he didn't die in a hospice but—'

Gilly covered her ears, shaking her head to dislodge Angus's words. 'Stop mentioning your brother,' she shouted, but Peter held up his hand.

'Gilly, it's time we faced the fact that we lost our way after Hugo passed,' Peter said before glancing at his son. 'Perhaps Angus more than anyone.'

'I feel like I've found it now, though. I really do.'

'Angus—' Gilly began, but Peter cut her off.

'The houses are yours,' he said, standing and squeezing his son's hand. 'We'll meet with my lawyer tomorrow to start putting things in motion.'

'Peter, you can't be serious!' Gilly objected, but her husband ignored her.

'You're going to do good things with this, Angus, I can feel it. Take the houses. Volunteer more. Find other ways you can help and use every resource at your fingertips. You have my backing, always.' With that, Peter turned to his wife. 'What about you, Gilly? Does Angus have your support?'

Gilly looked from her husband to her son and back again. 'The . . . the houses, Peter. We can't just give them away. They're worth millions.'

'I know, but I also know what it feels like to lose someone you love. If we could turn that tragedy into helping someone, shouldn't we do that? Shouldn't we have done that all along?'

Angus watched the lines on Gilly's forehead deepen. Even after all this time, Angus saw the same pain in his mother's eyes as he had the day Hugo passed. Gilly thought she hid it behind her putdowns and quick wit, but it was there. Sneaky and cruel, it was there.

Suddenly, Gilly met Angus's gaze. 'No, Angus doesn't have my support,' she said, before sweeping out of the room.

Her departure felt like a punch, but Peter didn't allow Angus long to be hurt by it. Striding over to him, Peter lay his hand on his son's shoulder. 'Your mother struggles with the idea of death being such a big part of life, Angus. I suppose we all do, after Hugo, but she will come around.' Pushing past the pain of his grief, Peter forced a smile. 'You should call the venture Hugo's House. It would be a fitting tribute.'

'Hugo's House,' Angus repeated. Somewhere inside, the words clicked. From one look at his father, Angus knew they'd clicked with Peter too.

31

Layla

Although she'd lived in London for a few years, Layla had never participated in the activities put on each year in the run up to Christmas. No glittering window display captured her attention enough to enchant her. No festive menu enticed Layla enough to nip inside for a bite to eat.

That was until Angus entered the picture. Now, Layla found herself bundled in a hat and scarf on her way to do the definition of a winter activity: ice-skating in the park. Cheesy and cute, like something from a Hallmark Christmas film, she couldn't wait.

Layla had never skated before. She wasn't sure she had the skills. In fact, when she'd called her dad earlier and told him what she was doing, he'd laughed. 'You? On ice? Really? Now *that* I would love to see.'

Even though she'd scoffed at his words, the idea of gliding around a patch of ice terrified Layla. What if she fell? What if she was terrible at it?

What if, what if, what if . . . Somehow, when Angus was around, that question wasn't quite so prevalent.

Layla saw him before he saw her. Up ahead, standing under the entrance to the park, as promised. Angus wasn't scrolling on his phone while he waited like most would. He was alert, scanning the crowd for Layla. And, as his face broke into a wide smile, Layla knew he'd spotted her. Her stomach flipped. That smile . . . It was enough to make Layla weak at the knees. A terribly timed reaction considering she was about to ice-skate for the first time.

'Are you excited?!' Angus enthused as soon as she drew near enough to hear him.

'Of course! A little nervous too,' Layla admitted.

Grinning, Angus swept her into a hug. As his capable arms pressed her body against his, Layla wished more than anything that Angus would hold on longer. Brush her hair back from her face. Lean in and kiss her . . .

But, ever the gentleman, Angus didn't push his luck. Their hug was one of friendship and warmth, even if Layla could swear it sizzled with the sparks of wanting more.

'Come on. Let's join the queue before you talk yourself out of it,' Angus said.

'Or before the rink gets too full,' Layla replied, eying the crowd. It seemed like half of London had come to the park with the same idea. People old and young, families and couples, all ready to skate as if they were invincible. Layla didn't know where they got the confidence, but as Angus slipped his arm through hers, she felt her own self-assurance rise. Another few minutes in Angus's presence and Layla wouldn't be surprised if she believed she could rule the world.

The queue was surprisingly quick. Wrapped around the rink, it allowed people to see what they were signing up for. Lights flooded the icy surface and festive music blared, giving life to a scene that was already brimming with people.

'Look at her,' Angus marvelled, pointing to a woman who was skating on one leg. 'Isn't she amazing?'

'I hope you don't expect me to do that,' Layla said.

'I reckon you could do it. I'll hold your hand for support.'

Layla's stomach flipped at the thought of Angus's hand around hers. 'I'll only drag you down.'

'I wouldn't mind. If there's one person I'd let pull me to the ground, it's you.'

As her butterflies fluttered into overdrive, Layla itched to reply, *You're the only person I'd let do that too.* But like always, when it came to admitting her true feelings to Angus, she held her tongue.

A couple skated past at that moment, dancing to Wham's 'Last Christmas'.

'I love their confidence,' Layla commented. 'I wish I could dance in public like that.'

'Well then, that's what we'll do,' Angus replied, stepping forward as the queue moved. 'Tonight, we won't just skate. We will become ice dancers.'

Layla laughed. 'Do you really think I'll be able to stand long enough to dance?'

'I reckon we'll be able to make our own moves up, for sure. They might be more Bambi-on-ice than graceful, but who cares?'

Layla felt like she was floating when Angus talked about them as a unit. Ever since their first meeting, daydreams of 'us' and 'we' and 'ours' had filled her mind.

Stop, her brain warned. *Think of your death date.*

But as Angus paid their admission, Layla silenced the thought. For one night, she didn't want to think of the end. She wanted to think of right here, right now. Of lacing skates alongside a man who made her feel like anything was possible.

'You okay?' Angus asked as his steady hand guided a wobbling Layla towards the entrance to the rink.

'I'm okay. Terrified, but okay.'

'Don't worry,' Angus said, stepping onto the ice and stretching out his hand for her. 'I've got you. What's the worst that could happen?'

A list of scary possibilities flooded Layla's mind. She could prove her death date wrong by falling and breaking her neck, for one. She could be wiped out. Split her trousers. Break a limb. Humiliate herself in front of the biggest crowd she had ever been in.

Or . . .

Or she could take Angus's hand and glide.

Reaching for him, Layla put her foot on the ice and trusted.

While Angus appeared to have the skills of a pro, Layla's skating technique wouldn't be described as graceful. It was the opposite, in fact. Angus ended up with one hand holding hers, and the other around her waist to keep her upright. But the many near-falls and jerking sweeps of her skates didn't matter. Layla was skating. She was floating on a cloud of happiness. Flying, even. All because of Angus.

'Where did you learn to skate so well?' she marvelled as Angus swooped them smoothly around a corner.

'I don't know,' Angus replied, his cheeks turning pink from the cold. 'I went a lot when I was a kid. I guess muscle memory has taken over.'

Layla opened her mouth to ask more, but as the first few bars of Band Aid's 'Do They Know It's Christmas?' tinkled through the speakers, Angus squeezed her tight.

'Come on,' he said. 'It's time to dance.'

'Angus, I don't dance,' Layla protested, 'and certainly not on ice!' But when Angus began to shake his hips, giggles overtook her. Layla had no idea how Angus was able to move like that and stay upright.

'Come on,' Angus cheered, moving Layla's arm so she could dance with him. 'It's fun, I promise. No one's looking.'

Glancing around, Layla saw that a few people nearby were in fact looking, but in that moment, she didn't care. Let them look. Let them laugh. She was soaring on the arm of the loveliest man she had ever met.

Grinning, Layla moved her hips too. She even threw a jazz hand. Then, when the motion made her wobble, Angus twirled her into his arms and held her upright. In all of Layla's life, she had never experienced a moment so romantic.

'That was smooth,' she breathed, watching her breath fog the sliver of air between them.

'I'm trying to impress you, aren't I?' Angus replied, blushing as he glanced at her lips.

Layla knew the moment was dangerous. She knew it blurred the lines of friendship she insisted they drew. Sense told Layla to pull away, but she couldn't. If Angus was the flame, then she was the moth.

Suddenly, a child whooshed past them, too close for comfort.

Gasping, Layla rested her hands on Angus's chest and held on tight. She knew she was steady now, but nothing about the moment felt steady. Her eyes traced Angus's frosty breath, watching it mingle with hers. Dragging her gaze from Angus's mouth to his eyes, Layla watched his face transform with a smile.

'I told you I wouldn't let you fall,' he said.

Internally, Layla laughed. Angus had no idea. She was already falling. She had been from the moment they met.

32

Angus

In the corner booth of his favourite French restaurant, Angus read the document Layla had emailed for a second time. He knew from their FaceTime earlier that she wanted feedback.

'Seriously, whatever you say, I can take it,' she said. 'Whether it's something small, like a missed piece of punctuation, or something big, like you hate any of the ideas, tell me. I trust you.'

'You do?' Angus had replied, flashing his cheekiest smile. Hearing Layla say she trusted him made him feel giddy, but he forced himself to concentrate on her ideas for improving workplace conditions.

Last week, Layla and Angus had seen each other four times: first for an ice-skating adventure on Monday, followed by Angus teaching Layla how to cook vegetarian lasagne on Wednesday. Thursday evening they made a post-work trip to the cinema, and on Saturday they went for a walk and some drinks.

Each time they'd seen each other, Angus watched Layla come to life as she talked about the project.

'This is only the beginning,' she said the other night in the cocktail bar. 'But if it helps one person access a fairer, safer, more supportive workplace, it will be worth it. No one should have to fight to get through the day like my dad did. When he couldn't do manual work because of his injuries, the company he'd been working at for years just let him go. All those hours he'd put in for them meant nothing. No one should be made to feel so worthless.'

'I couldn't agree more,' Angus had replied, marvelling at the woman opposite him. 'It's amazing listening to you, you know. You really care about effecting meaningful change.'

Layla's cheeks tinged pink as she nodded. 'We should all care about making things better for others. It's why I got into law in the first place, but I think I forgot that somewhere along the way.'

'Well,' Angus said as he reached for his glass to toast the sentiment. 'There is no doubt in my mind that your work is going to benefit many people.'

Angus had been sure of that as they clinked glasses, but reading Layla's ideas now, he was surer than ever. The ideas she had collated were good. They were excellent, actually. Flexible working, support through life-changing moments, incentives for high-performing staff . . . Angus knew this project had the potential to change her colleagues' lives for the better.

Honestly, it's brilliant, he typed. *My only suggestion would be to add that you deserve a huge pay rise for all your hard work x*

Angus smiled as he imagined Layla giggling and shaking her head at him. Pressing send, he looked up across the restaurant.

His parents were late. Only by five minutes, but that was unusual for the Fairview-Whitleys. Sticklers for good manners, being on time, if not a minute or two early, was vital in their eyes.

Opening his messages again, Angus fired off a reply to Jasper confirming his attendance at badminton later, then checked his thread with Peter. Their last exchange confirmed their lunch plans. Since then, nothing.

There wasn't a message from his mother, either. Chewing his lip, Angus wondered if his charity idea was to blame. Gilly still wasn't on board with Hugo's House, but the purpose of this lunch was to sway her.

Beside Angus was a folder of research. It had been his secret project for the last week. He worked on it whenever he wasn't volunteering at Haven or seeing Layla. Collating businesses he could partner with and generating a list of potential donors . . . it was the biggest project Angus had ever worked on.

While he wished he could have asked Layla to cast her discerning eye over it, Angus knew he couldn't. She still had no idea of his plans. He had no idea how he was going to tell her without unveiling his list of lies, but that was a problem for another day. Today was all about impressing his parents.

They just needed to show up first.

When Angus craned his neck to check his parents weren't waiting at the bar, a waiter approached him. 'Is everything okay, sir? Can I get you a top-up, perhaps?' he said, nodding to Angus's almost empty whisky glass.

'I'm fine, thank you. Although perhaps you could bring a bottle of champagne for the table.'

As soon as the words left his mouth, Angus regretted them. Champagne was a celebratory drink. He didn't want his mother to think that he wasn't taking this seriously or that he was partying before he'd crossed the finish line.

'Actually, make that a bottle of white. Sommelier's choice,' he corrected.

'Right away, sir,' the waiter replied before retreating. But by the time the wine was brought to the table, Angus's parents still hadn't arrived. Taking his phone from his pocket once more, Angus called Peter. The phone rang three times before cutting to voicemail. When Angus tried Gilly, the same thing happened.

Embarrassment singed Angus's cheeks. Scanning the restaurant, he saw that no one was looking, but Angus felt as if every eye were on him, laughing that he had been stood up.

On the table, Angus's phone pinged with a message.

Sorry son, something came up. Your mother and I will have to miss lunch.

A disbelieving laugh escaped Angus. Closing the message without replying, he set his phone down and glanced at the folder beside him.

How stupid could he have been to think that he could create something like Hugo's House? A project like that wasn't for a fuck-up like him. It was for someone who knew what they were doing. Someone people could get behind and support.

Someone like Layla.

It was as if thinking her name had conjured her, because Layla chose that moment to call.

'Hey,' Angus said, snatching his phone from the table to answer it.

'Hey yourself,' she replied. Her voice sounded echoey, as if she was speaking from the bottom of a well.

'Where are you?' Angus asked with a laugh. 'The sound quality is so bad it's like you're calling from the 1950s.'

Layla responded with a giggle. 'I'm in the stairwell at work.'

'What are you doing in there?'

'I didn't want anyone to hear me make a personal call, but I couldn't not thank you for reading my ideas. I really appreciate it.'

The knot that had tightened Angus's chest unfurled. 'You don't have to thank me. I'll check anything you want, you know that.'

'Anything? Even under my bed for monsters?'

Now it was Angus's turn to laugh. 'Name the day and I will be there with a sword and a suit of armour.'

'How chivalrous. Noble costume choice, too,' Layla teased. 'In all seriousness, though, thank you for making the time for me. It means a lot.'

As Angus's eyes travelled to the door that his parents hadn't walked through, his smile widened. So what if his parents didn't value him enough to show up to an important lunch? So what if walking out of this restaurant was going to be embarrassing? Layla appreciated his time. Layla wanted him around.

Layla doesn't know who you are, remember? his brain snarled. *She thinks you work in IT.*

But no matter how dark Angus's thoughts got, he shook them off. Those worries were for another day. Another Angus. The Angus he was right now was too busy enjoying sitting in a restaurant, sipping wine and talking to a woman who coloured his every waking thought.

33

Layla

'What do you think – too short? Not short enough?' Maya asked as she emerged from the fitting room in a sequin dress with a fur trim.

Instinctively, Joanna laughed, but Layla's response was a little more direct.

'Too "I dropped out of theatre school and stole this before I left",' she replied.

Turning to face her reflection, Maya burst out laughing. 'Now you've said it, I can't unsee it. I look like a pantomime dame.' Giggling, she headed back into the fitting room.

'Why's she picking such wild clothes, anyway?' Layla asked Joanna.

'Jayden told her she dresses like the other mums at school. Maya thinks it wasn't a compliment. So, she wanted to make this visit to London a shopping trip.'

'I thought you came to see me?'

'That's why I'm here, but for Maya, the bigger draw might have been Oxford Street.'

Laughing, Layla watched Joanna's eyes drift to the rail of items others had tried on and declined purchasing. While Maya was picking the more outrageous pieces in the store, there were undoubtedly some beautiful items available. The shine in Joanna's eyes told Layla that she thought the same too.

'Why don't you try something on?' Layla encouraged, but Joanna laughed at the suggestion.

'Don't be silly, love. No one wants to see me in a dress like that. Not with my legs.'

'There's nothing wrong with your legs,' Layla protested, but Joanna silenced her with a shake of the head. There was something about Joanna's defeated stance that tugged at Layla, but Maya interrupted the moment by exiting the fitting room.

'Come on,' she instructed. 'Time for more identity-crisis shopping.'

Following Maya back onto the shop floor, a terrible cover of 'All I Want For Christmas Is You' filtered through the speakers to greet them. Although it wasn't December just yet, retail stores were acting as though Christmas was tomorrow. Memories of her family's penny pinching in the lead up to past Christmases flooded Layla's mind, but as the chorus kicked in, she gave in to the enjoyment of the song. However poor the cover was, the tune was still too catchy to resist humming along.

When Maya sighed in frustration that a dress she liked wasn't available in her size, Layla moved closer. 'If it makes you feel better, I'd swap clothes with you any day.'

'That's because you dress like a sex-starved librarian,' Maya replied.

'Charming,' Layla muttered, but she wasn't angry. She knew Maya had a point.

Maybe you should invest in new clothes, Layla thought as she inspected a slinky black dress. No sooner had the idea sparked than it died. It was hard to get excited about a shopping spree when in a few short years, Layla would no longer be around to wear the clothes.

'I can't believe Angus fancies you in that outfit,' Maya teased. 'The sex must be great.'

'Maya!' Layla hissed, glancing around the store self-consciously. 'We're not having sex!'

'Doesn't mean you don't want to, though,' Maya replied with a wink.

Layla knew there was no point in arguing. Mostly because, lawyer or not, she never won against Maya, but also because Maya was right. Lately, whenever Layla's mind wandered, it went to one thing: the thought of Angus's lips on hers. The thrill she would feel as his hands roamed her body . . .

'Oh my God, you're imagining having sex with him right now!' Maya cried, pointing at Layla.

'I am not,' Layla protested, but as Maya waggled her eyebrows, she realised resistance was futile. 'Fine, maybe I am. A little, anyway.'

'I knew it! Layla's in love!'

Layla opened her mouth to respond, but the burn in her cheeks and Maya's unfiltered joy made her fold.

'For what it's worth, I'm sure he feels the same,' Maya said when she registered her sister's blush. 'No one hangs out with someone this much if they don't want things to develop.'

'I don't know about that.'

Maya shot Layla a dead-eyed glare. 'Layls, please. Save the humble attitude for someone it suits. Why don't you invite Angus round tonight and tell him how you feel?'

As her death date flashed before her eyes, Layla winced. 'I can't, Maya.'

'Why not?'

'Because I can't,' she snapped. Moving her attention away from her irritation, Layla focused on her mother. Joanna stood a few feet away, touching a pair of printed trousers with a longing look in her eye. 'Is Mum okay?'

'Mum? She's fine,' Maya replied. 'Why do you ask?'

'She seems sad, that's all. When we were in the fitting room, she was being negative about her legs.'

'Layla, we've been over this. Mum's always harsh about her body,' Maya dismissed, but Layla was tired of accepting that. Most of all, she was tired of seeing her mother act as though she was someone to be ashamed of.

In the next few stores, Layla watched Joanna interact with her surroundings. She observed her being drawn towards colour and print and beautiful fabrics, only to retreat and find the plainest, baggiest, darkest thing in the store. Even then, Joanna didn't touch the item. It was almost as if she didn't think she deserved it.

At first, Layla wondered if money was the problem. While her parents weren't experiencing the same financial difficulties they'd had when David wasn't working, they still had debt. Filling her lungs with air, Layla decided that if her mother picked up an item and loved it, she would buy it for her.

The problem was, everything Joanna's eyes wandered to, she didn't reach for.

Eventually, Layla snapped. 'Come on,' she said, plucking a dress Joanna had been looking at off the rack. 'You're trying this on.'

Joanna's expression looked like Layla had asked her to undress in the middle of the shop floor. 'Layla, I can't!'

'Yes, you can. Maya, grab that purple dress over there and that floral jumpsuit. Mum was looking at them earlier.'

'Layla,' Joanna cried, but Layla didn't give her mother another second to argue. Instead, she dragged her to the fitting room.

'This is so exciting,' Maya cheered as the two sisters sat opposite the fitting room curtain. 'I haven't seen Mum get dressed up in ages!'

'That's because there's no point dressing this body up,' came a muffled response from the other side of the curtain. 'It looks terrible no matter what.'

As Layla's eyebrows dipped, Maya shrugged and checked her phone. 'Dad says he's having a great time with Jayden. Their boys' weekend is going well.'

'I bet Dad's exhausted. Jayden will have him playing game after game.'

'Too right. Dad never tells him no, though. The other day, Dad took Jayden to the park while I was at work and it started raining.

Jayden was upset because his feet got wet so Dad carried him all the way home.'

No matter how sweet the story was, anxiety still gnawed Layla's stomach. 'He shouldn't be doing that, Maya.'

'I know, but he'd walk through fire for Jayden. For any of us. You can't stop Dad being himself. You've just got to love him for it.'

'I guess,' Layla replied, trying to silence the nagging feeling in her gut. The thing that distracted her, though, was a snort of disgust coming from inside her mother's fitting room.

'Yep, as hideous as I imagined,' Joanna called out.

'Show us,' Layla replied.

'Trust me, you don't want to see this.'

'Mum, come on.'

'Don't say I didn't warn you,' Joanna quipped before throwing open the curtain. 'Ta-da!' she sang, waving her hands to announce herself as the punchline to a joke.

Maya looked up from her phone and frowned. 'What's hideous about that?'

'My hips are too wide for a dress like this, to start with.' Joanna turned back to the mirror, lingering on the way the fabric embraced her. 'And look at my arms!'

'What's wrong with your arms?' Layla asked.

'They're hardly toned, are they? No, I can't wear this,' Joanna replied, slipping into the fitting room once more. Layla and Maya exchanged a look, but neither said anything.

A few minutes later, Joanna emerged again to show her daughters the next outfit they had selected. This dress was prettily patterned and more structured, with a hemline that stopped above Joanna's knees.

'Another no,' she said with a grimace.

'What's wrong this time?' Maya asked.

'A dress like this needs to be worn by someone who doesn't have chubby legs. That's definitely not me and my thunder thighs.'

It was the so-called joke that did it.

It made Layla recall every time her mother had put herself down because she was afraid that if she didn't, others would get there first. Layla remembered it all so vividly: the diets, the starvation, the detoxes. The times Joanna skipped ice creams on hot days or said she was too busy to eat dinner, even though she had spent the last hour making it. The way Layla would catch her mother eying her reflection as if it was something she couldn't stand.

Sometimes, Layla caught herself staring at her own reflection like that.

Before Joanna could return to her fitting room, Layla spoke. 'We have the same legs, you know.'

'What?' Joanna asked, frozen midway through closing herself into the box of bad lighting and criticism.

'We have the same legs,' Layla repeated, louder this time.

'Layla, we do not! My legs are three times the size of yours,' Joanna dismissed, but before she could close the curtain on the conversation, Layla stood and opened it wider.

Joining her mother in the fitting room, Layla hitched up her own trouser leg until it reached her mid-thigh. 'See how your knees stick out? Mine do the same. Our thighs are pretty much the same size too, and our calves.'

Joanna looked at her legs, then at Layla's. 'I don't see it.'

'Come on, Mum,' Layla urged. 'Look. They're the same!'

'I . . . I suppose now you've pointed it out, our knees do look a little similar. Only your skin's much less rippled with cellulite than mine.'

'Cellulite's your issue?' Maya said, bursting into the fitting room to join them. Pulling up her skirt, she showed her thighs, paved in dimples from her knees upwards. 'Doesn't stop me wearing a skirt, though.'

'That's because you dress well. Besides, your legs are lovely. They aren't things to hide!' Joanna cried.

'Neither are yours,' Layla said. 'You always say you hate your legs, but that mine and Maya's are lovely. How can you think ours are lovely when they're the same as the ones you hate?'

The question struck Joanna across the chest. 'What?'

'It's a genuine question, Mum,' Layla replied. 'You tell me I'm perfect and beautiful, but you don't talk about yourself like that. In fact, you say the opposite, but we look the same. We have the same nose, see?' Layla moved closer, pointing to Joanna's nose. The same nose Layla had spent years wishing was smaller because she'd heard her mother say that about her own all her life. 'My hair is thin like yours too. When I gain weight, it goes to my stomach, the same as it does with you.'

'I . . . I guess we have similar traits,' Joanna stammered, flustered.

'We have more than that, Mum. We look alike. Everyone says so. I'm proud of that, but I don't know if you are. I mean, all the things you hate about yourself are things I've inherited from you.'

'Layla,' Joanna breathed. 'You're beautiful, you know that, don't you? You and Maya both are.'

Layla shook her head. 'We're not asking for compliments, Mum. We know you think we're perfect, but we also know we look like you. Every time you say something bad about yourself, you might as well be saying it to one of us.'

Joanna opened her mouth to argue, but what could she say to that? As her chin dimpled, Maya reached for her.

'We're not saying this to upset you, Mum,' she soothed.

'I know, I just . . . It's so hard. No one tells you how fast your body changes or how quickly you age. One minute you're twenty-one and dancing with friends in bars, the next you're caring for a husband who nearly died and worrying how you'll care for two children if he does.' Closing her eyes, Joanna breathed the memory away. 'For so long I was fighting to keep our family afloat, then one day I looked in the mirror and didn't recognise the person staring back at me.'

'Mum,' Layla whispered as she watched the first of many tears slide from Joanna's eyes. 'Mum, you're so beautiful.'

'But I don't feel it, Layla. I don't feel it in here.' Joanna tapped her chest to prove her point. 'I hate how I look, then I hate myself for feeling like this. I should be thinking of more important things than my appearance but I'm not. It's always, always on my mind. Everywhere I look, I'm told I'm not good enough. Not thin enough. Not pretty enough.'

'You're more than enough,' Maya cut in, grabbing Joanna's hand. 'In every way, you're more than enough.'

'Maya's right,' Layla added. 'There's so much about you to love, Mum. Don't waste your life acting like there's not.'

A waterfall of tears threatened to pour from Joanna at her daughters' words. She turned back to the mirror to hide them, but instead found herself facing her reflection with new eyes.

'You are a woman who has lived an incredible fifty-four years on this earth,' Layla said. 'You have worked, laughed, cried and loved. You single-handedly held this family together when everything fell apart, when it felt like the world would never be the same again.'

'Exactly,' Maya said. 'You're our hero, Mum. That stomach you say is too big? It grew me and Layla, gave us life, and a bloody good one at that. The arms you think are too wobbly carried us to bed a million times. The lips you think are too thin have given us so many kisses, we have enough love in us to last a lifetime. If that's not the perfect body, then what is?'

'Oh, girls,' Joanna sobbed, leaning her head on Layla's shoulder.

Together, the Cannon women looked at their collective appearance in the mirror. They saw all the ways they were different and all the ways they were the same. They saw the long line of women who had gone before them, and imagined the ones who were to come, and realised it was time for change.

It started with an apology. Nothing loud, nothing flashy, just a moment to maintain eye contact and apologise to the tired, insecure, afraid little girls that lived inside their chests. They said sorry for hiding. Sorry for becoming so small and quiet that they weren't sure they existed anymore. Sorry for softening bits of themselves because they were too much for some, only to be told they weren't enough for others. Shape-shifting, morphing, changing . . . losing parts of themselves every time.

'This is it,' Layla said, pressing a kiss to Joanna's forehead. 'We are kind to ourselves from here on out.'

'Always,' Maya agreed.

'Always,' Joanna whispered.

Always, Layla thought.

34

Angus

The contracts lay on the table in front of Angus. The language was complex. Confusing, even, but Angus knew no one was trying to trip him up. Unlike his bad investment history, this was a good choice. He was dealing with a lawyer he knew. The properties were in excellent condition. And in a few moments, they would be his.

As Angus absorbed the enormity of the occasion, his eyes drifted across the wooden table in his lawyer's office. Decades old with a dark stain, the piece was steeped in history. Angus wondered how many people had sat at it over the years. How many decisions had been made in its presence? How many conversations had happened around it?

'If you could sign here,' Morgana said, pointing to the line awaiting Angus's signature. Parallel to it was Peter's swooping cursive, sealing his decision to hand two properties to his son.

The gesture, and the trust it implied, brought a lump to Angus's throat. It had been there ever since Peter agreed to the exchange. Angus knew it wasn't a decision his father made lightly, especially with Gilly insisting it wasn't a good idea. Angus knew his parents had argued about it, but the decision had been made in Angus's favour. That could mean only one thing: Peter had faith in him.

Emboldened by his father's confidence, Angus added his signature to the page and that was it – the transaction was complete.

'Congratulations, son,' Peter said, smiling the kind of smile Angus had long dreamed of earning from him. 'The next phase of your plan begins.'

Reaching across the table, Angus went to shake his father's hand, but Peter shook his head. Before the snub could wound Angus, Peter strode around the table and hugged him. Angus blinked in surprise, then held his father tightly.

The men had hugged before, but this one felt different. When the moment ended, Angus ordered himself to remember the way pride was woven into the embrace . . . and to notice how small his father's bulk felt when in his arms.

Shifting out of the hug, Angus's eyebrows dipped as he realised that the change in Peter wasn't only in his imagination. His father did look smaller. Thinner. Sadder.

'Is everything okay?' Angus asked.

'Okay? Angus, think of what we've done today. Everything is brilliant. Come on,' Peter said, clapping Angus's shoulder and steering him away from the table. 'Walk me out.'

After thanking the lawyers, Peter and Angus stepped out of the office. They didn't stop walking until they reached the streets of Kensington.

'Do you have any plans tonight?' Peter asked as they walked side-by-side to where Peter's driver was parked further down the road.

'I'm seeing Layla soon.'

'Celebrating the news?'

Angus nodded because it was easier than admitting that Layla knew nothing of his plans for Hugo's House.

'Glad to hear it, son. Moments like this deserve to be commemorated. You'll regret it if you let them slide by unnoticed.'

As the men reached the car, the driver opened the door, but Angus wanted to tell him to close it. Peter Fairview-Whitley didn't talk of regrets. He was a man who oozed confidence, not melancholy.

Willing himself to be brave, Angus moved closer to his father. 'Is everything okay?'

'You've already asked that,' Peter replied.

'I know, but is it?'

The second between Angus's question and Peter's dismissive laugh was short, but loud. 'I'm fine, Angus,' Peter said, evacuating himself from the conversation. 'Don't worry. Keep working hard and visit your mother and me at the weekend. We'd love to hear your updates.'

Before Angus could command his father to stay and speak to him, Peter slid into the car.

In the time it took the driver to return to his seat, Angus could have opened the door. He could have demanded answers from his father, but his arms stayed fixed to his sides, too afraid to ask the questions his gut told him he must.

From the pavement, Angus watched as his father was driven away. His eyes remained on the vehicle until it turned at the end of the road. Even when it was out of sight, Angus kept staring ahead, hoping that an answer might appear through the mist.

Inside the pocket of his overcoat, Angus's phone began to vibrate.

'I'm leaving work now,' came Layla's slightly breathless voice when he answered the call. 'Michelle said to cut out an hour earlier after the last few late nights. Fancy meeting for a drink before the show?'

The casualness of her tone jarred with Angus's anxiety, so much so that the world felt like it was splitting in two before his very eyes.

'Angus?'

Layla's voice cut through his unease. 'I can meet you at The Castle again, if you'd like?' he said.

'The Castle sounds great. I can be there in half an hour, if that works for you?'

'It works for me.'

There was a pregnant pause, and then Layla asked, 'Is everything okay?'

Was everything okay? Angus had no idea. In some ways, his life was the best it had ever been. He had found a purpose and fostered relationships in a way he never had before. In others, he was drowning in lies and worries. He couldn't shake the feeling that he was sinking, and that nothing and no one could save him.

'I . . . I think there's something wrong with my father.'

It was only when Layla responded that Angus realised he'd said the words out loud.

'What do you mean?' Layla asked.

'I . . . I think he's sick.' Emotion cracked Angus's speech. 'He's changed, Layla. Every time I see him, he's thinner. He talks more openly. If you knew my dad, you would know how weird that is. I don't know what to do.'

'Where are you?' Layla replied, her tone measured.

'Kensington.'

'Send me the address.'

Dumbstruck, Angus sent the address to Layla.

'Stay where you are and stay on the line,' she said. Even in his despair, the instruction made Angus smile. Where did she think he would go? These calls were what he lived for.

For the next twenty minutes, Layla and Angus talked as she made her way to him. While Layla recapped her day and wondered out loud about the play they were to see later that evening, Angus's worries levelled out. By the time a taxi pulled up and Layla emerged from it, he had almost forgotten them completely.

'Layla,' he breathed. Angus had barely finishing saying her name before her arms were wrapped around him.

'It's okay,' she whispered. 'It's all going to be okay.'

Softening into Layla's body, Angus allowed himself to be held until the world found balance once more.

35
Layla

The Life Experiment: Daily Questionnaire
Property of OPM Discoveries

How would you rate your level of contentment today? (1 represents low contentment, 10 represents high)

1   2   3   4   5   6   7   8   (9)   10

How would you rate your energy level? (1 being very low energy and 10 being very high energy)

1   2   3   4   5   6   7   8   (9)   10

What are two things you are grateful for today?
1. Angus's cooking. He brought me a box of cookies he'd baked yesterday that were AMAZING! And, speaking candidly, talent in the kitchen is quite attractive . . .
2. Maya sending me a photo of Jayden in his school uniform. He looks so grown-up, it hurt my heart (in a good way!)

What are you struggling with today?
I'm enjoying my job so much more, but it's still a heavy workload

Do you have any additional notes on what you would like to discuss in your upcoming counselling session?
How I can support Angus. He's worried about his dad – something I know a lot about! – but I want to make sure I'm saying the right things

'Is something burning?' Angus called out from the living room.

Dropping her phone mid-reply to Michelle, Layla glanced at the risotto simmering on the hob. Or the risotto that had been simmering a moment ago, at least. Now it was sticking to the pan.

'Shit,' Layla whispered. Scurrying to the cooker, panic set in. With Rhi at work and the apartment free, she'd convinced Angus to let her cook for him, but now Layla realised what an error that was. She didn't have his culinary skills. In fact, she didn't have any culinary skills.

Grabbing a wooden spoon, Layla tried to stir the rice, but it was no use. The bottom layer had cemented to the pan.

'Is everything okay in there?'

Angus's shout made Layla grimace. She'd ordered him to stretch out on the sofa with a glass of wine when he arrived at her apartment. Her aim had been relaxation. Hilarious, given that a few more minutes of Layla ignoring the stove could have resulted in a fire.

'Everything's fine,' Layla replied, failing to disguise her stress.

Scraping the spoon harder, Layla tried to chip charred rice from the bottom of the pan. Chunks of risotto flew everywhere, splattering the kitchen tiles with dull, soggy blobs of rice.

'Are we redecorating?' came a chipper voice from the doorway.

Blushing, Layla faced Angus. 'I swear I only turned away for a second.'

'A second is all it takes,' he replied, placing his hands on Layla's hips and nudging her out of the way. His touch made her face flush, but Angus was distracted, laughing at the damaged dinner. 'For someone so intelligent it's like you've never seen a kitchen before, let alone cooked in one.'

'Well, we can't all attend cooking classes in Italy, can we?' Layla teased. She knew Angus had gone to Italy a few years ago, but she'd only learned about the cooking classes earlier that evening. Layla hadn't stopped joking about it since. Cooking retreats in Italy sounded like something the Senior Partners at work did. Incredible trips, and something Layla would love to do, but dreams like that had always seemed out of reach.

Lately, though, Layla had started wondering if that was true or if it was her self-doubt talking. After all, if two years was all she had left, why not splurge on cooking classes and bottles of wine and experiences that would make her heart sing?

Maybe you and Angus could go together, her brain suggested. Bristling, Layla ignored the thought before she became too attached to it.

'It's a good job I like my risotto crispy,' Angus said, turning off the hob. 'Do you have another pan?'

From the cupboard under the sink, Layla pulled out a pan that gleamed like new. 'Before you say this looks like it's never been used, let me remind you that takeaways are my best friend,' she said as she handed it over.

'You think I don't know that?' Angus replied, transferring the least burnt bits of risotto into the new pan. 'I'm going to introduce cooking to your skillset, Cannon, just you wait.'

Giggling, Layla rested her head on Angus's shoulder, as if it was the most natural thing in the world. She inhaled his scent. Mint body wash combined with an aftershave that smelled expensive and clean, it matched Angus perfectly.

As Layla breathed Angus in, his hand caught her wrist. She lifted her head but remained close enough to see the flecks of brown in his blue eyes. Angus's thumb rubbed gently across her skin, causing goosebumps to cover every inch of Layla's body. Her heart thrummed at the base of her throat, telling her to stop before things progressed further, all the while begging her to lean in even closer.

But as Angus dragged his gaze to Layla's parted lips, she finally came to her senses. 'Well, whatever you do, be careful,' she said, taking a step back. 'We can't ruin another pan. Not tonight, at least.'

Angus cleared his throat, blushing lightly. 'Yes, chef.'

When he offered Layla a mock salute, she sighed internally. So much for her 'just friends' rule. Layla suspected her last session with Saira was to blame for making breaking it seem like a good idea.

In Saira's office, with her heart in her mouth, Layla finally braved bringing up the possibility of lifestyle improvements changing her death date. She'd been meaning to ask the question for the last few sessions, but her nerve always buckled at the last minute. If she didn't know the answer, Layla could cling to the hope that bettering her relationship with work might mean the next two years wouldn't end in goodbye. But as soon as she asked the question and got a definitive answer? Well, there was every chance it could be game over.

'Your results showed conclusive stress-related damage,' Saira replied tactfully. 'That's not to say that with amendments things couldn't be improved, but that would require another round of testing on top of significant lifestyle changes. Some of which I know you're attempting to make.'

'But are they enough?' Layla pushed.

'I can't answer that, Layla. All I can say is that your result was accurate given the data we collated.'

'But there's a chance I could have changed things?'

The smile Saira gave Layla was laced with a sadness Layla couldn't decipher. 'Perhaps, but I can't say either way.'

Layla understood the diplomacy of Saira's response, but Layla had to believe there was hope. And standing in her kitchen, watching Angus salvage dinner, she was filled with so much hope she could float away.

Ten minutes later, Layla and Angus were sat at the dining table, eating the non-burnt bits of risotto.

'Is it okay?' Layla asked when Angus took his first bite.

'Okay? I think you mean heavenly. You did well, Cannon.'

Grinning, Layla topped up their wine. 'I'm glad you like it. I've got to say, even I'm impressed. Maybe I'll be a chef one day too.'

'I thought your future was in making the workplace better for everyone?'

'That's a bit dramatic,' Layla replied with a giggle. 'You're making me sound like a superhero.'

Angus stopped with his fork suspended inches away from his mouth. 'Wait, your name isn't Super Layla?'

Layla cocked her eyebrow. 'You think if I was a superhero, I'd be called Super Layla? That's a lame name!'

Angus did his wide, unashamedly happy grin, Layla's favourite smile of his. There was something about the way it transformed his entire face that made her heart sing. But then again, to Layla there was something special in all of Angus's smiles.

'What would your name be, then?' he asked. 'Corporate Woman? Suited Slicker?'

'Suited Slicker sounds like a villain,' she replied, chewing a mouthful of risotto. 'Yours should be a cooking-based pun. You have too many skills in the kitchen for it not to be your superpower.'

'Really? I was thinking more along the lines of being an all-round top guy. Something like Angus the Great.'

'Angus the Great is boring!' Layla cried, stifling another bout of laughter. 'Why are you so terrible at creating superhero names?'

As Angus snorted, Layla's stomach flipped. How good it felt to make someone laugh so freely, without inhibition. How good it felt to laugh like that too.

'Forget cooking, then. Maybe yours should be work-related,' Layla suggested. 'Hit me with a techy nickname all the IT guys will love.'

Something about her comment froze Angus's smile. Not for the first time, Layla wondered if Angus didn't like his job. He wouldn't be the only person to feel that way, and definitely not the only person who worked in IT.

Maybe that's why he doesn't talk about work much, Layla thought. She wanted him to. She wanted to know who he sat next to, what happened in his meetings and what problems he'd solved that day, but Angus never seemed to share that side of himself.

Layla opened her mouth to ask if disliking his job was the reason for Angus's quietness, but then he beamed. 'Modem Man,' he said. 'That would be my superhero name. After all, who doesn't love alliteration?'

'Modem Man sounds like he would have useless powers.'

'Oh, he would be a very boring, very useless superhero. Not on posters in anyone's bedroom, that's for sure. You, on the other hand, would be on a poster in mine.'

'Did you mean for that to sound creepy?' Layla teased, trying to hide her delighted blush as best she could. 'Anyway, stop being so nice to me. I'm only trying to improve conditions at Mayweather & Halliwell. It's hardly changing the world,' she dismissed, but Angus shook his head.

'Don't diminish what you're doing, Layla. It's important. No one can change the entire world, but we can make our corner of it better. Not many people try to do that, but you are. It's impressive.'

Layla chewed her dinner while mulling over Angus's response. 'I've never thought of it like that before.'

'Well, maybe think about it like that from now on. Be proud of yourself. I know I'm proud of you.'

Layla beamed. She couldn't help it. Sure, having a man compliment her looks was nice, but compliments about her brain? Her drive? Well, they meant the world. They meant that Angus really, truly saw her.

The truth was, Layla *was* proud of herself. More than that, she was finally finding work interesting. Michelle had taken Layla under her wing, and Layla could feel herself thriving there. She was learning how to be a better lawyer and leader. She was growing and evolving. Understanding when to ask questions, when to listen, and when to use her voice.

Things with the project were going well too. Layla and Michelle had consulted with staff across Mayweather & Halliwell about their work–life balance and the changes they wanted to see. That morning, they had booked their first meeting with the Senior Partners to discuss the feedback and their ideas.

'Change is coming, Layla. I can feel it,' Michelle said as they pressed send on the invite. Layla knew exactly what Michelle meant. She felt it every morning when she woke up. Getting out of bed had never been easier. Even commuting was less hellish.

'I wish I was more like you, you know,' Angus said after taking a sip of wine. 'You're amazing. You don't wallow or wait or talk yourself out of things. You know your worth. You're ambitious.'

Instinct made Layla wince. Life had been cruel in teaching her the lesson that being labelled 'ambitious' was usually anything but a compliment. Years of working in a corporate field had shown Layla that she could work hard and aim high, yes, but be seen as ambitious? Absolutely not. When describing her male colleagues, the word connoted drive and passion. When describing her, it was an insult. An ambitious woman was ruthless and single-minded. She was hard. Unlikable. Difficult.

And there Angus was, putting that label on her. As if reading her mind, he cocked his head. 'You don't like being called ambitious?'

'Not really,' Layla admitted. 'I know it's what I am, but I don't love the way it's been used to describe me. It's never been said with the most positive intention.'

'Well,' Angus began, his fingers brushing the stem of his wineglass and throwing Layla's thoughts to his hand on her wrist in the kitchen. 'When *I* call you ambitious, I mean it as the highest compliment. I mean it to describe a hard-working, determined and intelligent person. Someone I want to know inside and out.'

'You want to know me inside and out?' Layla replied, doing her best to ignore the thumping of her heart in her ears.

Across the table, Angus held her gaze. 'Absolutely.'

At that confession, something in Layla's gut kicked. *Tell him*, it screamed. *Tell him you'll die in two years!*

The idea of waiting until the end of the experiment to tell anyone, especially Angus, seemed impossible. Worse than that, it seemed wrong. Every moment they spent together felt precarious, like it was teetering on a tower of lies.

Layla looked across the table at Angus. 'I . . .' she began.

I'm dying.

I'm falling for you.

I'm dying.

I'm falling for you.

Both things were true. Both needed to be said. But dread tightened Layla's throat. As Angus's gaze flooded with desire, Layla made her choice. 'I'll get more wine,' she said before rushing from the table.

In the kitchen, Layla leaned her forehead against the fridge and closed her eyes. She tried to tell herself she hadn't said anything about her impending death because telling Angus meant opening herself up to a potential lawsuit, but Layla knew the real reason for her silence. Telling Angus meant losing him. And as ambitious and brave as she was, that was something Layla couldn't risk.

36

Angus

Potential logos for Hugo's House were spread across Angus's dining table, but he couldn't decide which one felt right. There was something slightly off about each design. A line that didn't sit right or an illustration that appeared too cartoonish.

Or maybe the fear of choosing the wrong one is getting to you, Angus's brain chimed. The voice in his head sounded a lot like Saira's. Angus smiled at the fact that she was cutting through his bullshit, even in his imagination.

That didn't stop the bullshit from being there, though. Sighing, he rubbed his temples and waited for one image to stand out as the right one. It never did. Even when Angus got a drink of water and returned to the table with fresh eyes, there was no obvious choice.

The temptation to snap a photo of the mock-ups and send it to Layla for her opinion was strong. *Maybe this is the point you tell her,* Angus's brain suggested. *Stop with the lies.*

The thought was more tempting than ever. The little white lies Angus could once justify were not so little anymore, and Layla didn't deserve deception of any kind. What started as a way of hiding his shame had become the most shameful thing Angus had ever done.

Studying the designs once more, Angus made a vow. The next time he saw Layla, he would tell her about Hugo's House. From there, he would tell her the rest. If he explained, maybe she would understand. Maybe they could have the future that Angus couldn't stop picturing.

For now, though, all Angus could do was focus on the task at hand. Reaching for his phone, Angus fired off a text to his father: *Which of these logos do you like best?*

Sitting back in his chair, Angus picked up one of the printed graphics and studied it closely. While it didn't feel quite the right fit for the charity – Was it the colours? The way the font filled the entire outline of a house? – there was something about it that made him pause.

Angus had come up with the idea for Hugo's House. He had found an opportunity and chased it. The vision in his head was coming to fruition. Builders would start constructing self-contained units in the properties as soon as planning permission was granted.

Hugo's House was coming to life, yet Angus had no one to share the good news with.

Checking his phone once more, Angus was dismayed to see no response from his father. With a sigh, he left the table and poured himself a whisky. A solo celebration, of sorts. It felt as lonely as it sounded.

Taking the first sip of his drink, Angus trailed through his penthouse. At the window, he stopped and watched a blanket of darkness unroll over London until he heard his phone ring. Gulping the rest of his whisky, Angus headed back to the dining table. A smile took over his features when he saw Peter's name on the screen.

'What did you think of them?' Angus asked when he answered the call, but he was met with a thick silence.

'Angus.'

There was something in the way Peter said his name that made Angus feel sick. Gripping the back of a chair to steady himself, Angus willed himself to speak. 'What's going on? What's wrong?'

'Angus, it's your mother.' Peter's words sent a white-hot poker of fear through Angus's chest. 'She's not well, Angus. She hasn't been for a while.'

Angus heard the words, but they wouldn't compute. His grip on the chair tightened, white-knuckling the fabric like it was the only thing keeping him tethered to the ground.

'You need to come to the hospital,' Peter said.

Instinctively, Angus shook his head. Gilly was fine. Gilly was always fine. She was Gilly Fairview-Whitley, for crying out loud. She was strong, invincible . . . Wasn't she?

On the other end of the phone, Peter steadied his breathing. 'Cromwell Hospital, ward—'

'Stop,' Angus cried. 'What do you mean, Cromwell Hospital? What's going on?'

'Angus, your mother has cancer. She's been undergoing treatment for the last few months. She asked me to keep it between the two of us, but she's caught an infection. It's not looking good, son. You need to be here.'

Angus was aware of Peter giving directions to Gilly's ward. He knew he should be noting the instructions, but all Angus could focus on was the blood rushing to his head as he processed the news.

Gilly had cancer.

She had cancer, and Angus didn't know.

'You didn't tell me?' he heard himself whisper.

Peter paused before responding. 'Your mother didn't want to worry you.'

'Didn't want to worry me, but waiting until she's in hospital with an infection to tell me this news is okay?' Angus knew he was being petty. The hows and the whys didn't matter right now, but still, he couldn't stop himself from clinging to them.

'Your mother wanted to deal with this in her way,' Peter replied, wearily. 'My role wasn't to tell her how to do that, but to support her. Which is exactly what you should be doing now.'

'Now you want my support? Not in any of the months before, just when Mother is in hospital?'

'Angus—'

'No, I'm serious! You wanted to have me over for dinner and pretend everything was fine and—'

'Do you want to know why we didn't tell you, Angus?' Peter cut in furiously. 'Fine, I'll tell you why. Your mother wanted to keep this to herself because she didn't think you could handle the truth.'

For the second time in a matter of moments, Peter's words punched Angus in the gut. 'What?'

'That's right, you heard me. Your mother didn't think you had the maturity to deal with this news in a helpful way. And judging by your reaction tonight, it was the right choice to make! I do not care if you are upset that you were not told sooner. I do not care if you are angry. All I care about is your mother. You will come to the hospital and you will hold her hand and you will be there for her.'

When his father hung up on him, Angus stood staring blankly at the dining table in front of him. The desire to shy away from the moment called to him, telling him that seeing Gilly would be hard. That it would hurt, and that a night out with Jasper was only a phone call away.

But as Angus grabbed his coat, he knew there was only one place he would go.

Rushing from his penthouse, Angus jumped in his car and raced through a congested London. He drove erratically, weaving in and out of traffic. When Angus arrived at the hospital, he paced at the reception desk, willing himself to be patient as the elderly lady ahead of him spoke with the receptionist about the weather.

Eventually, when it was his turn to be seen, Angus said his mother's name so quickly he had to repeat it twice for the receptionist to understand him.

'Fairview-Whitley, let me see . . .' she said as she typed. As soon as she said the room number, Angus was off, rushing to the stairs and striding to the ward. He only slowed when he reached Gilly's room.

When she came into view through the glass door, Angus froze. Asleep, exhausted, and with skin greyer than he'd ever seen, Gilly looked . . . ill. Angus's body iced over. He'd never seen his mother look so vulnerable, not even after Hugo's death.

Spotting him on the other side of the door, Peter stood and opened it. 'Angus,' he said.

Numbly, Angus entered the room, his gaze fixed on his mother. 'It's bad, isn't it?' he whispered.

For once, Peter didn't hide the truth. 'Yes, Angus, it is.'

Reaching for his father, Angus crumpled.

37

Layla

Layla knew from listening to true crime podcasts that a late-night visitor was never a good thing – especially during a storm. As rain lashed the windows and wind howled deafeningly, the buzz of Layla's intercom made her clutch the book she was reading to her chest. When the intercom rang for a second time, Layla shook the fear away. *You live on the fourth floor, relax,* she reassured herself as she stood to answer the call.

'Hello?' she said into the intercom.

'Layla? Can I come up? I need you.'

Layla didn't need to ask who it was, or what was going on. The tremor in Angus's voice was enough for her to buzz him into the building without another word. Stuffing a pair of trainers onto her feet, Layla left her apartment to reach Angus quicker. She rushed to the lift, watching the numbers climb.

Then, when the doors opened, Layla simply opened her arms.

Angus's body sagged into hers. The sudden weight nearly knocked Layla off her feet, but she planted herself firmly and held him like it was the last hug they would ever share.

'Are you okay?' Layla whispered, but when Angus's response was an unsteady breath, she realised it wasn't the time for questions. 'Come on,' she said, weaving her arm around his waist. 'Come with me.'

Layla led Angus to her apartment. The cosy nights they had shared there flashed before her eyes, but Layla knew tonight wasn't going to involve jokes over wine or teasing her lack of culinary skills.

Before Angus collapsed with distress, Layla peeled the damp coat from his shoulders. 'Sit,' she instructed, taking the coat and resting it over that back of a dining chair.

Stemming her worry as best she could, Layla joined Angus and laced her fingers through his. When she felt how cold he was, she gasped. Using her other hand, Layla brushed her fingers over Angus's skin, willing it to warm.

Slowly, Layla dragged her eyes to Angus's face, gulping at what she saw. His skin was pale. His eyes were vacant. Damp hair feathered over his forehead, drops of rain dripping from the tips. Layla's fingers itched to brush them away, but that would mean letting go of his hand, something Layla couldn't bring herself to do.

'Do you need a drink?' she asked.

'I'm not sure getting drunk is a good idea,' Angus replied hoarsely.

'I meant water.'

'Water's not strong enough.'

Something in Angus's voice scared Layla. Inching closer, she squeezed his hand.

'What is it, Angus?' Layla pressed. 'What's happened?'

For the longest time, Angus could only stare at their intertwined fingers, but then he spoke. 'My mother has cancer.'

Shock overcame Layla. Her mouth twitched to find words, but no sound came out.

'Gilly . . . She's in hospital with an infection,' Angus continued. 'I've just been to see her. Sat there for over two hours, and not once did she wake up. She's on so many meds, they've knocked her out. She . . . she looked so small, Layla. My mother's never looked small before.'

As emotion splintered Angus's voice, Layla went to speak, but he cut her off.

'She's had ovarian cancer for the last few months. Stage two. She's been secretly getting treatment and didn't want me to know. She didn't think I could handle it, apparently.'

'Oh, Angus,' Layla breathed, but her distress only lit an angry fire within him.

'What kind of person, what kind of mother, discovers news this big and keeps it from her child?' Angus sounded angry, but his jagged breathing betrayed the pain he felt.

'I'm sure she had her reasons,' Layla soothed, but Angus shook his head.

'I'm her son, Layla. Her *son*. I deserve to know if she's sick. I deserve the chance to be there for her. That's all I'd have wanted to do, you know. I'd have gone to appointments. I'd have taken her food. I'd have . . . I'd have . . .'

As the enormity of all the things he was trying to say crushed Angus, he bowed his head and pulled away. The move was gut-wrenching. Layla watched Angus rest his elbows on his knees and clasp his hands together. The rigidity of his stance appeared impossible to break, but Layla couldn't let him shut off without a fight. Moving forward, she reached for Angus's hand once more. Gratefully, he accepted it.

'I know this can't be easy for her, but she's my mother,' he croaked, tightening his hold on Layla's hand while he spoke. 'How could she not tell me? Her not trusting me hurts almost as much as knowing what's going on.'

'I'm sure it's nothing to do with how much she trusts you,' Layla began, but Angus shook his head.

'It's exactly that. A person doesn't find out something like this and not tell their loved ones. What, was she just going to die one day and expect me to be okay with it? Was I meant to accept the fact that she'd known it was coming all along, but kept it from me?'

One of Angus's tears splashed the side of Layla's hand, making her flinch. As it trailed down her skin, guilt trickled down Layla's spine.

Gilly wasn't the only one keeping shattering secrets from Angus – Layla was doing the same thing. Her death date was another secret, another lie. The shame of what she'd withheld winded Layla so brutally she had to look away from Angus.

'Clearly I'm not the son she wants by her side through this,' Angus continued. 'She probably wishes I'd died, not Hugo.'

'Angus,' Layla gasped. 'Don't say that! Your mother loves you.'

'You don't keep a secret like this from someone you love. That's not what love is.'

'Angus, love is lots of things,' Layla protested, but Angus shook his head.

'No, Layla. I know what love is. I know it from . . .' As Angus trailed off, his eyes locked on Layla. Her heart leapt into her throat. She waited for him to finish his sentence, but Layla didn't need to hear the words. She could see it in his eyes. It was all there, laid out bare for her: fear, sadness and desire.

So much desire.

Angus leant in further, leaning his forehead against Layla's and breathing deeply. Sense told her to pull away, but Layla found she couldn't. Here, she could almost feel Angus's mouth on hers. Almost taste him. Everything she wanted was right in front of her.

There was no point denying it. There had been no point in denying it for a long time: love was what Layla felt for Angus. Love was all she would ever feel for Angus.

The tilt of his head professed Angus's intentions before he moved. His breathing slowed as he leaned in, waiting for Layla to meet him halfway. Caught in the trance of the moment, Layla moved closer. *Just one kiss*, her body begged. *One taste* . . . but Layla couldn't give in. Not like this.

Drawing back, Layla untangled herself from Angus. 'I don't think that's a good idea,' she whispered. 'You're upset. You're—'

'Of course,' Angus said, stiffening. 'I'm sorry, I didn't mean to cross a line. I know friends is all you want us to be. I'm sorry.'

'It's okay,' Layla replied, resting her hand on Angus's arm even though touching him cracked her heart. 'Really, it's okay.'

But no matter what Layla said, she knew nothing about the situation was okay. Thanks to her death date, it never would be.

38

Angus

The Life Experiment: Daily Questionnaire
Property of OPM Discoveries

How would you rate your level of contentment today? (1 represents low contentment, 10 represents high)

1   2   3   (4)   5   6   7   8   9   10

How would you rate your energy level? (1 being very low energy and 10 being very high energy)

1   2   3   4   5   (6)   7   8   9   10

What are two things you are grateful for today?
1. Layla making a shit time less shit
2. The distraction of Hugo's House

What are you struggling with today?
My mother not telling me about her cancer. I knew we weren't close, but this is a whole new level of dismissal

Do you have any additional notes on what you would like to discuss in your upcoming counselling session?

Hugo again. I hadn't realised how much his death still impacts me, but now I've scratched the surface, I keep being reminded of it. I don't know how to process it all

---

The bouquet filled Angus's arms. The flowers hadn't smelled quite so pungent in the florist, but in the confined lift of the hospital, their scent clogged the air. They were an over-the-top gesture, Angus thought as he saw his reflection in the lift's mirrored door, but he hadn't known what else to do when he'd heard the news.

After two days of constant worry and bedside vigils, Angus finally received the news that Gilly's fever had broken. She was awake and lucid. The moment felt like it needed marking, but what to buy someone who was in hospital? Flowers felt more appropriate than something like grapes, Angus had surmised when he ventured out for a gift. Now, though, walking through the white-washed walls of the hospital, the choice seemed foolish. Flowers might look beautiful, but in a few days they would wilt and rot, a reminder of the imminent presence of death.

Gilly might have won this battle, but she hadn't won the war. Far from it.

Angus had spent the last few days googling ovarian cancer. He'd read about treatments and prognoses and survival rates. He'd petrified himself, then calmed himself, then petrified himself all over again.

In that time, Peter finally told Angus the hidden truths of the last few months. Angus learned that Gilly had undergone surgery to remove her ovaries and fallopian tubes earlier in the year. Disguised as a two-week health retreat, the surgery had been a success.

Then the chemotherapy began. Gilly was partway through treatment, but it was taxing. Her body was weak. She was tired.

The revelation cast Gilly's protests about Hugo's House in a new light. She had wanted to shield herself from more talk of death, hospitals and pain. Understandable, really. But no one had trusted Angus enough to tell him.

Clutching the flowers tighter, Angus made his way to his mother's room. Well-designed and exclusively for Gilly, it was as comfortable as people might expect from a private hospital. But even with its calming décor, there was no denying that it was still a hospital.

Through the glass door, Angus studied Gilly. She lay in bed, looking out of the window. She looked sick. So sick that the temptation to run beckoned Angus, but Gilly must have sensed his presence. Turning, she raised an eyebrow. Angus entered the room before she could see the trepidation in his eyes.

'You seem better today,' he commented as he moved towards the bed.

'That's because I am better,' Gilly said, sitting up with a struggle.

'I brought these for you,' he said, thrusting the flowers forward.

'Of course you did. They were hardly for the nurses, were they?'

Tension twanged in the air. Angus didn't know if the comment was a joke or a barb. It was hard to tell when Gilly's sarcasm often verged on insulting. And now the secret of her illness had been outed without her consent, Gilly was more prickly than usual.

Resting the flowers on the bedside table, Angus took a seat beside Gilly's bed.

'Aren't you going to decant them into water?' she asked, nodding at the flowers. 'There's a jug over there you can use.'

'Would you like me to?'

'I would like you to do whatever you feel you need to, Angus.'

A flare twitched at Angus's nostrils. He didn't understand it. How could Gilly be so cold and obstinate, even in this moment? He was there, wasn't he? He was there even when she had tried to make it so he couldn't be.

Anger pushed Angus to reach for the flowers. The fury in his movements made Gilly smile. 'There, I knew we'd get emotion out of you somehow,' she said.

Angus's bones locked. 'What?'

'You're as taught as a drum, Angus. Let it out. You're clearly angry with me.'

'I have every right to be,' Angus retorted.

'That's one way of looking at things,' Gilly said, but as she performed her usual dismissive sniff, something inside Angus cracked.

'You're not serious, are you? You don't think I have a right to be upset in all of this?'

'I think you have a right to feel however you want, Angus, but I also have a right to feel how I feel. Do you think I want everyone knowing that I sleep in a cold cap to try to stop my hair from falling out? That I can't keep food down? That I'm terribly sick? I don't need to hear people say how sorry they are, then go home and have a good old gossip behind my back.'

Angus shook his head in disbelief. 'But I'm not "people", Mother. I'm your son!'

'Yes, my son who should be throwing all his effort into his new venture, not sat by a hospital bed talking about the weather.'

Angus's eyes locked on Gilly's. 'That's it, isn't it? That's the real issue. You don't want me here.'

'Angus, don't be absurd. I want you to be wherever you want to be.'

It took everything in Angus not to scream. 'There is nothing absurd about it! It's the truth. It's always been the truth. You've never wanted me around, ever! You sent me away to boarding school as soon as you could.'

'As soon as I could? Angus, you were eleven!'

'An eleven-year-old who had just lost his brother! Then a few weeks later, he lost his home and his family.' Fire flashed in Gilly's eyes, but Angus was angry too. 'What, when Hugo died, did you want to check out of being a parent altogether? Was leaving me at boarding school easier than admitting that I was the son you didn't want?'

'It was for the best.' Gilly spoke through gritted teeth, but her reaction only made Angus scoff.

'Sure, because every grieving child wants to be shuttled off to a strange place miles away from home.'

'It was for your own good!' Gilly shrieked. The pain in her voice hit Angus like a slap. He backed away from the raw emotion, but Gilly held Angus in her gaze. 'Do you think I wanted the one child I had left to be removed from my care? No, not at all, but you deserved better than a mother who couldn't get out of bed. You were only a child back then, Angus. You won't remember what it was like, but I do. After we lost Hugo, I couldn't even get dressed. I couldn't eat. I lost so much weight I was hospitalised, did you know that?'

Swallowing hard, Angus shook his head.

'I didn't want you to see me like that. I couldn't be the mother you deserved, never mind the one you wanted. So, I did what any mother would do – I protected you. I sent you away and shielded you from the worst of it because I loved you.' Raising her bony hand to her chest, Gilly beat it against her heart as she spoke. 'I. Love. You. Angus.'

With the thud of her words ringing in his ears, Angus's shoulders caved, but Gilly shook her head.

'Don't you dare fold in on yourself. Don't you dare shy away from what I am saying. I love you, Angus. My God, I love every hair on your head. I love you in all the times you mess up and all the times you struggle to like yourself. I know I don't show it in the way you expect. Trust me, I am well aware of my shortcomings, but guess what? Love doesn't always look like it does in films. It isn't running through airports to stop a plane, but make no mistake, Angus – I love you. Always have. Always will.'

As Gilly's breath hitched, Angus reached for her hand. 'Stop. It's okay. I'm sorry I shouted,' he tried to protest, but Gilly shook her head.

'No, Angus, clearly you need to hear this. Love isn't just the big things, it's the little things too. It's listening to your son say he wanted a bike and visiting every bike shop south of the Thames to find the right one. It's sending him chicken soup to eat when he's ill, even though he's a fully grown adult. Your whole life, I've listened to every whim, every flight of fancy, every dream you ever had. You may not realise it, but I've moved mountains to make you happy, and I will continue to for as long as I can. That is love, Angus.'

Leaning his head against his mother's hands, Angus fought to steady himself. 'I love you too,' he croaked. 'I'm sorry I don't always show it.'

'For goodness' sake, Angus, we're Fairview-Whitleys,' Gilly said, sniffing once more. 'We don't give into ridiculous displays of affection.'

Choking on a laugh, Angus gripped his mother's hand tightly. To his surprise, she held his just as tight.

39

Layla

Guilt ate at Layla as a vision of Angus's grief-stricken, tear-soaked face flashed in her mind. Gripping tighter onto Saira's plump sofa cushion, she willed the image to disappear, but it lingered.

'Start from the beginning,' Saira instructed.

Layla nodded, but the problem was, she didn't know when things had begun. Was it finding out about Gilly's sickness, or when she first made the choice to have Angus in her life? A choice that had always felt selfish but seemed worse in light of Gilly's cancer.

'It doesn't matter where the start is,' Layla rasped. 'I can't add to his pain, Saira. I can't be another person who lies to Angus, knowing one day I am going to leave him.'

'Everyone ultimately leaves, Layla. It's a fact of life,' Saira said, but the statement made Layla close her eyes. Of course Layla knew that people left those they loved eventually. Divorce lawyers and funeral directors would be out of business if that wasn't the case. But there was a big difference between knowing life would end eventually, and knowing specifically when it would happen. If Layla knew when her end was, was it fair to make a beginning with someone who didn't?

'Our friendship is false,' Layla said. 'It has been from the start. Angus met me and saw someone he liked. I know he hopes for more. I know he feels the same spark I do. The problem is, he doesn't know about my death date. I do. I know that every moment we spend together brings us one step closer to the end, but I've been seeing him anyway. I'm choosing my happiness over his heartbreak.'

'Layla,' Saira interjected, but Layla shook her head.

'You can't make me feel better about this, Saira. I know it's your job to show me different perspectives, but there isn't much to unpick here. It's simple – I like Angus. No, scratch that – I love him. All I want is to be around him. So, that's what I did, because I didn't want to die not knowing what it felt like to be by his side. But how is that fair to him? Is this really the way to treat someone you love?'

Tears fell thick and fast as Layla ducked her head. They landed on the patterned skirt she was wearing, bleeding into the material. Layla's hands trembled as she remembered Angus spotting it when they were out last week.

'That would look great on you,' he said as they passed a boutique window.

Layla laughed at the idea of wearing such bold colours, but her eyes stayed on the skirt. 'It is pretty,' she agreed. For a second, Layla imagined herself wearing it out with Angus.

That second was all Angus needed. 'Come on,' he said, putting his arm around her and steering her into the store. 'Let's see if I'm right.'

Layla didn't protest. Mostly because the skirt was divine, but also because Angus's touch rendered her unable to breathe, never mind speak.

'Layla, I know this is hard,' Saira said as Layla peeled her gaze away from her tear-stained skirt. 'Gilly's diagnosis was a shock, but that doesn't mean you have to walk away from Angus. Why not see what happens between the two of you?'

'I can't do that. It's cruel.'

'Cruel would be cutting something magical short because of fear.'

'It's not fear – it's practicality. No,' Layla said, shaking her head. 'I can't do it, Saira. I can't hurt Angus. You didn't see how upset he was when he told me about Gilly.'

'But surely that's an indicator that Angus needs you in his life now more than ever.'

'He does, but if I help Angus through this, we'll grow closer. I'll become someone he leans on. Relies on.'

'Is that such a bad thing?'

It took everything in Layla not to scoff. 'Do you really need to ask that?'

'It's my job to ask questions, Layla. Especially when someone's actions don't reflect their desires. If you want Angus in your life, why are you making the decision to walk away from him?'

'Because I won't be here in two years' time!' The hideous words burst from Layla in a screech.

Saira watched with an expression that mirrored the heartbreak Layla felt. 'Layla,' she said, but her soft tone made Layla rigid.

'This is the right thing to do, Saira. For me, for Angus, for everyone. Please don't try to convince me otherwise.'

Pursing her lips, Saira leaned forward. 'I'm not so sure. Perhaps we should talk—'

'No,' Layla interrupted. 'All we ever do is talk, but talking doesn't fix this. There's nothing for me to do but walk away. Angus doesn't need someone else he cares about lying to his face. He needs to focus on his mother.'

With that, Layla rose to her feet.

'What are you doing?' Saira asked, confused.

'I need to go,' Layla replied, reaching for her coat. 'I need to do this before I talk myself out of it.'

'Layla, we have more than half the session to go,' Saira said, but Layla headed for the door without another word. 'Layla! *Layla!*'

Saira's cries followed Layla down the corridor. Her concern was touching, but it wasn't enough to shake Layla's conviction that she was doing the right thing. Layla was tired of lying. She was tired of running from her death date. But most of all, she was tired of waking up every day knowing that she was going to devastate the man she loved.

40

Angus

Seeing Layla was always the highlight of Angus's day, and after a tough visit with Gilly he sorely needed the comfort of her presence. Despite showing signs of improvement over the last few days, Gilly's health seemed to have dipped again. She was weak, with beads of sweat pinpricking her skin as she shivered. Not for the first time since learning of her diagnosis, Angus looked at his mother and thought, *She might not get through this.*

Shaking off the devastating thought, Angus headed to Regent's Park and focused on the evening ahead. With everything that had happened recently, telling Layla the truth had slipped by the wayside. Stopping to let a jogger pass, Angus tried to reason with himself that he wasn't in the wrong for that. He still planned on admitting to the bits of himself he had hidden. One day. Soon. He just needed things to settle first. Right now, Angus couldn't risk losing Layla. Not when her presence was the only thing that soothed him.

But the second Angus saw Layla, all thoughts of a comforting evening evaporated.

Something was wrong, he could tell. Layla was too serious. Too rigid. Angus's legs sped up to reach her quicker. 'Is everything okay?' he asked. 'Has something happened?'

The half-smile Layla gave him might have been the saddest smile Angus had ever seen. 'Walk with me?' she said, holding out her arm for him.

'Always,' Angus replied.

With their arms linked, the pair entered the park. Wind whipped around them, bristling Angus's already fraught nerves. Willing himself to be brave, Angus searched for the words to ask Layla what was on her mind.

But Angus never had the chance to speak because to his left, someone called his name, throwing his world into chaos.

'I thought it was you,' came Clarissa's eager shout from several metres away.

Layla leaned to look at the woman bounding over in expensive gym gear. Clarissa's eyebrows dipped as she spotted Layla's arm intertwined with Angus's.

'Oh,' she said, her expression falling flat.

'Oh?' Layla said, looking from Clarissa to Angus. 'Who is this?'

Angus panicked. 'This . . . this is Clarissa.'

Layla paused, seemingly trying to place the name. 'From work?'

As Angus cringed, Clarissa barked a laugh. 'Clarissa from work? Is that really who you tell women I am?'

Sickened by dread, Angus braved a look at Layla. As soon as he registered the hurt in her eyes, he wished he hadn't. 'Layla, it's not what you think—'

'Is Clarissa your colleague or not?' she snapped.

Angus opened his mouth to reply, but Clarissa got there first.

'Yes, Angus, am I your colleague? I'd love to know what job we supposedly do together.' With that, Clarissa faced Layla. 'Angus is a Fairview-Whitley. He doesn't work. He doesn't need to. His family could buy this park and the buildings surrounding it ten times over.'

Angus heard Layla's sharp intake of breath as she removed her arm from his. 'Layla, I can explain,' he croaked.

'Which part – lying about your career, or how you apparently have a girlfriend?'

'Clarissa's not my girlfriend. We used to hook-up, but we haven't in months! Not since way before I met you,' Angus protested, but from the way both women reacted, it was clearly the wrong thing to say.

'A hook-up? Good to know that's all I am to you,' Clarissa retorted.

'I didn't mean it like that,' Angus said, looking from Layla to Clarissa and back again. 'I just . . . fuck, Layla, this is not how I wanted you to find out any of this.'

'Any of what, Angus? Exactly what have you lied about?' Layla asked.

'Everything, by the looks of things,' Clarissa replied on his behalf.

Angus wanted to tell Clarissa to stop, but he knew his anger was misplaced. He wasn't furious with her – he was furious with himself.

Angus had always known he would have to come clean at some point. It wasn't like he could get away with the ruse forever. He didn't want to, either. He wanted the world with Layla, including dinners with his parents and overnight stays at his penthouse. He'd always wanted to tell Layla the truth. He just wanted to do it once he wasn't full of self-loathing.

'Maybe we should find somewhere private to talk,' Angus suggested, but Layla's eyes narrowed.

'I don't want to go somewhere private. I want to know the truth. So what, are you an investment banker? A crypto-genius? A trust-fund baby?' When Angus couldn't reply, Layla exhaled through her nose. 'Come on, Angus. Tell me who you are.'

'I . . . I'm Angus Fairview-Whitley.'

'And?' Layla demanded.

Gulping hard, Angus unravelled. 'My family have money, Layla. Lots of it. We're descended from nobility. I grew up on a country estate in Buckinghamshire.'

Stumbling as if she'd been shoved, Layla gripped her stomach. 'Are you joking?' she asked, but Angus's sombre expression answered her question. 'Why wouldn't you tell me that, Angus?' Angus's silence only served to infuriate Layla further. 'Was I not good enough? Is it because my family isn't wealthy? Are you embarrassed by me?'

'It was nothing like that!'

'Then why lie?'

Seeing the hurt in Layla's eyes, something inside Angus shattered. 'I never wanted to lie to you. It just . . . happened.'

'Lies on this scale don't just happen, Angus. Every moment we spent together, you were editing who you were. There's nothing accidental about that.'

'I didn't lie about everything, I promise,' Angus protested.

'Just most things,' Clarissa chipped in.

'It's not all lies, I swear!' Angus argued. 'Everything I told you is based on the truth. I'm still me. I'm still Angus who likes to cook, and who knows you enjoy having two chocolate digestives and a cup of tea when you read.' Angus prayed the personal detail would make Layla soften, but her expression made it clear she didn't believe him. 'Layla, this had nothing to do with you and everything to do with me,' he continued. 'I wanted to be worthy of you. I wanted to be someone who did something with his life, who worked hard, who achieved things. I was lost before we met. I didn't know who I was or what I wanted, but I do now. I want you, Layla. *I want you.*'

Angus moved towards Layla, but she stepped away and wrapped her arms around herself. 'You lied to me, Angus.'

'I didn't mean to!' Angus cried, which only made Clarissa snort.

Angus thought he'd feel no greater shame than admitting to his lies, but watching Layla shrink back from Clarissa's derision crucified him. The agony doubled when she looked at Angus through large, tear-filled eyes. Layla's pain was there in plain sight, but beneath it was a firm resolve that terrified him.

'I should be thanking you,' Layla said, sniffing back her distress. 'You've just saved me from wasting more of my time on a person who isn't worth a second of it.'

'I'm so, *so* sorry,' Angus said, stepping closer. 'What can I do? I'll do whatever it takes. Please, Layla. You're everything to me. I can't lose you.'

Layla looked away, shaking her head. 'I don't think I can see you again.'

'Layla, *please*. None of this was a reflection on you, it was about me! About how I saw myself, about how I hated—'

'Do you hear yourself?' Layla cried. 'I, I, I . . . that's all you can see, but I've just found out the last few weeks of my life were a lie! Do you have any idea how that feels?' The look Layla fired at Angus sliced him in two. 'You need to grow up, Angus, and I need to put myself first. That starts right here, right now.'

'*Layla*—' Angus didn't know what he could say to keep her here, but it was too late. She was already striding away, back towards the park's entrance.

Stumbling after her, Angus opened his mouth to call her name, but Clarissa clutched his arm.

'I wouldn't bother,' she said. 'She's done. Can you blame her?'

Turning to Clarissa, Angus saw himself reflected in her eyes. A coward. He was everything he hated, personified, and there was no one to blame but himself.

41

Layla

The Life Experiment: Daily Questionnaire
Property of OPM Discoveries

How would you rate your level of contentment today? (1 represents low contentment, 10 represents high)

1 (2) 3 4 5 6 7 8 9 10

How would you rate your energy level? (1 being very low energy and 10 being very high energy)

1 2 (3) 4 5 6 7 8 9 10

What are two things you are grateful for today?
1. How busy my job keeps me
2. I don't know. Chocolate muffins? Or maybe finding out Angus was a liar before I got in too deep. Let's stick with the muffins

What are you struggling with today?
Everything, I guess. Everything is difficult

Do you have any additional notes on what you would like to discuss in your upcoming counselling session?
Why I am such a gullible, clueless idiot

Nerves rattled through Layla as she inspected her appearance in the bathroom mirror. With beads of sweat tracing her brow, Layla dreaded to think what her heart rate was. Saira would probably see her data and panic.

While Layla wouldn't say she felt awful, she didn't feel good either. Public speaking always made her underarms prickle with sweat. Usually, she could feign confidence and push through the moment, but Layla had never presented to the entire board of Senior Partners at Mayweather & Halliwell.

'All you can do is your best, kiddo,' David had said when Layla called him last night.

'What if my best isn't good enough?'

'Well, it's always good enough for me and your mum.'

Layla had to fight an eye-roll at the unhelpful sentiment. 'That's sweet, but you're not the ones who pay my wages.'

'So what? What do those stuck-up lawyers know, anyway?'

Despite herself, Layla laughed. 'They know a lot.'

'Not as much as my little girl. I always say you have the brain of ten men. Go prove it.'

After hanging up, Layla felt she could do exactly that, but now that the presentation was ahead of her, she wasn't so sure. Her confidence in the yellow suit Maya convinced her to wear was wavering too, even if Michelle had called it a 'power move' when Layla walked into the office that morning.

As she gnawed her lower lip, Layla wished more than anything that she could call Angus. His calm, measured tone would soothe her in an instant.

No, her brain snapped. *No thoughts of Angus. Not now. This is too important.*

But it was no use. All Layla seemed to do was think of Angus. His broken expression, his assertion that he wanted her . . . For what felt like the hundredth time since their showdown three days ago, Layla wondered if she should have heard him out.

While there was no denying her fury at Angus's lies, there was something in the way Angus spoke about himself that broke her heart. How could someone with as much going for them as Angus think they were a failure? Did he really live with so much shame? Layla didn't know, and she hadn't given Angus the time to explain. She'd shouted and fled, but with every step she took, Layla's gut told her that she was making a mistake.

But fleeing was easier. Fleeing meant that Layla would never have to see the look on Angus's face when she admitted to her death date.

See, he's not the only one who's been lying, her conscience pointed out. *Can you really judge him?*

As a bitter sigh left Layla's lips, Rashida burst into the bathroom. 'Don't even think about doubting how great you look,' she commanded.

'Rashida's right,' Sinead agreed from close behind her. 'I've never seen you look so on point.'

'Or so nervous.' Approaching her friend, Rashida reached into the cosmetics bag Layla had set down beside the sink. 'Here, let me help.'

As Rashida touched up Layla's makeup, Sinead smiled. 'You've got this, Layla. What you're doing will change this company forever.'

'It better. The working group didn't put so much effort in for you and Michelle to mess up at the last hurdle,' Rashida joked, sweeping a sheen of highlighter across Layla's cheeks.

Suddenly, there was a knock on the door.

'Layla, are you in there?' Michelle's voice rang from the hallway.

'She is,' Rashida confirmed.

Stepping into the bathroom, Michelle eyed Layla's nervous expression. 'I thought I saw you dash in here,' she said before turning to Rashida and Sinead. 'Would you mind giving us a moment?'

Nodding, Rashida and Sinead headed for the door, but not without giving Layla a thumbs up first.

When the door had swung shut behind them, Michelle approached the sink and started to tidy Layla's makeup away. 'I'm not going to ask if you're ready for this, but I am going to tell you you're ready. I want you to tell yourself that too. The way we speak to ourselves has more power than we realise. So, assure yourself that in a few minutes we are going to go into that boardroom, and we are going to be heard.'

'But what if the Senior Partners don't listen?' Layla asked, raking her teeth over her bottom lip.

'It's our job to make them listen. Now, come on. Let's make today one that will go down in Mayweather & Halliwell history.'

With that encouragement flowing through her, Layla followed Michelle out of the bathroom and across the office. Every eye was on them, but Layla didn't flinch from the scrutiny. Instead, she ordered herself to stride on like she was completely in control.

Together, the women headed to the top floor meeting room where the Senior Partners were waiting.

'Michelle, Layla,' each said as they shook their hands.

As Layla returned their greetings, she tried not to think of how much power was in the room. Or how as fast as those men could shake her hand, they could also fire her.

Then, when all the greetings were done, it was time to begin.

Michelle spoke first, as rehearsed. She ran through their presentation, giving an overview of her career and the challenges she had faced along the way. The partners appeared to be listening, but it was when Michelle ran through statistics about Mayweather & Halliwell's employment and promotion history that they really paid attention.

By the time Michelle presented the low scores generated from a well-being and satisfaction survey Layla had sent to all staff, the Senior Partners were hooked.

'Gentlemen, none of this should come as a shock,' Michelle said, 'but it should be a call to action. From the evidence presented, we can see firsthand that inequality exists within this company, and that it greatly impacts the staff we claim to value. But it doesn't have to be like this. We can change it, and improve not just our company culture, but our output too.

'To speak more on that, I'm going to pass over to Layla. Many of you have had the privilege of working with her. You'll know firsthand how much Layla's passion, dedication and undeniable talent brings to Mayweather & Halliwell. Layla, over to you.'

As Michelle took a seat, Layla stepped forward. She eyed the long boardroom desk and the grey-haired, suited men who sat around it. Their expressions were stoic, their gazes sharp. Suddenly, Layla felt smaller than ever.

As her wide eyes roamed around the room, Wallace Horton nodded encouragingly at her. A Senior Partner she had worked with before, Wallace was firm but fair, tough but adaptable. And now there he was, nudging Layla to go for it.

'Mayweather & Halliwell is one of the most prestigious law firms in the UK,' she began. 'It attracts elite clientele and the most promising, results-driven staff. However, as Michelle pointed out, almost two thirds of employees are considering leaving the company in the next six months. They listed a poor work–life balance, lack of communication and an unfair hierarchy as the main reasons for this. These are all things that Mayweather & Halliwell has the power to change. Choosing not to will only lead to one thing: the talent pool we train moving to our competitors. The figures Michelle presented show that this has been happening at an increasing rate. This means our competitors are profiting directly from the state of our culture.'

A few of the Senior Partners leaned closer, their interest piqued.

'While getting ahead of our competitors is a compelling reason to implement change, there are other reasons for focusing on employee wellbeing,' Layla said, settling into the rhythm of her speech now. 'Would anyone like to guess what they could be?'

'Productivity?' someone called out.

'Growth?' someone else suggested.

'Absolutely, both outcomes can be achieved by improving staff wellbeing,' Layla replied. 'Another reason is that it's better for people's health. Creating a healthy workforce is in your interest. After all, long-term sick leave directly impacts the bottom line. Does anyone know what one of the leading causes for health-related leave is?'

Layla looked around the room, taking in the number of shaking heads.

'It's stress,' she said.

A low, knowing chuckle rang out, but Layla didn't find it funny anymore. She hadn't since the day Saira handed her that envelope.

'Stress is killing us day by day. It shouldn't be that way. No one goes into a career in law expecting it to be easy. None of us are ill-prepared for hard work, but over two thirds of staff report feeling stress at a level that affects their eating and sleeping habits, as well as their personal relationships. This must change.'

There was a strain to Layla's voice as she spoke. Everything she had squashed down, all the anger and animosity she felt towards this place, bubbled to the surface, ready to burst free should her voice not be heard.

So make it heard.

Tilting her chin higher, she addressed the room. 'At Mayweather & Halliwell, we attract the best and brightest, but the best and brightest can only remain that way when they are rested, supported and valued. That includes benefits like parental leave and flexible working arrangements, visible praise, rewards and incentives, and an unbiased promotion review period.

'Several studies have found that when people feel appreciated and have a manageable workload, both their productivity and satisfaction increases. The aim of this meeting is to outline our proposal, but over the next few weeks, Michelle and I will present plans that could transform this firm and the lives of those working for it. Our ultimate goal is to make Mayweather & Halliwell an organisation people want to work at for a lifetime, not a short time. Thank you.'

Ducking her head, Layla stepped backwards, but Michelle placed her hand in the centre of Layla's back, holding her in place.

Her speech was met with silence until Bernard Addington cleared his throat. 'That was very rousing,' he drawled, 'but everyone at this table did late nights and took work on holiday with them. It's part of the job. If people aren't prepared for that, maybe they should question their decision to work in law in the first place.'

The knot in Layla's stomach tightened as several people around the table nodded in agreement, but with Michelle's steady presence beside her, Layla cleared her throat. 'Just because something happened in the past, it doesn't make it right and it doesn't mean it should happen in the future. Progress can't be made if we stick to the status quo.'

Bernard's mouth lifted into a smirk. 'The status quo has served everyone here well.'

'That may be so,' Layla replied, 'but if Mayweather & Halliwell wants to remain one of the best firms in the industry, attitudes need to change. People need to adapt.'

Another beat of silence echoed through the wood-clad room, this one more static than the one before. *Oh shit*, Layla panicked. *This is where they fire you.*

But then Wallace stood up, his six-foot frame towering over the other partners. 'Well, Layla, we have a lot to consider, but it's safe to say you've woken the dinosaurs at this table from their slumber. Well done.'

As Wallace reached out to shake her hand, Layla grinned. The instant she allowed herself to feel the joy of the achievement, Layla's mind wandered to the one person she wanted to share it with . . .

Suddenly, the colourful moment turned sepia.

42

Angus

The Life Experiment: Daily Questionnaire
Property of OPM Discoveries

How would you rate your level of contentment today? (1 represents low contentment, 10 represents high)

   1   2   3   4   5   6   7   8   9   10

There is no option for 0

How would you rate your energy level? (1 being very low energy and 10 being very high energy)

   (1)   2   3   4   5   6   7   8   9   10

What are two things you are grateful for today?
1. The invention of premium liquor
2. The fact that I own a lot of premium liquor

What are you struggling with today?
The knowledge of all my fuck-ups

Do you have any additional notes on what you would like to discuss in your upcoming counselling session?
No

Peeling his sticky eyelids open, Angus stared at the ceiling above his bed. A mild panic set in as he realised his tongue was glued to the roof of his mouth, but Angus knew he only had himself to blame. No one else had poured multiple tequila shots down his throat.

In fact, Jasper had repeatedly tried to pry the bottle of Don Julio 1942 from his hands. 'I'm worried about you, my friend,' he said as Angus stumbled away, clutching the bottle to his chest.

That was Angus's last memory of the previous night.

Stretching his weary shoulders, Angus thought of Jasper. Would he want to go out again later? Angus hoped so. Jasper was never one to shy away from a good time, although the last few days had been a lot, even for him.

From the bedside table, Angus's phone rang. Like all the times before, Angus ignored it, even though the vibrating device felt like someone jackhammering inside his skull.

Curling into a ball, Angus winced as his stomach somersaulted. When he'd crawled into bed at 4 am, he thought vomiting had expunged all last night's alcohol from his body, but clearly not.

Running through the patches of the night he could remember, Angus tried to find the positives. He had survived his third bender this week. He had made it home. That was good. At least he wasn't in a gutter somewhere, choking on his own vomit, or locked in a police cell. Or worse, waking up in a bed that wasn't his or Layla's.

A sweat-dampened shiver rattled Angus's body at the thought of making that hellish mistake. It would have sealed the end of him and Layla, but Angus had to hope it wasn't too late for them. His heart still ached at the thought of her.

Suddenly, panic gripped Angus. Snatching his phone from the bedside table, he checked his call history and groaned. Five calls to Layla were logged. Each were made after 2 am. None had been answered.

Sighing, Angus debated tossing his phone in the bin, but his phone began ringing. A photo of Peter filled the screen. It was only then that Angus noticed the time.

His stomach dropped. Lunchtime had long passed, and so had the time Angus was meant to visit Gilly while she underwent her next round of chemotherapy. He'd promised he would be there.

Don't make promises you can't keep, Angus, Gilly had said during their phone call the previous morning, but Angus had been adamant that he would be there. He wouldn't let her down.

Only, he had.

Guilt overwhelmed Angus as he imagined his mother in hospital, staring at the door, waiting for him to arrive. Pressing his palms against his eyes, he berated himself for his enormous fuck-up. *Why are you like this? Why, why, why?*

His thoughts were only interrupted by the sound of his intercom screeching to announce a visitor.

Swaying as he rose to his feet, Angus searched for clothes to throw on. Last night's shirt, crumpled on the floor beside a pair of tequila splattered jeans, lay before him. Rank, but when the door buzzed again, Angus threw them on and shuffled towards the intercom.

'Hello?' his sandpaper voice croaked into the speaker.

'It's your father,' Peter's stern voice stated simply. 'Are you going to let me up or am I going to have to use my key?'

Sighing, Angus buzzed his father into the building then trailed to the window for a moment of peace before the inevitable showdown began. Leaning his forehead against the cool glass, he watched as rain fell over London. Small figures on the ground rushed to escape the elements. Angus wished he could trade places with one of them.

Behind him, Angus heard his front door open, followed by the sound of footsteps marching towards him.

'So, this is what you're doing instead of supporting your mother. What an excellent way to spend your time.'

As Peter's rage simmered behind him, Angus kept his gaze fixed on the window. He tried to focus on a single raindrop, to watch it trail down the glass, but the rain was too heavy.

'Look at me,' Peter said coolly, but Angus didn't move. 'I said look at me, dammit!'

Angus flinched at his father's tone, then he turned, slow and weary.

When his furious eyes locked on his son's defeated stance, Peter's lips parted. 'Jesus, Angus. What's happened to you?' he breathed, his anger fading.

Opening his clenched jaw, Angus hunted for the words to explain, but there were none. There had been no words, no joy, no life since Layla walked away. 'I don't know,' he admitted.

Angus's teenage years had taught him that one thing Peter hated was vagueness. When Angus purposely hit a golf ball through the kitchen window and couldn't say why, when he took bottles of Peter's rare whisky to a house party and paired them with Coca Cola . . . Peter demanded a solid reason every time. But this time, he didn't push.

This time, Peter strode forward and enveloped Angus in his arms.

Slowly raising his arms to hug his father back, Angus began to cry. 'I'm sorry,' he sobbed. 'I really am. I didn't mean to let anyone down. I'm so, so sorry.'

Peter didn't lie and say that it was okay. Instead, he held his son tightly, rubbing his hand over Angus's back the way he had when Angus was small. 'Whatever it is, son, we can fix it,' Peter said.

Angus knew Peter couldn't erase Gilly's hurt or the pain Angus had caused Layla, but his father's words helped nonetheless. Soon, Angus's tears subsided.

When the men drew apart, Angus trailed to the kitchen for a glass of water. From the living room, Peter watched.

'Your mother needs you, Angus,' he said.

'I know,' Angus replied, gripping the sink for support as the water landed heavily in his stomach.

'I don't think you do, Angus. Do you have any idea what she is going through?'

Rubbing his forehead, Angus tried to wipe the stress away, but it clung on. 'I'll be there next time.'

'Next time isn't good enough. You should have been there today. She was waiting for you while you were out doing God knows what with God knows who.'

'I've said I'm sorry. It's . . . I'm going through something right now.'

'And your mother isn't?' The question hung in the air, spiked with a truth Angus couldn't deny. 'She needs you. *I* need you. Not this drunken husk of a person standing before me. I need the man who came to us with an idea that could help people.'

Pushing himself upright, Angus lifted his head and glared at Peter. 'But that's not who I am, is it? I'm the other guy. Drunk Angus. Off-his-face Angus. Fucked-up Angus. That's all I'll ever be.'

Snarling the hateful words made Angus feel even sicker. Reaching for his water, Angus went to swill the acrid taste away, but Peter stepped into the kitchen and knocked the glass out of his hand.

As it clattered to the floor and smashed, Angus's jaw dropped.

'What?' Peter snapped. 'Do you want me to pander to you because you've had too much to drink again? Well, I refuse. You've made some bad choices in life, Angus, I get it, but so what? You're not the only one. Do you know what I do when I'm sat in hospital with your mother? I hold her hand and tell her stupid stories, but all the while I sit there thinking of the times I could have been a better husband. Worked less. Listened more. Removed the pressure of this life. I burn with regret for my mistakes, but guess what? I don't let it stop me from waking up every day and trying to be better. And right now, I'm trying harder than ever because that's what your mother needs. She needs me by her side, and she needs you there too.'

'I . . . I can't see her like that,' Angus croaked. 'It kills me.'

'Don't you think it kills me too? But this isn't about me or you, it's about your mother. It's about the ways you can distract her from her pain. Make her laugh. Be there for her in the ways she would be for you, if you were the one in that hospital bed.'

As Angus's shoulders caved, a memory came to mind. One he hadn't thought of in years.

Aged twelve and battling glandular fever, Angus had been sent home from boarding school. Already distanced from his parents after losing Hugo, Angus assumed he'd be left alone to recover, but Gilly insisted on Angus sleeping in the master bedroom with her so she could keep an eye on him. Peter had been banished to a spare room. Every feverish dream Angus woke from, his mother was there. Gilly might not have fussed over him or doled out hugs, but she was there, quietly beside Angus when he needed her.

Lifting his head, Angus faced his father. 'I haven't been a very good son, have I?'

'No,' Peter replied. Bluntly, brutally.

Honestly.

'I'm sorry,' Angus said. 'I'm going to do better. I promise this won't happen again.'

Angus resolved that it was a promise he would keep. No more excuses, no more hiding, and definitely no more lies.

43

Layla

It seemed to Layla that London had never been busier. The assault on her senses was rough as she followed Michelle out of Mayweather & Halliwell's Westminster office. Drunken cheers rang out from pubs, Friday night mayhem taking over every establishment along the street.

'Watch it,' a tipsy man leered as he knocked into Layla. Or maybe she knocked into him, she was too overwhelmed to tell.

When Layla stumbled, Michelle grabbed her arm. 'Come on,' she said. 'We'll be late for dinner if you keep dawdling.'

Layla allowed Michelle to drag her along, grateful to have someone lead the way. Moments later, a venue lit by fairy lights came into view ahead. The women crossed the road, weaving through queues of traffic with reckless abandon. As they ducked under a sprig of mistletoe pinned above the restaurant door, the scent of oregano infiltrated Layla's lungs. Remembering her first dinner with Angus, Layla's heart twinged.

Brushing aside her sadness, Layla moved through the bustling venue towards a long table where Sinead, Rashida and a few others from their team were waiting.

It was Michelle's idea to set up a 'Women in Law' dinner to celebrate the end of the year. When it was first suggested, Layla had been excited at the prospect of an evening with her colleagues. But back then, Layla's heart hadn't been broken.

Greeting her colleagues, Layla forced a smile that was becoming harder to fake. Taking a seat beside Nidhi, a junior lawyer in their division, and Priscilla from the accounts team, she pushed herself into the conversation.

'Michelle's outdone herself tonight,' Layla commented.

'Hasn't she?' Priscilla said, pouring Layla a glass of red wine. 'I can't remember ever getting together like this. Isn't it exciting?'

'So exciting,' Layla replied, somewhat flatly.

Layla couldn't understand it. A social outing with the people who made work bearable should have brought her to life, but as Rashida began recounting a client's recent cutting feedback, all Layla could think was, *Does any of this really matter?*

The wins, the woes, the work . . . did it matter? Did the world stop turning if a client didn't receive an answer within twenty-four hours? Did anyone truly value the effort everyone at this table put into their work? What difference did they actually make?

Rubbing her eyes with her palms, Layla tried to push the questions away, but they went nowhere.

It was so unfair. Ever since that day at the park, Layla's darkest thoughts had come back with a vengeance. It seemed like the moment Angus disappeared from Layla's life, all her focus had turned to the glaring holes in it.

The unfulfilling work.

The question mark over what she really wanted.

The empty bed she crawled into every night.

Internally, Layla sighed. *Enough,* she thought. A line had to be drawn under what happened with Angus at some point. She'd had a big year. The project was thriving. She deserved to celebrate with her friends, even if celebrating was the last thing on her mind.

Squaring her shoulders, Layla took a sip of tepid wine and watched the others shriek with laughter. At first, she felt like an outsider looking in, but soon she settled into the conversation. By the end of dinner, Layla was almost enjoying herself.

Layla thought she'd done a good job of muddling through the night until Michelle paused at her chair. 'Layla, I'm going to go pay. Come with me?' she asked.

Nodding, Layla pushed her chair out and followed Michelle to the counter, unsure why she'd been invited along. Her confusion grew when Michelle exchanged small talk with the waiter without including her. Standing there awkwardly as the card machine loaded, Layla wondered if it was possible to slip away.

When the transaction went through, Layla made a move to dash back to the table, but Michelle caught her arm. 'Hang on a second. I asked you to come with me so we could talk away from the others,' she said. 'Is everything okay? You don't seem your usual self.'

Layla's eyes darted to the floor. 'I'm fine.'

'Layla,' Michelle said, her tone not dissimilar to Joanna's when she knew Layla wasn't being entirely honest. 'I've come to know you well over the last few weeks. I know when something isn't right.'

Tears burned Layla's eyes, so she kept her gaze downcast, afraid that if she looked at Michelle, she wouldn't be able to contain them.

'Come on,' Michelle coaxed. 'We're not just colleagues – we're friends. As your friend, I'm worried about you. Please talk to me.'

Something in Michelle's plea made Layla give in. 'I don't know, Michelle. Things in my life just don't feel right at the minute.'

'In what way?'

Layla paused, wondering how to reply. 'Do you ever wonder what the point of it all is?' she asked, glancing back to her colleagues in time to watch Sinead finish a story that had the rest of the table in stitches. 'Work. Networking. Acting like what we do changes the world.' The words were tumbling out of Layla now, but she couldn't stop them. 'That was what I wanted to do, you know. It's why I went into law. I wanted to make the world a better place, starting with families like mine.'

'Families like yours?'

'When I was young, my dad was in an accident that nearly killed him.'

A wave of sympathy rolled over Michelle's face. 'I'm so sorry, Layla. I can't imagine how tough that was.'

'It was hell,' Layla admitted. 'My family lost everything, but we were happy. We didn't need fancy dinners or new clothes – we just needed each other. I feel like somewhere along the way, I lost that. I searched for the wrong things. I mean, why am I going to work every day and making companies richer when I could be using my degree to help people like my dad? Why am I acting like I don't know what it's like to be shaped by hardship?' A tear fell from Layla's eye, but she wiped it away furiously. 'Do you know, working on the project with you is the first time I've felt passionate about what I'm doing in years. It shouldn't be like that. I just . . . I don't know if this is what I want, Michelle,' she croaked. 'I've tried to make this big-city, corporate identity fit, but I'm not sure it's me. I want to be safe and successful, but I want to be a good person too. I want to do good things.'

'Layla, you're leading a project to change the work environment at Mayweather & Halliwell. Many people will benefit from that,' Michelle pointed out, but the response made Layla shake her head.

'It's not enough. It's not what I want to do.' As soon as the words left her, Layla met Michelle's gaze. 'It's not what I want to do, Michelle,' she repeated. 'I love law, but I think I'm working in the wrong sector. I want to do good. Real, meaningful good. I want to help families like mine. I want to ensure people are working and living in safe and healthy conditions. Be someone twelve-year-old Layla would be proud of.'

Michelle's features softened. 'I have contacts in legal aid and employment law, you know. I could put you in touch with them. It's not too late for you to take your career in a different direction, if that's truly what you want.'

The future split before Layla's eyes. Both visions had their appeal. Both were not without their challenges, but one spoke to her more. As scary as change might be, The Life Experiment had taught Layla one thing – her time was precious. She had to use it wisely.

Taking in a deep breath, Layla nodded. 'I'd like that, Michelle. Thank you.'

44

Angus

Flexing his fingers, Angus approached his parents' house. Flanked by two stone pillars, the front door loomed tall. Gripping the bag in his hand tighter, Angus pushed it open and entered.

'Hello?' he called out.

From the back of the house, clipped footsteps could be heard. They drew closer until Ms Tillman came into view. 'Angus, what a lovely surprise! I didn't know you were visiting today.'

'It was an impromptu thing. I'm here to see Mother.'

Ms Tillman nodded like she expected as much. 'She's resting at the moment. Would you like me to go up and tell her you're here?'

'No, thank you. I'll go to her.'

As Angus approached the staircase, Ms Tillman moved to stop him, but then stepped aside. Angus understood her almost-objection. Gilly Fairview-Whitley prided herself on appearance above all else. Would she want anyone, even her son, to see her in bed in the middle of the afternoon?

But Angus didn't care about appearances anymore. All he cared about was righting his wrongs. And, as he ascended the sweeping staircase, Angus was determined to do exactly that.

At the door to his parents' bedroom, he knocked gently.

'I'm fine for a drink, thank you,' Gilly called from inside, but Angus entered anyway.

The number of pillows surrounding Gilly made her appear smaller than ever. The sight was painful for Angus, but ever since starting chemotherapy, he knew Gilly's skin had felt hot and irritated. Enveloping herself in soft furnishings seemed to be the only way she could get comfortable.

'Angus,' Gilly said, struggling to sit upright. 'What are you doing here?'

'Don't get up,' Angus replied, moving closer.

'I should have been up hours ago,' Gilly said, but Angus reached her side before she could swing her legs from the bed.

'Mother, please. It's only me. Rest. Relax.'

Gilly paused but gave a small nod and settled back into her cushions. Only when she seemed relatively at peace did Angus exhale. He moved to sit in the chair beside Gilly's bed, but as he did, the bag he was carrying banged into his leg.

Gilly frowned. 'Have you been shopping?'

'I have. For you, in fact.'

Gilly's eyebrows shot up. 'For me? What on earth have you done that for?'

'I've been thinking about what you said. About listening to everything I've ever said, all my throwaway comments and dreams. It got me thinking about how we've been with each other in the past.'

A frown flashed across Gilly's face. 'Angus, I'm tired. I don't want to fight.'

'Neither do I. I want to show you something.'

'Show me what?' Gilly asked warily.

'Well,' Angus replied, clearing his throat. 'I want to show that I've listened to what you've said over the years too.'

Lifting the bag onto the bed, Angus reached inside and pulled out a set of items.

'When you were young, you used to paint,' he said. 'The illustration you did of your garden is one of my favourite things in this house, but all my life, I've never seen you pick up a paintbrush.'

'My father told me that a lady doesn't have paint on her clothes.' Gilly sniffed. 'I could hardly host dinner parties while covered in acrylics, could I?'

'Exactly. You didn't put yourself first, ever. We let it happen, but we shouldn't have. We should have signed you up for a painting class and made sure you had the chance to do the things you loved. Well, I went out and got you a sketchbook and some watercolours. I thought you could use this time to paint, if you wanted to. When you're feeling better, we can look for a class to join too, if you'd like.'

Dumbstruck, Gilly stared at the A4 sketchbook and paints Angus placed in her hands.

Next, Angus pulled an oversized shirt from the bag. 'Last summer, you hosted a garden party on the sunniest day of the year. You burned your shoulders, but Corinne Smythe didn't because she brought an overshirt with her. You wanted one to throw over your outfit on hot days too. So, I bought you one. If it's not right, we can return it, but I think it will look good on you. When you feel up to it, try it on and let me know.'

As the buttery soft material slipped through Gilly's fingers, she choked on a disbelieving laugh.

The third item Angus held in the air was a book. 'You've always said you want to read *Pride and Prejudice*, but never got around to it. When the film played on ITV last Christmas, you said you would only watch it after reading the book first. So, here's a copy. When you've finished it, we can watch the film together. I'll even make popcorn.'

Placing the book on top of the paints, Angus went back to his bag. His hand paused on the next item. He knew how hard saying this would be, but as he heard Gilly struggle to swallow back tears, he knew he had to.

'My favourite childhood memories are of you, me and Hugo baking together. We always made such a mess, do you remember?' Angus braved a look at his mother.

Tears filled Gilly's eyes, but she ignored them. 'Chocolate cake was Hugo's favourite,' she said simply.

'It was. The day of his funeral, you cried and said you would never eat chocolate cake again.' The memory seared Angus, but he didn't shy away from it. 'We never baked one after that. In fact, we stopped baking altogether, but we shouldn't have. We should have made chocolate cake every year on Hugo's birthday. And we should have talked about him. Kept him with us. Shared that pain.'

'We should have,' Gilly agreed, closing her eyes as her tears escaped.

'It's not too late to start,' Angus said, pushing through his emotion so he could speak. 'I bought a Nigella cookbook. The lady at Waterstones said there's a great chocolate cake recipe in there. We can bake it later, if you feel up to it.'

'Oh, darling,' Gilly whispered as he added the book to the stack on her bed.

'I think it's time we stop hiding from the pain, and from each other,' Angus continued. 'I want to spend time with you, and talk about Hugo more. Make new memories.' With the paper bag now empty, Angus folded it in his hands. 'I know some of this stuff is silly. I just wanted you to know that I care. I'm sorry I ever made you feel like I didn't. I'm also sorry if they're not the right supplies. I'm not a painter or baker or—'

'Stop, Angus,' Gilly interrupted, leaning forward and catching her son's hand. 'They're perfect.'

A smile lifted the corners of Angus's mouth. Reaching forward, he wrapped his mother in his arms, holding her gently. A moment later, Gilly's arms found Angus too.

45

Layla

The Life Experiment: Daily Questionnaire
Property of OPM Discoveries

How would you rate your level of contentment today? (1 represents low contentment, 10 represents high)

1   2   3   4   ⑤   6   7   8   9   10

How would you rate your energy level? (1 being very low energy and 10 being very high energy)

1   2   ③   4   5   6   7   8   9   10

What are two things you are grateful for today?
1. Michelle putting me in contact with her friend in legal aid. We've only chatted once, but I felt more excited after that call than I have in ages
2. Maya visiting for the weekend. It will be nice to not be alone

What are you struggling with today?
Being excited for the future when I know I won't be around long enough to enjoy it

Do you have any additional notes on what you would like to discuss in your upcoming counselling session?
I guess we should talk about Angus, but honestly, I don't know where to begin

Layla didn't know what was more irritating – Maya barging into her bedroom or Maya throwing her curtains open. 'Stop!' Layla protested as the bright light burned her eyes.

'Don't be such a misery guts,' Maya argued, jumping on the bed and throwing her arms around Layla. 'When I said I was coming to London, I pictured going to cocktail bars and sightseeing, not Rhi working all the time and you sulking in your bedroom like a moody teenager.'

'I told you, I'm tired.'

'And I told you, I don't believe you,' Maya replied, pulling back Layla's duvet. 'Come on, Layls. What is it? What's wrong?'

The words filled Layla's throat, but they were too difficult to say. She chose to stare at the radiator instead, hoping the silent treatment would be enough to fend off Maya's questions.

Layla should have known better.

'Is it work?' Maya pushed. 'I thought your project was going well? Didn't you just get a miscarriage leave policy approved?'

Layla sighed. 'We did, yeah.'

'So, what's the problem? Why are you in bed when it's almost lunchtime? Is it to do with Angus?'

Layla shot her sister a sideways look. 'Not everything relates to men, you know.'

'I know that. Christ, I've not had a boyfriend in years and look how happy I am! All I'm saying is, last time I saw you, you and Angus were talking nonstop, but you've not messaged him once since I arrived. Is he away or something?'

Layla's shoulders tensed at the innocent question. 'Drop it, Maya.'

'No,' Maya said, shuffling closer. 'I'm worried. Talk to me. Please.'

Layla thought she could ignore her sister's pleas, but when Maya pulled at the duvet once more, something inside Layla snapped. 'I said drop it! What part of that don't you understand?!' she cried, sitting up so quickly she nearly knocked Maya from the bed.

'Watch it,' Maya protested, but her anger faded as she eyed her sister. Concern dipped Maya's brows. 'What's going on, Layla? And don't dismiss me. I know you. I know when something is wrong. What aren't you telling me?'

A rebuttal sprang to Layla's mind, but she couldn't bring herself to push Maya away again. As Layla looked into her sister's sharp eyes, the words she had struggled to contain since learning her death date bubbled in her throat.

Layla knew she couldn't say anything. There were just under two weeks left of the experiment. She had to stay quiet. If she didn't, she would break a legally binding contract. She would leave herself ineligible for the experiment's benefits.

But Layla was tired of carrying this secret alone. She was so, so tired.

'I only have two years left to live.'

The words erupted from Layla as if a dam had broken. In the aftermath, Layla waited to feel guilt or dread or any of the other awful feelings she had convinced herself she would feel if she let the truth out.

Instead, Layla simply felt at peace.

Maya stared at Layla for what felt like an eternity. 'What?' she asked, a strange, disbelieving smile stretching her mouth. 'What are you talking about?'

'I only have two years left to live,' Layla repeated.

'Layla, you're scaring me now,' Maya said, her voice wobbly.

Taking a deep breath, Layla came clean about the experiment. She broke every clause of her NDA, but she was past caring about legalities. Let Saira sue her. She'd probably be dead by the time the case made it to court, anyway.

But the more Layla spoke, the more Maya's face relaxed. After hearing Layla's explanation, Maya simply looked up from the OPM Discoveries website Layla had loaded on her phone and blinked.

'Is this supposed to convince me it isn't bullshit?' she said.

'You don't believe me?'

'I don't believe any of this crap. It's like going to a fortune teller and believing you'll meet a handsome stranger when you least expect it.'

'It's not like that at all. They did tests and everything.'

Maya scoffed. 'Come on, Layla. I thought you were smarter than this.'

'Maya, it's a legitimate study. OPM Discoveries is a research lab. They've won more awards than I can count. They ran a million and one tests.'

'So? Tests are wrong all the time. Tests can't take into account every random part of life. Think about it. You could walk across the road tonight and get hit by a bus.'

'The experiment analyses your biological date of death. Obviously OPM Discoveries can't control the randomness of life, but they can make an assessment based on health data and—'

Maya's wry laughter interrupted Layla's train of thought. 'Surely you can't really believe this?' she asked, but when Maya looked into her sister's terrified eyes, she saw that she did. Turning the phone to Layla, Maya pointed to a photo of Saira. 'This is the person in charge of the study? Saira Khatri?'

Layla nodded.

'If she's in charge of a biological study, why are her qualifications in psychology?'

Layla's hands trembled as she took her phone back. Saira's list of accomplishments flashed before her. A degree, a masters, a doctorate. So intelligent, so educated. 'Saira does the counselling,' she explained. 'She's here to support us through the aftermath of our result and analyse our reaction to it.'

'But why would a psychologist lead this experiment, not a biologist?' When Layla failed to find a response, Maya reached across the bed and took her sister's hands in her own. 'Listen to me, okay? This is bullshit. No one can tell you when you're going to die, not even people in lab coats.'

'But they—'

'No, Layla,' Maya interjected, holding Layla's hands tighter. 'You went into an experiment unhappy and unfulfilled. You'd have believed anything they told you because you needed a wake-up call. Fuck OP-Whatever-They're-Called. How can they tell you that you'll die of stress in two years when, right now, you're not stressed at all?'

Tears spiked Layla's eyelashes. 'You think I've changed my results?'

'I think your results were like your life – yours to determine,' Maya replied. 'I mean, look at us. I wanted to be a hairdresser, so I became a hairdresser; you wanted to be a lawyer, so you became a lawyer. We worked hard and we made our dreams happen.'

'But my job is killing me. It said so, in my results.'

'Layla, you're not listening. There's no way this study can actually predict when exactly you'll die. What if you decided to only eat junk food from now on? What if you threw yourself into training for a marathon? There are lifestyle patterns that can influence your health, sure, but nothing as definitive as this.'

'You really think so?' Layla asked, her voice lifted by hope.

'I know so! Don't live your life on a countdown, Layls. You are no more on a clock than the rest of us. Enjoy yourself. Keep working hard and being a good aunt to Jayden. Date Angus and see where it takes you.'

At the mention of Angus, Layla's head bowed. 'What if it's true, though? What if I do die in two years? How can we be together if I know the end is coming?'

'Layla, there's no relationship on earth that doesn't have an expiry date. Whether it's a break-up or a death, an end is inevitable, but that's not what matters. What matters is the bit in between. Who cares if what you have with Angus goes on for two months or two decades? Just enjoy yourself.'

Layla raised her head. 'I'm scared.'

'Well, that's okay. Life is scary, but the Layla I know doesn't believe in letting fear rule her. Not enough to stop her going for what she wants, anyway.' Leaning closer, Maya wiped a tear from Layla's cheek. 'Call Saira. Ask her if it's real.'

Layla blinked. 'I can't do that.'

'Why not?'

'Because. What if she says it is, that I really do have two years left to live? Then what?'

Shaking her head, Maya pushed the phone into Layla's hand. 'Call her.'

With Maya's encouragement, Layla braved calling Saira.

She picked up after three rings. 'Layla, is everything okay?'

Even through her professional tone, Layla could hear Saira's concern. She had every right to worry about an unscheduled call. *Especially from someone she gave two years to live*, Layla thought bitterly.

'Is it real?' she asked. 'The experiment, is it real?'

'Layla, has something happened?' Saira asked.

'The experiment,' Layla repeated through gritted teeth. 'Is it real?'

The pause on the other end of the line told Layla everything she needed to know. As the air was knocked from her lungs, Layla folded at the waist. Maya's hand rested on her back in a gesture of comfort, but Layla was in so much shock, she barely felt it.

'How could you?' she whispered. 'How could you let me think I was going to die?'

'Layla, that was never our intention, but—'

'Never your intention?! You told me I had two years left to live!'

'Layla, it's okay,' Maya soothed, but Layla didn't want her sister's platitudes. She wanted Saira's answers.

'Why do this, Saira?' she demanded. 'Why torture people?'

'The purpose of The Life Experiment was never to make you obsess over when you would die, but to make you think about how you wanted to live,' Saira explained desperately. 'Our aim was to assess how candidates responded to the news and hopefully help them grow. Make positive changes. Trust themselves. Believe me, Layla, it came from a good place.'

'A *good place*? You think putting me through this hell has helped anything? You think making me lie to everyone I love has been a positive experience?' Layla closed her eyes as the exhaustion of the last few weeks ploughed into her. The days she had lost, crying in bed over a fate that wasn't real. The pain in her chest as she carried the enormous burden alone.

'You told me I was dying, Saira,' Layla stated acidly.

'Only to help you face your fears. You weren't happy, Layla. Your body was telling you what to do, but you didn't trust yourself enough to listen. We aimed to provide a nudge in the right direction. You were going to find out the truth soon,' Saira added, as if that made it better. 'The plan was to tell candidates the true purpose of the experiment when the ten weeks were up, then evaluate the progress they'd made in that time.'

'Progress?' Layla spat. 'My life isn't better than it was before, Saira. The world feels scarier than ever now. I thought you'd become a friend. I thought you were on my side.'

'Layla, I am on—'

'No!' Layla's shout made Maya jump. 'I participated under false pretences. I deserved the truth.'

Saira's excuses echoed down the line, but Layla was no longer listening. Without another word, she hung up.

Seconds later, her phone lit up with a call from Saira. Layla watched it ring out.

'Layla,' Maya said gently, nudging her sister. 'Layla, it's okay.'

'It's not,' Layla replied, tears welling in her eyes. 'I let him go for nothing, Maya. I let him go.'

46

Angus

The construction team were already outside the house in Bloomsbury when Angus parked his car. He checked the time. He was ten minutes early, but he supposed Roy, Antonia and Savannah wanted to make a good impression. Renovating the four-storey Victorian property into the first block of Hugo's House accommodation was a big deal for them all.

Not wanting to keep anyone waiting, Angus left his car. When the trio spotted him, they moved forward in a huddle to greet him.

'It's good to meet you in person, Angus,' Roy said, shaking Angus's hand. A lifelong tradesman, Roy had a thick South London accent, a patchy head of hair and was in charge of bringing Antonia's architectural design to life.

Antonia was a friend of Gilly's who Angus had known for years. He greeted her with a kiss on the cheek before shaking the hand of the woman beside her. Early in their discussions, Antonia supplied Angus with portfolios of interior designers she trusted. The first few were flashy, with sleek lines and marble in every design. Chic aesthetics, but none created the kind of homely feel Angus wanted for Hugo's House.

Then he opened Savannah's portfolio. Unafraid of using a rich colour palette and layering soft furnishings, Savannah created homes, not art. Her vision was exactly what Angus wanted.

'Well, it's a fine property to work on,' Savannah said as they all turned towards the entrance.

'It will be even finer when we're through with it,' Angus replied. 'Come on, let's head inside.' Taking out the keys his father had given him earlier, Angus led the trio into the building.

Even though the property belonged to Angus's family, Antonia led the tour. She'd spent so many hours looking at floor plans, she knew the layout best. 'This wall will be knocked down to create a reception area. Think light, bright and breezy,' she said as she led the team through the building's downstairs apartment. 'Originally, I wanted to extend further into the back, but that would mean culling a communal space. Angus wants to keep admin spaces small and resident spaces big. That way, Hugo's House can accommodate as many people as possible.'

'A vast entrance is great, but its only purpose is for first impressions,' Angus added. 'This place needs to offer comfort, community and respite.'

'Exactly,' Antonia agreed before steering the group through to the next room.

For the next forty minutes, they worked their way around the building, comparing sketches and sharing ideas. As they assessed each room, Angus saw flashes of Hugo's House coming to life. The existing apartments would be rejigged. The garden would be landscaped. The building would have new life breathed into it.

Standing in the attic space, Angus allowed himself a moment to acknowledge all he had achieved with the project so far. He was still at the start, but so much had happened already. In no time, Hugo's House would be inviting guests through its doors. Sure, there were building regulations to adhere to and permissions to apply for and so much paperwork to complete that Angus felt like he was drowning in it, but none of that mattered. The thing Angus had spent his life searching for was in front of him.

'Is there anything else you wanted to run through, Angus?' Antonia asked as they completed their inspection.

'No, I think we've covered it all. Feel free to roam about the space, though. We told the tenants we'd be here for a couple of hours, so there's time if you want to look around again.'

One by one, the team left until the only person in the vast property was Angus.

He moved about the attic, thinking of Layla and how he wanted to share this day with her. Angus wanted to hear her opinions on the plans. He wanted to take her by the hand and lead her through the rooms. He wanted to stop and pull her in for a kiss when the moment called for it.

Leaning against a nearby wall, Angus hung his head. He missed Layla so much. He missed messaging her as soon as he woke up and kissing her soft cheek when they parted at night. He missed the way she frowned when she was reading. He missed the excitement he felt whenever she called or messaged. He missed . . . everything.

Trailing wearily down the stairs, Angus reached the ground floor. Stopping, he took in his surroundings. He told himself to remember this moment and all the promise it held.

Then, in his back pocket, Angus felt his phone buzz.

47

Layla

The Life Experiment: Daily Questionnaire
Property of OPM Discoveries

How would you rate your level of contentment today? (1 represents low contentment, 10 represents high)

1   2   3   4   5   6   7   8   9   10

How would you rate your energy level? (1 being very low energy and 10 being very high energy)

1   2   3   4   5   6   7   8   9   10

What are two things you are grateful for today?
1. Stop calling, stop texting and definitely stop sending these stupid surveys. I am not part of this experiment. I wish I never had been.
2.

What are you struggling with today?
Your audacity

Do you have any additional notes on what you would like to discuss in your upcoming counselling session?
There won't be one

Twisting her body this way and that, Layla studied her reflection in her bedroom mirror. Her mouth scrunched. This was the sixth outfit she'd tried on, but it still wasn't right.

What the hell do you wear to tell the man you love that you made a mistake? Layla wondered, but deep down she knew that what she wore didn't matter. What mattered was what she said. And, after messaging Angus, Layla knew he would be expecting her to make some kind of statement.

> *Hey Angus – I hope this isn't too out of the blue, but I keep thinking about that day in the park and all the things I could have done differently. If you'd like to meet, there is something I'd like to tell you. I'd like to hear all the things I never gave you the chance to say too x*

Only a couple of minutes passed before Angus's reply came through.

Yes. I absolutely want to meet up. Just tell me when and where. xx

The response made Layla smile. There were no games, no pretence, no playing hard to get. Just two people ready to lay everything on the table.

Layla just had to figure out exactly what she wanted to say.

Anxiety had crippled Layla all day. Pacing her flat, Layla had been so flustered that she knocked over a glass of orange juice. As the syrupy liquid seeped into Rhi's favourite rug, an ill-timed call from her dad came through. Even though Layla had promised David they'd catch up this week, she let the call ring out. She was too busy panic-cleaning to chat. Besides, Layla could hardly make coherent conversation when all she could think about was what to say to Angus.

What *did* someone say to win over the person they loved?

I'm sorry was the first thing that came to mind. *I'm sorry for shouting, for walking away, for never letting you get too close.*

Angus needs to apologise too! an indignant part of her brain protested. Layla knew the voice had a point.

She also knew the voice was trying to conceal her fear.

It was easy to be angry at Angus. Blaming him for their downfall felt better than blaming herself, but the dust on their argument had settled. Now, whenever Layla thought of that day in the park, she didn't see Angus as spiteful or deceitful. She saw him as someone who was lost. Scared. Someone who knew so little about themselves, they hid behind someone else because they thought a falsehood was safer than reality.

Layla knew she hadn't imagined the bits about Angus that she loved. His easy-going laugh, his staunch belief in her, the vulnerability he showed when talking about his brother . . . So what if Angus had hidden his wealth? Layla had hidden her death date. They had both entered the relationship on shaky ground.

But today, Layla was going to ask if they could draw a line under it all. She was going to walk into a wine bar in Soho that Sinead insisted was the best in London, extend her hand and hope that Angus would accept it.

She just needed to find an outfit first.

'The nunnery called. It wants its jumper back,' Maya commented from the doorway.

'Very funny,' Layla replied, pulling the jumper over her head before eying Maya's outfit. Pyjamas, despite it being four in the afternoon. 'Shouldn't you be dressed? You've a train to catch.'

'I'm not going home today,' Maya said, throwing herself on Layla's bed. 'I changed my train to tomorrow. Mum and Dad said they're okay to look after Jayden for another night.'

'I didn't realise you wanted to stay longer,' Layla said, perching on the end of the bed.

Maya shrugged. 'Neither of us know how tonight's going to go with Angus. I thought you might want someone to come home to if things don't work out. Rhi's not exactly warm and fuzzy, and I didn't want you to be alone.'

Layla smiled . 'You're staying for me?'

'Of course. What are sisters for? But for the record, I don't think it's going to go badly. In fact, I'm expecting it to go so well that you don't come home at all. Don't worry, I won't tell Mum and Dad about your adult sleepover.'

'Maya!' Layla protested, but there was no fighting her giggles.

Grinning, the sisters shared a moment before Maya reached across the bed for a knitted jumper dress Layla hadn't tried on. 'This would look good with those boots I brought with me,' she commented.

'You're willing to lend them to me?'

'I figure it's the least I can do to make up for when I inevitably spill pad Thai on your duvet,' Maya replied.

Laughing, Layla grabbed the dress and threw it on. A quick look in the mirror earned a satisfied nod from both sisters. Next, Layla reached for her cosmetics bag, but Maya shimmied off the bed and stopped her.

'Let me,' she offered.

Layla hesitated. While it was appealing to have help when her hands were so shaky, Maya's idea of glam was the opposite of Layla's. A firm fan of red lips and luscious lashes, Maya loved to put on a full face of makeup, but Layla didn't want to look different to how she usually did. She and Angus had spent too much time being other people. Tonight, she wanted to be completely herself.

'Don't look so worried,' Maya said, leading Layla back to the bed. 'I promise I'll do your makeup exactly how you like it.'

Taking a seat, Layla closed her eyes and let her sister work her magic. A playlist of pop anthems from the noughties filled the room.

'There,' Maya said eventually, stepping back to inspect her handiwork. 'If he turns you down after seeing you like this, then the man has lost his mind.'

Heading to the mirror, Layla half expected to see a clone of Maya, but her lips parted at the result. Maya's work was subtle, highlighting Layla's features but keeping her looking very much like herself. 'I love it,' she breathed.

'I'll try not to be insulted by how shocked you sound,' Maya replied, clicking the lid onto a lip gloss and dropping it into Layla's bag. 'Now go or you'll be late.'

Layla's brain told her legs to move, but they chose to listen to her nerves instead.

Maya's head tilted to the side. 'You're not talking yourself out of this, are you?'

'No,' Layla replied, a little too quickly. 'It's just . . . Maya, what if it's too late? What if I messed up too badly?'

'Then it's too late and you messed up too badly,' Maya replied. As Layla's face fell, she shrugged. 'What do you want me to say, Layla? That it won't happen? That things will work out? We don't know that. But one thing we do know is that if you don't tell Angus how you feel, you will spend the rest of your life wishing you had.'

Flexing her fingers, Layla forced herself to nod. 'I hate it when you're right.'

'I know. Being the smart sister is a blessing and a burden, but I carry it well.'

Maya's banter was enough to push Layla out of the bedroom and into the living room. Nerves jittered her stomach as she plucked her phone from the coffee table. The screen brightened, displaying messages Layla had missed in her rush to get ready.

On my way. I can't wait to see you xx

Instinctively, her lips curled into a smile at Angus's text, but her smile froze at the notification beneath it.

Layla call me back
It's urgent

Frowning, Layla opened her mother's message. A queue of notifications loaded before her, the tone growing more and more urgent. But one particular message stopped Layla's heart altogether.

It's your dad

Layla's stomach dropped. Time seemed to slow, warning her that something was coming. Something big. Something she was not prepared for. But before Layla could process the feeling, her phone lit up again, her mother's photo filling the screen.

With a shaky breath, Layla swiped to answer the call. 'Mum?'

'Layla,' Joanna croaked down the line. 'Oh, Layla.'

As Joanna descended into a fit of heart-wrenching sobs, Layla's head swam. She didn't need to hear more. As soon as she heard Joanna's voice, Layla knew. She knew, she knew, she knew.

'He's gone,' Joanna cried. 'Your dad, he . . . he's gone.'

With the words ringing in her ears, Layla screamed Maya's name, her chest heaving in shock. She didn't stop screaming when Maya ran into the room, nor when she snatched the phone to hear what Joanna was saying.

Layla's screams didn't stop, even when Maya dropped to her knees and sobbed.

48

Angus

The Life Experiment: Daily Questionnaire
Property of OPM Discoveries

How would you rate your level of contentment today? (1 represents low contentment, 10 represents high)

1 2 (3) 4 5 6 7 8 9 10

How would you rate your energy level? (1 being very low energy and 10 being very high energy)

1 2 (3) 4 5 6 7 8 9 10

What are two things you are grateful for today?
1. The team of oncologists working with Mum. They're miracle workers
2. How busy Hugo's House is keeping me

What are you struggling with today?
Missing Layla. Same as yesterday, and the day before that, and the day before that

Do you have any additional notes on what you would like to discuss in your upcoming counselling session?
Unless you know how I can win Layla back, the answer is no

Sunlight filtered through the trees, illuminating Gilly and Peter's dining room with soft light. Angus smiled at the brilliant blue sky. It looked like a snapshot of summer, not winter. An illusion of the most beautiful kind.

'Are you going to bring me that water or stand there like a statue?' Gilly called from across the room.

Stifling an affectionate eye-roll, Angus made his way to her. 'You know, you're quite bossy when you paint.'

'I'm not bossy. I'm commanding.'

'Are you? I hadn't noticed.' As Angus handed his mother her drink, they shared a smile. Going toe to toe with Gilly, Angus had learned, was a way to earn her smiles.

Standing back, he watched his mother take a drink. There was life to Gilly's features that hadn't been there a few days ago. Two pink splodges coloured her cheeks, a relief to Angus and his father. In fact, things with Gilly were going so well, Peter had even gone out for the day to play golf.

As Gilly took another sip of water, her eyes traced the canvas on the easel in front of her. She had been working on something all morning. So far, Angus hadn't been allowed to look at it. It was one of the things that surprised him most after gifting Gilly the paints. In all other aspects of life, Gilly Fairview-Whitley was confident and self-assured, but when it came to her creativity, she was surprisingly shy.

When Angus perched on the edge of the dining table, Gilly set down her paintbrush. 'Have you given Manet a run for his money?' he asked.

'His title is secure, but I must say, I'm quite proud of this.'

Angus's eyebrows raised. 'Really? May I see?'

'I suppose you had better, seeing as I painted it for you,' Gilly said.

'For me?'

'Yes, you. Don't look so surprised, Angus. I have been known to do nice things from time to time.'

Unable to hide his smile at this unexpected turn of events, Angus lifted himself from the table. But before he could reach the canvas, Gilly put out a hand to stop him.

'Before you look, I want to say that you don't have to use it. I know you've been having trouble finding a logo for Hugo's House, that's all. I thought if I can't steer you away from a life surrounded by death, then I might as well do my part. So, I gave designing a logo a go.'

If Angus thought his mother painting something for him was touching, then it being for Hugo's House was something else entirely. Stepping closer to the canvas, he took in his mother's creation.

A simple structure of a house, not quite cartoonish but not quite realistic either, sat in the centre of the space. With one side green and the other blue, the colours blended into each other in seamless, fluid brushstrokes to create a solid, undeniable building.

'I used your favourite colour and Hugo's,' Gilly said. 'It's a simple palette. You can change it if you like, but—'

'It's perfect,' Angus breathed. 'You've brought Hugo's House to life.'

Turning to his mother, Angus watched happiness light Gilly up from the inside, until the sound of approaching footsteps broke the moment. There was a jarring urgency to them, making Angus want nothing more than to stop whoever was coming from entering the room.

Especially once he saw who it was.

'Jasper, Clarissa, what a pleasant surprise,' Gilly enthused. Angus was surprised to hear how sincere Gilly sounded. The Marshall-Halteses and Dowesses had learned of Gilly's cancer after her infection forced Peter to come clean. Still, Angus would have thought his mother would baulk at the idea of anyone seeing her in her dressing gown near midday.

'Lovely to see you as always, Gilly,' Jasper boomed, striding into the space. Angus bristled as Jasper inspected the canvas. 'Well, you've certainly been keeping busy.'

'Hello,' Clarissa said, avoiding Angus's gaze as she smiled warmly at Gilly. 'Mother sends her love. She'll pop in when she's back from Edinburgh on Thursday, if you're free.'

'I suppose I could make time,' Gilly replied, but her delight shone through her haughty tone.

'Wonderful, I'll let her know. What are you painting?'

Angus cut in before his mother could answer Clarissa's question. 'What are you both doing here?'

'Well, obviously, we wanted to visit Gilly,' Jasper replied. 'But also, we need to talk to you.'

Confused, Angus prepared to take them elsewhere to talk privately, but Gilly grabbed his arm. 'Stay. It's been so long since I've had a visitor. I would love to catch up with you all.'

Unable to deny her, Angus gestured to the table and chairs. Jasper and Clarissa took a seat, and Angus followed suit. As he moved, he noticed how tight Clarissa's shoulders were.

'Is everything okay?' Angus asked once they were seated.

'That depends,' Jasper replied. 'What's your definition of okay?'

Angus's lips pressed together, worried. There was a playfulness to Jasper he didn't trust. No doubt he was there to rope Angus into some harebrained scheme or night out, but Angus hadn't touched a sip of alcohol in days. He wanted to keep it that way. He felt clearer, sharper, more level-headed. Besides, the last time he'd had a drink, he'd been sat in a wine bar, waiting on Layla.

She'd never arrived.

Angus had called. Texted. Called again, but no reply ever came.

It had taken him two hours to accept that Layla wasn't coming. Two hours for heartbreak to sink its teeth into him once more. Downing the rest of his drink, Angus left the bar.

When he reached home, worry hit. Was Layla hurt? Had something happened to her en route? He tried contacting her again with the same result.

A few days later, Angus saw three dots indicating Layla was typing. She never sent a response.

As his fingers moved to text Jasper and see if he wanted to meet for drinks, Angus had stopped, unnerved. He didn't want to go drinking to numb his pain. He didn't want to rely on that crutch or be a person who couldn't process their emotions. For years, Angus had lived with the consequences of that. His behaviour had already let his family down once. He wouldn't let it happen again.

So, the no-drink rule was implemented. It was a vow Angus planned to maintain, no matter how convincing Jasper was.

As an impish grin took over Jasper's face, Angus's patience wavered, and he steeled himself for the finest display of manipulation he'd ever been on the receiving end of.

'You're going to love me,' Jasper chimed, leaning back in his seat and grinning.

'Jasper, we already love you,' Gilly joked, but when she looked between her son's flat expression and his friend's cheeky one, her smile faltered. 'Is everything okay?'

'It is now. Not that you'd know it from looking at Angus. Don't be so serious, my friend,' Jasper chided. 'This is a good thing! Clarissa and I have found the key to ending your moping.'

'I'm not moping,' Angus protested, but Jasper shook his head.

'You're a moper, Angus. It's quite annoying, especially when you won't say why. I've been trying to figure out what could have gotten you so down. We know it can't be money, so what could it be? Then I bumped into Clarissa.'

A subtle blush coloured Clarissa's fair skin when she spoke. 'I told him about our run-in at the park, with your friend Layla.'

'Who's Layla?' Gilly asked.

'Exactly!' Jasper replied. 'Who is she and why has she broken my best friend's heart?'

Heat burned the back of Angus's neck as he felt his mother's eyes on him.

'Your heart is broken?'

'I know, Gilly. I didn't think he had a heart to break either,' Jasper quipped. 'Anyway, I wanted to find out who this mysterious Layla was. See about fixing things for our boy here. And seeing as you so rudely never introduced us, I had to do a little digging. With Clarissa's help, of course. You should see her skills, Angus. It's quite frightening, actually. Five minutes on social media and bingo! She found her.'

'It helped that I'd seen her, too,' Clarissa added.

'Needless to say, we now know everything there is to know about Layla Cannon. The next step is to use that knowledge to get you back together,' Jasper said, pulling his phone from his pocket, but Angus groaned.

'Jasper, please. I messed up with Layla. There's no going back.'

'There you go moping again. How do you know that?'

'She was supposed to meet me the other day. She never turned up. If that doesn't prove that she's done with me, I don't know what will.'

A small frown furrowed Jasper's brow. 'When exactly was this?'

'Why does that matter?'

'It matters more than you might think. What day did she stand you up?'

Sighing, Angus stuck out his jaw. 'Tuesday.'

Jasper nodded as if he expected as much. Biting his lip, he flicked through his phone. When he handed it over, Layla's sister's Facebook profile was loaded.

'Why are you showing me Maya's social media?' Angus asked.

'Just look,' Jasper replied.

'What is it?' Gilly asked, but Angus could barely hear her over the pounding in his ears. It grew louder as he read the text on the screen. A screenshot of Maya's status announcing the death of David Cannon and the details of his funeral.

'Layla's . . . Layla's dad died?' he whispered.

Jasper nodded. 'A heart attack. I'm guessing you didn't know?'

It took everything in Angus to find the energy to shake his head.

As Gilly quizzed Jasper about Layla, Angus's eyes closed. He thought back to his many conversations with Layla about her family. Her father was her hero, that much was clear. Every word she spoke about him dripped with love and respect . . . and now he was gone.

'Why are you showing me this?' he said gruffly, pushing the phone away.

'So you can go to her,' Jasper replied, like it was simple, but Angus shook his head.

'I can't.'

'Don't be ridiculous, of course you can! Didn't you read the death notice? David's funeral is in three days. It's in Hull, another place to cross off your bucket list.' Jasper laughed at his own joke, but his smile faded when he saw Angus's pain. 'Look, I know I'm not always the best friend. In fact, most of the time I'm a shit one. A bit like you've been recently.'

Angus smiled weakly. 'Can't say I don't deserve that.'

'You do, but it's okay. Friends forgive each other. They also point out when their friend is being an idiot. Well, right now you're being an idiot, Angus. I saw how much you cared for Layla. I'm guessing she felt the same. Trust me, "friends" don't talk on the phone as often as you two did. It's the twenty-first century – we communicate through emojis and likes. But you two? It was sickening.' Jasper grunted as Clarissa nudged his side. 'Sweet, though, I guess. If you've found someone you want to talk to that much, don't walk away from it.'

'I'm sorry I didn't realise that when I met her,' Clarissa added softly. 'I was shocked to see you with someone. Hurt too, I suppose.'

'Don't worry, one day it'll all be water under the bridge,' Jasper replied, patting Clarissa's hand. 'All that matters is that Layla forgives Angus for being an idiot.'

Angus tried to find the words to reply, but his throat was tight. Painful memories of Layla stirred in him. Lingering glances and shy smiles and firework touches and the constant, pressing thrill of butterflies . . . Angus's time with Layla had meant everything to him. Everything.

But thanks to his lies, it was over.

'No,' Angus replied, crossing his arms. 'Layla wouldn't want me at her dad's funeral.'

'Of course she would! You clearly love her!' Jasper protested, but Angus shook his head.

'I hurt her, Jasper. I'm not showing up on the hardest day of her life and doing it again. I appreciate your efforts, but they were wasted.'

Despite Jasper's protests, Angus stood and began to walk away.

'Angus,' Gilly called. Something in her voice stopped him. 'Angus, remember what we spoke about. Love is being there. It's showing up, especially when things are hard. It's saying, "I'm here if you need me". It's loving them more than you love yourself.'

'But Layla won't want me there. I ruined everything between us.'

'Did you? Or did you simply give up?'

Anger flamed in Angus, but his retort died on his tongue. Had Angus ever told Layla what she meant to him? Had he ever rested her hand on his chest so she could feel the way his heart pounded when she was close?

Had Angus ever told Layla, plainly and simply, that he loved her?

As his shell-shocked gaze met his mother's, Gilly offered Angus a gentle smile. 'Go to her, Angus.'

Swallowing hard, Angus nodded. Gilly was right. He had to go to Layla or he would spend the rest of his life wishing he had.

Maybe now wasn't the time to delay or ask questions.

Maybe now it was time to do something.

49

Layla

Through swollen eyes, Layla stared at the dinosaur poster pinned to Jayden's wall. Once again, she was commandeering his bedroom, this time for entirely different reasons.

It had been seven days since David's passing. In that time, Layla had learned more about grief than she ever wanted to know.

Layla had learned that a house could feel completely empty, even when it was filled with people, all because it was missing one vital person. Her childhood home had transformed into a mausoleum. Every room Layla entered was filled with reminders of her dad. His slippers, still perched beside the sofa because no one could bear to move them. His favourite coffee cup sitting in the drying rack, waiting for him to use it. His toothbrush, still in the holder beside her mother's.

Then there were the bits of David that weren't visible but were everywhere. The silence where one of his jokes would have been. The absence of a goodnight hug or ruffle of the hair. Jayden's sad, wide eyes as he looked for his best friend, not understanding why he was no longer there.

In the days since she received the news, Layla had been on autopilot. After that first, heavy cry, she'd wiped her face, helped Maya up and got them on the first train to Hull. She hadn't left since.

By the time Layla thought to message Angus to explain what had happened, three days had passed.

The queue of notifications on Layla's phone was proof he was worried, but Layla didn't know what to say. How the hell was she meant to explain everything that had happened?

It wasn't like she hadn't tried. Night after night, she sat with her messages open, waiting for the words to come to her. But every time her fingers moved to type, Layla stopped. Explaining meant typing the words 'my dad died'. Words that, even after seven days and several meetings about David's funeral, Layla still couldn't bring herself to say.

Huddled under the duvet, Layla remained cocooned until her body ached with hunger. Forcing herself to get up, she made her way downstairs, moving with slow, trudging steps.

At the front door, Layla spotted David's trainers. Flinching, she looked away.

'There you are,' Joanna said, appearing in the hallway at the sound of Layla's footsteps. 'I wondered if I should wake you.'

Even though it hurt, Layla forced herself to look at her mum. Joanna was dressed, but she didn't look right. The buttons on her cardigan were misaligned. Her hair was bedraggled, and her skin looked bare and dry. The last seven days had aged Joanna, and Layla knew nothing she could do would change that.

'Would you like a cup of tea?' Joanna offered, already moving towards the kitchen.

'No, Mum. Let me make it,' Layla replied, rushing past her. Joanna protested, but Layla shook her head. She may have lost her father, but Joanna had lost her husband, the man she'd had by her side for more than thirty years. The least Layla could do was make her mum a drink.

As Joanna lowered her weary body onto a dining chair, Layla flicked the kettle on. 'I need to ring the florist soon,' Joanna said, staring out of the window.

'I can do that,' Layla replied. 'Please. Let me take some things off your plate.'

Twisting to face her daughter, Joanna forced a smile. 'Well, only if you're sure.'

The kitchen fell into silence as Layla plopped teabags into two mugs. Gathering milk from the fridge, she calmed herself with the routine of making tea until Joanna next spoke.

'Will that man you were talking to be coming to the funeral?' she asked.

Layla's shoulders stiffened. Unlatching the kettle, she filled the mugs with water. 'Angus and I aren't speaking anymore.'

Joanna's eyebrows arched. 'Why not?'

'I don't know, Mum. Things didn't work out, that's all.'

As she handed Joanna a mug, Layla did her best not to imagine Angus waiting for her in the wine bar that day. The image was haunting.

'You should talk to him,' Joanna said as Layla joined her at the table. 'See if you can fix things.'

'Mum, please. I don't want to talk about Angus right now.'

'But talking about Angus is exactly what we should be doing. Your dad said he'd never seen you as happy as when you were speaking to him.'

Blinking, Layla dragged her eyes to her mother. 'He did?'

'He did.' Across the table, Joanna reached for Layla's hand. 'You and Angus, what you shared . . . it meant something to you, I can tell. I know you, Layla. I know you don't spend hours talking to just anyone. He must have been special.'

Layla's heart ached as she thought of Angus's slow, breezy smile. 'Maybe he was, once upon a time, but it's over now,' she said, trying to sound braver than she felt.

Joanna took a sip of tea like she knew better. 'I once said that about your dad, you know. It's true,' she added when she observed Layla's shock. 'We dated for six months before we split. We'd gone out one night and got into a silly argument. Too many drinks, too many emotions flying about that we were too young to understand. So, we called it quits. We barely lasted two weeks without each other.'

Suddenly, Joanna squeezed Layla's hand.

'Layla, I would give anything for one more night with your father. If you've found someone who makes you feel like that, don't give up on them. Please. We only get a few shots at happiness in life. Your dad would want you to take every one that comes your way.'

It was those words that broke Layla. 'I miss him,' she wailed. 'I miss him so much.' Layla didn't know who she was speaking about, Angus or her dad, but it didn't matter. She missed them both, and having either of them back in her life felt equally as impossible.

50

Angus

The Life Experiment: Daily Questionnaire
Property of OPM Discoveries

How would you rate your level of contentment today? (1 represents low contentment, 10 represents high)

1   2   3   (4)   5   6   7   8   9   10

How would you rate your energy level? (1 being very low energy and 10 being very high energy)

1   2   3   4   5   (6)   7   8   9   10

What are two things you are grateful for today?
1. Jasper and Clarissa's sleuthing. They're pretty great friends. I should probably tell them that
2. Mum's latest results. Things seem to be heading in the right direction

What are you struggling with today?
Not knowing how Layla will react when she sees me

Do you have any additional notes on what you would like to discuss in your upcoming counselling session?
Depending on how today goes, we could have a lot to discuss

Angus tugged at the collar of his shirt. It was a tailored fit, but suddenly it felt too tight. As he manoeuvred his car into one of the last free spaces in the crematorium car park, he wondered if he would make it to the funeral before the shirt choked him.

Turning off the ignition, Angus eyed the congregation waiting in the drizzle. It was a big crowd filled with people of all ages, shuffled closely together in their grief. Angus felt a lump in his throat simply observing their sadness.

Was it right that he was here? Angus didn't know. It wasn't like he knew David personally, and he definitely hadn't been invited. The worries were almost enough to make him drive away, but then Angus thought of Layla. He needed to see her. Just one look to see that she was okay.

Just one chance to be there for her.

With that thought, Angus sealed his fate. He walked across the car park to join the crowd. As he did, he noticed the gentle chatter fade into silence. Self-consciousness prickled Angus's skin, but then he heard the distinct roll of tyres. Without turning, he knew the funeral cars were arriving.

Tucking himself into the crowd, Angus watched on, waiting to see Layla.

A strangled breath escaped him when she stepped out of the car. Wrapped in a sleek black coat and wearing pointed boots, she looked beautiful – and sad. So incredibly sad. Her body was rigid with composure, but Angus knew it was an armour.

As Layla extended her hand back into the car, a small hand accepted it. Seconds later, a young boy emerged.

Jayden, Angus thought. He recognised him from Layla's photos. The woman following him was Maya. With similar features to her sister, Maya too was stiff as she clutched onto her son's shoulder.

When one final person emerged from the car, Angus's chin dimpled. Joanna was pale-faced and curved inwards as if aching with pain. Angus's heart broke for her.

As the family made their way towards the crematorium, all Angus could do was watch. It amazed him how he could name all the significant people in Layla's life at a glance. She had shared her world so openly with him, but he hadn't done the same.

Before the shame of that could destroy him, Layla looked up from straightening Jayden's collar and locked eyes with Angus.

Angus's heart thundered. His palms dampened with sweat, and all he could think was, *How the hell have I survived a single day without looking into those eyes?*

Time remained frozen until Maya nudged Layla into action. Flustered, she tried to move forwards but stumbled. Even though he was too far away to catch Layla, Angus's body jerked to steady her, but Maya got there first.

Turning to her sister, Angus watched Layla whisper something. Maya's eyes darted to the crowd, picking through the funeralgoers one by one until she spotted Angus. Her eyes widened. Then, despite the events of the day, she smiled.

Ducking her head, Maya whispered feverishly to Layla. At one point, she even pointed to Angus.

Shit, he panicked, wondering how he could have got it so wrong. Of course he shouldn't have intruded on Layla's family and their grief, but it was too late now.

The sisters shared a look before Layla darted away from the crematorium. Angus watched her go. Instinct told him to follow her, but he was paralysed by the fear that he had really, truly fucked up. Again.

'Layla must need a minute,' the man in front of Angus said. The sudden interruption jolted Angus. He turned to hear the rest of the conversation, but his eye was caught by someone making their way towards him.

'Maya,' he said when she reached him. 'I'm sorry, I didn't mean to upset Layla. I just wanted to—'

'Go,' Maya interjected, jerking her head in the direction Layla fled. 'I'll give you two minutes. We've got big things to do today, aside from you two finally admitting you love each other.'

Angus stomach flipped. 'Layla . . . Layla loves me?'

The comment earned him an eye-roll. 'Honestly, for smart people you're both pretty dumb,' Maya said, before glancing back to Joanna. 'You have two minutes before Layla needs to be back here. Go.'

Angus didn't need telling again. He followed Layla, racing down pavements interspersed with moss and ducking through memorial gardens. Charging down a set of stone steps, Angus's heart flipped when he saw Layla at the bottom of them. Head bowed, she was leaning a hand against a tree for support.

'Layla,' he called.

Spinning on her heel, Layla faced Angus. She blinked once, twice, then exhaled an unsteady breath. 'I wasn't sure if you were really here or if my imagination was playing a cruel trick,' she croaked.

'I'm here,' Angus confirmed, taking the last of the steps. At the foot of them, so close he could see each of Layla's freckles, Angus slowed. 'I'm so sorry about your dad, Layla. I thought about messaging you, but I had to see you in person. I had to know you were okay.'

'I'm not,' Layla admitted, doing all she could to fight the wobble of her chin. 'I'm not okay at all.'

'That makes two of us,' Angus joked weakly. 'Layla, I'm so sorry. I wasn't sure you'd want me to come today, but I couldn't not. Even if there was a chance you'd kick me out, I had to be here for you.'

Layla's mouth opened, but no words came out. Taking her silence as a good sign, Angus willed himself to keep going.

'I know today isn't about me or us, but I wanted to say I'm sorry. I never wanted to lie to you. I just wanted to be worthy of you. From the moment I met you, I was in awe. I'd have done anything to be near you. Gone anywhere you wanted, became anyone you liked, but I realise now that the only person you ever wanted me to be was myself. Well, here I am. Angus Fairview-Whitley, charity founder, fuck-up and all-round okay person who is trying to be better. I should have introduced myself as him from day one. I'm sorry it took losing you to make that happen, and I'm sorry for all the hurt along the way.'

'You're sorry?' Layla echoed. 'Angus, I'm the one who should apologise. I didn't give you a chance to explain, then I stood you up.'

'None of that matters, Layla. Not after what I did. A few cross words and a bit of ghosting is the least I deserve,' Angus replied, but Layla shook her head.

'It does matter, Angus. I'm sorry too. I never should have run away or kept you at arm's length.' Tears spilled down Layla's cheeks, each one a hammer to Angus's heart.

'Layla, I don't care about the past,' he said, stepping closer. 'I just care about you. What can I do to help you get through today?'

A sad, startled laugh made Layla choke. 'You want to help me after how I acted?'

'Yes. All I care about is being beside you. If you would like me there, that is,' Angus replied, then he bit his lip. 'I know this isn't the most romantic time or place, but I need to tell you something. Something I've been wanting to tell you for a while now. I love you, Layla.'

Shock coloured Layla's expression. 'You love me?'

'I do. So much. I love everything about you. Even the fact that you burn risotto.' At this, Layla laughed tearfully. 'I'm sorry I haven't been there for you through this,' Angus continued. 'I'm sorry—'

'Don't,' Layla said, eliminating the space between them. 'We've both apologised enough. I don't want to look back anymore. I only want to look forward. To the future. Our future.'

With a coy smile, Layla took Angus's hand in hers. Her other hand rested on his chest, feeling his racing heart beneath her palm.

Swallowing hard, Angus tucked a stray strand of hair behind Layla's ear. She was so close now, all he had to do was lean in . . .

And for the first time in his life, Angus Fairview-Whitley didn't listen to doubt or worry. Instead, he trusted. He leaned in.

Falling into him, Layla did the same.

The kiss was slow at first. Tender. Filled with everything Angus had been carrying inside of him for weeks. And as Layla's arms wrapped around his neck, Angus drew her closer, until he wasn't sure where he ended and she began.

51

Layla

As she lay her head on Angus's chest, Layla took the advice her dad had once given her. She closed her eyes and paid attention to the way Angus's breathing mirrored her own. Noticed the way her nerve endings fizzed as he toyed with her hair. Took a mental picture of this moment so she could carry this sense of peace with her always.

Sighing contentedly, Layla snuggled deeper into the crook of Angus's arm. The pair had been coiled together on Layla's sofa ever since returning from Hull two hours ago. Stillness was needed after the last four days. Post-funeral life had been taxing in ways both good and bad. There was joy in watching her family bond with Angus, but it was shadowed by the sadness that David wasn't there to meet him too.

As if sensing Layla's thoughts had wandered to grief, Angus pressed a kiss to the top of her head. 'You're amazing, do you know that?' he whispered.

'I do. You keep reminding me,' she teased, her cheeks lifting as she smiled.

Tightening her grip around Angus, Layla made herself a promise – every day, she would fight for this feeling. However big, however small, she would take a moment to stop. To breathe. To revel in the love she felt.

Layla was about to tell Angus this vow when the intercom to her apartment buzzed.

'No,' she groaned, burrowing into his chest. 'I don't want to get up. I'm too cosy.'

'Let me,' Angus replied, pressing another kiss to her head and shimmying off the sofa. At the intercom, he held the answer button and called, 'Hello?'

'Is Layla there? Layla Cannon?' a voice called back.

Shock forced Layla upright as she registered the voice, but what shocked her more than Saira's appearance was Angus's reaction to it. The instant he heard her, all colour drained from his face.

Layla didn't give herself long to process that, though. Scrambling to her feet, she ran and joined Angus at the intercom. 'Don't let her in,' she commanded.

For a moment, the pair simply stared at each other, but then Angus broke the silence. His gaze traced over the fierce blush in Layla's cheeks. 'How do you know Saira?' he asked tightly.

Blinking, Layla studied the man before her. Slack-jawed, as surprised as she was. 'You . . . you know Saira too?'

Before Angus could answer, the intercom buzzed once more.

Watching Angus flinch at the sound, an indignant frown took over Layla's features. 'How do you know Saira?' she demanded.

'I . . . I'm not sure I should say.'

'Well, I'm not sure you should stay silent either,' Layla snapped, folding her arms across her chest as if doing so could quash the panic rising inside her.

When Layla's interrogative stare became too pressing to ignore, Angus cracked. 'I don't know what I'm allowed to say,' he cried, in time for the intercom to ring again. Before Layla could refuse Saira entry, Angus reached out and buzzed her into the building.

'What are you doing?!'

'Getting an answer to your question,' Angus replied. His measured tone stoked Layla's fury, but her anger wobbled as she watched him chew the corner of his lip.

He's nervous, she realised. Drawing back, Layla wrapped her arms around her trembling body.

'Don't look at me like that. Please,' Angus begged, but Layla couldn't help it. The idea that Angus was somehow connected to Saira was overwhelming. Layla had already forgiven him for lying once. She couldn't do it again.

Side-by-side and locked a tense silence, Layla and Angus waited for Saira.

When her knock came, Layla opened the door. Saira stood on the other side, meeker than Layla had ever seen her before. 'Hello, Layla,' she said softly. 'It's good to see you.'

'Good' was not the word Layla would use to describe that moment. Before she could respond, though, Saira gasped.

'Angus!' she cried. 'I was hoping you'd be here. I've been reading your updates in the questionnaires.'

Layla's head snapped to Angus. 'The questionnaires? Were you part of the experiment too?'

If Layla was surprised, then Angus was well and truly shocked. 'Wait, what?' he said, his eyes darting from Layla to Saira and back again. 'Are we . . . Are we okay to talk about this?'

As Layla drew a sharp intake of breath, Saira smiled. 'Angus, I think the only thing we can do is talk,' she said. 'Shall we sit?'

Robotically, Layla stepped back from the door and allowed Saira inside. Accepting the invitation, Saira moved about the space like she knew it well. The day Saira first came to the apartment flashed in Layla's mind. So much had happened since then. Looking back, that day felt like another life, another Layla.

Stumbling to her sofa, Layla was vaguely aware of Angus following her. 'I don't understand,' she said, collapsing into her seat. 'What's going on?'

'I think I'm the best person to answer that,' Saira said, settling into Layla's armchair. 'What you suspect is true. Unbeknown to each other, you and Angus were both participants in The Life Experiment.'

Layla's jaw dropped. She didn't have to look at Angus to know his face mirrored hers.

'From your counselling sessions and questionnaires, I've followed what's been going on between the two of you from the start. Every meet-up, every interaction . . . It's been beautiful to witness. Secretly, I've been championing a moment like this for weeks. I'm so happy you found your way back to each other.'

With an unsteady hand, Angus reached for Layla, but his touch woke the rage within her.

'That's not all Saira's been doing,' she snapped. 'Have you told Angus the truth about the experiment yet, or is he still caught in your web of lies?'

'Lies? What lies?' Angus echoed, turning to Saira.

The happiness lighting Saira's features dimmed. 'Angus, when you signed up for The Life Experiment, you were only told a partial truth. Yes, the work we are doing has incredible implications, but not in the way you think. OPM Discoveries can do many wonderful things, but we cannot tell you when you're going to die. The death date you were given isn't real.'

Bowled over, Angus sat back in his seat. 'I . . . I don't understand. You lied about my death date?'

When Saira nodded, Angus's head drew further back.

'Why would you do that?'

'There are many good reasons, let me assure you,' Saira replied. 'We live in a world where people are crippled by struggles and where comparison is the thief of joy. We wanted to evaluate what would it take for people to separate themselves from those pressures. Our aim was to assess how people respond to being confronted by death, and whether it would trigger them to appreciate their lives more. We wanted to study their reactions and the changes they made. Participants were always going to be told the truth as soon as the experiment ended.'

'Like that makes it okay,' Layla muttered.

'You convinced me you knew when I was going to die,' Angus said quietly. 'Why put me through that if it wasn't real?'

A flicker of sadness undermined Saira's usual self-assurance. 'It was necessary in order for the experiment to yield accurate results, Angus. I'm sorry we couldn't be truthful from the outset. Really, we were hoping you'd find the experience inspiring.'

'Yeah, because telling someone they'll die in two years is *so* inspiring,' Layla couldn't help snapping.

Angus whipped around to face her. 'Two years? That's how long they said you had left to live?'

'That's why I said we could only be friends,' Layla replied, fighting the urge to cry. 'I didn't want us to become more and then have to say goodbye. I couldn't do that to you.'

Layla watched Angus piece everything together. His face crumpled. 'This whole time we've known each other, you thought you were inching closer to death?' he whispered. When Layla nodded, Angus breathed her name. Letting go of her hand, Angus drew Layla into his side, hugging her tightly. 'I am so sorry you were dealing with that on your own.'

'That's your response?' Layla replied, mouth agape. 'You find out the last ten weeks of your life have been a lie and all you can think of is me?'

'Layla, you're all I ever think of.'

A startled laugh escaped Layla. She pulled back from the hug to smile at the man she loved, but then her eyes narrowed. 'Wait, how long were you given to live?'

She heard Angus gulp. 'Sixty years.'

'Your worst fear was living for another *sixty years*?' Layla cried, but Angus's sombre expression made her chest hurt. 'Oh, Angus. I had no idea you were in so much pain.'

'I was,' Angus admitted. 'I was lost, confused, full of self-loathing . . . just despondent, to be honest. But all that changed when I met you.'

Layla's face flickered with a smile, but then her eyes widened. 'The day we met . . . that cafe . . . I wasn't in Birmingham because of work. I was there because of the experiment.'

'I was there because of the experiment too.' Angus replied. 'I was a mess the day we met, Layla. I'd just learned my death date. I needed to sit and process having a long life and no idea what to do with it.'

Layla's lips twitched. 'Me too, only my life wasn't quite so long.'

'No wonder you were so sad,' Angus said, his face dropping. 'I wish I'd known what you were going through. I wish I could have made it better.'

'You did. Strangely, somehow, you did. If I hadn't met you . . . if you hadn't shown me a glimmer of happiness . . . well, my thoughts were so dark, I don't know what would have happened.'

A juddery breath rattled in Angus's chest. 'Thank goodness for cafes in Birmingham, I guess.'

It was only when Saira let out a gentle laugh that Layla remembered they weren't alone. Turning to Saira, Layla was surprised to see there were tears in her eyes. 'I know you might think little of me,' Saira said thickly, 'but you need to know that the aim of the experiment was pure. I only wanted to help.'

'By making us think we were going to die?' Layla asked, but even she could hear that there was less anger in her voice.

'By helping you realise how precious life is,' Saira replied. 'Think about your life over the last few weeks, Layla. You reconnected with your family. You put in place building blocks to make a better work-life for yourself. And, looking at you and Angus, it's clear that you opened your heart to love.'

Glancing at Angus, Layla's lip quivered. He loved her. That was all that mattered.

'The woman I met back in September was as lost as the man sitting beside her,' Saira continued, 'but you both worked and fought and found yourselves. You built futures to be proud of, and you've begun crafting a solid relationship. My methods might not be conventional, but—'

'But they work,' Layla interrupted, finishing Saira's sentence for her.

Deep down, she knew there would come a day where there would be no anger in her heart for Saira, only gratitude. The Life Experiment had made Layla brave. It had given her permission to rest as much as it had pushed her to go for what she wanted.

And, most importantly, thanks to the experiment, Layla had found Angus. She would sign up all over again if it meant there was even a 1 per cent chance of finding him. So there could be no anger. No fear, no regret, just excitement and hope for a future Layla prayed she would share with Angus for a long time to come.

52

Saira

'I'm home,' Saira called out as she entered the house. When no response came, she slipped off her shoes and padded in stockinged feet through to the kitchen. There, she plucked a half-full bottle of wine from the fridge and poured herself a glass, because why not? Today was a day of celebration, after all. The Life Experiment had officially come to an end. All that remained was for Saira and her team to disclose the true aim of the experiment, then for all involved to take the lessons they had learned and implement them. Saira included.

'This is the defining work of your career,' one of her senior researchers said. He was right. The experiment had been everything Saira hoped it would be when she had the idea three years ago. Maybe even more. The growth shown by participants was phenomenal. Lives had changed for the better. Everything Saira had wanted to achieve was complete.

So why did she not feel complete herself?

The first sip of wine slid smoothly down her throat as she ventured back through the house. At the door to the living room, she paused. Inside, Saira knew her sofa was waiting, as was the latest BBC police procedural she was invested in. Her shoulders relaxed at the idea of bingeing the rest of it, but Saira found herself heading upstairs instead.

Outside the third door on the landing, she stopped. Habit almost made Saira knock, but at the last minute, she stopped herself. There was no point. Saira knew she wouldn't get a response.

Saira entered the room anyway. It smelled faintly of the polish she used once a week to keep the space clean and tidy. Well, tidy enough, if you ignored the school blazer lying rumpled on the floor. It was meant to be hung over the back of the desk chair, or preferably in the wardrobe, but the floor was usually where it ended up.

Dodging the discarded blazer, Saria made her way to the bed. Purple bedding, beautifully patterned. *Grown-up*, she thought, the words puncturing her lungs.

Tentatively, Saira sat, careful not to spill her wine. 'The experiment finished today, can you believe it? The end came too quickly, if you ask me. What am I going to do with my day now? Other than annoy you, of course.'

The silence was deafening. Saira's shoulders slumped, but she continued. 'I saw Layla and Angus earlier. Remember them? Throughout the experiment, they were smitten and ... actually, I should stop spilling their secrets. Confidentiality and all.' Saira laughed before inching further up the bed. 'They were shocked and angry at what I'd done, but that soon faded. After going through something like this, you can't cling to the bad, can you? That's the point of the experiment, to make people stop being ruled by nerves and insecurities and doubts. And, most importantly, to make them see their worth. Seeing that is one of the hardest things, isn't it? We both know that.'

Saira closed her eyes as the words she wanted to say caught in the back of her throat.

'If only I'd helped you see yours,' she whispered. 'If only I'd helped you first.'

As Saira touched the empty pillow before her, she closed her eyes and imagined Harpreet's face. The long, thin nose, a mirror image of Saira's. Fierce brows that furrowed when she studied. The smattering of acne scars on her left cheek. Harpreet was so insecure about them. Saira told her they were her skin telling the story of her life. Maybe she should have told her that more. Made Harpreet see her beauty. Taken her bitter comments about her body more seriously.

But Saira hadn't listened enough, hadn't done enough, hadn't been enough to save her little girl.

Now the tears had started, they wouldn't stop. They ran down Saira's cheeks, a waterfall of grief so crushing her lungs lost the ability to breathe. 'If only I could have shown you how much joy you brought to the world. If only I could have made you see,' she sobbed. 'I'd give anything for a chance to fix things. You know that, don't you?'

Saira's hand curled into the pillow, the knot of pain burning too bright in her chest. Seven years later, her grief still felt so fresh.

It was the cruellest of tricks, how someone could be made to think that ending their life was the answer to their pain. The people left behind were cursed to spend their lives wondering how it happened. What they could have done to stop it.

People said Saira couldn't have known, that Harpreet hid her pain well, but Saira hated their platitudes. She was Harpreet's mother. She was a psychologist, for goodness sake. Every time Harpreet bought a new outfit to try and fit in, every time she added another layer of makeup, every time she skipped a meal . . . She should have known.

She should have *known*.

Sniffing back her emotions before they consumed her completely, Saira sat tall. 'Enough of that, eh? The important thing is that the participants know their worth now. Those mothers and fathers, those daughters and sons, those friends and colleagues, they know how much the world needs them. They know how much life they have left to live.'

On the pillow, Saira's hand unfurled. For a moment, she debated stroking the air as if it were Harpreet's cheek, but she stopped herself.

'We're doing amazing work together, you and I,' Saira said softly into the silence.

Lingering a moment, Saira smoothed her daughter's pillow. Then she rose to her feet and drew a line under her sadness. For tonight, at least.

Before she left Harpreet's room, Saira took one last look at the empty bed. 'Goodnight, sweetheart,' she whispered. Closing the door behind her, Saira walked away, safe in the knowledge that she had tried. And for the rest of her life, she would continue to try to show people that they had value. That they were loved. That here on earth, alive and kicking, was exactly where they belonged.

Acknowledgements

It might be a little unorthodox to start acknowledgements with a story, but here I go.

The idea for *The Life Experiment* came to me in 2020 during a pandemic-induced time of self-reflection. For the first time in years, I stopped, looked inwards and faced some of the things I'd been running from. Mainly the fact that in my early 20s, I lost my friend James to cancer. His death shook the foundations of my life in the most immense way. Even in his final moments, I simply couldn't bring myself to imagine a world without him in it.

James's passing forced me to realise that 'one day' isn't guaranteed. Out of nowhere, all the dreams I had about travelling Australia and writing novels became tentative. Terrified, I threw myself into making my dreams reality, ploughing forward as if it was the only way to go. It wasn't until Covid forced the world to stop that I processed my loss and how it shaped me. From there, *The Life Experiment* came to life.

With that in mind, I have to start these acknowledgements with James Knox. James, every word in this book traces back to you. I hope they show what a wonderful human you were, and how loved and missed you are. Thank you for being the truest friend I have ever known. For the time you brought me water, snacks and meds when I was sick and home alone. For the time you picked me up after a night out when my purse was stolen. For every time you were there with a hug, a laugh, a night out. I'm not sure what I did to deserve you in my life, but I'm grateful that you were such a big part of it.

Now to the rest of my acknowledgements, which are no less heartfelt.

First and foremost, I have to thank my wonderful agent, Dan Pilkington. When Dan and I met for lunch on my last day in Sydney, I mentioned that I'd been 'working on a thing'. Dan read it and told me that *The Life Experiment* was not a 'thing'. It was, in fact, a book I was meant to share with the world. Dan – thank you for believing in my writing even more than I do. You are the agent of dreams!

To the wonderful team at Simon & Schuster . . . where do I begin?! To my publisher, Anthea, who loved Layla and Angus from day one. Thank you for seeing all their story could be, and for all your guidance with helping them get there. I feel blessed to be working with you! To my wonderful editors Rosie and Celia – your keen eye and insightful observations made this book ten million times better. Thank you! To Jasmine, Fleur and the rest of the S&S team, thank you for all you have done for *The Life Experiment*. You are a team of superstars!

With publishing in mind, I have to thank the wonderful writing community in Australia, the UK and around the world. For years, I looked at the world of writing and wished I could be part of it. To everyone who welcomed me so warmly into this space and taught me how to celebrate every milestone . . . thank you! An extra special shout out must go to the wonderful Jo Dixon, my Tassie safe space and dear friend. Writing retreat soon, please?!

A huge thank you to the bookstagram community around the world and all my friends in it. There are no words to describe how special the support and love you show authors is! I feel so lucky to have connected with so many of you . . . thank you!

I cannot write a set of acknowledgements about this book/time of my life without thanking my wonderful friends. Leaving some of you to move to the other side of the world and build a life from the ground up is tough, but it became easier because of your support. Robyn, Aidan, Beth, Chris, Katie, Tom, Brigid, Alyse, Aaron, Helen, Madison, Catelyn, Sarah, Andy, Amy, Al, Amy, Grace, Laura, Rachel, Sanch, Gemma, Heloise, Lauren, Lyndsey, Kirsten, Sophie, Hannah, Vic . . . you make every day bright.

To the Hobsons (and my favourite cousin, Jazz!). Thank you for being my home during the lead-up to publication and making sure I stop to enjoy every moment along the way. I'm not sure where I'd be without you, but it definitely wouldn't be here.

To my family in the UK . . . you've no idea how much I miss you! James, Lauren, Victoria, Poppy, Mick and Lesley – I hope you know how big a piece you are in the jigsaw of my life. A special mention must go to my parents. Thanks to my dad for being my hero, always. Thanks to my mum, who reads my stories first. Because of you both, I grew up believing that I could reach the stars I so often looked up at. I don't know if you realise how powerful that message was, but I do. This book is proof of that.

And lastly, to you, the person reading this . . . thank you for taking a chance on Layla, Angus and *The Life Experiment*. I hope this story stays with you for a long time to come.

Reading Group Questions

1. *The Life Experiment* is written from the perspectives of Layla and Angus. Is there another character you'd like to see join the experiment? Why did you pick them?

2. If you were given the same news as either Layla or Angus, how would you react?

3. So much of Layla's growth came from reconnecting with her family. Do you think this is always true of time spent with family?

4. How do you think wealth impacts the experiences of the two families in *The Life Experiment*?

5. The experiment aimed to help candidates re-evaluate their attitudes and perspectives on their lives. How successfully do you think it did this?

6. What do you think would have happened to Layla and Angus if they didn't join the experiment? Would they have made changes to their lives? Would they have connected in the same way if they still crossed paths?

7. Where do you think Layla and Angus will be in ten years' time? What makes you say this?

8. Do you think Saira's motive for creating the experiment justifies her actions? Why/why not?

9. Grief and loss are as much a part of this novel as hope and dreams for the future. Which theme came across stronger to you – grief or hope?

10. Would you join The Life Experiment? Why/why not?

About the Author

Jess Kitching is an avid reader, writer and binge-watcher. After graduating Huddersfield University with a First in English Literature, Jess worked as a primary school teacher before becoming an author. Her three thriller novels have been internationally published and described by readers as 'thrillers with heart'. Originally from Bradford, England, she lives in Canberra, Australia. To find out more, visit jesskitchingwrites.com or Instagram @jesskitchingwrites.